PRAISE FOR
SONYA BIRMINGHAM

"Sonya Birmingham's star burns brightly in the field of romantic fiction."

—Rendezvous

"Sonya Birmingham has a rare talent, able to blend humor and tears to create a moving story."

—The Time Machine

"Endearing characterization and expressive language."

—The Paperback Forum

SONG OF THE LARK
"A rich, rewarding story of unselfish love and unbridled passion."

—Affaire de Coeur

"An unforgettable, sensuous page-turner."

—Rendezvous

SCARLET LEAVES
"A compelling Civil War masterpiece."

—Rendezvous

"A high-tension love story, set in the darkest days of the Civil War."

—Romantic Times

FROST FLOWER
"Frost Flower is sure to steal your heart."

—Romantic Times

THE BEST OF EVERYTHING

"Don't I have dreams and wishes, just like the fine ladies you eat dinner with every evening?"

"And what are those dreams?"

She met his twinkling eyes. "I want to stand on my own feet—take care of myself, and never ask a blessed soul for a thing. And I want a chance to learn, learn everything I can. Whatever I do, from making beds"—she glanced at her journal—"to hooking words together, I want to be the very best. There's something that delights the heart about being the best, isn't there?"

Lassiter remained silent, but she noticed a warm, satisfied expression on his face. He gently took her by the shoulders, and his eyes deepened until they were the color of the starry, moonlit night sky. "You're a beautiful girl, Molly Kilmartin, and a brave one, too."

A new softness glazed his face and her pulse fluttered crazily. "Of course," she chirped playfully. "Didn't you know that already?"

Shivery excitement raced through her as he cupped her chin. "What a joy you are."

He loosely gathered her to him, and the warmth of his body and the scent of tobacco clinging to his clothes released a raw, primitive feeling buried deep within her. His smoky eyes held her captive, and when he lowered his head, her heart pounded as if it might burst through her rib cage. He was going to kiss her, she thought, trembling with sweet anticipation.

THE BRIGHTEST FLAME

SONYA BIRMINGHAM

LEISURE BOOKS NEW YORK CITY

A LEISURE BOOK®

August 1999

Published by

Dorchester Publishing Co., Inc.
276 Fifth Avenue
New York, NY 10001

Cover Art by John Ennis

ISBN 0-8439-4564-8

Printed in the United States of America.

*This book is dedicated to the memory of
Cora Hester Shehann, my plucky Irish grandmother, who
had such a great influence on my childhood and
adolescence. How brightly the flame of life burned in her
laughing blue eyes.*

An Irish Blessing

May you have warm words on a cold evening,
a full moon on a dark night,
and a smooth road all the way to your door.

The Brightest Flame

Chapter One

The Atlantic—1883

Molly Kilmartin caught the scent of a man's cigar and whirled about. From her place by the *Saxonia*'s railing she spied a tall, well-built figure crossing the first-class saloon deck, now shrouded with night shadows. Soft light spilled from the steamship's ballroom, washing over the man's huge form and tousled hair.

Her heart pounding, she guessed it was one of the ship's officers coming to tell her she had no business up here when she belonged in steerage. If he caught her, he'd escort her below and demand a fine she could ill afford to pay. Trembling, she turned and stared at the dark sea, knowing the man would soon be right behind her. Caught like a rabbit in a snare, she thought miserably.

In her haste to flee, she pivoted and actually bumped into the man's hard chest. "Excuse me," she gasped, her legs turning to jelly. "I-I'll just be moving on now."

The man flashed a smile, sending her pulse fluttering wildly. Dressed in a fine tuxedo that outlined his broad shoulders to perfection, this tall stranger was clearly no ship's officer, but a passenger like herself, although so self-assured and richly dressed, he took her breath away. To make matters worse, he possessed a reckless, wild-blooded look that made her feel all soft and vulnerable inside.

Lines creased the corners of his laughing blue eyes, and she shivered with excitement that anyone so high-born would grace her with such a beautiful smile. And heaven knew she hadn't expected the fire in his eyes or the appealing cleft in his strong chin. He was nothing like the swains in her simple Irish village, but from his polished manner, she could tell he was exactly the sort of man her mother and Father Riley had warned her about.

He clamped a glowing cigar between his strong, white teeth and in the smoothest, deepest voice Molly had ever heard said, "I'm sorry, miss, I didn't mean to startle you."

"Y-you didn't startle me," she stammered. "I-I always look this way."

The man laughed and glanced at the twinkling stars. "Beautiful night, isn't it?" he remarked in a friendly tone.

All was silent except for the waves lapping against the ship's hull, and the sound of music and feminine laughter floating from the ballroom.

"That it is," Molly answered, trying to put some

starch in her voice. "There's a nice breeze up here, not like—like—"

The black-haired scamp took the cigar from his mouth and held her gaze, setting off a tingling excitement in the pit of her stomach. "Like down below?" he asked, cocking a knowing brow.

"Y-Yes, that's right." Saints above, he'd known she was from steerage the moment he'd clapped eyes on her. And here she stood with her hair all tangled and the breeze whipping her gown about her body indecently, no doubt revealing every curve she had. "I should go," she muttered, a hot flush creeping over her cheeks.

She walked away, but the gentleman followed and laid his hand on her shoulder. He turned her around, and, wrapped in the spicy scent of his cologne, a warm tide of arousal ran over her.

"Hold on a minute, Irish. Won't you stay? I'd enjoy having a little company while I smoked."

Faith, how could she possibly entertain such a fine gent? Molly wondered. He was obviously rich and American, while she was Irish and desperately poor. He epitomized the languid world of the privileged, while until a few days ago, she'd never been out of County Galway.

His questioning eyes roamed over her, shattering her defenses. "The smoke doesn't bother you, does it?"

She went weak all over. No male she'd ever known had been gallant enough to ask her if he could smoke in her presence. "No, it doesn't. It's just that I—"

"Don't belong?" A dazzling smile streaked across his face. "Don't worry, I won't give you away," he promised, eyeing her with blatant sexual appraisal.

Sweet heaven! Did the good-looking devil think

she'd sneaked up to the saloon deck for his personal enjoyment? She might be poor, but God hadn't put her on this earth to provide amusement for this bold rascal. "Shouldn't you be getting back to the party?" she asked sternly, grasping at a last chance to get away.

Laughter burst from his lips. "No, not at all. I've been to a hundred balls and danced with thousands of women in my time. I'd rather talk to you."

Molly hesitated, but he clasped her arm and guided her back to the rail, the warmth of his fingers burning through her thin gown. When he blessed her with another blinding smile, to her chagrin, she had to struggle to hold back a smile of her own.

With an air of easy confidence, he leaned against the rail, hard muscles rippling under his expensive tuxedo jacket. "You're from the west, aren't you?" he asked in a tone alive with warm feeling.

She laughed with surprise. "Yes, Ballyshannon. How did you know?"

"I heard it in your voice. I've just been in County Sligo doing some salmon fishing."

"But you're not Irish. I know you're not."

"How?" he chuckled.

"Your clothes, your accent," she answered, realizing she was actually carrying on a conversation with the man now.

"No, I'm not. I'm American and my name is Burke Lassiter. And who might you be?"

"Molly Kilmartin. I'm going to New York City to work in my Aunt Agatha's boardinghouse," she blurted out, too late remembering Mam had warned her to never give personal information to strangers.

14

A smile tugged at the corner of Lassiter's sensual mouth. "A little girl like you? Are you sure you're up to it?"

She raised her chin a notch higher. "Talking never brought the peat home, did it now? Working's nothing new to me. Done it all my life."

Lassiter smoothed back her windblown hair, making her blood race hot and strong. "And where is this boardinghouse?"

"On the east side of Manhattan. A place called Murphy Street."

His expression lit with interest. "Yes, I've been there."

Molly decided he might have been there, but he certainly didn't *live* there, for her aunt had written Murphy Street was located in a poor but decent section of Manhattan, honeycombed with small businesses and Irish boardinghouses. Why, this man looked as if he'd never done a hard day's work in his whole blessed life.

"You'll love New York," he told her easily, his eyes bright with pleasure. "It's the most exciting city in the world."

An inner voice warned Molly against getting involved with the American, but her curiosity overrode it. "Is it true that trains run on the rooftops in New York, and the shops are chock-full of pretty gowns?" she inquired, becoming more comfortable in his presence by the minute. "And is it true everyone has all the milk they can drink, and nobody goes hungry? And—"

Lassiter clasped her hand with strong fingers. "Hold on a minute. One question at a time. The trains that run on the rooftops are called elevateds, and they run *over* the roofs, not *on* them," he explained, amusement moving over his rugged features. "Most of them converge at a place called Battery Park."

He idly caressed Molly's fingers, seemingly unaware that his touch was spreading drugging heaviness through her limbs like warm honey. "And yes, the shops are full of lovely gowns," he continued, "but you must have the means to buy them—and the same goes for milk and food."

Lassiter looked down at the lovely girl standing beside him, marveling at her innocence. Dressed in a ragged russet-colored gown, she was tall and willowy and had a wonderful figure—a small waist and lush breasts that sped warmth through his veins. Even in the shadows, he noticed her complexion was as smooth as jersey cream and the light from the ballroom caught in her soft auburn hair, burnishing it with coppery highlights. So far she'd been the only surprise, the only bright spot in the whole excruciatingly predictable voyage that would soon be over.

Molly slipped her hand away, seemingly set back by the depressing news. "But I thought America was the land of abundance. Now you're after telling me it's not!"

He gazed into her large, emerald-green eyes, trying to soften the blow he was about to render. "Yes, America is a land of abundance, although everyone isn't rich. Far from it. But if you have the grit, you have a good chance to get ahead. Unlike Ireland, you can't be held back because your father wasn't born in a manor."

Hanging on his every word, Molly pulled a small book from her skirt pocket, and began scribbling across one of its ragged pages.

"You're writing that down?"

"Yes, in my notebook."

He grinned, totally intrigued. "Don't tell me you're keeping a journal."

An impish grin played over her lips. "And why shouldn't I? I promised Mam I'd write everything down so Father Riley could read it to her," she answered in a husky Irish lilt. "It was he who taught me to read when I was cleaning his rectory, don't you know. He said I had more ability than any blockhead altar boy he'd ever known." She shook her slender finger. "Don't say anything else until I get this down. I wouldn't want to miss a blessed word."

Lassiter smiled to himself as she wrote, thinking her directness was typical of Ireland's west coast. Most people there said whatever came into their head without a thought of editing it. How refreshing that was after a crowd of overdressed socialites fawning on his every word.

Molly started to put her journal away, but he thought he might use the little book to advance their acquaintanceship, for somehow this amusing snip of a girl had managed to alleviate his crushing boredom as well as warm his loins. "Would it be possible for me to read your journal?" he asked, clasping her hand. "I'd like to get your viewpoint of the voyage. You see, I'm a reporter," he lied easily, deciding to keep his position as a newspaper publisher a secret in case it might frighten her away. "Perhaps I could use a few of your observations in a story sometime."

Her lashes flew up. "A reporter, are you?" She slid him a dimpled smile. "Saints above, I can't let you read my scribbling, then. You might laugh at my spelling!"

"*Never,*" he returned, noticing she looked excited at the possibility of her words being published. "It's ideas I'm looking for."

She flushed, and for a moment he thought she might refuse, but after carefully sizing him up, she slowly placed the journal in his hand. "All right, but I'll be wanting that back soon, you understand."

Already looking forward to enjoying her sprightly company at least one more time, Lassiter nodded. "Very well, I'll meet you here night after next"—he paused thoughtfully—"that is unless you're afraid to come."

"*Afraid?*" she laughed throatily. "I'll worry about telling the devil good day when I meet him." She tossed him a sly grin. "And so far I haven't seen hide nor hair of him."

"Brave girl," he said, thinking how different she was from his fiancée, Daisy Fellows, who was anxiously waiting in New York to enfold him in her lily-white arms.

Molly gazed up at his handsome face, slightly surprised she'd promised to meet him again. She nervously searched the deck, then transferred her attention back to him. "An officer might come by any minute. "I-I have to go below now."

"Very well. Good night, Molly Kilmartin of Ballyshannon. Sleep well. I'll see that your journal is returned."

Molly wondered if he was mocking her, but found no guile in his eyes. She desperately wanted to say something witty, something clever, but in his magnificent presence, her mind had gone totally blank.

He shot her another devastating smile and she

backed away, hoping she wouldn't trip over her own feet. "I'll be saying good evening to you, then." Deeply shaken, she turned and hurried toward the companionway that would lead her to the second-class deck, then down into the bowels of the ship where five hundred other desperate souls like herself had sold all they had and bought themselves a piece of the American dream with a one-way ticket to America.

The next morning, scores of weary steerage passengers rose from their bunks totally dressed, for there was no chance of privacy here. Children squalled, their cries rending the fetid air, while frazzled mothers nursed their babies and potbellied men scratched and adjusted their suspenders.

"Molly, are you up yet?" came a voice two bunks down from her own.

With no chance of a bath, Molly slipped from her bunk, wiped her face with a damp rag and smoothed back her hair. Her friend Clara was calling and she sounded even weaker than the morning before. Always slim and fragile, Clara, who was two years younger than herself, lay in a middle bunk, dark smudges under her eyes. With the tossing sea, the girl had heaved out of an empty stomach until she was little more than skin and bones and almost too weak to walk.

"Are you feeling better today?" Molly asked her, privately deciding she looked worse than ever.

"No, not at all," the girl whispered through cracked lips. "I feel so weak, and all sick inside."

"I see." Molly rubbed Clara's arms with the damp rag she'd used on her own face, then made her way to the communal barrel to fetch a can of water.

There was a forest of faces, an excited babble of voices, plus the smells of oil, and the groaning, creaking sounds of the immense ship. Here in steerage, no attempt was made to trick a person into believing they were relaxing in a country home as on the saloon deck. It was all steel—massive expanses of it—the very sinews of the ship, riveted and bolted, exposed for all to see.

Back at Clara's bunk, Molly raised the girl's head and gently eased water between her parched lips. "You'll be fine once you get off the ship," she offered encouragingly, noticing a flicker of hope light her friend's face.

A sick woman close to Clara called for water and Molly went to the great barrel yet again, then helped a lady with a child, giving the toddler a bit of taffy that her mother, Kathleen, had made as a farewell gift. Twenty minutes later, she'd eaten a chunk of hard, dry bread for breakfast and was with Clara talking about America again.

The young girl gazed at her with eyes full of hope and longing. "Do you believe all the stories?" she asked, her face aglow with wonder. "Do you think New York will be as fine as they say?"

Lassiter's statement about America's bounty being available for the right price hovered on the tip of Molly's tongue, but she knew these words would do the girl no good. She'd promised Clara's mother back in Ballyshannon that she'd see the homesick lass safely to her brother, Paddy, in America, and what she needed now was a sustaining dream to hold on to. "I'm sure it will be," she answered, brushing back Clara's limp hair and hoping she was right. "We've heard so many fine tales, some of them just have to be true, don't they, now?" she offered, infusing her voice with a sense of glowing promise.

They were quiet for a while and the girl looked at her with worshipful eyes. "You were on deck late last night."

Molly blushed, for she'd dreamed of Lassiter, dreamed of his bewitching eyes and enticing smile. "Yes. It was so hot I couldn't sleep," she answered, trying to pass off her actions lightly. "I had to get a bit of fresh air, you know."

Clara nodded in calm acceptance. The pair talked awhile longer before the frail girl closed her eyes and drifted into fitful slumber once more.

With gentle hands, Molly adjusted a ragged sheet about her, then went through her morning routine, still thinking of Lassiter. She thought of him as she ate her ration of salted herring at lunch, and when she took a turn on the packed orlop deck near twilight.

Raking back her windblown hair, she gazed at the sea, now shimmering gold with the sunset's last rays. Saints above, would she ever see Mr. High and Mighty Burke Lassiter again? More important, would she ever get her precious journal back? What a foolish thing she'd done, giving it to him in the first place. She must be careful, so very careful where this man was concerned, for he radiated the same mesmerizing appeal her father had used to ruin her mother's life.

Johnny Kilmartin had been a charmer, too, handsome of face, graceful of form, and able to bewitch any woman alive with his silver tongue and flowery words. Hadn't her poor mother supported the family while he drank away his problems and seduced all the colleens in the county with his special brand of magic? And what agonies her mother had suffered when he'd run away with another woman, only to come back three years later, full of sickness and despair to die in her arms a few months later. Molly wondered if her mother had ever forgiven him, for she knew she couldn't.

Molly jostled her way through the noisy crowd and tightened her fingers about the ship's rail. Lassiter had said he'd attended a hundred balls and danced with thousands of women. Slept with half of them too, she told herself, thinking she'd seen his kind at close range in the form of her own father.

When she married—if she ever did—it would be to some hardworking, responsible man with good habits, a man with selfless, patient ways, a soft-spoken man who'd cherish and revere her. After all, handsome is as handsome does, she sternly reminded herself.

One by one, lights bloomed on the saloon deck, their reflections spilling over the tossing sea. Molly turned and glanced upward, realizing the swells in first class must just be sitting down to dinner. She imagined Lassiter pulling out a chair for some beautiful girl dressed in a gown that cost more than Molly could earn in a whole year. Well, they were welcome to each other, she thought, standing a bit taller.

She, Molly Kilmartin, would never allow some good-looking scamp to steal to her heart and ruin her life. Still, even as she said the words, just thinking of Lassiter's face prompted a staggering flash of pleasure, so strong it left her weak.

"And how is the newspaper business, Mr. Lassiter?" the silver-haired captain asked in a clipped British accent.

Lassiter leaned back in his velvet-upholstered chair, and met the officer's gaze above a white cloth set with expensive china and goblets sparkling with light. "It's doing well. The *Telegram*'s circulation is increasing daily," he lied casually, deciding this was no place to air his financial problems.

The lady seated to the captain's right leaned forward, providing a striking view of her powdered bosom. Still attractive though middle-aged, a red silk gown clad her slender body and her black hair had been swept into an elegant chignon, decorated with red plumes. "One thing is for certain," she affirmed, flirtatiously snagging Lassiter's attention, "your readership should be growing, for New York is bulging at the seams." She laughed airily. "Then again, I suppose that type of person doesn't read."

Lassiter groaned inwardly for he'd talked with the lady before and tagged her as a bigoted bore, obsessed with status and position. *"That type of person?"* he echoed, knowing perfectly well whom she was talking about.

Fine lines streaked across the socialite's brow. "Yes—I'm referring to immigrants, of course. They're pouring in by the thousands and have no skills at all." Her voice rose above the polite murmur filling the room and several passengers turned to stare.

"They're able to offer muscle power—hard labor," Lassiter countered, thinking the city was presently being built with Irish labor.

"Well, yes, if you count that," the woman scoffed, pausing to sip her white wine. "But we have our own blacks for that, don't we?"

23

Several of the elegant women seated at the table nod-ded, jewels sparkling at their ears and throats.

A bald-headed man two chairs down from Lassiter coughed, signaling his intention to join the conversation. "The Irish are a clannish lot, flocking to themselves like they do and cutting off everyone else who wasn't born on the old sod."

Lassiter laughed to himself, thinking they had little choice. Like the rest of the immigrants from Russia, Italy, and eastern Europe, it was that or risk hostility and rejection in the more established communities that fiercely guarded their turf from intrusion by outsiders. "Well, at least the Irish are friendly devils," he joked, trying to turn the conversation aside.

"Too friendly if you ask me," the woman in red prat-tled on, sharply nodding to emphasize her point. "They're breeding like animals in those ghettos and so many of them have tuberculosis. Pugnacious hooligans is what they are," she added with a toss of her plumes. "No one can deny it!"

The bald-headed man gave a crack of laughter. "Did you hear the joke about the Irish servant girl who was sent by the lady of the house to fetch a bed comforter?" His watery eyes glistened with mirth. "She promptly returned with one of the grooms!" he chortled, to be joined by a chorus of male guffaws.

Apparently seeing the conversation was getting out of hand, the captain raised his bushy brows. "Well, I must admit the Irish have been a plus for the Red Star Line," he offered smoothly. "We used to carry cargo in the steerage compartment, but immigrants are much more profitable."

The lady in red demanded Lassiter's attention. "I know everyone who really matters in New York, and the Lassiters are solid stock—one of our founding families. Won't you give us your opinion on this topic, sir? I'm sure we'd all like to hear it."

Lassiter felt his jaw tighten. "Really, ma'am, I don't think I could give you a fair answer."

"Yes, please go on. Let us know what you think."

He paused meaningfully, not caring too much what he said. "Certainly you must realize that at one time all of our ancestors were immigrants."

Red splotches spread over the socialite's cheeks. "Yes, b-but that's different," she stammered, clasping the base of her jeweled throat in embarrassment. "I was born in New York. *I'm* a native American."

Lassiter stood and laid his napkin aside. "You're a native American? Technically speaking, I'm afraid the Indians are the only ones who can call themselves native Americans."

The woman spluttered, obviously offended.

Lassiter gazed at the captain's stricken face, knowing his presence would no longer be required at this exalted table. "Thank you, captain," he offered with a genuine smile, having no quarrel with the officer. He locked gazes with the lady in red and formally bowed his head. "If you will excuse me."

Surprised murmurs followed his swift footsteps into the adjoining lounge. Irritation rose within him as he realized most of the city's upper crust, including Daisy Fellows, shared the socialite's opinions. Taking a few more steps, he slammed his stateroom door behind him, then entered an impressive sitting room decorated with easy chairs and a magnificent bed crowned with a silken canopy.

Vaguely troubled and dissatisfied, he poured himself a glass of brandy, took a sip, then placed the drink aside. He'd left his paper in the capable hands of his city editor and taken a month's trip to Ireland to settle his mind and sort out his financial problems, but he'd found no answers. A generous trust fund would always insure him a comfortable life, but he was in serious jeopardy of losing his beloved newspaper. And it wasn't just his problems with the *Telegram* that troubled him.

Although he'd finally relented to Daisy's insistent pleas that they become engaged, he had to face the fact that their relationship wasn't all that he desired. Most men in his position would be joyous, for Daisy was beautiful, rich, and well-connected, but he was looking for something more, something that at this point he really couldn't identify or put into words.

He flopped into a chair and spied Molly's unread journal on a table beside him. He'd harbored no intention of actually reading it, but out of sheer curiosity, he began scanning her large, rounded handwriting. Her written voice was so strong it seemed as if she were standing before him, speaking in a clear Irish lilt that very minute.

We were all herded on the ship like cattle the day we sailed from Queenstown. While the first- and second-class passengers walked up a high fine gangplank like kings and queens, we marched into a door low on the side of the ship like rats scrambling over a line. They shut us away in steerage compartments like sardines in a tin can, and it was so hot that evening everyone near perished for lack of air.

There are no portholes and we sleep in compartments six feet high, crammed with two tiers of metal bunks with straw mattresses. There's nothing but a few thin blankets tossed over a line to separate the men from the women, and what a desperate racket of snoring and belching and pissing goes on during the night!

Misspelled words, poor grammar, and underlined words riddled the journal, all inked in a bold hand. On the positive side, the writing was strong and colorful and held the ring of truth.

While the toffs eat, drink, and dance their way across the Atlantic, we in steerage eat food that would choke a goat. Mainly they give us barrel after barrel of salted herring. Herring! Herring! Herring! And garlic on bread! They say it will keep a person from being seasick, but it doesn't, for I tossed up everything but my toenails for the first five days of the voyage. I never want to eat herring again. Like Lot's wife. I may soon turn into a pillar of salt!

Lassiter turned a page.

When they want to give us a treat they offer bread pudding. I'm sure they make it from the scraps the lords and ladies leave on their plates. I don't know what they're eating in first class, but I'll bet it's not salted herring!

The passage made Lassiter think about the dining room he'd just left, a late Georgian oasis with a marble fireplace at each end of the cavernous room where plaster cherubs kept a watchful eyes on passengers as they sipped their after-dinner cognac. Overall it attested to the exclusiveness that money could buy—a place for conspicuous consumption and snobbishness.

He devoured more of the journal and laughed to himself.

We have no stewards or deck chairs on the orlop deck. Everyone just sits on their bums staring at the sea—but at least the air is fresh—better than the compartments below. Being seasick in steerage is terrible. The sour odors and the pounding of the engines and waves made me so numb-headed I could scarcely remember my own name. Father Riley, I've already had a glimpse of hell, and I never want to go there again!

The next entry penetrated Lassiter's heart.

I'll be so glad when I can help myself and depend on no one's charity. It's terrible to be trapped at the bottom with no path to work your way up, but by your own wits and muscles. God help me, perhaps someday I can do better.

Still holding the ragged notebook, Lassiter stood, sipping his brandy. He'd lied about wanting to get her reactions to the voyage, but now found himself strangely touched by her frank words. He thumbed through the rest of the ink-splotched journal with its scores of mistakes and regiments of unnecessary exclamation points that marched over the pages like stiff-backed soldiers. The writing had fire and spunk. Crude as it was, it shimmered with originality.

He knew the dog-eared notebook had to be important to the girl. She'd be looking for it, expecting him to bring it to her tomorrow night.

He smiled to himself, for just the thought of seeing her again prompted a pleasurable glow within his chest.

Chapter Two

Late the next evening Molly slipped up to the first-class deck, once again impressed with its magnificence. The vast ship was the most incredible thing she'd even seen. It went on forever: a maze of decks and companionways, a towering mass of funnels, immaculate stewards, officers, all gold braid and medal ribbons, and self-important passengers, strolling to the sound of muffled dance music.

Anticipation bubbled within her. Would she speak with the charming Mr. Lassiter again tonight? Would he bless her with that flashing smile that had so much force she felt as if an ocean wave had just rolled over her? Well, it didn't matter, she lied to herself. She'd just come to get her journal, then she'd be on her way, leaving the rich American to amuse himself as he might.

When she came to the spot where she'd originally

met Lassiter, he was nowhere in sight, and her spirits dropped like a rock plunging to the depths of the sea. She neared a porthole and peeked into a columned ballroom filled with gorgeously dressed ladies with swan's down fans and gentlemen in black tuxedos. Saints above, did these people do anything but amuse themselves? Molly wondered, still searching for Lassiter, but not finding him in their midst.

A lump in her throat, she strode from the porthole. It was time to go back to steerage. How foolish she'd been to believe the man's promise! Why he'd probably laughed at her journal and tossed it away, promptly forgetting about her. Her pride cut to ribbons, she marched ahead, then as she rounded a boat housing, her heart lurched, for there, only twenty feet away, stood Lassiter absorbed in conversation with another well-dressed gentleman. The man scanned Molly, prompting Lassiter to turn and catch her gaze himself. When he started toward her with purposeful strides, her nerves jangled with excitement.

"Molly Kilmartin of Ballyshannon, I believe," he greeted her, taking her slender arm as if she were a great debutante. "I've been looking for you," he proclaimed with another of his enticing smiles.

"And I've been looking for you too!" she chimed in saucily.

His eyes lit with amusement. "I thought you weren't coming."

She swung her gaze about the deck, then back to him. "Of course I was coming," she returned, her sensibilities offended that he'd doubted her word. "I had to come, you know. I had to get my journal."

A snooty lady swished by in silks, dropping her

glossy lids in callous disgust at the sight of Molly, who stiffened her spine, refusing to be intimidated by the haughty socialite or the rest of the passengers who gave her questioning stares. The Good Lord had fashioned her as well as any person on the ship, she kept reminding herself when her courage flagged. She might not have money, but she had a heart full of dreams and the good common sense and self-respect her mother and Father Riley had put into her head, and that was enough for anyone.

Once the lady had passed, Lassiter guided Molly to the rail. He pulled the tattered journal from his vest pocket and gave it to her. "Here, this is yours I believe," he announced, observing how small and out of place she looked on the saloon deck, dressed in a shabby black gown with frayed cuffs. But her back was ramrod straight, he thought with approval, and she carried her head with a proud tilt—a tilt that told the world she believed in herself.

"Well, what did you think of it?" she inquired, lovingly tracing her fingers over the worn volume. "Only your honest opinion will do, for your face will speak the truth even if your tongue doesn't."

Lassiter laughed, remembering some of the journal's outrageous sentences. "I liked it—very much, in fact."

Her face fell like a wilted flower. "But you're laughing."

"Laughing is good. It's hard to make people laugh."

They began walking again. "Is it now?" she prodded, a suspicious look passing through her dazzling green eyes. "Tell me, then, what's so special about making people laugh?"

"I think," he began slowly, "that humor often makes people see the truth. Sometimes people can be reached with laughter when they can be reached no other way."

Molly grinned. "I suppose you're right. But it's best to dress up the truth a bit, don't you know. There's an old Irish story about Truth," she rambled on, clutching the journal to her curvaceous bosom. "Would you like to hear it?"

He nodded, knowing he was going to hear it whether he wanted to or not.

"Well, hundreds of years ago," she began, "the Good Lord himself sent Truth to the villages of Ireland to tell people they were being slothful. They must work harder or there would be a famine year." Her eyes glinted with mirth. "When Truth knocked on the villagers' doors they were opened, but then slammed in his face. Not knowing what to do, Truth went to the archbishop of Dublin himself with the problem."

She paused, amusement playing over her lovely face. " 'Why am I not accepted?' Truth asked, beating his chest boastfully, 'After all I'm the Truth!' The archbishop took one look at him and blushed, seeing he didn't have on a stitch of clothes.

" 'But lad,' he explained with a kind smile, 'can't you see you're stark naked? Who'd want to look at your hairy little body, now?' " Molly's eyes twinkled playfully. "The archbishop was a wise man. He dressed Truth in fine clothes—folktales of scarlet—and sent him out again. This time Truth was invited into the cottages and offered tea and a warm place beside the peat fires. The people finally listened to him and were saved," she finished with a pleased sigh.

Lassiter smiled, thinking the story was typically Irish. "That's a charming story. I'll have to tell it to my children one day."

A cautious look crept over Molly's face. "You're married, then. You have children?"

Lassiter chuckled, amazed she'd taken his statement so literally. "No, I'm not married and I don't have any children—at least none that I know of. I simply meant I'd have to remember it for the future—for when I do have children."

She held his gaze intently. "And how many would you be wanting?" she asked, as if he might be ordering up cords of wood.

"I haven't given that question much thought," he chortled, offering her his arm again. "I've been far too busy to consider it."

She wagged her head. "That's a pity, for no man ever wore a neckcloth as fine as his own child's arm draped around his neck."

They walked on in silence, but when Molly could stand it no longer, she glanced at Lassiter, still amazed that a real reporter had read her work. "So you like my writing, then. You think it's all right?"

He smiled down at her, warming her heart with his approval. "Yes, it's fresh, and vivid too. I especially liked the part about the salted herring."

"Oh, don't mention it. I may be sick!"

The sound of the waves kept time with their strolling footsteps. "I didn't write the first night, you know," Molly finally admitted, surprised she was becoming so comfortable with the American.

He looked at her thoughtfully, but said nothing.

"I lay on that hard bunk and cried my eyes out," she

confessed, embarrassed that she'd been so weak. "I kept wondering if I was doing the right thing. If I'd ever see Mam again. If I'd be a burden to Aunt Agatha." She bit her lip. "I have to make it, you know. Da is dead, so I'm the only hope Mam has."

Lassiter frowned. "Isn't there anyone else to take care of her? Don't you have brothers?"

"Yes, I have two brothers, but they're both off in the Queen's army in India. And they're as tight as tuppence in a market woman's purse, so it doesn't matter anyway," she answered, remembering their neglect with disgust. "They never send a farthing home." She heaved a great sigh. "I gave myself a good talking to that first night. I told myself other people had made it in America, and I could too."

She noticed a warm look in Lassiter's eyes. "Tell me more about your father," he gently prompted, holding her arm a little tighter.

"Well, when Da was alive, he cut peat and did piddling jobs here and there, but his main business was drinking." She rolled her eyes, warming to her story. "Faith, if holy water was whiskey he'd be at mass every day. He was a fine, handsome black-haired man, but looks and charm don't make the pot boil, do they?"

Molly looked up at Lassiter, suddenly realizing she was on the verge of revealing all of her family problems. An officer's brass glinted in the dull light and she gazed at the sea until the man had passed. She glanced at Lassiter again, amazed she'd told him so much about herself, him being an American and all. "It's getting late, and I've talked far too much," she admitted softly. "I'd better be getting below."

Lassiter's eyes sparkled with curiosity. "Tell me,

Irish, why did you do it? Why did you risk sneaking up here the other night when it could only mean trouble?"

"Just got my courage up," Molly returned, considering the question for the first time herself. "You see, there's this little brass plaque on the companionway that leads up from steerage. It says, 'All Steerage Passengers Stay Below. Trespassers Will Be Fined.' Funny how a little sign like that can intimidate so many people."

She sighed, angry with the injustice of it all. "There was something about that sign I didn't like—something about it that made me want to climb those metal steps and see what was up here." She shook back her wind-blown hair. "Don't I have dreams and wishes, happiness and sadness, just like the fine ladies you eat dinner with every evening?"

"And what are those dreams?"

She met his twinkling eyes, compelled to tell him. "I want to stand on my own feet—take care of myself, and never ask a blessed soul for a thing. And I want a chance to learn, learn everything I can. Whatever I do, from making beds"—she glanced at the journal—"to hooking words together, I want to be the very best. There's something that delights the heart about being the best, isn't there?"

"Anything else?" he chuckled.

She laughed softly. "I wouldn't mind having a red velvet gown and a real fur muff one day."

Lassiter remained silent, but she noticed a warm, satisfied expression on his face. They'd arrived at a shadowy, deserted part of the saloon deck and he stopped walking and gently took her by the shoulders. His eyes deepened until they were the color of the starry, moonlit night sky. "You're a beautiful girl, Molly Kilmartin, and a brave one too."

A new softness glazed his face and her pulse fluttered crazily. "Of course," she chirped playfully. "Didn't you know that already?"

Shivery excitement raced through her as he cupped her chin. "What a joy you are."

He loosely gathered her to him, and the warmth of his body and the scent of tobacco clinging to his clothes released a raw, primitive feeling buried deep within her. His smoky eyes held her captive, and when he lowered his head, her heart pounded as if it might burst through her ribcage. He was going to kiss her, she thought, trembling with sweet anticipation.

There was a war going on within her, not of guns and cannons, yet a war just the same. How she wanted to surrender her lips to this gorgeous man! But she would be the master of her destiny. She would become a success in New York without the help or interference of any man, even one as charming as this. Sexual intimacy welled between them until it was almost a tangible thing, but using all her emotional strength, she pulled from Lassiter's strong arms.

A moment of charged silence filled the air; then his voice became light and casual again. "Do you like champagne, Irish?"

"Faith, what a question!" she laughed, her heart still stroking evenly. "You're asking *me*, who's never tasted a drop of the stuff?"

"Well, it's time you did." He took her arm and walked on as if nothing had happened. "You should have a glass to celebrate your arrival in America."

A warm glow worked its way about her heart. "Now that would be something, would it not? Me drinking champagne with a real gentleman. And where would you be getting this champagne, Mr. Lassiter?" she inquired, a sense of tingling expectation stealing over her.

He paused and idly caressed her shoulders, sending a pleasurable thrill down her spine. "From the farewell party, the last night out, of course. Meet me at this spot two evenings from now—the night before we dock," he ordered, glancing about as if to remember the spot himself. The urgency of his voice skittered sparkles of fire through her blood. He looked at her again, bold appraisal in his eyes. "Let's say eleven o'clock. We'll have our own farewell party."

Excitement poured through her. "Well, I'm not sure. I may be busy, you know, getting all my belongings in order. I understand a lot happens that first morning we arrive in New York."

He traced a knuckle over her cheek. "Yes, a lot."

His invitation was a passionate challenge, hard to resist. "If I have time, I'll meet you here the last night of the voyage, Mr. Lassiter. But only if I have time, mind you!"

He gave a deep, rich laugh, and she suppressed a smile, thinking her heart had taken wings.

The last night of the voyage, Molly stood at the rail and gazed at the brilliant stars that gleamed just above the horizon. Lush music wafted onto the deck from the ballroom, and a poignant sweetness hung on the light evening air and tugged at her senses.

She'd worn her Sunday gown, a plain blue cotton

dress with a scooped neckline and white lace cuffs salvaged from one of Mam's old gowns, and she knew she'd feel the biggest fool that God ever made if Lassiter stood her up. Then over the noise of the gently lapping waves, she caught the sound of heavy footsteps and whirled about.

Her heart pitched, for Lassiter walked toward her, every bit as rakishly good-looking as she remembered. She saw his black hair, untidy and mussed from a little breeze, his bronzed skin, his animal-white teeth flashing in the shadows. *Manly, potent, desirable,* were the words that instantly flooded her mind. Why, just the sight of his heavily muscled body moving beneath his tuxedo set off a shocking torrent of wicked feelings she could scarcely identify as her own.

In one hand he carried a huge bottle of champagne, while from the fingers of his other hand dangled two long-stemmed crystal flutes, gold-rimmed, and glimmering softly in the moonlight. His mouth quirked up in a friendly grin, and she laughed in spite of herself.

"Now what are you laughing about, Irish?" he asked, placing the champagne bottle and glasses on the rail where it thickened in front of a lifeboat.

"Saints above—a whole bottle! Glory be to God. Did you steal it off a serving cart?"

His eyes danced with amusement. "Yes, of course. Believe me, they'll never miss it." He considered her thoughtfully. "You look ravishing tonight," he commented lazily, caressing her shoulders as if he'd known her all his life. He ran a hand through her windblown locks. "And your hair feels like spun silk."

Him and his pretty words! Molly thought with a soft blurring of her senses. God help her, if he wasn't a silver-tongued devil, but being so unabashedly masculine, the trait only made him more appealing. Their gazes locked, and she wanted to tell him that just being near him made her feel warm and wonderful, but she bit her tongue, knowing she dared not.

He picked up the bottle and eyed the gold-swirled label. "Umm, *Chateau de Chandon*, a fine French champagne, dry and not too sweet. Do you like dry wines?"

Molly, who'd never drank anything but rough ale, started to tell him she had no idea what he was talking about, but simply smiled and whispered, "Yes, of course."

The champagne cork had already been loosened and Lassiter poured the bubbling wine into the delicately etched glasses. He offered her one, then held his before him. "I propose a toast," he announced, his eyes full of merriment, "a toast to Molly Kilmartin and her success in New York."

Molly twirled the icy-cold champagne flute between her fingertips, then sipped the wine, thinking her first taste of the elegant life was as smooth as silk. Before she knew it, she'd finished the glass and Lassiter had poured her another.

"Just think, me drinking champagne like a real toff," she observed, wondering why the light wine was making her feel so giddy. "No one will ever believe it!"

The "Blue Danube Waltz" floated from the ballroom and Lassiter placed her glass aside. "May I have this dance, Miss Kilmartin?" he asked, his roving gaze lazily appraising her.

She smiled her answer, and he led her from the rail.

He held her as if she weighed nothing, and began dancing, gliding over the smooth, polished deck. The music swelled and he pulled her closer yet, his warm breath upon her cheek. Shyly she met his gaze, and the hunger and open admiration in his eyes made her tremble.

Molly had been to a few Christmas dances in Ballyshannon and thanked the Lord above that she knew enough steps to keep up with his practiced moves. During those country dances, her mother and Father Riley had beamed on in approval as she stiffly moved about the room with some young man as awkward as herself. But this was different, so different, for there was power and assurance in Lassiter's huge body. He swept her about the deck, and she wanted him to keep holding her, keep dancing with her, and from the look on his face, he wanted it too.

He pulled her so tightly against his chest, she could feel his starched white shirt, smooth against her cheek. His heart thudded rhythmically and a wild sensual feeling swelled within her, prompting her to follow his lead until they danced as one person. Tonight life itself sang through her veins in a golden flow.

After another waltz, Lassiter's arm draped casually about Molly's waist as they rested at the rail and drank more champagne. By now, Molly felt as if she'd known him all her life—as if she could tell him anything. They laughed and talked about New York and in her mellow, softly tipsy mood, she found herself revealing the contents of her heart with no inhibitions whatsoever.

"I need to save money," she confessed, now completely at ease with him. "I have to scrape up Mam's passage, and quickly too."

41

His eyes moved over her assessingly. "Aren't you being a little hard on yourself? Give yourself some time."

"No, I must have it in three months," she blurted out, feeling the pressing obligation fall squarely on her shoulders. "Before . . . before . . . "

"Before what?" Lassiter asked, brushing a tendril of windblown hair from her forehead.

"Before the squire evicts her!"

Softness gathered in his sensual eyes.

Saints above, she'd told him, Molly thought with a pang of regret. She lowered her gaze, then looked up, deciding he might as well know it all. "You see, Mam sold almost everything she had to give me a chance at a new life," she sighed, sick at the thought of it. "She makes a little lace to get by, but she's really too sick to work—too brokenhearted. She has enough to keep her for three months, then the squire's men will put her on the road." She swallowed back a rush of tears. "S-So you see, I've just got to have that passage and have it soon."

Lassiter gazed at her thoughtfully, but said nothing.

"I'm sure she'll be happier in America," Molly whispered, trying to master her emotions. "Maybe the change will mend her heart."

He tenderly gathered her in his arms. "And what broke her heart?"

"I told you about my older brothers, but I didn't tell you about my younger brother—about Cossi. Twelve he was. We lost him last year from scarlet fever." She heaved a heartfelt sigh. "Mam hasn't been the same since. She just can't stop grieving for him."

Lassiter's heart quickened with feeling. How ridicu-

42

lously young and innocent the girl looked—too innocent to shoulder such a burden. He thought of the socialite in the red gown and wondered if she'd ever been faced with such a challenge. Molly trembled and he flicked a sparkling tear from her face, wanting to comfort her, wanting to give her courage.

Gently, he eased her away, then slipped a business card from his vest and placed it in her hand. "Take this," he said quietly. "If there's some way I can help while you're in the city, let me know."

A frown skittered over her smooth brow. "I won't be needing a loan, if that's what you mean," she returned in a hurt tone. She tried to give the card back to him. "I can stand on my own two feet as well as anyone else, you know."

Lord, damn that Irish pride of hers, Lassiter thought irritably. He closed her fingers over the card. "No, that's not what I mean. If you need someone to talk to—if you need a friend—"

Without glancing at it, she reluctantly took the card and slipped it into her skirt pocket.

It was just as well, Lassiter thought with a weary sigh. Why should she know he published and edited the New York *Telegram* and lived in the palatial Regency Hotel on Fifth Avenue? Let her think he was a reporter for the evening. It made things so much simpler. He offered her a smile and another glass of champagne, hoping to divert her sadness.

"*Four,* Mr. Lassiter? No, I couldn't!"

"Call me Burke," he suggested, watching moonlight play over her delicate features.

She sent him a shy, sidelong glance. "I-I think just plain Lassiter suits you better."

"Very well," he chuckled, determined to make her smile again. He placed the glass in her hand. "Go ahead and have a sip. This is a special evening."

Once the champagne glass touched her lips, he began telling her amusing stories about New York, all engineered to lift her spirits. In a few minutes she was laughing, and he laughed with her, happy to see her eyes sparkling once more.

When the orchestra began playing "Auld Lang Syne," he scooped her into his arms before she had a chance to put down the champagne flute. He scanned her upturned face, her large eyes, her sweet moist lips. Primal urges flared within him, and he knew he couldn't blame it on the glow of the wine, for the feeling was too profound. He feathered his hands down her slim back, trying to forget Daisy Fellows was waiting for him in New York, trying to puzzle out why this delicate girl affected his emotions so deeply.

Damn it all, if this little spitfire wasn't the most desirable bit of femininity he'd ever seen—and she was so alive, so vibrant, so authentic. He gazed into her questioning eyes, shaken by the passion that flashed between them. For him, the prolonged anticipation of kissing her was almost unbearable, and he gradually stopped dancing and drew her close.

Despite his best efforts, he could feel his discipline crumbling like wet sand. At this particular moment, he wasn't thinking of Daisy Fellows or any other woman he'd ever known; all his thoughts, all his life force, all his desire, were centered on Molly alone.

Lassiter lowered his head and, before she could protest, devoured her lips. He'd always taken women as the lightest of diversions, but a strange feeling he didn't understand stubbornly lodged in his chest. With her, all the passion of his younger years, all the romance the world had tried to beat out of him came surging back in a hot, passionate flow.

He held her quivering body tighter yet, cradling the back of her head as he deepened the kiss. Trembling, she stepped back, but he strengthened the embrace and refused to let her go. "Open your mouth, little one," he coaxed in a penetrating whisper, his loins already warm with desire. He lightly flicked his tongue over her lips, and when they relaxed, he slipped it between them.

Molly melted into his embrace, unable to fight her aching desire any longer. As his tongue traced her teeth, then plunged deep into her mouth in a long, searching caress, a swooning sweetness flooded over her. She felt her body yearning hotly to burst into bloom, and trembled with erotic need. Days of suppressed longing suddenly surfaced within her and moisture welled between her legs. The champagne flute crashed to the deck as she tightly circled her arms about his neck.

He tore his lips from hers and she yielded to a profusion of kisses on her hair, her neck, her throat. Each place he kissed, he worshiped with adoring words of love, and she sighed deeply, her body thrumming with sexual hunger. She struggled to fight back her raging need, but the sensations his lips elicited were so delectable, pangs of desire flashed through her like sheet lightning.

"You have the face of an angel," he murmured as his hands smoothed down her arms, leaving them warm and glowing. He pulled her against him roughly, his lips slanting over hers again. She felt his tongue, thrust-

45

ing deeply and possessively, darting in and out of her mouth, and a hot flush stung her face.

His fingers traced her collarbone; then a deep thrill ran through her as his warm hand slipped into her bodice and cupped her breast. He rolled an aching nipple between his fingers and she whimpered with violent pleasure. A fire began in the palpitating center between her thighs and spread over her quaking body. Her nipples went hard as coral and she became exquisitely languid and drugged as if she'd taken a powerful opiate. Her joints were melting, her head reeling.

She felt his thick manhood strain long and rock-hard against his trousers and blood roared in her ears. Every nerve in her body throbbed and rapturous sensations swept through her in a glorious rush of sexual pleasure. Relentlessly, he flicked his fingertip over a swollen nipple until she thought she might actually faint with delight.

Confused feelings stormed against her heart. Her body pulled her one way, while her mind pulled her the other. Who was this gorgeous stranger who'd stolen the spirit right out of her so smoothly she'd scarcely known it had happened? And saints above, why did she feel so weak and as helpless as a kitten when he touched her?

Then with a shaft of insight, she realized this perfect ecstasy had dissolved all her inhibitions, and an obstinate warning voice echoed through her mind. Had she lost every grain of sense she had? After all of Mam's and Father Riley's labors to turn her into a lady, what would they think if they could witness this little scene?

God help her, she was acting no better than a slatternly tavern wench. And what of Lassiter? Why would a rich American like himself be kissing her if he didn't have more ambitious plans in mind? Why, the rascal had plied her with French champagne no less—urged four glasses of the stuff on her to break down her resistance to his advances. How could she have been so blind? A gentle kiss on the lips was one thing, but this was something else altogether—something she had to stop this very minute!

Her heart pounded wildly and she twisted away. She stared at his puzzled face, tears stinging her eyes. "A farewell party, is it now?" she said, her voice breaking with huskiness. Humiliation rolled through her in great waves. "I should have known what you really wanted, but fool that I am, I thought you were a gentleman!"

He tried to embrace her again, but she pulled away, then slapped his face so hard, her fingers stung like they'd been burned with fire.

Lassiter gazed at her evenly. "Molly, wait a minute. Let me explain. You don't understand."

"*No,* it's you who'll be doing the waiting, and I understand the situation just fine. I'll have you know, my mother thinks as much of me as yours does of you!" Tears rolled unbidden down her face. "God above, have you no heart in you?" she sobbed, still so attracted to him that her body ached passionately for his touch.

He grabbed her arm, but she jerked away. Tears choking her throat, she ran toward the companionway leading to steerage, hating him with all her heart, but knowing she'd remember every line of his handsome face for the rest of her life.

Chapter Three

The *Saxonia* had just passed through the Narrows, and crying gulls wheeled over the ship and climbed into a dawn sky, trailed with apricot and rose. Molly had thought of Lassiter most of the night, but with the first sight of land, her attention became riveted on New York's smudgy skyline. She put her arm about Clara, who stood by her side trembling with anticipation. "We've finally arrived in America," she murmured in an awed tone, pointing at the distant buildings wrapped in haze. "There's New York. Just think of it."

An excitement that Molly felt herself rippled through the laughing crowd thronged about the girls. Each man, woman, and child had all they could carry, and many looked like pack animals with their belongings strapped to their backs. Molly smelled the tang of the harbor and experienced a thrill of triumph. Her long-awaited arrival in America loomed like a golden promise, only moments away now.

After the Narrows, the ship glided down the East River to the noisy South Street docks. Craft of all kind from great steamships to small skiffs dotted the sun-dappled water. "Oh, look at that," Clara exclaimed, indicating three tugs, all blowing their rasping horns and rubbing against the vessel as they guided it into port.

Escorted by the tugs, the ship moved past the cargo docks packed with great tin-roofed warehouses and laboring stevedores. All about Molly, fathers lifted children to their shoulders, and there was a general clatter and hubbub with strangers embracing and kissing like old friends. Clara laughed happily and Molly decided their arrival had given the girl a temporary burst of energy, but dreading their upcoming medical inspection, she wondered how long it would last.

The steamer's whistle gave a shrill blast and she felt the bumping tugs position the vessel to slide into its berth. The quay swarmed with moving figures, and a trio of young port officers in smart uniforms gazed up thoughtfully as the huge steamer finally docked to the sound of clanking chains and clattering winches.

Molly scanned the dock area and noted fine carriages and well-fed horses, their satiny coats gleaming in the morning light. Elegantly dressed men, and women with dainty parasols, began alighting from the smart broughams and strolling in the direction of the great steamship to greet their well-heeled relatives and friends. All at once, Molly wondered if someone was waiting for Lassiter.

Thinking she might see him, she dragged her battered suitcase to the rail, and craning her neck, stared upward at the first-class deck. By now the saloon passengers, dressed in their finest, filed forward to leave the ship, all chattering pleasantly. Ladies waved lacy handkerchiefs and men shook hands and said their last good-byes as porters followed, pushing trunks on squeaking trolleys.

Lassiter suddenly appeared, a long cigar jauntily clamped between his white teeth. He carried a briefcase while a porter walked behind him toting two expensive suitcases with brass buckles. Never taking her eyes from Lassiter, Molly watched him proceed down the busy gangplank. She wore the same gown as the night before, and remembering his card, retrieved it and read, BURKE LASSITER, PUBLISHER, EDITOR IN CHIEF, *NEW YORK TELEGRAM*. Her heart turned over in her bosom. Saints above, he wasn't a reporter as she'd thought, but a publisher, worth millions, no doubt!

She gnawed her lip, thinking of all the things she'd said the night before. How gauche she must have appeared, telling him of her personal problems while he couldn't have cared less. She'd stood emotionally naked before him, while the man had wantonly toyed with her for his idle sexual pleasure. When he disembarked, and a beautifully dressed blond lady rushed forward and threw her arms about his neck, sickness swirled in Molly's stomach. Who was the beautiful creature, and what was her relationship with Lassiter? Could they be romantically involved?

What did it matter? she thought, angrily sailing his card over the rail and watching it swirl downward to float on the foam-specked water. Him and his offer of friendship! She knew exactly what kind of friend he'd be—the kind who'd take her to bed, but never offer a wedding ring. She stood on her toes to snatch a last glimpse of him as he and the fashionable lady melted into the milling crowd. *Well then, Mr. High and Mighty Burke Lassiter, good-bye forever and good riddance to you!*

Clara gazed at her strangely. "That fine-lookin' gentleman that just left the ship. Do you know him, then?"

Molly shook her head. "No, not at all."

"Funny. The way you were starin' at him, I thought you might."

"I haven't the slightest idea who he is. Just some swell who caught my eye," Molly said more sharply than she'd intended.

"It must be nice to have money," Clara remarked wistfully. "I'd love to meet a man with money."

"*Why?* If you put a fine suit on a goat, he's still a goat, is he not?"

Clara looked shocked, but before she could reply, an impressive officer swaggered onto the orlop deck, his face all business. Pushing people aside, he made his way through the crowd where wide-eyed children clung to their mother's skirts in wonderment and fear. When the man was in the very center of the deck, he stood on a trunk and in a loud, gruff voice announced, "You people will be transported to Castle Island on a barge and processed there. Do what they say and give them no trouble."

A questioning murmur ran through the assembled immigrants, who gazed at one another expectantly.

"Take everything with you," the dour officer continued in a businesslike tone. "Leave nothing behind. You won't be coming back unless you fail the tests. Remember, no pushing and shoving!"

The steerage gangplank was lowered with a thud and the immigrants moved forward in one surging mass. Families struggled to stay together, but often became separated. Mothers fanatically tried to keep up with toddlers, and grown children with their doddering elders. Everyone was so mixed up, Molly wondered if the families would ever get back together again.

She glanced at the busy harbor and spotted the approaching barge, outfitted with a canvas shade, and on its side, lifesavers and coiled ropes. In the distance, through the haze, lay the island itself and the huge round building that she must pass through before she met Aunt Agatha. In a few moments, she, Molly Kilmartin of County Galway, would actually set foot on American soil, and her pulse raced with anticipation. She and Clara hoisted their heavy suitcases and milled toward the gangplank, their bodies pressed, shoved, and gouged by the exuberant crowd.

Molly knew she should be the happiest person on earth, but for some unexplainable reason, she thought of Lassiter and tears stung her eyes. She blinked them away and ordered herself not to be so foolish. She wouldn't give him a second thought. The black-hearted rascal meant nothing to her. Absolutely nothing.

"Oh, I'm so glad you're back. I could just squeeze you to death!" Daisy Fellows cried, throwing her arms about Lassiter and kissing him deeply as their brougham rattled toward Fifth Avenue.

Suffocating in the scent of her heady jasmine perfume, he pushed her away. "For God's sake, Daisy, control yourself," he said, swinging his gaze over her.

With her low-cut pink silk gown, perky bustle, and white kid gloves, she was a vision of the dressmaker's art. A saucy chapeau crowned one side of her head, and with every turn of the creaking carriage, golden ringlets bounced against her delicate shoulders.

A month away had sharpened Lassiter's perception of her. Before his trip, she didn't seem any worse than the other vapid socialites who swarmed about him at the endless cotillions he was forced to attend—but she now seemed insufferable. Why should that be, he wondered vaguely?

She snapped a closed fan against his sleeve. "Honestly, Burke, I thought you'd be more glad to see me. Why did you rush off to Ireland in the first place? I can compete with any woman alive, but not with a salmon stream, it seems." She gave him a flirtatious pout. "And how could you have spent a whole month over there? I'll never forgive you!"

"Sometimes a man needs to be alone."

"And sometimes a lady needs companionship! Let's go to Delmonico's for lunch. All our old friends will be there."

He heaved a deep sigh, thinking he should have extended his vacation several weeks longer. "Maybe tomorrow. I need to go home, then spend the rest of the day at the *Telegram*."

Daisy rolled her china-blue eyes. "Oh, yes, that dreadful paper!" She pulled a wad of bills from her beaded reticule and waved them in front of his face. "Forget about the paper today. We'll spend Daddy's money. He has five million stacked in the bank just moldering away. Why it's practically our duty to spend it—to keep the economy going!"

Scarcely taking a breath, she prattled on about trivia that had happened while Lassiter was in Ireland. Lord, how insipid she could be, he thought. He groaned inwardly, now clearly remembering why he'd gone abroad in the first place.

Why didn't Daisy make him feel alive and vital as Molly had? He considered the girl again, remembering her flashing eyes and saucy words. What a little spitfire she was! he laughed to himself, tracing a hand over his jaw and recalling her stinging slap. Damn stuffy social convention to hell, he thought with a snort of disgust, deciding she'd appealed to him more than any socialite he'd met in ages. What a pity, he'd probably never see her again.

He studied Daisy's perfectly powdered face, perfectly glossed lips, and perfectly corseted eighteen-inch waist, and decided she looked like a fragile wax doll. That was the problem. He couldn't imagine her on a fishing trip, even in misty Ireland; she'd wilt like a flower in the noonday sun. Actually the *real* problem with Daisy was she had one focus—herself and herself alone. An original idea had never entered her head, and as for a sense of humor, he could forget it. Telling her a joke or sharing an amusing story was like trying to bounce a ball off a snowbank, he decided, recalling Molly's tale about the naked truth.

Lord, what had happened last night, anyway? They'd been wrapped in an erotic dream, then damn it all, if she hadn't suddenly made an one-hundred-and-eighty-degree turn, even suggesting that he'd plied her with champagne to break down her resistance. When all was said and done, he couldn't have helped kissing her if he'd tried, and the Lord knew he wasn't sorry he had, just puzzled that it had all turned out so badly.

"Burke, why are you so preoccupied? Why aren't you listening to me?"

Daisy stripped off a kid glove, then lifted her long, white fingers and admired her costly engagement ring. "Really, Burke, I think we should consider trading this stone for a larger one, don't you?"

Any larger, he thought, and she wouldn't be able to hold up her hand.

She cuddled against him and clasped his arm. "And we need to think about a date. We *must* set a date, you know."

Lassiter knocked on the carriage roof, signaling the driver to stop.

Daisy fluttered her long lashes. "What in the world are you doing? I thought we were going to Delmonico's."

Lassiter opened the carriage door and glanced at the impressive columned mansion belonging to Daisy's father, William Thornton Fellows the Third, of the Connecticut Fellows, all descended from the Founding Fathers. "You don't listen very well," he returned as he gathered up the tail of her long skirt and forcefully guided her from the carriage.

Daisy's pink lips trembled with rage. "Burke, what are you doing? What in heaven's name is wrong with you? No, stop, I don't want to go home!"

"Good-bye, Daisy." Once she was safely on the pavement, he slammed the door, then knocked for the driver to proceed down the avenue.

He lit an expensive cigar to dissipate the heavy jasmine scent that still lingered in the carriage, then glanced over his shoulder to see Daisy standing on the sidewalk, stamping her dainty foot.

"Burke, come back!"

He leaned against the soft plush seat and chuckled, thinking of their wedding date, a possible necessity to keep the *Telegram* afloat, but an event he could forestall for years if necessary. He took a deep draw from his cigar, finally facing the unvarnished truth about Daisy Fellows: When all was said and done, she was nothing more than an insurance policy against bad times.

It had been said every man had his price, but Lassiter prayed with all his heart that his wouldn't be sacrificing his freedom to marry William Fellows's only daughter.

Clara shuffled by Molly's side, a tendril of hair drooping over her tired, shadowed eyes. "We've been on our feet for hours," she lamented with a weary sigh. "Do you think we'll ever get to sit down?"

Molly took Clara's suitcase in one aching hand, while she carried her own in the other. "We can't sit down now," she answered in a comforting tone. "We have the whole blessed day ahead of us."

The handles cut into Molly's hands and she thought of the rich women on the *Saxonia*'s saloon deck who'd disembarked so easily, carrying no more than a handbag. Three hours had passed since the vessel had docked, but outside of changing their small treasure of money into American dollars and coins, the girls had made precious little progress.

Now near nine o'clock, Molly guided Clara through the babbling throng of humanity filling the huge Castle

Island immigration building that became increasingly warmer with each passing hour. And the smell of the place! Odors surged about them: closely packed bodies, cheap tobacco, and the earthy aroma of dirty clothes and unwashed hair.

With the excitement of coming into port, most of the children hadn't eaten breakfast and were hungry and fussy. Many of the older people couldn't stand any longer and had slumped on benches or simply sat on the floor, their heads resting against one of the pillars that supported the great glass-domed roof.

"Over there, miss!" an important-looking man wearing a big homburg shouted at Molly. He stabbed his finger at a row of never-ending lines. "Get in one of those lines and wait your turn."

The girls stood for another two hours, then passed an officer whose duty it was to register their name, birthplace, and destination in a large folio. The inspector asked Molly a long list of personal questions: What was her nationality, was she married or single, how much money did she have, had she ever been an inmate in a prison or an insane asylum?

After they'd been interrogated, they found the dining room, and ordered milk, bread, and a thick soup with meat. Such an abundance! Molly thought, being careful not to spend too much of the money she'd knotted in an old handkerchief. After the pair had satisfied their hunger, Molly lugged both suitcases to the sight of their next trial, the medical inspection area, where they patiently queued up with hundreds of other weary souls.

She noticed the stern-faced inspectors watched every

step the immigrants took. They watched to see if they slipped, or stumbled on the many steps they had to climb, or were otherwise unfit for life in America. The weak ones were sent aside for further inspection. Immigrants were also checked for mental problems, partial blindness, deafness, heart trouble, tuberculosis, and trachoma.

Clara tugged on Molly's sleeve. "Faith. What's happenin' there? Why are those people takin' on so?"

Molly tilted her head and tried to see what was going on. "Someone from the family has been rejected," she explained as easily as she could. "They'll have to go back." Two crying women walked past, their backs marked with chalk. "The chalk marks means something is wrong with them. They'll have to be held in detention until a ship arrives to take them home."

Clara blanched and clutched Molly's arm a little tighter.

By late afternoon Molly was so tired she could scarcely stand. Her body drooped with weariness and her ears throbbed with the noise and clatter that constantly echoed through the massive building. She closed her eyes, and seeing flashes of Lassiter's face as he held her in his arms, fought back a sense of aching regret.

Faith, had she done the right thing last night? With a spurt of defiance, she told herself he'd given her no choice. His manner—thoughtless and aggressive— couldn't be tolerated. If she didn't follow her dream, she couldn't live with herself. But if she'd done the right thing, why did her heart ache as if it was tearing apart?

"Miss, step forward!" A white-robed doctor signaled

her to approach and stand before him for the trachoma inspection.

She straightened her shoulders and swallowed back her tears.

The doctor roughly pulled back her eyelids, checking the inside of them for infection. It hurt terribly and she wanted to pull her head away, but stood stoically still.

"Go to the next station," he ordered before she had a chance to wipe the streaming tears from her cheeks. "The other doctors will finish your physical there."

Desperately worried about Clara, who was in line behind her, Molly moved on.

The new doctor ordered her to do some sums in her head and read a bit. The man told her to press her hands on a table so he could see if her fingernails were a healthy pink or turned blue, indicating heart trouble. He forced her mouth open to inspect her teeth and throat, and most humiliating of all, ran his hands through her hair, and peered at her scalp, searching for lice. Finally, he weighed her and recorded her height.

Molly smoothed her tangled hair and watched Clara go through the ordeal she'd just endured. Suddenly the delicate girl's face went white as paper, and three doctors clustered about her, gesturing with animation. Molly's stomach churned with anxiety. Something was wrong, desperately wrong, she thought, moving to her friend and taking her arm.

Tears welled in Clara's glassy eyes. "They say I don't weigh enough, that I'm too weak," she blurted out hysterically. Her face a picture of anguish, she flung her arms about Molly and sobbed deeply. "They want to send me back. If only Paddy were here!"

"You can't see anyone until you've finished processing," a gray-haired doctor told her curtly. "No friends or relatives are allowed in the building."

Molly comforted the girl as best she could, then approached the man with a pounding heart. "She only needs a bit of good food and some rest and she'll be fine," she insisted, gazing at him through a blur of weariness. "The food on the *Saxonia* was terrible, mostly salted herring and a little dry bread. Faith, she was so seasick and couldn't eat and—"

"We have rules here, miss," the doctor cut her off in an officious tone. "She must be up to a certain weight for her height or we can't let her through."

Molly's throat tightened with fear. "Can't you bend the rules a little? I've known her all my life. She's a hard worker. Her brother will take care of her until she's better—and I'll help her too."

"New York's charity rolls are already too full," the tired man snapped as if he'd heard the story a thousand times. "We can only permit the able-bodied to enter America."

"Saints above, I'll be responsible for her myself. I promise I will. Just let her pass!"

The man's face softened a bit. "Are you ready to sign a bond that you'll be responsible for *all* her medical expenses?"

Clara clutched her shoulder. "No, you can't do that. I won't let you. I-I'll have to go back."

Molly had no idea how she'd get her mother's passage, yet how could she refuse to sign the bond? If she did they'd send Clara back for sure.

She gripped the girl's shoulders and gently shook her, trying to get her to stop crying. "No, you won't go back. I won't see your mother lose the price of your passage. I'll sign the bond, Paddy will take care of you until you're stronger, and everything will be fine."

Molly turned to meet the doctor's skeptical gaze. "Get the papers. I'll sign them. And be quick about it," she added, tossing back her hair defiantly. "We have lots of things to take care of, don't you know."

After Molly signed the bond with a flourish and the girls had walked away, Clara burst into a fresh gale of tears and had to be calmed down yet again. Molly put her arm around her friend, and said a silent prayer, fervently hoping the last of their troubles were behind them.

Beyond the lines and the desks of the medical inspectors great pens stretched across the rest of the building. Into one enclosure those who were going to New York or its suburbs were lead; into the other were put all those going on to the interior of the United States. Everyone was tagged like a parcel, and a bedlam of languages swirled about them as passengers were given directions and handed letters from relatives with money and instructions on how to proceed.

After Molly had passed the last desk and answered the last question, she waited for Clara, then together they walked from the building into the fresh evening air, where a scarlet twilight mingled with the first city lights. In the large fenced compound the sounds of laughter and sobs filled the air and hundreds of voices burbled over with wonder and amazement.

All at once someone tried to wrench a suitcase from Molly's hand. "I'll be takin' you colleens to a good clean boardin' house, now," a ragged man told her, the scent of whiskey flowing from his slack mouth. Hair hung in his eyes, and a strange sick look glittered in his bloodshot eyes. "I made the trip meself," he continued, still fighting Molly for her suitcase. Another ruffian grabbed at Clara's suitcase, but Molly yanked it back, wondering how she could fight off the pair.

"I know how tired ye must be, the both of you," the first man said, a false smile pasted on his lips. "Jest come with us. Don't be givin' us any trouble now!"

Runners, Molly thought with a rush of alarm. Aunt Agatha had written about them in her letters to Ireland. They were wild drunks who tried to steer immigrants into filthy boardinghouses near the port area where they would be charged exorbitant prices, if not robbed. She wrenched back the suitcases and kicked wildly at the runners' legs, hitting one in the shins and making him howl in pain.

Clara, who'd shrank back in alarm, broke and ran forward, crying, "Oh look, there's Paddy!"

Dressed in a ragged tweed cap and dirty working clothes caked with mud, a robust young man with flashing eyes strode forward. He yelled and shook a muscled arm at the runners, who turned tail at the sight of him.

Clara and Paddy embraced, and blood stung Molly's cheeks as the girl poured out the story about the bond.

Paddy swept a thick arm across his grimy brow. "It's obliged I am to you, Molly, for seein' me sister safely through. Don't be worryin' your head about that bond, now." He clutched Clara to his side. "She's a little stick of a thing, but I'll be fattenin' her up, soon enough. Just see if I don't."

Talk flew thick and fast between them for a while, then addresses were exchanged, and Paddy hoisted his sister's suitcase. A concerned expression passed over his tired face. "Will ye be all right, now? We can stay and—"

"No, you go on and take Clara home," Molly said, noticing the girl was almost swooning with fatigue. "Bless her soul, she's all done in, and my aunt will be here any minute now."

Molly kissed Clara good-bye, and with last waves of farewell, the girl and her brother disappeared into the noisy crowd, leaving her standing by herself. In truth, she'd been totally on her own since she'd left Ireland, but now that they'd gone, she experienced a strange sense of loss. She thought of Lassiter and the lovely lady just sitting down to dinner at an elegant restaurant, and a great loneliness swept through her, leaving her hollow and aching inside.

No sooner had she taken a deep breath to calm her nerves than she was accosted by another runner, who tried to yank her suitcase away. "No, no. Get away!" she cried, her attention focused totally on the rough-looking man who fought for the possession of her luggage. She tugged back with all her might. "No—you can't have it!"

Faith, where was Aunt Agatha? She'd written she'd be right here, outside the exit of the immigration building the day the *Saxonia* berthed, and a sense of panic steadily built in Molly's chest. Saints above, how could she hold out against the powerful brute? Even now she was seconds from losing the battle.

Chapter Four

A walking stick whacked down on the man's knuckles and he gave a sharp yelp, jumping back in surprise. "That will be enough of that, you filthy scoundrel! God preserve us, decent people can't walk the streets with you louts about!"

The ruffian lunged through the crowd and Molly turned to see Aunt Agatha shaking her brass-handled walking stick at the man's running legs. *"That's it.* Get back to the saloon where you belong, you rascal!" she scolded, her half spectacles slipping down her nose.

Molly hadn't seen her plump, silver-haired aunt for ten years, and although she now sported a fine lavender dress and a hat with quivering black feathers, her snapping blue eyes and proud carriage hadn't changed one iota.

"Aunt Agatha," Molly sighed as she was swept

against the old lady's soft bosom in a loving embrace, "I thought you'd never come!"

"There, there, don't take on so," her aunt whispered, smoothing back Molly's disheveled hair, then holding her a little tighter. "I have you now." The old lady kissed her cheeks and graced her with a tender smile that reminded her of her own mother's. "Welcome to America, my darlin' girl, welcome to America."

After a few more hugs and kisses, Aunt Agatha took Molly's suitcase and guided her away from the crowd milling around the immigration building. "Sorry I'm late, my dear, but we'll soon be leaving this wretched place."

Once they'd passed through a tall gate, the old lady bought them both a ticket on the East River ferry. On the way across the dark water, they stood on the crowded deck and talked excitedly about Molly's trip and all the folks in Ireland. Before the girl knew it, they'd landed at a Manhattan pier, and she saw a long line of hacks, their round headlights swinging gently as they rolled forward to pick up passengers.

Aunt Agatha spoke with a driver, a ragged man wearing a homburg, then helped her niece into the open carriage and climbed in beside her. Molly heaved a shuddering sigh and relaxed against her aunt's soft body, weak with relief that they were finally on the way to the boardinghouse.

The rattling carriage cut through a district bordering the water that reeked of dirt and filth, and was filled with loathsome underground chambers, rotting beams, and broken windows. Here tavern doors were thrown open, and Molly saw men playing billiards and heard raucous feminine cries. Ragged children ran across the street, and she spied an inebriated old man traversing the broken sidewalk in carpet slippers.

Ten minutes later they were in a better area, and her spirits lifted as she noticed a jumble of gabled frame houses, small businesses, and a grocery on every corner. The busy street was filled with carriages and horse-drawn omnibuses and there were pedestrians everywhere. *Saints above, so many people—they're like ants!* she thought to herself.

Aunt Agatha traced her gloved fingers over Molly's cheek. "You look so tired, my girl, quite overcome."

"Y-Yes," Molly stammered. "I'm afraid I'm all done in."

"Surely the day's been too much for you." The old lady smiled affectionately. "I'll soon have you home, and in a good soft bed. You'll feel much better tomorrow. I'll wager you that."

Now there were alternate blocks of tenements whose five stories were decorated with iron balconies, and rambling old wooden houses, feeble lights gleaming through their bay windows.

"We're almost there," Aunt Agatha informed Molly, patting her hand. "The boardinghouse isn't anything fancy, but it's clean and decent."

As Aunt Agatha had predicted, the carriage soon turned down Murphy Street, flanked with leafy trees and old frame houses situated on tiny city lots. A Victorian home, looking much better than those around it, shone in the light of a street lamp, and the vehicle creaked to a halt.

The peak of the old place's roof, trimmed with wooden cutouts, was silhouetted against a bright moonlit sky, and in the shadows, Molly saw a wide porch spanning the front and sprawling around to the side. A porch swing hung at one end. Aided by the street lamp, she spied rosebushes bordering the house's walks and a filigreed iron fence surrounding the neat lawn.

"Well, here we are," Aunt Agatha announced cheerfully. "It took me ten years of backbreakin' work, but it's mine now."

She stiffly exited the carriage, and Molly followed, seeing the driver hoist her suitcase from the boot and place it on the cobblestones. After being paid, he wheeled the carriage about, and Molly followed her aunt through the open gate and up the walk, the suitcase handle cutting into her palm.

Once they were inside the sizable, high-ceilinged entry, Molly smiled with delight. The boardinghouse had steep front stairs and fireplaces everywhere. The one in the parlor, situated to the left of the entry, was especially beautiful with gleaming tiles of burgundy and bright blue. Mahogany settees, gleaming with lemon oil, had been placed about it to catch the fire's warmth on winter nights, and crocheted doilies graced an old couch, overstuffed chair, and a battered upright piano.

Aunt Agatha glanced at the stairway lit with dim gasoliers. "I'll show you to your room, child," she said with a lilt in her voice. "Right on up," she continued, as Molly dragged the heavy suitcase up the carpeted steps. "That's right, it's on the third floor. Your room is just ahead."

The chamber was lit with a soft light glowing from a china lamp decorated with painted roses. Molly took in the scarred, salvaged furniture, noticing everything was spotlessly clean. There was a shiny brass bed and wardrobe against one papered wall. Lace curtains at the dormer windows and a few houseplants gave the homey room a touch of warmth.

"There's some leftovers on the back of the stove," the old woman offered. "I'll bring you up a tray. By the way you're lookin', you won't be able to keep your eyes open much longer," she remarked, already walking to the door.

Molly had scarcely had time to open her suitcase and hang a few things in the wardrobe before Aunt Agatha was back with a tray of food, along with a pot of tea, and a glass of whiskey and water. "Here's some pork and picked beans, and a few potatoes mashed with butter. Eat everythin', child. You need your strength."

By now ravenously hungry, Molly sat down on the bed to eat, holding the tray on her lap.

"It bein' Thursday evenin', all my gentlemen boarders are at Finnegan's playin' billiards," her aunt said, easing down beside her, "but you'll be meetin' them first thing in the mornin' at breakfast."

Molly nodded, her mouth too full to speak.

"I'll be wakin' you early. We begin cookin' at daybreak. Then I always scrub the floors, and clean house good on Fridays to spruce up things a bit for the weekend."

After Molly had eaten, a wave of tiredness rushed over her and she felt desperately weak.

The old lady patted her hand. "I'll be payin' you two dollars a week, child," she explained in a soft voice. She slowly rose. "It isn't a fortune, but you couldn't be earnin' that in Ireland."

Molly smiled up at her. "No. There's no way I could earn such a sum in County Galway," she replied, standing as her aunt prepared to go. At the same time, she mentally winced at the length of time it would take her to earn her mother's passage—and the Lord help her if she should be called upon to pay Clara's bond.

"Now you drink that whiskey and water before you go to sleep. After a day like you've had, you'll be needin' somethin' to relax you." She walked to the door, then turned in farewell, a tender expression on her face. "You'll be doin' fine in America, Molly Kilmartin. Just fine."

After her aunt was gone, Molly noticed a pitcher of water and a basin on a table beside her bed. Placing her tray aside, she rose and removed her gown and petticoat. Dressed in a thin chemise and an old pair of bloomers, she picked up a bar of soap and started taking a sponge bath, thinking the water felt wonderfully soothing sliding over her throat and aching arms.

After she'd finished and dried off, she took the glass of whiskey to the room's open dormer window where cooling night air sloughed in over her freshly washed skin. As she sipped her whiskey and looked at New York, the moonlight shimmered over the old houses and decrepit tenements like silver, giving the city an ethereal air.

The whiskey relaxed Molly's body and set her thinking of dawn when the *Saxonia* had berthed. Blurred images of Castle Island, poor little Clara, the runners, and the city streets all coalesced in her tumbling mind. She clutched the windowsill, thinking she might swoon with weariness. Heaving a huge sigh, she realized she'd lived through the hardest day of her life, but she was in America, and with God's help, she'd brought Clara with her.

She finished the whiskey, then took off her shoes and blew out the flame flickering in the china lamp. Totally exhausted, she sank to the bed and stretched out. During the moment before sleep, she saw the image of the beautiful woman who'd thrown her arms around Lassiter. Who could she be, and what was she to him? she wondered, experiencing an unbidden sense of rivalry just before she tumbled into comforting darkness.

The next morning Molly woke up to the sound of a rattling wagon and sat up in bed just as Aunt Agatha entered the room, her face wreathed in a tender smile.

"And what kind of night did you have, my girl?" she asked laughingly. "That whiskey should have sent you right off, and I'll wager you're feelin' much better this mornin'."

Molly stretched her arms, noticing they were still sore from carrying hers and Clara's luggage the day before. She reached out her hands to clasp those of her aunt. "I had a wonderful night's sleep. Why, I feel like a new person!" Filled with excitement, she slid from the bed and padded to the window. Rosy summer light bathed the run-down section of New York in a tender glow and softened its more disagreeable aspects, making Molly think it was the loveliest city she'd ever seen.

The rattling milk wagon that had awakened her creaked to a halt in front of her aunt's boardinghouse. The burly driver, walrus-mustached and top-hatted, leaped to the ground and swung a metal can to the curb.

The old lady clucked her tongue. "That's my first delivery of the day," she announced matter of factly, already turning to leave the room. "I'll be goin' down to pay the man," she said, moving toward the door. She paused and raised her brows. "Hurry on down to the kitchen, child, and we'll start breakfast. Your mother wrote you were a good plain cook, and we have five hungry men to feed, don't you know."

Molly washed her face and hands, then pulled a clean gown from the wardrobe and slipped it on. Afterward she stood before a little cracked mirror to brush her hair and hastily pin it atop her head, feeling wonderfully revived after her good night's sleep.

Her skirt flying, she went down the creaking stairs, passed the dining room, and guided by the scent of coffee, found the cluttered kitchen, hung with brightly polished pots and pans. There was a singing teakettle on the enormous wood-burning stove, and the old linoleum was cracked and peeling, but buffed to a high gloss. In the corner, a dish of milk was set out for the house cat—a fat tabby with thick, soft fur.

Her aunt, who was frying bacon, wiped her hands on her long apron. "I'll be startin' the oatmeal, and there's a bowl of peeled potatoes on the table you can start slicin' up," she said over her shoulder. "Shamus will be down first, and he always likes a few home fries with his breakfast."

"All right, then," Molly answered, tying on an apron herself. She hurried about the pleasantly scented kitchen, following her aunt's directions and listening to the sound of the old boardinghouse coming to life. There was the muffled noise of coughing, footfalls, and someone slamming a door, telling her she'd soon meet her aunt's boarders. Her spirits, already exhilarated by the interesting morning, lifted further at the prospect.

"Agatha, me darlin', do ye have my breakfast ready, then?" came a loud call from what Molly knew was the dining room.

"Yes, Shamus, just a moment, my love," her aunt called, her face blooming with pleasure.

Molly smiled to herself as she watched her aunt load a plate with fried eggs, bacon, and home fries, before turning from the smoking stove. The woman started across the kitchen, then paused, and gazed at Molly with twinkling eyes. "No, you take it to him. I'll be goin' along to introduce you. Yes, that's it, the dining room is just to the right," she added, piling three pieces of buttered toast onto the already heaping plate.

From the sound of his voice and the amount of food she carried, Molly expected Shamus to be a huge man of enormous girth, but when she walked into the neat little dining room, decorated with lacy curtains and blooming houseplants, she bit back a smile. No more than a hundred and thirty-five pounds, the lean working man sat at the head of Agatha's table, scanning an open newspaper.

"This is Molly, my sister Kathleen's girl just over from County Galway," Aunt Agatha announced proudly. "She's come to help me out."

Molly rewarded the little man with her warmest smile, and the moment she set the plate before him, he stood and kissed her hand, his full mustache brushing against her fingers. "And what a beautiful young thing she is, Aggie," he said, his blue eyes snapping as he reseated himself to tuck the end of a linen napkin into his collar. He took a bite of potatoes, then let his dancing eyes play over Molly again. "Oh, ye won't be keepin' her long. No ye won't! Some young man will snap her up quick as a wink. Before ye know it, she'll be married and danglin' a babe on her pretty knee."

Aunt Agatha, who was all tenderness one minute, and stern and commanding the next, put her hands on her hips. "*Married?*" she hooted. "And I thought you weren't in favor of that particular institution, Shamus."

The little man squirmed on his seat. "Now, Jelly Bean, you know I'm not against marriage in general, but in certain cases a man's finances just won't permit it." He shot her an ingratiating grin. "Why, I'd marry you in a minute if I were only able. I vow, I'll—"

"Yes, yes!" Aunt Agatha sharply interposed. "I've heard it a thousand times—you'll marry me the day you win the lottery!"

Shamus leaned forward, an earnest look on his face. "Yes, and that's a vow I'll keep, my love. That I will!" he said, turning the newspaper to the front page and running a blunt finger over a list of winning lottery numbers.

By now other boarders had drifted into the dining room, and familiar with what they ate, Aunt Agatha gave their orders to Molly as she rushed back and forth to the kitchen, serving up plates of eggs, bowls of oatmeal, and platters of buttered toast that seemed to disappear as fast as she put them on the table.

The boarders, their forthright emotions written on their plain Irish faces, all spoke in a heavy brogue and reminded her of men she'd known in Ballyshannon. Nearly rushed off her feet, Molly poured a last round of coffee, then wiped a hand over her brow as they finally left, thinking she could eat her own breakfast now.

She started to clear the dishes away, when her aunt clasped her arm. "We have one more, my dear. Fergus will be comin' down any minute now. He's always last. Stays up half the night readin' those books he gets from the library. It's a blessed wonder he makes it to work at all." Her aunt brushed back a straying piece of hair. "The lad will be wantin' a scrambled egg, two strips of bacon, and a piece of toast, so you might as well be fetchin' it now."

Molly went back to the kitchen and brought the order out, only to almost bump into a thin, dark-haired young man as he hurried into the dining room.

"This is Molly, just in from Ireland," Aunt Agatha said matter of factly, moving a pot of marmalade in front of the young man's plate. "And this young gentleman is Fergus O'Flaherty from Dublin Town."

Fergus pushed up his sliding, wire-rimmed spectacles and smiled awkwardly. He projected none of the male allure that she'd found so attractive in Lassiter, but intelligence snapped in his eyes, and there was a certain refinement about him that spoke of books and universities. She could tell he was terribly shy, and her heart went out to him as he began speaking, for he stuttered badly.

"G-glad t-to meet y-you, Molly. I-I hope you like New York."

She nodded and saw him glance at the wall clock as he wolfed down his food. Only half finished, he tossed down his napkin hurried off to work.

Aunt Agatha began clearing up the dishes and Molly helped, taking time to smear marmalade over a piece of toast and eat a few bites.

"Saints preserve me, I don't know what's goin' to happen to that boy," her aunt lamented over the sound of clattering dishes. "Sometimes I think he'll stumble over his own shadow."

Molly stacked some cups on a tray and smiled to herself. "He reminds me of someone I know."

"And who might that be?"

"A girl who came over with me on the *Saxonia*. Her name is Clara."

"What a pair they'd make!" the old woman laughed.

"Actually," Molly remarked, sweeping into the kitchen with the tray of dishes, I think they'd make quite a fine pair indeed!"

Aunt Agatha began boiling water on the stove. "Well, we have more to do than arrange romances today, my girl. We have to wash these dishes, change the linen, clean the linoleum, and polish the furniture."

Molly experienced a sinking sensation, then quietly admonishing herself, thought, *Well, you won't be be earning your mother's passage just standing here, will you? Get on with it now.*

Taking a deep breath and bracing her shoulders, she strode purposely across the kitchen to help Aunt Agatha wash dishes.

That Saturday afternoon Molly had half a day off and after pinning on her hat, walked to the entry only to see Fergus standing there with several books crooked under his arm. "I was going out too," she said impulsively, feeling completely at ease with him as she walked at his side. "Thought I'd explore the neighborhood a little," she went on, having no particular agenda for herself that afternoon.

"I-I'm going to the library," he remarked with an

embarrassed grin. "It's only five blocks from here. I-I'll show you where it is—that is i-if y-you want to c-come with me."

Fergus's kind eyes touched her heart, and she decided he'd be a perfect escort for showing her about the neighborhood. They left together and walked along Murphy Street, which was flanked by private dwellings, boardinghouses, and small businesses indiscriminately mixed together.

Carriages rattled past them as they strolled along the broken sidewalk, and the high voices of boys playing hon-pon rode the warm summer air. Molly learned that Fergus had attended two years at a Dublin university and now worked part time in a box factory about a mile from the boardinghouse while he went to college in the city.

The pair talked pleasantly about the neighborhood, and Fergus showed her where she could catch omnibuses, then pointed out a little cubbyhole store where one could buy baked goods and candy for special occasions. Used to rural life in Ireland, Molly scanned the shabby neighborhood with relish, thinking it offered many hidden delights. She loved all of it: the long street perspectives, the colorful fruit stands, the crisp lights and strong, sharp shadows, the warm musky scents, for they all meant life and hope.

"T-There's the library—j-just there," Fergus announced, indicating a columned brick building, surrounded by shrubs and covered with climbing vines. "I-It's a branch of the N-New York Central Library."

They went in, and the scent of old paper and ink immediately touched Molly's nostrils, producing a pleasant little thrill down her spine. She let her gaze play over the library, overwhelmed with the sight of shelves and shelves of books that rose to the high ceiling.

"What does it cost to read a book?" Molly asked, having never entered a library before.

Fergus pushed up his spectacles with a bony finger. "*Nothing*. It's all free. I-Isn't that grand?"

Molly stared up at him. "Saints above, a person can read all they want for nothing? Why, I can't believe it!"

Fergus turned in his books at the reception desk, then guided Molly to a long reading table where they both sat down. "T-Tell me what you're interested in, and I'll find you a book."

"Oh, I don't know," she laughed, somewhat nervous at the thought of being in a library when she'd never even been inside a school. "Men, women, children, families, I guess."

The tall lad peered at her keenly. "For a girl alone, m-making the trip from Ireland was a courageous thing to do. I'd g-guess a person such as yourself might be interested in women's rights."

"*Women's rights?*" she echoed vaguely, noticing her cheeks heat with embarrassment.

He gave her an amused grin. "Yes, did you know there's a group here in N-New York even lobbying for a woman's r-right to vote?"

Molly sat up a little straighter. "Why, I've always been for that! The Lord knows a woman can think just as good as a man"—she felt her face grow hotter—"even if her plumbing is different. And if the truth be told, most of the families in my village were kept together by a woman, not a man."

Fergus nodded. "I-It was the same in my part of Dublin." A thoughtful look raced over his face, then he stood, gazing down on her with his soft, kind eyes. "Wait here. There's a newspaper I want you to read. I-I'll just get it for you."

He returned only moments later and laid a newspaper in front of her with a banner reading *Woodhull's and Claflin's Weekly*. The newspaper was edited by a woman named Victoria Woodhull.

Fergus had selected a book for himself, and as they sat there reading together, Molly thought of her mother and all the people she'd known in Ballyshannon. How impressed they'd be to see her sitting in this fine library, less than a week after she'd arrived in America, reading a newspaper. For the hundredth time, she silently thanked Father Riley for teaching her to read—for giving her such a wonderful gift.

She was delighted to find that Miss Woodhull believed in equal rights for women and a single standard of morality for both sexes. Presently she came upon the word *chauvinist* written in italics. Guessing it was a foreign word, but having no idea what it meant, she whirled the newspaper about, traced her finger under it, and raised her brows.

A gentle smile touched Fergus's lips. "The word is French. It's pronounced *show-vi-nist*."

"Thank you very much," Molly whispered, "but what does it mean?"

"In this case, it means someone who has an attitude of superiority toward members of the opposite sex."

Molly batted her eyes, digesting everything. "Do you mean a pigheaded male?"

Fergus laughed softly. "Yes, I believe in this instance Miss Woodhull is referring to pigheaded males."

Molly sank back against her chair, Lassiter's handsome face flooding her mind. She could see him offering her his card, his friendship, all in what she considered a manipulative, condescending manner.

"I see," Molly softly replied, meeting her new friend's questioning gaze. She thoughtfully tapped her fingers on the table. "Well now, I think I'm beginning to understand what the women's movement is all about."

Chapter Five

Lassiter gazed into the clear blue eyes of the *Telegram*'s chief accountant, Tom Perkins, asking the question he had dreaded since returning from Ireland. "Well, how do the figures add up? Are we making any money?"

Tom rose from his desk chair and ran a hand through his sandy-blond hair. A stocky, medium-built man, he projected a look of quiet efficiency as he paced about his small office, a pencil shoved behind his ear. With a heavy sigh, he paused and scanned his employer apologetically. "No, sir, I'm afraid not. Actually we're running a few dollars in the red. The paper manufacturers have raised their prices and circulation has gone down." He loosened his tie. "You know the *Metropolitan*—"

"Yes, the *Metropolitan* is beating us into the ground," Lassiter groaned, knowing his competition across the street was slowly but surely putting him out of business with a series of investigative features, journalism's newest sensation. "That rag prints some damn sensational stuff these days. But the writing is so flashy, it's practically irresistible."

Lassiter talked to the accountant awhile longer, then left the man's office and walked through the *Telegram*'s huge press room filled with scribbling reporters, trying to make their deadlines for the paper's next issue. At last he entered his huge, well-furnished office, and took a seat behind his desk. With a frown, he picked up the latest issue of the *Telegram,* scanned the front page, then disgustedly tossed it atop yesterday's issue.

His father had been the original publisher of the newspaper, and in one sense, he'd inherited the enterprise, but it was far more than a business to him. Occupying most of his waking thoughts, it meant a tremendous amount to him emotionally, for he'd always had great aspirations for the paper, hoping he'd eventually be able to effect some much needed social changes with its publication.

He'd seen enough of the idle rich who frequented establishments like Delmonico's and the other fashionable restaurants and clubs of the metropolis, that he didn't want to be like them. Morally bankrupt and mentally lazy, they had no real goal but idly enjoying themselves, and he shuddered at the thought of joining their numbers. Life should be lived with verve and purpose. Somehow he had to hold on to the *Telegram* and make it something to be proud of, something that would kindle people's intellects and make New York a better place to live.

The paper's circulation had never been lower—no

doubt about that. He desperately needed to come up with something to grab the readers' attention—something to make them eagerly look forward to the *Telegram* each day. After leisurely lighting a cigar, he paced about the room, then paused at a huge window, thoughtfully watching the sun set over New York in a swirl of scarlet and gold. Over the usual rattle of carriages and rumble of omnibuses, the sound of a beating drum rose from the street three stories below, and he peered through the twilight shadows to see what was going on.

It seemed a group of militant ladies, one with a bass drum no less, was demonstrating for the right to vote. Carrying neatly painted placards, they marched in a circle before the *Telegram* building, partially obstructing the busy flow of traffic down Broadway. Surly teamsters pulled their vans to a halt while angry salesmen with satchels paused in order to heckle the demonstrators.

"We want the vote and we want it now," one of the women shouted, to be joined by the others in agreement.

Lassiter caught snatches of the speaker's words and his lips twisted with amusement. Lord, these amazons wanted more than the right to vote—they wanted equality with men in every aspect of life.

"Women are just as capable as men, and always have been!" the feminine speaker shouted to a burst of applause and a boom of a drum.

Lassiter leaned his shoulder against the windowsill and crossed his arms, thinking he hadn't seen such a gutsy female since he'd first clapped eyes on Molly Kilmartin.

A burly teamster jumped from his freight wagon and

raised one arm into the air. "Aw, go back to the kitchen," he hollered, to the approving guffaws of several men.

Lassiter took a draw of his cigar, noticing a flash of excitement race through his body that he knew had nothing to do with the expensive tobacco he was smoking. Damn, if this little drama wasn't getting more interesting by the second.

Of course, he knew about the feminist cause. Some of his reporters had even written small unimportant pieces about the Feminist Movement as it was now loftily called, but he'd never taken it seriously. He listened to the woman's speech with an open mind, but when she mentioned that females would one day be mayors and governors, he had to chuckle, imagining Daisy Fellows as the mayor of New York. Nonetheless, he heard the passionate ring in the speaker's voice, and noticed the men's laughter was underlaid with an all too apparent thread of fear.

With a burst of acuity, he realized this was an issue both sexes cared about more deeply than he'd imagined. He turned from the window, a grin on his face. This was a topic as old as Adam and Eve, a topic that engendered deep feelings in every human being in New York, a topic that would dramatically increase circulation.

His brain buzzing with ideas, he sat down at his desk and jammed his pen into an inkwell, then pulled out several pieces of smooth paper. The nub of the pen scratched over the paper and he wrote quickly, the ink of one paragraph scarcely drying before he'd composed another.

Thoroughly enjoying his cigar, he created the most inflammatory editorial he'd ever written, intended for

front-page publication. Everyone with a grain of sense
knew that females could think as well as men, but for
the sake of argument, he wrote down every scurrilous
chauvinist argument against feminism that he'd ever
heard, ideas he'd picked up everywhere from fashionable pulpits to Bowery taverns.

Certain that the city's better-educated classes would
realize the editorial had been written tongue in cheek,
he poured on the adjectives, and when he was finished,
decided Harriet Beecher Stowe and Charles Dickens
working together couldn't have produced such a masterpiece of sentimental, gilt-edged, purple prose.

Getting a brainstorm, Lassiter jotted down a last
paragraph, inviting female readers with differing view-
points to write him personally, promising selected letters would be printed.

He leaned back in his chair and blew smoke rings
into the air, relishing his triumph. Let old man Babbage, the publisher of the *Metropolitan,* try to outsell
him now. He'd hit on a topic that would shake the city
to its very roots and shoot the *Telegram*'s circulation to
the stars, he congratulated himself, affectionately tapping his ringed hand over the newspaper's front page.

Late the next morning, Molly briskly walked back from
the fresh-air market carrying a tote bag of vegetables
she was going to prepare for dinner. The sun shone
brightly and a little breeze wafted through her loose
hair, lifting her spirits and making her feel especially
light and buoyant.

Only half a block from the boardinghouse, she spotted a young boy, about ten, hawking that day's newspaper. Ragged clothes garbed his slight frame, broken

boots shod his feet, and a tattered tweed cap was pulled down jauntily over his curly hair. Her heart turned over in her bosom for not only his physical appearance, but his whole sprightly demeanor reminded her of her brother Cossi. As she neared the young scamp, she caught an Irish lilt in his voice and saw his blue eyes dance with life and fire.

"Buy a paper, miss?" he called to her, pulling a thick newspaper from the canvas sack strapped over his shoulder and brandishing it in her direction. "It's only a nickel. You can't go wrong there, can you, now?" he winked, his face animated with amusement.

Molly let her gaze float over the boy. Since she'd been in New York she'd seen dozens like him—scrappy Irish newsboys who got by on luck, determination, and one sparse meal a day. But there was something in this child's stance and the tilt of his head that spoke of pride and a fierce determination to survive—and it was this quality that most reminded her of Cossi.

"There's more good readin' in the *Telegram* than any paper in the city," the boy went on encouragingly. "My regular customers swear by it. Say they wouldn't read nothin' else."

Molly's pulse raced faster. "The *Telegram*, is it?" she echoed, shifting the weight of the bag so she could take the paper from his hand. She studied the child more closely, thinking he not only needed a good washing, but a lot of good meals to put some meat on his slight frame. "What's your name, lad?"

"Brian," he came back with another smile, doffing his cap flirtatiously. "Brian O'Neal fresh from County Cork, miss."

"Well, Brian O'Neal, I just arrived from Ireland

myself," she laughed, enjoying the boy's bright personality and twinkling eyes. "And wasn't it a wicked hard trip?"

A look of sadness passed over the boy's face. "That it was. My mam took sick on the way over and passed away right after we got here—bless her sainted soul."

Molly's throat tightened with emotion. "Oh, I'm sorry to hear that," she replied sympathetically. "So now there's just you and your da?"

The boy stood a little taller as if to shield himself from her pity. "Just me and my stepdad. Not that I'm complainin', mind you," he said with a casual offhand air, trying to dismiss the situation lightly. "Ain't lookin' for no handouts. I been gettin' by sellin' papers, and I'll be gettin' into construction soon, I'll wager."

Words of sympathy trembled on Molly's lips, but she bit them back. Recognizing a kindred soul, who wanted no pity, only a chance to make it on his own, she simply nodded in understanding.

"Well are ye goin' to buy the paper, miss?" the boy asked jovially, steering the conversation back to his livelihood. He swept a grimy finger over a large headline on the front page. "See here, Mr. Burke Lassiter himself wrote this piece about women havin' the right to vote. I can't read much, but best I can make out, he's dead set agin it."

The boy's words galvanized Molly's gaze on the front-page editorial, and as she swept through the first paragraph a gorge rose in her throat. "Why the blackhearted rascal," she mumbled under her breath. "Him and his fine airs. I should have pushed the rascal overboard while I had the chance!"

"What's that you're sayin', miss?"

Molly, suddenly remembering herself, pressed fifty cents into Brian's palm. "Never mind. I was just talking to myself. You keep the change, now."

The boy widened his eyes and drew himself up in a manly fashion. "Wait a minute, miss. You gave me too much. I done told you, I don't want no handouts."

"I'm just paying you in advance." Molly pointed at the boardinghouse. "You see that old house over there? It belongs to my aunt and it's where I live. I expect a fresh copy of the *Telegram* on the porch every morning at seven o'clock for a week. Spend the rest of the money on a hot meal tonight."

"But—"

"No buts about it!"

The boy smiled broadly and shook his head. "Yeah, sure, but we haven't been properly introduced yet. What's your name?"

Molly walked away. "Molly—Molly Kilmartin," she called over her shoulder. "You do as I say now."

Molly skimmed over Lassiter's editorial as she walked, head down, dodging pedestrians and once again muttering to herself. "Why the nerve of the man," she said, almost bumping into a heavy matron, who glared at her hotly. How could he have written such a passel of rubbish when he seemed so charming on the ship? she wondered, feeling betrayed afresh. "Why he's no more than a . . . a . . . " She pressed her lips together, searching for a word despicable enough for him. "What's the word now? Chauvinist, that's it. He's a flaming chauvinist, that's what he is!"

She flopped down on Aunt Agatha's porch swing to finish the editorial, her blood pressure soaring by the minute. At last she read Lassiter's request for female readers who disagreed with him and felt a flame of outrage burn its way through her soul.

She drew in a long breath. Well, the rascal would surely get a letter from her, or her name wasn't Molly Kilmartin.

That evening after she'd washed all the dinner dishes, Molly went to her room and gathered her writing supplies. Sitting on her bed with her legs crossed and a tablet in her lap, she wrote and wrote that night, her temper rising with every completed sentence. How dare Lassiter appear so charming on the *Saxonia,* when in reality he was nothing but a pigheaded male chauvinist! Recalling passages from Victoria Woodhull's newspaper, she borrowed several ideas from the feminist writer to add to her own disorganized harangue against him.

Biting her lips as she composed her thoughts, she wrote about families she'd known in Ireland, families that would have gone on the charity rolls if it hadn't been for the forthright leadership of the lady of the household. Getting an idea, she fetched a Bible, and faithfully copied the complete passage concerning the worthy woman whose price was above rubies. King Solomon, the wisest man in the Bible, had written that. Did Lassiter think he was smarter than him?

She wrote with such fury that she had to cross out several words, but continued doggedly ahead, ignoring the ache between her shoulders and the cramp in her fingers. Lassiter had once praised her humorous writing tone. Well there was no humor in this letter, only truth! Zealous rage inspired her words, and her pen fairly flew over the pages, gushing words that she underlined and sentences she ended with dark exclamation points. The oil in the lamp burned low, but one by one the long pages piled up, and she carefully laid them on the carpet so the ink could dry.

On and on she wrote, asking Lassiter if he had a growth on his brain or if his intelligence was just abnormally low. She pondered over all the history lessons kindly Father Riley had given her. Had Lassiter never taken *any* history classes at all? Surely he knew how Elizabeth had guided England through its finest age, and then there was the other great Elizabeth, Empress of Russia who'd almost singlehandedly saved her country from destruction. And what about Cleopatra, who'd been so much more capable than her weak, indecisive brother?

Around ten o'clock, Molly took a short break to pace about the room and get a drink of water, then getting another idea, she sat down to write again, ignoring the fact that she'd already composed nine long pages of blistering rhetoric.

Did Lassiter think that whiskers and "superior sexual equipment" made a man smarter than a woman? She railed hotly against the argument that women were too emotional to be given the vote. Why, overall, women were as emotionally balanced as men, and the truth be told, they could endure a lot more pain. Saints above, everyone knew that if men had to give birth, civilization would quickly die out!

Prompted by an ache in her shoulders, she paused to take a deep breath and noticed that the boardinghouse was dead quiet. Not a soul was stirring. She glanced at the clock and saw that it was already midnight. Knowing she must be up at six, she wound down the letter, but not before calling Lassiter a stiff-necked, addlepated nincompoop, who was completely unfit to be an editor, much less a publisher. She underlined this sentence three times.

She gathered her long missive together and read it out loud to herself, deciding it was the best thing she'd ever written—even better than the journal she'd composed on the *Saxonia*. Pride warming her heart, she signed her name with a large flourish at the bottom of page twelve.

Her better judgment told her she should ask Fergus to check her letter for spelling and grammar, but motivated by a burning passion she didn't completely understand, she decided that would take longer than she wanted. The letter must get to Lassiter as quickly as possible. Someone, namely herself, needed to bring the blockhead down several pegs.

She hastily addressed an envelope, then folded her letter, stuffed it inside, and licked and closed the bulging package. She'd get stamps from Aunt Agatha in the morning, then hurry down to the mailbox on the corner and post the letter right after breakfast.

Two days later Lassiter sat at his desk, which was piled high with angry missives from female readers. As he'd expected, his editorial had stirred a hornet's nest of controversy the likes of which the *Telegram* had never seen. His secretary had scanned many of the letters, and selected one as "so hot it burned my fingers."

Lassiter's heart had leaped with joy when the woman told him the letter was from a Miss Kilmartin, and he now devoured the correspondence, chuckling deeply as he finished one florid page and began another. He laughed until tears came to his eyes when he read the passage asking him if he had a growth on his brain, and thought the bit about Cleopatra's weak, indecisive brother was especially effective.

He chortled heartily over the phrase *superior sexual equipment* and decided the whole disorganized mess was one of the most amusing things he'd ever read. He thoughtfully leaned back in his chair, knowing he had to publish the letter even if it was a twisted literary deformity. He'd have the spelling and grammar corrected and put it on the first page of next Sunday's feature section, for his readers were bound to enjoy it as much as he had.

He turned the envelope over, and finding Molly's address, an exciting idea blossomed in his mind. He now knew where to find the little spitfire and could hardly wait to see her. He'd just pay Miss Molly Kilmartin a visit and invite her to write more letters to the *Telegram* expressing her vivid opinions. Her writing was bound to increase circulation, and who knew where their renewed relationship would take them, he thought, happier than he'd been since he first bumped into her on the *Saxonia*.

Two nights later Molly had just finished washing a huge pile of dinner dishes, and she brushed back a lock of hair from her damp forehead. The kitchen was intolerably hot and she looked her worst with circles under her arms and food stains streaked down the front of her apron.

She heard a knock at the front door, but ignored it, knowing Aunt Agatha would receive the visitor who was undoubtedly another working man looking for lodging.

Presently her aunt walked into the kitchen, a puzzled look on her face. "There's someone at the door and he's askin' to see you, dear."

"*Asking to see me?*" Molly returned, wondering who it could be.

"Yes, and he's a fine gentleman too."

Molly hadn't met any fine gentlemen in New York yet and was completely taken back by her aunt's statement. She wiped off the counter, then laying her rag aside, slowly ventured into the hall and made her way to the entrance, noticing with some unease that her aunt had vanished.

Molly's heart lurched, for standing in the entry was Lassiter, dressed in elegant clothes. He gazed down at her with twinkling eyes and slowly took off his hat. "Molly, I've found you at last," he said in a warm, amused voice as he laid his head covering on an entry console.

Overcome with shame at her appearance, she brushed back her unbound hair, desperately wishing she'd had some notice of his arrival so that she could have changed her clothes. "W-What are you doing h-here?" she stammered, her pulse racing wildly.

"I got your letter," he answered simply.

"Oh, you did, did you," she replied, having the presence of thought to raise her chin a bit higher. "Well, I'm sure you didn't like what I wrote, but I meant every word of it!"

He laughed softly. "I'm sure you did." He glanced at the parlor that was presently empty. "May I come in and talk awhile?"

Molly blushed as she pulled off her dirty apron and gestured at the room where a small lamp burned invitingly. "Suit yourself. All of my aunt's boarders are at Fennigan's tavern playing billiards. All except Fergus, that is. He's upstairs reading."

They walked into the room, and seeing Lassiter seat himself upon a stiff little Victorian settee, she pulled off her dirty apron and rolled it into a ball. She took a chair across the room and pushed the apron under the cushion, trying to hide it. They stared at each other in silence for a moment, then Lassiter gave her a flashing smile, the same kind that had made her knees weak on shipboard. Damn the man for coming here and catching her like this! she thought, hoping he couldn't see how terrible she looked sitting across the room from him in the half shadows.

"Actually I liked your letter very much," he went on graciously. "In fact, I plan to publish it in next Sunday's feature section."

"Next Sunday's issue?" she whispered, thinking she hadn't heard him correctly.

"Yes, it was wonderful," he laughed, and I'm sure most of the women of New York will agree with you wholeheartedly. I especially liked the part about King Solomon. And what was that phrase now," he asked, thoughtfully rubbing his chin—*stiff-necked, addlepated nincompoop*? He grinned roguishly. "By the way, the last time I checked, I didn't have a growth on my brain."

Molly swallowed hard. "Well, I—"

"There's no need to apologize."

"I wasn't! I—"

"You expressed yourself very well. You do have a way with words, you know." He laughed softly. "We'll be forced to give Victoria Woodhull credit for her thoughts, though. Her work is very well known."

"Mr. Lassiter," she replied, stiffly rising, "if you came here to chastise me—"

"I thought you were going to call me just plain Lassiter," he interrupted in a teasing tone. "I'd appreciate it if you would." He raised his brows. "In fact, I came here to see if you'd consider going out to dinner with me tonight."

"*Going out to dinner?*" she echoed incredulously. "Why, I've already eaten," she said a little more sharply than she'd intended. "It's seven-thirty. Poor people eat early, don't you know. They *have* to eat early so they can go to bed and get up early for work the next day."

Lassiter had the grace to look contrite. "I see. My mistake."

Realizing she sounded rude, she ventured, "If you'd care to come into the kitchen, there are some leftovers on the back of the stove—some pork and cabbage, and some boiled potatoes. I could give you that."

To her surprise Lassiter stood, saying, "Yes, I'd enjoy that."

Straightening her back, and wondering what Aunt Agatha would think if she knew the editor in chief of the mighty *Telegram* was going to eat leftovers in her kitchen, she ushered him into the hot little room as if it were a fine restaurant. Putting on a fresh apron, she gestured for him to sit down at the table and began fixing him a plate and a pot of coffee.

Lassiter ate with relish, then looked up at her and grinned. "This is very good. Did you cook it yourself?"

Molly smiled and sat down beside him, enjoying his

company greatly now that she was over the shock of his appearance. "Yes, I did, as a matter of fact." They talked pleasantly for a while about the boardinghouse and her duties there, then burning with curiosity about the mystery she'd pondered over for so long, she slowly ventured, "I saw you when you left the ship the day we arrived." He smiled at her. "Oh, you did?"

She bit her lip, trying to make her next question sound casual, trifling even. "Yes, w-who was that pretty lady who met you at the dock?"

Lassiter put down his fork, a look of surprise moving over his face. "Oh, her?" He coughed a little. "That was just my cousin. We grew up together."

Molly sensed that the question had startled him, and for a moment she considered pressing the issue, then she decided to accept his explanation, and experienced a sense of relief that left her weak.

After he'd fished eating, he reached over and took her hand, sending a little thrill up her arm.

"Now that we've both eaten, how about accompanying me for a carriage ride up Broadway? I'll take you to Central Park too."

"A carriage ride?" she asked, secretly thrilled at the prospect. "With me looking like this? No, I couldn't!"

"You look fine, but I'll wait for you to change your gown if you'd like. I really wish you'd go because I want to talk to you about a business proposition."

"And what might that be?" she asked, her voice rising with surprise.

He threw her a teasing wink. "I'll tell you when we get to the park."

After hesitating for a moment, she slowly stood,

wondering if the rascal had anything up his sleeve. Then being so desperate for funds, and knowing she could always refuse if she didn't like his proposition, she boldly decided to go. "All right—since you insist," she allowed grudgingly. "Just give me a few minutes to tidy up."

"Very well. I'll just sit here and drink my coffee. Take your time," he answered with a relaxed smile.

She hesitated at the kitchen door, thinking she should back out of the invitation, but he nodded for her to be on her way, and she hurried upstairs, her knees trembling beneath her. Halfway up, she met her aunt and blurted out, "I'm going on a carriage ride. I-I don't know when I'll be back." The old lady stared at her with wide eyes, but not giving her a chance to ask questions, Molly rushed into her room and closed the door.

She pulled her best dress from the wardrobe, and smoothed out the wrinkles with her hands, wishing she had time to iron the garment. After changing, she dabbed some powder on her face, glossed her lips, and brushed her hair, trying to ignore the fact that her hands shook.

Lassiter met her at the foot of the stairs and gallantly escorted her from the boardinghouse, telling her Central Park was lovely at this time of the evening.

His smart open carriage with yellow painted wheels impressed Molly mightily. Doubtless it cost a fortune, but what could she expect from a rich man like himself? He probably had *three* fine carriages and a whole stable of blooded horses.

Lassiter regaled her with stories of New York as their carriage rolled toward the center of the city. Once on

Broadway, Molly was met with the sound of hundreds of wheels on the resonant pavement, a rhythmic symphony of noise. Keenly interested in everything she saw, she sat forward staring at the main artery of the metropolis, lined with tall buildings made of brick, granite, and brownstone.

On the sidewalks she saw well-dressed gentlemen, poverty-stricken working men, and a fluttering stream of feathers and petticoats. What a melange of nationalities! she thought, spying saucy-faced flower girls and shabby immigrants with bent shoulders.

Lassiter indicated the tall spire of Trinity Church that soared into the deep blue night sky, and a few moments later, Molly heard the chimes burst out strong and melodic over the avenue. Soon Lassiter pointed to a tall building whose fourth floor blazed with light, saying, "That's the *Telegram* building. Those lights are coming from the composing room where they're busy putting together tomorrow's edition."

"Why aren't you there?" she laughed.

"Being a publisher does have some privileges, you know."

They passed Union Square with its benches and splashing fountains, Madison Square with its flagstone walks and lamps hung among the foliage, then the great emporiums of Tiffany's and Lord and Taylor.

At last entering Central Park, they took a carriage road down the Ramble, passing a band concert, then came to the wider Mall, where Lassiter slowed his horse to a sedate walk. There were a few pedestrians, but most people were in carriages. A large open carriage rumbled past them, filled with chattering women in opera dresses and elegant men with cigars in their mouths, the tips of the cheroots glowing red in the darkness.

Lassiter stopped their carriage near the richly ornamented Terrace, saying it was the best place to view the array of horseflesh and vehicles passing through at this time of the evening, then turned his attention to Molly. He hadn't envisioned eating a dinner of leftovers in a hot boardinghouse kitchen, but actually the evening was going quite well, for the girl seemed totally relaxed, and it was apparent she was enjoying herself thoroughly.

The soft light of a street lamp glowed over her face, and he let his gaze flow over her. Her lithe body was garbed in the same gown with the white cuffs she'd worn their last night at sea, and although Daisy was always telling him that clothes made the woman, he decided he'd never seen a more beautiful girl. "Where did you read Victoria Woodhull?" he asked casually.

Molly smoothed back her hair. "Fergus took me to a library and showed me one of her newspapers." She widened her eyes. "American libraries are wonderful. All those books—and it doesn't cost a penny to read anything you want. Did you know that?"

Lassiter's chest filled with an unexpected warmth. As exquisite as a moonbeam, this young woman who was hardly more than a stranger had managed to work her way into his emotions without even trying. He was sure that now that he'd found her, he'd be avoiding Daisy as much as possible, for she'd been boring him to distraction. Despite her wealth and beauty, the shallow blond socialite couldn't hold a candle to this feisty Irish bundle of mischief. "How do you like New York?" he asked, suppressing an urge to touch her mass of silken hair that glinted like flames in the soft light.

She rolled her eyes heavenward. "Oh, I love it. It's so exciting, and you can purchase anything here! I buy vegetables for Aunt Agatha at the fresh-air market, and I love the little shops." A wry smile touched her lips. "There's such color here. Ireland is usually misty, but the sun shines here nearly every day. Everything is so bright. Sometimes I wish I were an artist so I could paint all the colors."

Lassiter smiled to himself, knowing he hadn't misjudged her. With her poetic soul and lust for life, she naturally had to like New York, even if she hadn't seen its more fashionable districts. Daisy had lived here all her life, and with her great advantages he'd never heard her talk about the city as this girl just had. Guilt twinged through him as he recalled the lie he'd passed off about Daisy while eating; then he told himself he'd done the right thing, for he'd protected Molly's feelings, and after all, the two women would never meet.

"Do you miss Ireland?" he suddenly asked.

A wistful look gathered in Molly's eyes. "Yes, of course. The countryside is green and lovely there, but life is so hard, people can scarcely exist." Her eyes softened. "Mostly I miss Mam. I write her all the time."

"Did you keep my card?"

Her expression turned dark. "No, why should I? You lied to me about being a reporter. I told you I planned to stand on my own two feet here anyway."

Laughter rumbled from his chest. "Oh yes. How could I have forgotten?"

She narrowed her eyes. "Did you really mean all those horrible things you wrote about women?"

"Well," Lassiter hedged, "not exactly, but I do think the feminists are taking their issue too far, and the editorial has increased circulation significantly."

"Increased circulation significantly? Is that all you think about!"

He gave a soft laugh. "I am in the business of selling newspapers, you know." He traced his fingers along her cheekbone. "Now let's talk about that business proposition I told you about," he continued forthrightly, watching a suspicious frown race over her brow.

She stared at him skeptically. "Yes, all right, go on."

"I'd like to publish more of your letters—that is if you'll write them."

She shifted upon the carriage seat. "Now you're making fun of me for sure!"

"No, I mean what I say," he chuckled, gently brushing back a lock of her hair. "Your writing is good. Editors are always looking for good writing."

She glanced down. "But I make lots of spelling mistakes," she admitted, clasping her hands. "I know I do. I-I should have asked Fergus to correct my letter before I sent it to you."

He raised her chin and gazed into her soft eyes. "I have a building full of people who can correct spelling errors, but good writers are much harder to find," he explained as she stared at him with disbelief. "Not everyone can put heart and soul into their writing like you can. It's a great gift—a gift you should accept."

She studied him thoughtfully.

"How about it, Irish? I'll pay you half a cent a word. Write another letter this weekend, and bring it to me next Monday morning."

Her expressive face went blank with surprise.

"You'll pay me half a cent a word just for writing you nasty letters? Why I never heard of such a thing!"

He chuckled deeply, casually putting his arm about her shoulders. "That's the going rate for freelance writing. Some people make a living doing that very thing," he added, mentally picturing her counting every *a, an,* and *the* she wrote, so he wouldn't shortchange her.

He studied her finely molded face. Her delicate features touched his heart, and at that moment, it seemed the most natural thing in the world to take her in his arms and caress her back. The sight of her green eyes shimmering with desire touched his emotions as strongly as the warmth of her body through her plain homemade gown enflamed his passion. He lowered his head, wanting to kiss her.

Molly noticed a now-familiar surge of desire sweep through her. Then it slowly dawned on her that he was trying to use her natural attraction for him to seduce her yet again. Why, the nerve of the man! And here she was beginning to trust him. Almost without thinking, she slapped him square across his face, only a little stunned at her action. "Don't think that you can work your way into my affections by promising to publish my work," she said firmly. "I've taken a measure of you already, and I know what kind of man you are."

This time Lassiter didn't even bother to rub his stinging jaw. "You do? And what might that be?"

"The kind of man that would take advantage of a poor working girl if she didn't watch out."

"I think you've misread me. I assure you—"

"And I assure you that you're wrong. You'll get your letters, Lassiter, but that's all you'll get. Just remember that."

"Why are you so suspicious of all my actions?"

She studied his questioning eyes. "Our lives have taught us different things. Your life has taught you to use your charm, your good looks, and fine manners to get what you want. Mine has taught me to be wary, to be on my guard." She straightened her back. "My instincts have always served me well, and as I see it, they'll continue to serve me well. Now take me back to the boardinghouse. I can't be out gallivanting about Central Park at night like some fine lady, you know. I have to get up at six in the morning and cook breakfast for five hungry men."

Chuckling to himself, Lassiter clicked to his horse, and began slowly turning the carriage around to leave the park.

Chapter Six

The next Monday morning, Molly swung off of an omnibus and stared at the section of Broadway that contained all the newspaper buildings: *The New York Times*, the *Metropolitan,* the *Telegram,* and a host of lesser publications, all concentrated in one bustling third of a mile. She crossed the busy street, dodging carriages and freight vans, and walked half a block to peer upward at the imposing *Telegram* building that soared six stories into the air. Steam came from its roof and the very sidewalk beneath her feet vibrated with the rumble and heat of its presses.

Grimy newsboys lounged on the steps of the building, and once inside its huge brass-trimmed doors, she spied an advertising clerk in an office on the ground floor. Taking the sweeping marble staircase, she passed ink-stained errand boys, harried telegraph messengers, and reporters, pencils shoved behind their ears.

After asking someone where Lassiter's office was located, she walked up to the third floor. Heads turned as she entered the smoky, high-ceilinged newsroom filled with dozens of bent, tired-looking reporters whose desks were littered with scribbled articles and papers from all over the United States and abroad.

She smiled at the men, trying to hide her nervousness. What would the exalted editor in chief of the *Telegram* think of her latest writing effort? she wondered, feeling anxious and very out of place. Would he like her second letter as much as the first, or would he send her away in disgrace to do rewrites?

Finally spotting Lassiter's gold-lettered name on an office door, she slowly approached a desk that seemed to be guarding his holy of holies. A heavy older woman with frizzy gray hair, obviously his secretary, sat behind the neatly organized desk rearranging some papers. She looked as if she hadn't smiled for fifty years, and with her air of efficiency and stern manner, she reminded Molly of a strict schoolteacher. Never cracking a smile, the secretary sighed and glared over the top of her half spectacles.

"I've come to see Mr. Lassiter, and—"

"Yes, you must be Molly Kilmartin. He's expecting you," the woman tossed out in a gruff voice. She nodded at the door, then quickly returned her gaze to the papers. "Go on in."

Molly let herself in the huge cigar-scented office that seemed to go on forever. Her gaze immediately flew to Lassiter, who sat behind the largest desk she'd ever seen. His eyes snapping with amusement, he rose with an air of authority, his large biceps rippling under his superbly tailored blue gabardine suit. "Hello, Irish," he said, walking around his desk with an easy stride. "Let's see what you brought me." He briskly extended his large hand to take the material.

Conscious of his scrutiny, Molly walked toward him, noticing the office was furnished with a beautiful Oriental carpet, leather chairs, and enormous bookcases filled with gorgeously bound volumes. *Saints above,* she thought, fishing the folded letter from her reticule, *the rascal must be as rich as John Jacob Astor himself.* Momentarily abashed with the magnificence of the room, she handed him the long missive amplifying her views on women's rights.

To her chagrin, he read her work silently, laughing to himself as he paced about the office.

Blood pounded in her temples. Now what was the man laughing about? she wondered irritably. She thought she'd expressed herself quite well, and she'd even asked Fergus to correct her spelling. Her breath quickened as she edged toward him. "W-What's wrong? Don't you like what I've written?"

Ignoring her, he fastened his gaze to the papers, chortling loudly. "Oh, this is good—even better than your first effort. This is great—very funny."

Heat stole to her cheeks. "But it's not supposed to be funny," she lamented, her voice rough with frustration. "It's supposed to be serious."

He glanced up, his dancing eyes holding hers like glue. "Don't worry. You've made your point."

Lassiter let his gaze float over Molly, thinking the

auburn-haired bit of muslin looked like springtime itself in a simple shirtwaist dress with a white collar and like-colored gloves. With great discipline, he steered his eyes back to her scrawled-out letter with its many exclamation points and crossed out words.

Her writing was wonderful, but sloppy—so sloppy. And Lord, would the girl ever stifle her desire to lavish on the exclamation points and superlatives? Would she ever rein in her passion for purple prose? If so, she could become an outstanding writer, the finest he'd ever read. If not, someone, probably himself, would always have to correct everything she composed. He sat down at his desk and asked her to join him there, then watched her warily approach, her eyes flashing with outraged defiance.

"I want to explain something to you," he announced, running his finger beneath a phrase on the first page of her letter. "You've used a double negative here and that's incorrect."

She gave him a hostile glare. "If it's a double negative that just makes it stronger. That means it's better," she sniffed defensively.

Lassiter rubbed the back of his neck. "*No,* you can't make up your own grammar rules," he said, trying to bridle the frustration in his voice. The *Telegram* doesn't publish writing with double negatives." He went on to discuss double negatives and how they could be avoided.

"And look at this," he added, boldly swerving his pen under a convoluted sentence. "Here's a dangling participle."

"What's it dangling from?"

Promising himself he wouldn't smile, Lassiter talked

about dangling participles, using a list of examples that Molly found amusing.

Gradually her mood softened, and tugging off her gloves, she expelled an exasperated sigh. "Why do I need to know about double negatives and dangling participles? she asked, pulling her brows into an offended frown. She shoved her gloves into her reticule. "You said you had a whole building full of people who could fix up my writing."

Lassiter stood to meet her challenging stare. "It's part of being a professional. Not more that fifteen minutes ago, you indicated you wanted your writing to be taken seriously. Right?"

Her face clouded up. "Yes, but—"

"Would you respect a carpenter who couldn't use his tools?" he asked, his voice heavy with reproach. "No? Well, this is the same principle. You must know how to use the English language correctly."

Molly gave a grudging nod and started paying more attention, but thirty minutes later, she blew back a dangling curl and frowned with impatience.

Lassiter bit back his desire to pour knowledge into her head like water into a jug. "All right," he conceded, placing her heavily marked-up letter aside. "That's all. Your grammar lesson is over—for today, that is."

She seemed relieved, then cleared her throat importantly. "Good. That will be four dollars and seventy-five cents then."

"What?"

She blinked at him as if he'd gone daft. "You did say you'd pay me half a cent a word, didn't you?" she said, impatience crackling in her eyes. "Well, I wrote nine hundred and fifty words, and I want to be paid for every blessed one of them." She roughly tugged on her gloves. "I'll try to make my next letter longer," she informed him, her mouth set determinedly.

He laughed, then pulled a bell cord and his secretary promptly entered, a frown marking her sour face. "Send Tom Perkins in," he ordered matter of factly.

A few minutes later, the accountant knocked and walked into the office, wearing a curious expression. His gaze first went to his employer, then swerved to Molly and lingered there. From his look of stunned delight, Lassiter could tell he was smitten at his first sight of her. Irritation rose in his chest; then he told himself that Tom's reaction had been entirely predictable. After all, the man wouldn't be human if he hadn't been affected by the charming girl standing so gracefully before him.

When Lassiter introduced the pair, the accountant nodded at Molly politely, then finally managed to transfer his attention back to his employer.

"Tom is the accountant for the *Telegram*," Lassiter told Molly, "and as such, responsible for writing all checks. He's located just across the newsroom next to the city editor's office. From now on, you should make all your requests for payment directly to him." He glanced at the accountant. "Miss Kilmartin is doing some freelance writing for the paper. "Give her a check this morning for four dollars and seventy-five cents," he ordered calmly.

Tom smiled pleasantly at Molly. "Very well. If you'll just accompany me to my office, I'll take care of your payment right away."

Not bothering to tell Lassiter good-bye, Molly left the office with Tom, chatting amicably.

After they'd gone, Lassiter reseated himself behind his desk and heaved a great sigh, realizing that only a blind man wouldn't have noticed how the accountant's eyes had lingered so appreciatively on Molly. Then he told himself again that it was only natural, and he had no right to be irritated. Molly wasn't attached and neither was Tom.

Still, to Lassiter's surprise, the thought of another man sharing a private moment with Molly and even accidentally brushing her hand with his made him feel uncomfortably anxious and perturbed the rest of the morning.

Saturday morning after she'd finished the breakfast dishes, Molly sat at Aunt Agatha's kitchen table putting the final touches on the third letter she'd just written for Lassiter. She found a dangling participle and corrected her mistake, secretly pleased with her new knowledge. How happy Lassiter would be to know that he'd actually taught her something, she thought, stubbornly deciding to leave in all her exclamation points. After all, there was no use in capitulating to all his high-handed demands. A few exclamation points never hurt anyone and never would.

She heard footsteps in the hall and Fergus walked into the kitchen, bright morning light streaming over his lanky form. "Do y-you think you could help me study for a history test?" he asked almost apologetically.

"Sure," she replied with a smile, liking him better the more she knew him. "She pushed her letter aside, making a place for them to work. "Sit down, and tell me what I have to do."

With a weary expression, he claimed a chair and shoved the thick history book in her direction. "A-Ask me these questions about the American Revolution," he said, polishing his glasses with a soft handkerchief. "The answers are at the bottom of the page."

She took him through the signing of the Declaration of Independence to the Battle of Concord. They worked hard with her rapidly firing questions at him until ten o'clock; then she suggested they take a break for a cup of tea. While she prepared the tea, she asked him to read her letter to Lassiter, paying special attention to the grammar.

"Molly, this is good," Fergus laughed as she came back to the table, the tea things on a tray. She sat down and filled two cups while he read the finely written pages with a smile, taking time to make a few corrections.

He favored her with a look of admiration. "You're a fine writer," he announced, carefully stacking the pages in order. "A person with your a-ability should be a regular feature reporter with a byline," he continued, his usually soft voice now strong with conviction.

Molly leaned an elbow on the table. "But what could I write about?" she asked, handing him a pitcher of cream. "I've said everything I can think of about stiff-necked male chauvinists." A worried feeling spread through her. "I think I'm running out of steam on that topic—if you know what I mean."

An easy smile played over Fergus's lips. "Molly, do you know what investigative reporting is?"

"No," she chuckled, liking the sound of the words anyway. "Tell me."

He took a sip of his lightened tea, then held her gaze, his eyes sparkling with excitement. "I-Investigate reporters dig into m-matters that people often wonder

110

about, but don't have the time and inclination to look into themselves."

She sat back in her chair. "Now *that* sounds interesting," she said, folding her hands on the table. "They more or less make up news instead of just reporting facts, right?"

"N-Not exactly," he laughed, adjusting his glasses. Investigative reporters seek out corruption and spotlight it. They're watchdogs for the common people. L-Last week the *Times* had a wonderful report on Castle Island."

"We could tell them something about that place, couldn't we?" she chuckled, sipping her tea. "That reporter should have talked to me."

A thoughtful look moved over Fergus's lean face. "That's just it. The *Times* reporter pretended to be an Irish immigrant just like us. I still have the story if you'd like to read it."

Molly rattled her cup into its saucer. "Umm, yes, I would." She felt herself blush. "Do you really think I could do this investigative reporting?"

"I'm sure you could," Fergus answered, his eyes twinkling affectionately. "You'd be great."

Just then Aunt Agatha walked into the kitchen, a wondering smile on her face. "Molly, dear, there's a young lady here to see you. "She's just a little bit of a thing and she says she came over with you on the ship. She's waiting for you in the parlor," she added, already walking away to do her usual Saturday morning cleaning.

Molly quickly rose. *Clara,* she thought excitedly, wondering how her friend had been getting along since they'd parted over a month ago now. She watched Fergus gulp down the last of his tea, then stand and pick up his book, preparing to leave the kitchen. She was almost out the door when she glanced back at him, wonderful possibilities suddenly blossoming in her mind.

She whirled about, and taking his history book, slammed it on the table. "I want you to come with me," she ordered, noticing his face cloud with uneasiness. "I want you to meet Clara. She's a sweet girl and I'm sure you'll like her."

"A-A girl," he stuttered, blushing beet-red to the roots of his hair. "N-No, I don't think so. I'll just be going up to my room. I-I need to study, you know."

"You can study later," Molly insisted, clasping his long, cold hand. "I want you to meet Clara. You two are so alike."

"*Molly*," he ground out, valiantly pleading his cause, "*No*."

She grasped his bony arm and steered him toward the parlor, surprised at how strong he was for his slight build. There was a final scuffling of feet, but before he could utter another word of protest, she'd gently shoved him into the freshly cleaned room.

Bathed in slanting sunlight, Clara turned about, a look of shocked surprise on her gentle face. She'd dressed carefully, and a modest blue muslin gown garbed her slender form, the pleats on the bodice enhancing her rather flat bosom. Blue ribbons and dainty flowers decorated her inexpensive straw hat.

When Molly was sure Fergus was far enough into the room that he couldn't make a graceful retreat, she hurried to her friend and embraced her. "Clara, it's so good to see you!"

Looking somewhat overwhelmed, the girl hugged her back, her curious gaze straying to Fergus as he tried to edge from the room.

In an instant Molly was at his side, clutching his arm. "Clara, here's someone I want you to meet." She placed her spread hand on Fergus's back and maneuvered him toward the wide-eyed girl. "This is Fergus. He's one of Aunt Agatha's boarders."

Fergus nodded at Clara, then shook her trembling, white-gloved hand. "N-Nice to meet you," he croaked, his Adam's apple bobbing like a fishing cork in his long neck.

"Yes, likewise, I'm sure," Clara whispered, looking as if she might faint at any moment.

Molly suggested they all sit down and talk. Disappointment darted through her when the nervous pair seated themselves as far apart as possible. Clara pulled off her gloves and twisted them anxiously while Fergus blushed and fiddled with his sliding glasses.

Molly talked to Clara about her brother, then just to keep some kind of conversation going, started reminiscing about Ireland. Clara answered in monosyllables, while Fergus remained completely silent, only shuffling his feet. Saints above! Molly thought, this was worse than pulling teeth. She sighed heavily, then happily recalled that Clara had always longed to go to Dublin.

"Fergus is from Dublin," she announced enthusiastically, hoping to open a fertile avenue of conversation. "He went to the university there, and he's terribly smart. In fact, I've never known anyone so intelligent."

Fergus turned a bright scarlet and stared at his feet.

"*Dublin?*" Clara timidly ventured, her face aglow.

"I've always wanted to visit that city." She leaned forward and smiled—just a little. "Did you enjoy living there?"

Fergus, looking like a condemned soul who'd just been ordered to walk the plank, finally started talking, trying to hold his stammering to a minimum. "Y-Yes, very much. Something interesting is always happening in Dublin," he muttered awkwardly.

Clara raised her delicate brows. "Oh, tell me everything you can remember, won't you?"

Fergus rose to take a seat closer to Clara, and as he gently began talking about his life in Dublin, Molly silently thanked God above for the miracle he'd just performed.

Standing, she quietly backed toward the parlor entrance. "I'll just get us all some tea and cake," she said, speaking softly so she wouldn't break the spell she'd worked so hard to create. "I won't be gone long. You two enjoy your talk, now."

Once in the hall, she heard the pair laughing and her heart soared. She leaned against the wall and crossed her fingers. "Oh, Lord, rain your mercy upon them," she prayed, glancing upward. "Guide them, for they need your help so much!"

Her prayer finished, she sauntered toward the kitchen, whistling softly.

Bright and early Monday morning, Molly walked into the *Telegram* building, and on her way to the third floor, met Tom Perkins on the marble staircase.

"*Molly.* What are you doing here so early?"

She grinned at him, so excited about her new idea, she had to tell him. "I came to ask Lassiter to make me a regular reporter—and not just any kind of reporter. I want to be an investigative reporter."

He clasped her arm and laughed. "Investigative reporting? Why, that's the latest thing, and what's more, I think you might have a knack for it."

Molly smiled, then lifted her skirt and started up the sweeping staircase again. "That's what I think. Wish me luck, now," she said over her shoulder.

His eyes glinting with admiration, Tom looked up at her and laughed. "Yes, of course. Let me know how the old man treats you."

Once Molly arrived in the newsroom, she noticed most of the reporters grouped about one of their comrades as the young man crossed swords with Lassiter's secretary who was seated at her desk, looking like a surly sergeant. "What do you mean, you need the day off?" the old lady asked in a disgruntled tone. "Weren't you supposed to cover the mayor's speech today? The chief won't be happy about this, Jenkins."

The frazzled reporter loosened his tie. "I can't help it. My wife is expecting, and someone just came by from our building to tell be she's having labor pains," he announced in a desperate tone. "Someone else will have to cover the mayor's speech." He coughed nervously. "W-Won't you go in and tell him that for me?"

The old lady glared at him fiercely. "No, I think not. "If you want him told, you can tell him yourself—that is if you have the nerve."

Molly sashayed toward the pair unable to believe what she was hearing. Could they *both* be afraid of Lassiter's wrath? After pushing her way through the reporters, she confronted the belligerent secretary head-on. "I'll tell Lassiter that Jenkins can't work today," she rushed out, her sensibilities offended with the injustice of it all. "Burke Lassiter may own the *Telegram* and be its editor in chief, but he's only flesh and blood, you know."

Seething with anger, she aimed herself at Lassiter's office door, drawing murmurs of wonder from the stunned reporters.

"*No*," the secretary warned, pushing herself up from her chair. "You can't barge in there unannounced."

"He's expecting me," Molly shot over her shoulder.

"Not before nine o'clock, he isn't. No one is allowed to see Mr. Lassiter before nine o'clock!"

Molly turned and permitted herself a withering stare. "Nine o'clock, is it? Well, the man needs to know the whole world isn't on his personal timetable, doesn't he?" She placed her hands on her hips. "Now tend to your business and let me tend to mine!"

The newsroom broke into a rousing cheer as Molly left the woman standing in slack-jawed wonder, then opened Lassiter's office door and walked into his private domain with no hesitation whatsoever.

Obviously hearing the reporters before she closed the door, Lassiter pinned her with a questioning glare. "What's going on out there?" he queried, astonishment touching his frowning face. "What's all that commotion about?"

Molly proceeded to his desk, trying to ignore her racing heart.

"To answer your first question, there's a young reporter out there named Jenkins who needs the day off." She cocked her brow in warning. "Don't say a word to the poor man because his wife is having a

116

baby," she said, shaking a finger at him. "You'll have to send someone else to cover the mayor's speech."

Bracing her courage, she continued staring him down. "Everyone out there seemed to be afraid to tell you, so I thought I'd just tell you myself," she finished, startled at the fire in her own voice. "To answer your second question, for some odd reason, that lot in the newsroom thought me coming in here was worth cheering about."

Lassiter stared daggers at her for a moment, then slowly lit a cigar. "All right, I have another question for you, then," he said, squinting through the swirling smoke. "What brought you to my office unannounced in the first place?"

Her footsteps took her the length of the sumptuous chamber as she tried to calm herself down. Pulling up her courage, she finally met his fiery gaze. "I came to tell you I want to write a regular Sunday feature," she announced forthrightly, thanking God her voice held steady. She approached him step by slow step, then looked directly into his glittering eyes. "No more of this half a cent a word stuff, either," she commented with some distaste. "As a regular feature writer, I expect to be paid at least three cents a word."

Lassiter gave her a sidelong glance of utter disbelief and she had to bite her lips to keep from smiling. Obviously her demands had shocked him speechless, but he finally had the wit to compose his features into that bland, sophisticated expression she knew so well.

Lassiter gazed into Molly's snapping eyes, wondering if she'd lost her mind. Amazed at her bravado, he walked across the soft carpet to the window and drew back the silken drapes, gazing at the busy street below and buying himself some time to think. Molly had only written a few letters to the editor and here she was demanding a regular Sunday feature, when some of his reporters had been writing for fifteen years hoping for just *one* Sunday feature.

He took a long draw from his cigar, admitting to himself that her writing had already increased circulation. The paper had received many letters expressing interest in her work, and he knew that people in taverns and public houses all over the city were talking about what she was writing. Not only were the poor Irish interested in what she had to say, but readers from the more affluent classes as well. Still, her demand was outrageous.

He turned and looked at her standing across the room, staring directly at him, her eyes shining with hopeful expectation. Damn it to hell, he thought, wondering who she'd been talking to. The little spitfire was a genuine sensation now, and what was worse, she was beginning to realize it. "My answer is no," he said, slowly bridging the distance between them. "I think you've just about exhausted this women's rights issue too."

"That's just it," she chimed in enthusiastically. "I want to be an investigative reporter."

"*An investigative reporter?*" he snorted, now knowing she'd lost her mind for sure. "The *Telegram* has never resorted to that kind of journalism," he added, thinking at the same time that the *Metropolitan* was doing quite well with investigative reporting.

"Oh, I'd get all my facts straight and do the pieces up real classy-like," she went on, gazing up at him with pleading eyes. "The readers would hardly think of it as investigative reporting at all."

She returned his scowl with a satisfied smile. "Evidentially the biggest paper in the city doesn't have any qualms about publishing investigative features. The *Times* did a feature recently on Castle Island that was excellent."

Lassiter had to admit that she was right, for he'd read the piece himself and was quite impressed with it.

He remained stoically silent and she took advantage of the opportunity to add, "I'd have all the features in early so you could look them over. If you didn't like a piece, we could drop it and I'd write something else."

Lassiter gazed at her thoughtfully, his mind churning wildly at the thought of the possibility of increased Sunday circulation. The little baggage might have just stumbled upon a good idea, and his pride dueling with his natural desire to save his floundering paper, he seriously considered her sensational idea for the first time. "Do you have anything in mind for the first feature?" he asked, rough challenge edging his voice.

Her face lit up. "I certainly do. The garment district is filled with sweatshops where immigrant women toil from dawn until late at night. Their employers only pay them a pittance—in fact they're hardly more than indentured servants." She arched a knowing brow. "I know how to sew, and I think it would be mighty interesting to get a job in one of those sweatshops and find out what's really going on."

Lassiter stared at her, beginning actually to become interested in the idea.

"I know what you're thinking," Molly added, nodding her head thoughtfully. "You're probably wondering how I'm going to work and still help Aunt Agatha at the boardinghouse. That's no problem. I'll get up early to help her before I go to work, and I can always lend a hand when I get home at night. And it'll only be for a short time." She smiled brightly. "Come on, what do you say? The feature will stir up loads of interest."

He was forced to agree with her. The feature would make a lot of businessmen mad, but it touched his social consciousness, and to the general public, the story would be irresistible.

He sat down at his desk, hiding his secret enthusiasm. If necessary, he could touch up the piece and even send someone to double-check her facts. True, the feature would be a calculated gamble, but if she pulled it off, it might be the beginning of a trend that would save the *Telegram* from going under.

He gazed at her, trying to look stern. "Very well," he conceded, "I'll try you with *one* feature, but it had better be the best thing you've ever done." He stood, making sure he had her complete attention. "If you muff this piece, you'll never write anything for me again— *not one blessed line.* Do you understand?"

"Yes, I understand," she answered evenly, her face aglow with triumph. "Believe me, you'll love it!"

"I'll withhold my opinion until I've read it," he came back dourly. "Just remember this deal can be undone instantly." He sat down and shuffled through some papers, scarcely believing the last moments had actually happened. "Now if you'll give me some privacy, I'm very busy."

Molly backed toward his office door, hoping that he couldn't see that she trembled ever so slightly. "You won't be sorry about this. I'll give some thought to the piece and bring you some written ideas tomorrow."

He drew his dark brows together. "See that you do."

She had her hand on the doorknob when he added, "And another thing, *never* barge into my office before nine in the morning again."

"*Nine o'clock?* Why that's a silly rule anyway. You should change it."

He stood and walked to her, a warning cloud settling on his features. "All right, I will just for you," he agreed with a wicked smile. "I expect to see your ideas at eight tomorrow morning."

Molly gulped back her surprise. "A-All right. I'll be here at eight on the dot."

He looked so stern she wondered if she should click her heels or bow before backing from the office. Her last glimpse of Lassiter was that of a marble statue fiercely gazing down at her from Mount Olympus. Filled with secret joy, she eased from his office and quietly closed the door behind her, weak with relief that the interview was over.

She had so much to think about. Just which garment manufacturer would she approach to get her job? What would she wear, how would she apply, and how would she conduct herself when she was being interviewed? Jesus, Mary, and Joseph, she thought with a sudden dart of alarm—what would happen to her if the owner suspected she was actually a reporter?

Once she was in the newsroom, someone grasped her arm, and she whirled about with a start to see Tom Perkins.

"I've been waiting for you," he said calmly, a benign

smile claiming his face. "I just had to know how you made out with the old man."

She chuckled throatily. "He's going to try me with one feature. Isn't it wonderful?"

"Yes, that's terrific," he answered, his eyes gleaming with warmth. "I'll pick you up about six this evening. We'll go out and celebrate."

Molly felt surprised and pleased all at the same time. "Oh, I'd love to, but I have to get some ideas together. Lassiter's depending on me, you know."

Profound disappointment flooded Tom's face. "All right, let's make it another night when you've had time to plan ahead."

"Fine, Tom. That would be wonderful," she replied, experiencing a warm, flattered sensation.

Molly looked at his soft brown eyes thinking what a really kind, gentlemanly sort of fellow he was—the kind who would always bring flowers, and never smoke in her presence, and never forget special occasions.

But even as she walked away, still shaken that she was now actually a reporter, it wasn't Tom's gentle eyes, but Lassiter's stern face that burned its image into her mind.

Chapter Seven

The next Monday morning, Molly and Lassiter stood by his desk looking at the previous day's issue of the *Telegram,* more specifically the Sunday feature, exposing sweatshops in the garment district. Lassiter finished rereading the piece with a glow of pride. How could he have ever doubted Molly's abilities? he wondered with a twinge of guilt, remembering the strict instructions he'd given her.

Not only was the writing first rate with no grammar mistakes, she'd given striking statistics and facts to back up her plea for better working conditions for the immigrant women who worked in the unpleasant little sweatshops, toiling sixteen hours a day. She'd produced a good story—a riveting story—that touched the emotions, and it had such spunk and heart, such great heart.

People were beginning to ask who Molly Kilmartin was and what publications she'd previously written for. Lord, how could he tell them the girl had just arrived by steerage class from Ireland and had absolutely no writing experience whatsoever? He gazed up from the feature, sensing an air of nervousness on Molly's part.

"Well, what do you think?" she asked softly, closing the features section and folding it neatly.

"It's great work," he said in a warm tone, trying to put her at ease. "I like it better every time I read it. "I received some good comments on it yesterday at dinner," he added, thinking of the people who'd stopped by his table to compare it with the *Times*'s feature on Castle Island.

"Really? That's wonderful," Molly replied, experiencing a glow of pride. Lassiter had liked the feature when he'd read her first draft, but having his rich, influential friends compliment it would only make him like it more.

He chuckled lightly. "No doubt we'll get some letters from angry sweatshop owners, though."

She raised her brows. "No doubt," she chuckled, tamping down the secret nervousness his close proximity aroused in her. "They were beside themselves when the *Telegram*'s photographers appeared unannounced last Friday."

"It serves them right," Lassiter growled with a little flare of temper. "The scoundrels need to be exposed for the no-accounts they really are." He ran an appreciative gaze over her. "You've written something that really matters—something that makes people think. You should be proud of yourself."

Somewhat embarrassed with his praise, she sauntered across the room, twisting the cords on her simple reticule. "Thanks," she murmured. "Thanks for printing it."

She heard him walking toward her, then felt his warm hands on her shoulders as he turned her about, and she pulled in a long breath, trying to ignore the strong allure his touch elicited. "you're looking mighty satisfied with yourself this morning, Irish," he said smoothly, his spicy cologne wafting over her. "I smell another Sunday feature boiling in that pretty head of yours."

She heaved a secret sigh of relief that there would actually be another Sunday feature. Last night she'd stolen enough time to write her mother and tell her she was now a real journalist being paid three cents a word for her articles. When she'd seen how the disadvantaged were exploited in the city, outrage had burned within her heart, and now she was helping to effect change with her work and it thrilled her deeply. She took a long, calming breath, thinking life had never been sweeter.

"You bet you smell a story cooking, and it's a doozy," she proclaimed, looking into his sapphire-blue eyes and knowing she had to put some distance between them. Her gaze riveted on him, she walked about his office just to build up the suspense a little.

He sat down on the corner of his desk and arched a questioning brow. "Well, spit it out," he ordered with a laugh, placing a spread hand on his knee. "I'm dying to know."

She searched his interested face, watching it for a reaction to her words. "I thought I might pose as beggar girl and stand in front of several of the theaters this week. I could see how the well-heeled gents treated me. I might run into some people whose pictures regularly appear on the society pages—people with names like Vanderbilt and Astor and Gould."

Lassiter's mouth twitched with amusement. "Yes, that's good, but the same people might say you'd quit reporting and gone to meddling," he came back, a teasing light in his eyes.

"You mean I can't do it?" she asked, surrendering to a rush of disappointment.

He laughed a little, liking the idea already. "No, I don't mean that at all. Suppose we do ruffle a few feathers. What the hell. I've always prided myself on printing the truth, no matter how embarrassing it might be to those in high places."

He rose and walked about, his mind churning with possibilities. "But we need to beef it up a little," he said, stroking his jaw. "You could talk to some real beggars and see how they live—where they sleep, how often they eat—what they have to go through to keep body and soul together. And let's take it a step further," he suggested, really getting into the idea as he thought of the snobbish lady in the red dress he'd crossed swords with on the *Saxonia*. "Why don't you write about the salaries of plain working people, and we'll compare it with the estimated net worth of the New York elite. The readers should lap that up like a Christmas pudding."

"That's what I was counting on." She graced him with a shy smile. "I love the power of the press, don't you?"

Lassiter curled an index finger under her chin and

looked into her dancing eyes. "Yes, I love it so much, it's damn scary."

He laughed, and tilting her head to the side, she joined him. He had to admit she had good instincts, for all the working folks would be interested in how the other half lived. If things went as he expected, the *Telegram* would soon be the talk of the town.

He gazed at her soft face and laughing lips, pondering the future with trepidation. He'd enjoyed the intimate favors of several sophisticated women, but as far as he could determine, he'd never been in love with any of them. Could he actually be falling in love with Molly? Certainly she was a charming Irish girl, blazing with the flame of life, and he thoroughly enjoyed her bubbling personality and fascinating mind, but did he seriously want to get involved with her?

He let his gaze roam over her lovely face. "You have a great laugh, you know."

"Thanks," she said shyly. "So do you."

Light streamed through the office windows, splashing over her coppery hair and creamy skin. What a striking effect she had on him, filling him with delight and pleasure, and a deep yearning to take her in his arms. Almost without thinking, he encircled her body and pulled her close, feathering gentle kisses over her cheeks and eyelids and the pulse in her throat.

Surprise flickered in her eyes, and her lips mouthed the word *no*. Then she forcefully pulled away. "I agreed to write for the *Telegram* and nothing else," she exclaimed, her bosom heaving with indignation. Her eyes flashed. "If I'm not mistaken, I recall telling you that one night in Central Park."

Lassiter moved away from her, silently cursing himself for letting his emotions get the best of him. He had to admit the rejection stung, especially when other women were clamoring for his attention. He turned about and, pasting a smile on his face, met her reproachful gaze. Making a strong, active decision, he told himself he wasn't sure if he actually loved Molly yet, but he did want to become involved with her, for he cared deeply for her. And in order to win her affections, he was willing to do some old-fashioned courting.

"My apologies, miss," he said, only a trace of sarcasm in his voice. He bowed his head formally, thinking he couldn't bear another evening with Daisy and that lamebrained crowd of hers that hung out in Delmonico's. "Please accept my apologies. To make up for my gaffe, may I invite you to dinner this evening? We'll do New York up right. Dinner and champagne, then dancing until the wee hours. I'll even bring roses," he finished with a chuckle.

A flicker of pleasure raced through Molly's eyes. "No, thank you," she coolly intoned, sending him a sharp glance. "I remember the last time we drank champagne very vividly." She strolled about the office, tracing her hand over the leather chairs, and gazing back over her shoulder. "Besides I couldn't possibly accept. I have another engagement."

"Another engagement?"

She met his gaze head-on. "Yes, Tom and I are going out."

Lassiter felt as if someone had hit him in the stomach. "*Tom?* Are you speaking of Tom Perkins?"

"None other."

"*Good God.* I didn't dream he'd get up the nerve to ask you."

Her eyes danced with pleasure. "Well he did, and I'm going."

Lassiter walked back to his desk, hiding his surprise and lacerated pride. "Well, I'll be damned," he muttered dourly, studying her satisfied face.

"Most likely you will," she chirped, a soft smile taking some of the sting from her words. With that, she swept to the office door, and just before leaving, announced, "I'll start working on the new feature today and give you an update Wednesday morning. You can send a photographer with me Friday."

"Fine," he answered, gracing her with a nonchalant smile.

After she'd gone, Lassiter lit a cigar, then flung the match into an ashtray, wondering what had happened— what he'd let happen—under his very nose, no less.

He sat down at his desk and tried to work, but he couldn't banish the image of Tom Perkins holding Molly in his arms. He wrote three paragraphs, rearranged the sentences, then scratched out everything. With a low groan, he tossed down his pen and rubbed his temples, knowing he was going to have a particularly bad day.

That evening Molly relaxed in Aunt Agatha's parlor as she waited for Tom to pick her up. She watched Fergus and Clara, who sat by each other on the settee holding hands as they talked pleasantly. Since she'd introduced them, Fergus had visited the pale girl at her home several times and he'd surprised both Molly and her aunt by inviting Clara to the boardinghouse for dinner that night.

It warmed her heart to see how well the pair was getting along, and lifted her spirits to know what the budding romance had done for both of them. A healthy blush glowed on Clara's cheeks and Fergus's confidence had already grown immensely.

Dinner would be served in ten minutes, and having nothing else to do, Shamus wandered into the parlor with a tray of elderberry wine. He offered Molly a glass, then handed one to Clara and Fergus before setting down the tray and taking a glass himself. When he cleared his throat and gazed at the pair affectionately, Molly knew he was going to make one of his famous toasts.

"My dear friends," he rumbled in a pleasant Irish lilt, "may you both be poor in misfortune, rich in blessings, slow to make enemies, and quick to make friends." He smoothed down his mustache and licked his lips. "But rich or poor, quick or slow, may you both know nothin' but happiness from this day forward."

Fergus nodded his head appreciatively. "Ah, that was very nice, Shamus."

Aunt Agatha, who'd been standing at the parlor entrance, listening, sent him a blistering glance. "Yes, that was very pleasant, but try as I might, I can never remember you offerin' a toast to the married life."

Shamus lifted his bushy brows. "Well, that must have just slipped my mind, Jelly Bean." He took a sip of wine, and with a wry grin, swept an amused gaze over her. "How about this: There's only one thing better than a good wife, and that's no wife at all!"

Fergus and Clara laughed, but Aunt Agatha entered

the room like a square rigger at full sail. "Listen to the man," she scoffed, her voice sharpening considerably. "Even the good Lord himself said that matrimony is a blessed state, did he not?"

Shamus ambled to her and patted her plump hand. "Now, now, Jelly Bean, haven't I promised you a thousand times that I'll marry you when I'm financially able?"

"Your promises are like piecrust," she spluttered, bristling with indignation, "very easily broken!" Her face softening, she gazed at Fergus and Clara, who now rose from the settee, seemingly understanding it was time to eat. "Dinner is ready, my dears. Why don't you two go on in the dinin' room."

Her demeanor growing in severity again, she glared at Shamus, who appeared quite pleased with himself. "I guess I'll have to feed you, too, old man," she conceded, surveying him imperiously. "Get in there and carve the roast."

Once the three of them had left the room, Molly stood and clasped her aunt's soft arm. "Are you sure you can get along without me?

The old lady took her by the shoulders. "Yes, yes, you just enjoy your evenin' with Mr. Perkins, dear." Her eyes lit with pleasure. "You look so pretty in your new gown. The blue silk goes so nicely with your hair."

Molly blushed at the compliment, feeling extravagant that she'd spent some of her carefully hoarded funds to buy a new garment for the evening.

Aunt Agatha headed for the dining room, then paused in the hall and raised her brows. "You deserve a bit of fun. Just see that this Mr. Perkins behaves himself like a gentleman. I'll be wantin' a whole report on the evenin' bright and early tomorrow mornin', don't you know."

Tom arrived a few minutes later with a large bouquet of roses, which he presented to Molly with great ceremony. A born accountant, he was alarmingly neat and fastidious. There wasn't a speck of lint on his fine blue suit and his shoes were polished to a high gloss. After some polite small talk, they left the boardinghouse in a gay mood.

Tom's carriage wasn't as fine as Lassiter's but much nicer than Molly had expected, considering his modest accountant's salary. The restaurant he'd chosen was an elegant place in the better part of Manhattan, and the ritziest eating establishment Molly had ever seen.

After they'd been seated, Tom gazed across the table with adoring eyes. "So, you see, Molly, by saving half of my paycheck each month, I've been able to amass a tidy nest egg." Color touched his cheeks. "I have a nice apartment too. Now when I marry, I-I mean if I ever marry," he stammered, "I would be able to buy a house—something quite comfortable, I'll wager."

Tom's lack of subtlety made Molly blush herself.

They talked of finances as they ate with Tom telling her he was a good money manager, and had even made some small investments that were doing well. It bothered her that he seemed so obsessed with money, even though it was natural, considering he was an accountant.

She breathed a secret sigh of relief when he changed the subject to the *Telegram*. "Your features have really increased circulation," he said, enthusiastically. "Believe me, that's something we needed badly."

"*Really?* The way you make it sound, the paper is on its last legs."

He gave a knowing nod. "It hasn't been doing all that well lately. The New York newspaper business is highly competitive, you know. Outside of the *Times,* the *Metropolitan* is our biggest rival. They nearly always outsell us."

Molly sat forward, keenly interested in what he had to say. "Why, I thought Lassiter was one of the richest men in the city."

Tom widened his eyes. "True, he inherited a fortune, but the *Telegram* hasn't added substantially to his bank account. In fact, there have been months when the paper actually ran in the red."

Molly twirled a wineglass between her fingertips, mulling over the information with a sense of alarmed surprise. Lassiter was a proud man and she realized he'd never tell her about his financial difficulties, but this was something she never expected. She stored the information in the back of her mind, thinking it might help her understand the enigma that was Burke Lassiter.

"You've really brightened up the newsroom," Tom went on with a winning smile as he leaned back in his chair. "The reporters tell me things have gotten a lot better since you've arrived. Everyone has always been afraid to cross the old man, and you don't seem to be intimidated by him at all."

"Believe me, he's only flesh and blood like any other man," she responded, thinking of his passionate kisses upon the *Saxonia.*

She and Tom continued their conversation, with him telling her he'd worked for the paper for six years. He proved very knowledgeable, and after talking to him for thirty minutes, she had a much better idea what it cost to produce a first-class daily paper.

When she decided to venture some friendly questions about his past, he fobbed her off with vague general answers, mildly surprising her. She persisted, but he skillfully sidestepped the subject, and put on a guarded expression that said *stay out, don't come any closer.*

As they left the restaurant, he gently draped her wrap about her shoulders, letting his hand linger just a moment too long on her arm.

On the way back to the boardinghouse, he boasted about his plans for the future. "Someday I will have my own accounting firm. I know the business inside and out, and I'm sure I could make a great success of it."

Molly smiled, thinking Tom was more ambitious than she'd realized. But the fact that he'd talked of money all evening while withholding information about his past gave her a vague uneasy feeling she couldn't explain.

On the boardinghouse porch, he searched her face, then lightly brushed his lips against her cheek. "Good night. Sleep well."

"Good night, Tom," she responded, relieved he hadn't tried to kiss her on the lips. "It was nice of you to invite me," she added to be polite, just now realizing that she'd never laughed even *once* this evening the way she laughed when she was with Lassiter. She watched Tom drive away in his expensive carriage, then went upstairs to her room, reviewing her evening in her mind.

Yes, Tom had all the qualities she'd always dreamed of in a man, all the solid, respectable qualities that would ensure a girl of a stable marriage, she thought while divesting herself of her gown. He was presentable, hardworking, and safe, and although he wasn't Irish, even her mother would like him. Sometime in the far-distant future he might make suitable marriage material—that is if she ever decided to marry. The accountant was just what she was looking for in a man, not a charming, irresponsible scoundrel like Lassiter.

She put on her nightgown and slipped into bed. In one sense, Tom seemed to be the perfect man, but their evening had left her with a host of nagging, unanswered questions. How could he afford the fine suit he'd worn tonight, and those costly roses? And how could he sport about in a fine carriage and live in an apartment located one of the better sections of the city?

Finding no answers to her troubling questions, she finally slipped into an exhausted sleep.

Molly's days had fallen into a routine. On Monday mornings, as every morning, she exchanged a few words with Brian as he brought the *Telegram,* then read the newspaper during her omnibus ride. As soon as she arrived at the huge newspaper building, she'd have a conference with Lassiter, then see him again on Wednesday mornings and let him know how she was getting along. She would spend the rest of the weekdays in the city interviewing people and taking notes.

When her long days were over, she'd come back to the boardinghouse to help Aunt Agatha prepare dinner for her hungry boarders. After that, she'd write in her room, and this way was able to produce her Sunday features, which were now receiving rave reviews.

Summer was playing itself out, and one pleasant

Monday morning, she stepped from the omnibus and briskly walked down Broadway to the *Telegram* building, a little breeze riffling through her hair. Feeling fantastic, she swept through the newsroom gathering bouquets of smiles from the reporters, who all greeted her warmly now.

As she approached Lassiter's office, his secretary glared up at her with her usual sour expression and announced, "He had to go out this morning. He wants you to meet him at eleven at the Press Club for lunch."

"The Press Club?"

"Yes, It's just around the corner. You can't miss it. He'll be waiting for you at table sixteen—it's his favorite." The woman sighed, then returned to her work, her eyes fastened to a roster of writing assignments for the upcoming week.

Molly remembered the look on Lassiter's face when she'd refused his night on the town and worried for a moment that he might be trying to steal his way into her affections again. Then remembering his perfect behavior of late, she decided he'd been all business.

More relaxed, she saw one of the reporters was away covering a story, and borrowed his desk to flesh out some ideas. She scribbled furiously until 10:45, then, still vaguely wondering if Lassiter had something up his sleeve, walked to the Press Club, an old three-story brick building with an imposing columned entrance and huge brass-plated doors.

Once inside, she was immediately enveloped in a cloud of cigar smoke and the sound of droning male voices. The club projected a potent masculine ambiance, and when a host of reporters gave her admir-

ing stares, she shifted uncomfortably, feeling somewhat ill at ease.

On one side of the pleasantly furnished entrance she
noticed a saloon bar with softly glowing lamps and a
brass-fitted bar, and on the other side of the entrance, a
billiard room. When a curious waiter approached, she
simply said, "Table sixteen," and was escorted down
the wide hall to a luxurious dining room awash with
the scent of delicious food and the sound of scraping
silverware.

Upon seeing her, Lassiter rose and, his eyes widening with pleasure, flashed a smile. After she'd been
seated, he ordered lamb and mint sauce for them both,
then reached across the table and enclosed her hand in
his. "Thanks for coming, Irish," he offered in a low vel-
vet-edged tone that reverberated straight through her.
"Sorry we couldn't have our usual Monday morning
conference, but I was talking to a very important person
about the possibility of an interview with the *Telegram.*

Molly took a sip of water. "And who might that be?"

Lassiter's eyes kindled with satisfaction. "John L.
Sullivan, himself."

"John L. Sullivan? The fighter?"

"No other. He's the talk of New York, and I've been
wanting to do a story on him for months."

"Then why aren't you having lunch with the sports
editor?" she murmured hastily, laying her reticule
aside.

He bent his head slightly forward. "Because John L.
wants *you* to interview him," he answered, tightly
squeezing her hand.

"He wants to be interviewed by a woman?" she
asked, wrinkling her nose in surprise.

Laughter rumbled in Lassiter's throat. "Not any woman—only you. He's read all of your features and loves the way you put words together."

"But I've never done an interview."

"That doesn't matter," he returned, waving his hand dismissively. "The man is Irish and he wants to be interviewed by someone fresh from the old sod." His mouth curved in a pleased smile. "His exact words were, 'I don't trust no one but Molly Kilmartin and she's the only one I'll talk to. She'll give me a fair shake.' "

Molly wanted to discuss an idea for another feature, but as they ate their meal, Lassiter continued talking about Sullivan and what a sensational scoop the story would make. "We'll schedule the interview for next month after his championship fight."

Molly had never seen Lassiter looking so self-satisfied and for a moment she thought he might actually pop the buttons right off his starched white shirt.

"Every newspaper publisher in New York will turn green with envy when this exclusive hits the streets," he went on, his excitement spilling over into his voice. He stared at her thoughtfully, his mind obviously spinning at ninety miles an hour. "Oh yes, I forgot to mention I'm giving you a pseudonym the public should love." His eyes snapped with pleasure. "What do you think about the Angel of Murphy Street?" He lounged back in his chair, obviously pleased with his publishing coup.

She stared at his amused face. "*The Angel of Murphy Street?*" she echoed, fluttering her lashes in surprise. "Don't you think that's a bit dramatic?"

Lassiter pushed back his plate and laughed. "No, it's

wonderful. The public will eat it up. The paper has been receiving a lot of letters about you lately, you know." He patted his chest, slipped his hand into his vest, and pulled out a thick wad of letters, then spread them on the table with a smile. "Here, just take a look at these if you don't believe me."

Surprised, Molly picked up one of the letters and read it, then scanned several more, filled with wonder and delight that people were so interested in her, that they would say such nice things about her.

Lassiter scooped up the letters and shoved them in her reticule. "Take them home and read all of them," he suggested, his mood rising by the second. "You'll see the readers are hungry to know details of your life, so I'm going to write a piece myself, dwelling on your Irish roots and mentioning how I met you on the *Saxonia*.

"I hope you don't tell them everything!" she laughed, feeling a blush roll up from her bosom.

"Don't worry. I'll simply mention you're working for your mother's passage to America and helping your aunt in her boardinghouse. With a name like Molly Kilmartin you're already a saint to the Irish, and the rest of New York will want to read about you, too, because your writing is so colorful."

Molly studied the contents of her plate for a moment, then slowly looked up at him. "And dubbing me the Angel of Murphy Street will sell more papers?" she asked, thinking he'd go to any length to increase the *Telegram*'s circulation.

"That's right," Lassiter came back jovially. "There's nothing wrong with selling papers, is there? And you did come to America to become a success didn't you?"

"Yes," she replied thoughtfully, slightly embarrassed

at his proposition, "but the Angel of Murphy Street seems a little heavy-handed, a little—" She paused searching for the right word.

"*Manipulative?*" Lassiter offered, a suggestion of annoyance gathering in his eyes.

"Yes, that's it."

He smiled knowingly. "Don't worry. People love to be manipulated. In fact, life is about manipulating and being manipulated."

"Yes, I'm sure you wouldn't hesitate to manipulate someone for a moment, would you?" she challenged dryly.

"Oh, I'd hesitate," he rejoined with a laugh. "I'd hesitate until I knew what they held most dear—then my efforts would be more effective." He patted her hand as if to dismiss the subject. "We'll use your new byline on your next feature."

"But—"

"I'll not hear another word about it."

Molly sighed and gave in, thinking she could hardly argue with him. Frustrated, she leaned forward to emphasize her next words. "Now if we're finished discussing Mr. Sullivan and your plans to manipulate the reading public with some melodramatic pseudonym, I'd like to talk to you about a new feature idea."

He raised his fingers to silence her. "Put it on the back burner, Irish. *I* have an idea for your next feature myself."

She placed her empty water glass aside. "*You do?*" she replied, a twinge of wonder in her voice.

"Yes," he answered, his eyes bright with pleasure. He clasped her hand and caressed it with his thumb.

"We're going to spend all day together tomorrow—and the evening too."

She stiffened at his words. "I thought I told you—"

"Don't be so defensive," Lassiter came back in a slightly reproachful tone. "I'm not asking you out socially, you hotheaded little mick. We're going on a field trip to research your next feature."

Molly pulled her hand away, his take-charge manner making her pucker her lips in annoyance. "Oh, we are, are we?" She rose and tossed her crumpled napkin on the table. "And just where are you taking me on this so-called field trip?"

Lassiter slowly stood and leaned toward her, playfully arching his brows. "I'm taking you to a place you're bound to like," he answered, his eyes twinkling like a boy's. "I'm taking the Angel of Murphy Street to Coney Island."

Chapter Eight

The excursion boat arrived at Coney Island late the next morning, and Molly watched with fascination as the passengers poured toward the famous amusement park. But Lassiter suggested they first take advantage of the fine day to explore the beaches and hotels, and visit the park that evening. By then, he said, its glowing gas lights would illuminate the booths and dance pavilions to their best advantage.

Waves lapped beside them as they traversed the boardwalk, and overhead, gulls cried and made lazy circles in the clear blue sky. There were hordes of strolling city folk here, bare-legged boys searching for fiddler crabs, and rows of bathhouses and shady wooden pavilions sheltering gay oompah bands whose brass instruments glittered in the sharp morning light. Seeing a bench, they sat down and Lassiter finally brought up the subject of the feature he'd mentioned at the Press Club the day before.

"Well come on and tell me," Molly teased, her curiosity driving her crazy. "I want to know right here and now. Just what kind of story do you have in mind for Coney Island?"

A slow smile worked its way across his lips. "I thought you might do a story about crime here on the island," he suggested, immediately snagging her attention. "You could start with the games in the amusement park."

"Go on," Molly prompted, already liking the idea.

"I want you to discover how the barkers are cheating their customers. Most people think the games are crooked, and with a little work, I'm sure you can dig up some interesting facts. "Seems to me the public needs to know the truth before they lay down their hard-earned wages."

Molly nodded, silently agreeing with him. Already she began to outline the feature in her mind, thinking it would be a great story, one that would stir a lot of reader interest. They set a deadline for the piece and a schedule for the photographer then rose and walked on, Lassiter laying his hand at the small of her back.

The September sun warming their bodies, they passed an old-fashioned bathing machine that looked like nothing more than a small covered wagon driven partway into the water at the edge of the sea, its canvas providing a sense of modesty for the shy bather inside.

Farther down the beach, there were pale-faced office girls sitting at the surf's edge, laughing and splashing water at each other's legs. Elsewhere mothers led barefoot toddlers to the ocean's edge, and couples relaxed against sand dunes, huge beach umbrellas over their heads. Some families picnicked out of wicker baskets, and in the distance, a laughing child rode a pony, led by a swarthy man with a gold ring in his ear.

About eleven-thirty Molly spotted the Manhattan Beach Hotel with its gingerbread turrets and spreading verandas, gleaming with snowy linen-covered tables.

"How about some lunch?" Lassiter suggested. "You should have worked up a good appetite by now, and I hear the hotel has the best restaurant on the island."

Molly felt her stomach growling, for she hadn't eaten since seven that morning. "You've got a deal," she laughingly agreed as they turned up a boardwalk that led to the sprawling hotel.

The lobby led to an impressive restaurant that was an oasis of feathery palms and potted flowers. The restaurant's walls were hung with rose-colored silk and its tables set with sparkling cut glass and creamy gold-rimmed china. Knowing this was a sight only the well-heeled were ever privileged to see, Molly drank it in with hungry eyes.

An attentive waiter seated them where they could look out over the white beach and blue water, then Lassiter ordered pheasant for them both along with a fine French wine. A steward brought the wine in a crested silver bucket, and after Lassiter had approved it, filled their glasses, then made his way to another table with the authority of a field marshal.

Lassiter thoughtfully sipped his wine, then sat back to run appreciative eyes over Molly.

"Did you ever think you might spoil me?" she asked, somewhat uncomfortable under his warm gaze.

"That's something I've been wanting to do for a long

time," he answered, his resonant voice as effective as a caress.

She blushed hotly. "Now I see how your mind works," she challenged, shifting in her chair. "This little trip was just an excuse to get me out for the day, wasn't it?"

"Call it what you like," he answered, a playful light dancing in his eyes. "I see no reason why we can't mix business with pleasure and enjoy ourselves. This is the New York you dreamed of, isn't it?"

As they ate, Lassiter beefed up his plans for the feature, suggesting Molly also write about the pickpockets who fleeced the crowds on the midway and the thieves who pilfered the bathhouses.

"I'll get a job in one of the booths," she said, digging into her meal with relish. "By keeping my eyes open and my mouth shut, I'll learn a lot."

Indecision clung to Lassiter's furrowed brow. "I'm not sure about that. This island is filled with shady characters."

"Don't worry," she insisted, putting down her fork with a decisive clink. "I think you're forgetting something."

"And what's that?"

"I'm Irish, and I've been looking out for myself most of my life."

"All right," he laughed, swirling his wine around in the glass, "get your job and write me a feature that will show up these thieves on Coney Island for what they really are. Too many people have been cheated already."

Molly considered Lassiter's handsome face. To look at him sitting there in his fine suit, drinking expensive wine, it was hard to imagine him as a crusader for the working masses—but perhaps he was, for he'd enthusiastically backed her features, which had all highlighted the trials and tribulations of the city's downtrodden.

Could there be another side of the man she knew nothing about? *No,* she finally decided, tamping down her growing enthusiasm. He was simply a good newspaperman who'd smelled another exciting story—one that would sell more copies of his beloved *Telegram.*

Yes, she knew Lassiter was all business and always would be as far as writing went. But matters of the flesh were another thing with him. As she listened to him talk about the upcoming feature, she thought of this evening and a warm tingle of anticipation floated through her blood.

After a leisurely luncheon, the pair took in an open-air concert, then Lassiter hired a carriage and they made a grand tour of the island, often stopping to walk out on a pier so they could get the best view. They had afternoon tea at the great Oriental Hotel, drinking a fine English blend. Toward sunset, Lassiter suggested they make their way to the amusement park proper.

Near the park's entrance, excursion boats unloaded battalions of poorer city folks and Molly and Lassiter were swept up in the babbling crowds streaming into the amusement park, an immense hodgepodge of shacks, carousels, freak museums, and gaudy sideshows. Molly took it all in with delight, thinking it was amazing, for she'd certainly not experienced anything like this in Ireland.

Golden gaslight illuminated the stalls and the music

of hand organs and calliopes enlivened the warm night air. Filled with cheap dolls and appealing trinkets, the rough booths faced a wide midway strung with glowing Chinese lanterns that moved gently in the light sea breeze, which also carried the pungent aromas of popcorn, onions, and frying potatoes.

"Want a hot dog?" Lassiter asked, eyeing a pushcart full of famous Coney Island Hots wrapped in thin white paper and oozing mustard.

"Sure," Molly answered, caught up in the carnival atmosphere. "I'm going to pretend I'm a kid tonight and eat everything I want." She grabbed his arm. "Before the evening's over, I want some popcorn and a candy apple too."

"All right" he laughed indulgently, "but it may give you a stomachache."

"Not a chance. Kids eat the stuff all the time."

"Yeah, but kids have iron stomachs."

They continued looking over the carnival, leisurely eating their hot dogs. For the little ones, there were rocking-boat rides, and a host of fanciful steam-powered carousels with beautifully painted and gilded hobby horses.

Some of the booths contained shooting galleries, and machines to test a man's grip and strength, while others housed dart games and win-a-cigar contrivances that Molly quickly noticed were rigged for the benefit of the barkers, who loudly urged passersby to test their skill and win a prize.

In a game of strength, Lassiter pounded a sledgehammer at the bottom of a scale, but as a marker soared upward, the barker quickly moved his hand under the counter. Seconds before the marker hit the top of the scale, it plummeted downward, denying him a prize.

Ignoring the man's plea to try the game yet again, Lassiter escorted Molly down the busy midway. "Did you see that?" he asked with a skeptical smile.

"I certainly did. That game had to be rigged, and I'm going to find out how it's done."

After trying a few more games they took in a sideshow with a sword swallower and a trio of dancing dogs. Later they bought candy apples and rested on a bench to watch the milling crowds pass by. Molly took a deep breath, then gazed at the star-sprinkled sky. Gaslight rippled over the sparkling ocean, and a cool sea breeze caressed her face and blew through her loose hair.

As Lassiter put his arm about her shoulder, she gazed upward at his shadowy face. "It's been a perfect day," she offered, thinking she owed him the compliment.

"Not so fast," he laughed, brushing back a lock of her windblown hair. "As soon as you finish your candy apple we're going to a dance pavilion."

Eight o'clock found them near a beer garden filled with new immigrants, who applauded the band loudly after each lilting waltz. "Are you ready?" Lassiter asked, taking Molly's hand and pulling her onto the wooden platform, already filled with couples, who good-naturedly made a place for them to stand.

Molly secretly admitted to herself that it was wonderful to feel Lassiter's strong arms about her, to be moved over the platform with such grace, to be swept up in the laughter and gaiety all about her.

"Get ready. We're going to take a dip," he ordered,

suddenly taking her into a reverse that made her laugh brightly.

"None of your fancy steps, now," she warned, clutching onto his shoulders tightly. "Remember I'm just a country girl."

"Nonsense. You're a born dancer," he replied, negotiating another complicated move that took to them to the very center of the platform.

When the waltz finished, the band struck up a polka, and the pair jigged over the wooden planks with the laughing immigrants. Nearby, a young man, a look of grim effort on his face, danced ramrod straight, holding his partner's arm out like a pump handle. Lassiter quickly adopted the lad's attitude, spinning Molly about in tight little circles until she burst out in unbridled laughter.

"*Stop,*" she pleaded, scarcely able to catch her breath, "I'm getting dizzy!"

After giving her a moment to recover, he led her from the platform and through the noisy crowd. Clutching her hand a little tighter, he headed for a shadowy pier that jutted into the dark ocean. Their footfalls sounded quietly over the well-worn planks as they slowed down and strolled toward the end of the quiet pier hand in hand, still slightly out of breath.

They listened to waves lap against the pier's underpinnings and watched whistling fireworks burst red and gold into the night sky. The scent of the sea wrapped itself about them and in the distance, there was the excited murmur of the crowd and the faint sound of a barker's call.

Lassiter took Molly into his arms and swept an affectionate gaze over her face. "Did you have fun today?" he asked softly.

"Oh yes," she whispered, knowing she couldn't deny him an honest answer, "the most fun I've ever had."

He studied her quietly, then gently asked, "What about those dreams you talked about on the *Saxonia*? Do you still have them?"

She arched her brows. "Of course I do. I'd never give up on my dreams."

Lassiter touched her face in a gesture she found almost irresistible in its tenderness. "No, I'm sure you wouldn't," he said, his velvety voice making her heart thud noisily within her.

He chuckled softly. "Holding to your dreams has paid off, hasn't it? You're not only a reporter, but write a regular Sunday feature now."

Molly giggled. "And all because I had the good sense to get mad at your editorial and write you a nasty letter!"

He laughed, then his expression slowly sobered and a thoughtful look kindled in his eyes. "How are you doing saving money for your mother's fare?"

"Not too well," she came back with a little frown, "I've had to buy some clothes and other personal items. But I am managing to put a bit back each week."

He ran his finger down the side of her cheek. "Yes, I'm sure you could use some help, so I've decided to offer The Angel of Murphy Street a small salary."

Molly pulled back from him. "Did I hear you say salary?"

"You did."

"How much?"

Lassiter chuckled heartily. "Enough. You're not in a

position to start haggling about money, yet, young lady."

Molly wanted to challenge him, but decided at the last moment to hold her tongue. "All right," she grudgingly agreed, "you win—but only this round, mind you." She tilted her head, studying his amused face. "Before I accept this salary, I'd like to inquire if it comes with any fringe benefits."

Lassiter gave a crack of laughter. "You never give up, do you? All right," he added, affectionately caressing the hollows of her back, "I think the Angel of Murphy Street deserves her own desk at the *Telegram*."

Molly stared at his twinkling eyes, not believing what he'd said. "D-Do you mean you're going to give me my own office?"

"It's more of a broom closet than an office," he answered dryly, "but if you want it, it's yours."

Overcome with joy, Molly forgot herself and hugged him tightly, then laid her head against his hard chest. "Oh yes, I want it. You'd better not give it to another soul but me."

Lassiter grinned, then cupped her chin so he could look directly into her eyes. "I named you well. You really do have the face of an angel, you know," he murmured, a mixture of tenderness and sexual interest playing over his rugged features. He raised her hand and kissed each of her fingertips. "Nevertheless, there's a challenging little gleam in your eyes that has nothing to do with the holy realms."

Molly fought the surge of tender feelings his words aroused, but felt herself weakening . . . giving in. His sapphire-blue eyes deepened in the moonlight and his breath feathered over the pulsations at her throat. At that moment she knew he was going to kiss her, and put in a soft mood by the wonderful day and her own raging desire, she couldn't find the will to resist him.

Gently cradling her chin, he raised her face and seared her mouth with a kiss full of wild desire. He tightened his arms about her and she was engulfed in the warmth of his body and the salty scent of his skin. She mentally fought the sensuous kiss, but noticed a deep warmth radiate over her back where his arm encircled her.

"You're so unspoiled," he murmured against her trembling lips. His deep, husky voice sent delicious tremors rippling through her body. "Just relax, little one," he coaxed softly, brushing her cheek with his thumb. At first she stiffened, but then gave in as his tongue played over her lips and finally slipped between them.

He plundered her mouth with a long, devastating kiss that left her trembling with emotion. Like a swift torrent, aching passion rushed through her, making her nipples swell and harden against her bodice. With a will of their own, her arms clasped his broad shoulders more tightly and her legs went weak beneath her.

She moaned as his tongue plundered deeper and he teased her nipple through the thin material of her cotton gown. The pebbly crest tingled sweetly and ached with unbidden pleasure. Aflame with desire, she now noticed a sharp pulse throb between her thighs, and she found herself kissing him back as if she couldn't get enough of him. Blood roared in her ears and her heart fluttered crazily.

At the same time, an angry part of her mind struggled against the sweet sensation. She knew what he was like, the same kind of man as her father, who ruthlessly used women, then carelessly cast them aside. But this evening she was only aware of the sinewy muscles that pressed against her and the passion he'd managed to ignite within her. Not many weeks ago, she'd pushed him away when he'd tried to take her in his arms, but tonight his kiss sent a tingly fire through her veins that evaporated every last drop of her judgment and common sense.

What did one kiss matter? she told herself, thinking the fireworks streaking over the ocean were nothing compared to those bursting within her heart. Tonight she didn't want to think about breaking the kiss or lecturing him about the day being strictly business. She didn't even want to consider the consequences of her actions or where they might lead her. She only wanted to feel his arms about her, holding her tight, and feel his heart beating against hers.

Five days later, Molly looked up from her writing as Lassiter illuminated several gaslights, which banished the gathering shadows engulfing his suite in the palatial Regency Hotel. She laid her pen on the huge mahogany table, where she was making last-minute revisions on her feature about Coney Island, to proudly announce, "I'm finished, if you want to take a look."

After gently caressing her arm, Lassiter sat down beside her, then began thoughtfully editing the pages she'd just finished, crossing out some redundant phrases. A lock of black hair flopped over his forehead as he loosened his tie and placed the first page aside.

Just being with him made Molly feel warm and secure, and strangely relaxed, she decided, thinking he looked very stylish in his starched white shirt, embroidered vest, and dark trousers. Noticing he was absorbed in his work, she stood, marveling at the beauty of the large parlor filled with the finest cut-velvet sofas and chairs and appointed with elegant French chests and a sparking chandelier that hung from the high scrolled ceiling.

She heard the distant rumble of thunder and walked to the rain-splattered window, looking out. Hazy twilight had settled over New York like a blue veil. Rows of street lamps glowed down Fifth Avenue, and on the street below, hacks with swaying headlights emerged from the ever-flowing stream of traffic to let out couples dressed in evening clothes.

When Lassiter had asked her to go home with him after work to finish the article, then go out to dinner, she'd experienced a pang of doubt, thinking well brought up young women didn't accompany men to their hotel suites without an escort. Surely Aunt Agatha wouldn't approve—but after all, they were only working on her feature, which had to be typeset early the next morning. Hearing shuffling papers, she turned to see Lassiter lean back in his chair with a pleased face.

"The article is good—superb in fact," he commented, rolling a cigar between his fingertips. "I especially like the section where you describe how the barkers rig their games so it's almost impossible to win."

Molly slowly returned to the table. "I haven't used too many adjectives, have I?"

"No, not at all," he answered, lighting the cigar leisurely. "It's good writing." He slowly stood and ran his warm hands down her arms, her heart turning over in response to his touch. The patter of rain had increased, and as thunder burst over the hotel, he slowly looked upward. "It's raining and windy outside," he commented in a light tone, transferring his gaze back to her face. "Instead of going out, why don't I ask room service to bring us dinner? It might be rather cozy."

Molly met his questioning eyes, thinking he had more in mind than dinner. But she was forced to admit he was right about the messy evening. Dinner in his suite would be quite cozy, indeed, she decided. "All right," she answered, thinking she'd leave as soon as they'd finished the meal.

Lassiter rang for room service, then ordered dinner and champagne.

"Champagne again?" she asked with an unbidden smile.

"Why not? This is America. We drink champagne here morning, noon, and night if we want to."

They enjoyed a fine roast chicken and vegetables, along with crème brulée served in little silver cups. As they ate, they continued discussing the Sunday feature, laughing about their experiences on Coney Island, and the champagne was almost gone by the time they finished dinner.

Lassiter poured the last of it, then stood and lifted his sparkling glass. "To the Angel of Murphy Street," he announced grandly, a contemplative expression claiming his face. "When this feature comes out," he speculated, "I predict you're going to be New York's newest celebrity."

Molly finished her champagne, then moved to the window again, noticing the sound of slamming carriage doors. Rain slanted down steadily outside now, making the street lamps look like soft halos. People hurried from the hotel, holding umbrellas over their heads, and she could hear their muffled laughter as they ran for a line of waiting hacks. "Celebrity, indeed," she chuckled softly. "As far as I know, I'll still be cooking dinner at Aunt Agatha's next week."

He walked to her and clasped her shoulders, and she turned, noticing his mild concern. "I've been wanting to talk to you about that," he commented, curling his index finger under her chin. "From now on, you'll need most of your time for writing. "I'm sure you'll still want to live at the boardinghouse, but perhaps your aunt can find someone else to help her with the cooking." A smile caught at the corner of his mouth. "Most celebrities don't have time for peeling potatoes, you know."

Molly had to laugh. "I suppose you're right. I'll talk to her tomorrow and see what we can arrange."

A warm intimacy welled between them, and for an agonizing moment she stood there watching him stare at her, his eyes glittering with hungry intensity. She drew in a ragged breath, but found she could not look away no matter how hard she tried. His sensuous lips whispered over hers in the slightest breath of a touch and she was seized with the same hungry longing that had beset her as they stood on the shadowed pier. Her discipline hovered at the breaking point, and the thought of what might happen if she completely let herself go made her legs go weak beneath her.

Wanting to remove herself from his tempting nearness, she moved to a green velvet sofa and sat down, only to see him walk to her side. She looked up at him through lowered lashes and the raw desire she saw on his face sent her heart hammering out of control. "I-I think I should go now," she murmured, luscious sensations unfurling deep within her soul.

An enticing smile crept over his mouth. "Why don't you stay a little longer? I'd enjoy the company," he challenged in a tone filled with appealing tenderness.

She stood, but his left hand slid down her ribs to settle on the indentation at her waist. It rested there for a moment before he put his right arm about her and pulled her so close she could feel his mounting desire for her. "Have I told you how beautiful you look tonight?"

Warning bells clanged in Molly's head and her pulse galloped wildly. Her common sense told her she should leave his hotel room, but she was drowning in an intoxicating sensation that had little to do with the champagne she'd consumed at dinner.

A sweet thrill ran through her as he lowered his head and slanted his mouth over hers, almost taking her breath away. With a sob of wanton pleasure, she raised her arms and slipped them around his broad shoulders, wanting him to continue the kiss as she'd never wanted anything in her life.

Chapter Nine

As he deepened the kiss, warmth coursed through Molly in a golden flow and the room seemed to whirl about her. One part of her mind told her that she should break free and run from his suite, but she felt absolutely rooted to the spot by the strength of his overpowering kiss.

She knew without a doubt that she was in love with him, not only physically, but on a deeper spiritual level. She was in love with his strength, his intellect, his wit, even that sensual gleam in his gorgeous eyes. The realization was so staggering it blotted out all concerns of modesty, and with a prickle of excited fear, she knew she was on the verge of completely surrendering to him.

His lips devoured hers, and his hand was on her back, creating a glowing warmth that radiated upward to her shoulders. She felt his thudding heart, then seconds later she could think of nothing else, for she burned with a white-hot yearning beyond description.

He slipped his tongue between her lips and plunged it into her mouth, and his hand fondled her breast. She could feel the warmth of his fingers through her bodice, and instantly her neck and face flushed with a tingly warmth and she trembled with excitement.

He pressed hot kisses over her closed lids, her cheeks, and the throbbing pulse in her throat. "I want to make love to you, Irish," he whispered in a caressing drawl as he slid his strong hands over her hips, kneading them tenderly.

When he lifted her in his arms and swung her feet from the floor, she drew in a tremulous breath. A thrill darted through her as he carried her toward his bedroom, where soft light spilled from the half-open door. She experienced a last-minute pang of doubt as she recalled how long she'd battled against this happening. But her desperate need quickly dissolved it, for she now truly believed with all her heart that this event had been ordained from the moment they met.

Before she knew it, he'd carried her into the high-ceilinged bedroom and she had a glimpse of a four-poster bed and red velvet drapes, both reflected by the huge mirror hanging over his massive dresser. Rain drummed steadily against the windows and a moist chill hung in the air. Soft light pooled from a bedside lamp and gleamed over the satin counterpane, and the room held the scent of wool clothing and his bay rum cologne. She heard the door close behind them and a sweet, sumptuous feeling overwhelmed her, consuming all thought and reason.

He reverently laid her on the mattress, his eyes mesmerizing her with the hungry desire she saw in them. She realized her capitulation was rash and reckless, but she'd come too far to return, and in her heart of hearts, she didn't want to. The fiery passion she'd harbored for so long had finally surfaced and demanded satisfaction.

Lassiter divested himself of his shoes, and with a rush of excitement, she watched him undress. Silhouetted against the soft backlighting, he was magnificent. Smooth skin covered his wide shoulders and his well-defined chest, and thick hair tapered downward over his sleek belly to his shadowed groin.

A tender smile caressed his lips, and for one glorious moment, it seemed she saw not only his physical appearance, but his spirit as well. Yes, here was all she could ever want in a man. Not only was he devastatingly handsome, she loved his wry sense of humor, his strength and commanding personality, his gentleness. She loved him as a total being.

He sat down beside her and his weight made the bed creak. A tender expression moved across his face as he leaned over to brush his lips against hers. A sensuous fire swept through her, and looping her arms about his neck, she boldly traced her tongue over his partially opened mouth. In return, his lips twisted over hers, and she moaned, savoring the taste of him.

When he finally broke the kiss, she heard his ragged breathing. "My darling, are you sure?" he asked throatily. Tears stung her eyes, and she nodded mutely, not trusting her voice.

He unbuttoned her blouse and pulled her lace-trimmed chemise down over her breasts, making her shiver with desire. As he slowly rolled her nipples between his fingertips, a groan of pleasure burst from her lips, betraying her burning need for him.

He slipped off her blouse and chemise, tossing them on the carpet, then eased up her skirt and petticoat, and in one smooth movement, pulled her bloomers to her knees. She gasped as he lovingly suckled her nipple while his warm fingers slipped into the soft tangle between her legs and fingered the moist seat of her desire. A sweet rush of passion rocketed through her in response to his teasing explorations.

After tenderly pleasuring her, he pulled her skirt and petticoat along with her bloomers over her feet and cast all the garments aside. Now dressed in black silk stockings and garters, she felt moist air kiss her skin. With sure fingers, he rolled down both of her lacy garters and skimmed them from her legs, then peeled off her silk stockings and kissed the arches of her feet. She gazed up at him, trembling with anticipation.

Lassiter scanned Molly, touched by the beauty of her finely sculpted face and shapely feminine contours. Lord, what perfection, he thought as he swept his gaze from the tips of her delicate feet to the crown of her head. Her eyes sparkled with vitality and wavy strands of auburn hair flowed across the pillow like a sea of molten copper. Long thick lashes cast shadows on her cheeks, and her delicate lips were slightly parted, as if in anticipation of a kiss.

Quickly obliging, he threaded his fingers in her hair and kissed her white throat, her quivering eyelids, her tender pink lips. He'd taken his pleasure from scores of willing women, but he'd never experienced this heart-stopping passion before, and troubling new feelings stormed within his heart.

Did he love Molly? That he hadn't decided, but she'd completely possessed his mind, blotting out the memory of every woman before her. She was a lovely, desirable woman, so full of life and courage that it shook him to the roots of his soul, and the thought of bringing this lush Irish rose to flower made him near mad with longing.

Even now his troubling relationship with Daisy Fellows flickered through his mind, but he mentally shrugged the problem aside, knowing he didn't love Daisy and never would. He'd make no commitments to Molly tonight, for he hadn't completely sorted out all his feelings for her, but he'd dedicate himself to making sure that her first taste of real passion was pure and sweet and filled with memorable tenderness.

When he slowly broke the kiss, she reached out to trail her fingertips over the lines of his face. He caught her hand and kissed it. "You're so lovely, my heart aches for you," he sighed, his voice rough with passion. "What a rare precious treasure you are."

He caressed her breasts, tugging her nipples and rolling them between his fingers. Her eyes grew soft, and with a sensuous sigh, she encircled his shoulders and pulled him close. He kissed her gently, then forced her lips open as he explored her smooth teeth and silky tongue. At the same time, he cupped a breast and noticed her nipple grow rock-hard under the flicking touch of his fingers.

Lovemaking had never been like this before for him, and with his heart beating heavily, he sensed he was being pulled down into a whirling tide pool of desire that threatened to consume him. What was he feeling? Was this saucy Irish lass the true love of his life he'd aimlessly searched for all these years? he wondered excitedly.

The scent of his cologne wrapped itself about Molly and she felt encompassed in a warm glory. As the kiss became more demanding, a deep sexual hunger possessed her, and she ruffled her hand through his thick black hair. With a spread hand, he traced over her breasts, her belly, the swell of her buttocks. An aching longing swept through her and when he firmly rolled her nipples between his fingertips once again, breathtaking passion overpowered her, leaving her defenseless against him.

As he gently teased her nipples with his teeth, his shaft rose long and hard against her abdomen, sending her heart thudding crazily. He kissed her stomach and when his warm lips nuzzled her inner thighs, hot blood stung her cheeks. A warm indolence crept though her, and it seemed her body was dissolving with pleasure. "Love me, Lassiter," she whispered, throatily. "Make love to me now."

She was vaguely aware of the sound of the rain against the bedroom windows, but melting with desire, she closed the distraction out and abandoned herself to a world of pleasure. A tremulous urgency ran through her and her arms encircled his shoulders in a gesture of total surrender. He slipped his tongue between her lips and plunged it in and out, sending a sweet fire bubbling through her veins.

His fingers slipped into the tangle of curls about her femininity, then relentlessly stroked the fount of her desire until a warm ache filled her throbbing womanhood. He kissed her with a hot passion that left her trembling, and surprising herself with her boldness, she returned his kiss with equal fire, her tongue battling with his.

Her head sank back on the bed as he spread her legs apart. She gasped as his fingers continued to tease her womanly softness, for his touch ignited a deep craving within her soul that she did not fully comprehend.

When his lips left hers, she saw him hovering above her, the muscles of his arms straining as he held himself at bay to protect her from his weight. Then his hips slid between her thighs, and she felt his hot shaft probing into her tender flesh. She experienced a second of burning pain, but moaned with pleasure as he fully entered her with one firm stroke. She wanted to make the glorious moment last for eternity, but her sumptuous feelings gave way to even more rapturous sensations.

His lips slanted over hers again as he began to move within her. She arched her trembling body toward his, accepting him, loving him with all her heart and soul. They moved together in perfect rhythm, and she caught her breath as a sharp burst of pleasure engulfed her, taking her breath away. She could feel herself melting, feel herself surrendering to each rapturous sensation that swept through her like a crashing wave. Each masterful stroke fueled her excitement, and she gasped and drew him closer yet.

Groaning, she dug her fingers into his back, and lifted her hips toward him. As he continued the tantalizing rhythm, she rocked up to meet him, exhilaration steadily building within her. Moaning with delight, she met each of his thrusts, transported to a starry realm of exquisite sensations. At last, a wave of overpowering desire surfaced from deep within her and she cried out in delight, experiencing the sweet pleasure of throbbing release.

Lassiter, clutching her shoulders tightly, finally joined her in fulfillment, and moaning deeply, shuddered against her.

Afterward she caressed his back and ran her hands through his glossy hair as their racing hearts, beating as one, slowed. He held her close for a moment, then rolled over and pulled her with him, tracing his hands over her back and gently kneading her hips. Wondrously satiated and content, it seemed she was floating downward, slipping into a dreamy, peaceful sleep.

She instinctively realized she'd taken a great gamble in surrendering her virginity, but she also realized that her heart and spirit had demanded it. No, Lassiter had made no commitment to her, but she was certain that he soon would, for beneath his suave, worldly manner she believed he was a decent man with a sense of honor. All her instincts told her so. She'd trust him with all her heart, for he'd never let her down.

The Monday after the Coney Island article appeared, Lassiter paced about his office, a cigar jauntily clenched between his teeth as he chuckled to himself. He paused to shoot Molly a delighted smile. "You've put us on the map, Irish. I talked to Tom Perkins this morning and he said circulation has never been higher."

"Well, what do you know," she replied, pleased that all her hard work had made the feature a success.

Lassiter continued strutting about his office, his hands now shoved in his pockets. "The feature was fantastic," he continued, beaming with pride as he took the cigar from his mouth and moved directly in front of her. "I've received compliments on the story for the last two days, not only from friends, but other editors—people who know a good piece of writing when they see one."

He loosely took her in his arms, his eyes sparkling with admiration. "Didn't I tell you you'd be a celebrity?"

Molly playfully tapped his chest. "Yes, I do believe you mentioned something like that just last Friday evening."

He laughed and kissed her on the forehead.

She'd hoped for something more passionate, but as he walked to his desk and picked up a copy of the *Telegram* she realized that this morning, the paper's increased circulation totally dominated his mind and attention. She thoughtfully watched him scan the first page, a lock of dark hair falling over his forehead. As far as her writing went, this had been the most successful day of her career, but, her high spirits taking a nosedive, she thought it seemed all Lassiter could talk about was his blasted newspaper.

In fact, since they'd made love, the man hadn't said a blessed word about their future, together or otherwise. Oh, he'd been tender and unfailingly polite and even romantic. He'd showered her with flowers and gifts, and invited her out for dinner every night, but he hadn't brought up one very important subject—namely marriage.

He moved to the other side of the office again, his face wreathed in jubilation. "Lord," he said, his low voice shot with pride, "we're on top now, but we've got to produce an even better feature for next Sunday." He ran a puzzled gaze over her. "Please tell me you have another great idea taking shape in that remarkable brain of yours," he drawled, his eyes gleaming with anticipation.

"Well actually I have given some thought to another story," Molly ventured, placing her spread hand on her bosom. "In fact, I wanted to talk to you about it before I did the Coney Island piece." She crossed her arms and tilted her head. "Why don't I look into some of the agencies that place servants? From what I hear, most of them charge both the domestics and their employers exorbitant fees."

She walked to his desk, and picking up the *Telegram*'s classified section, held it before him. "And there's gossip on the streets that some of the agencies even demand domestics to pay huge bribes in exchange for being placed in the best households." She pointed out one of the ads, then tossed the section aside. "Seems that little game could use some investigation."

Lassiter rubbed his hands together. "I like that," he answered with a big grin. "I like it a lot." His eyes gleamed with determination. "Take a look at some of the ads, then decide the agencies you want to home in on." His expression preoccupied, he sat down behind his desk. "You can give me a full report in the morning."

Molly experienced a twinge of resentment. Feeling she'd been dismissed, she walked to Lassiter's office door and opened it, just as he called her name.

"Yes?"

He jammed his cigar back into his mouth. "Think up another story for two weeks from now, and remember the Sullivan interview will we coming up soon," he warned, his tone making it perfectly clear how important he thought the event would be. "Talk to the sports editor when you have a chance. He can give you a couple of good angles on prizefighting games." He raised his dark brows and smiled. "Well get going, Irish. You have a lot of work ahead of you." Before she left, she noticed him going through some articles his secretary had brought him, without even giving her a second look.

She passed through the newsroom, feeling somewhat depressed by her matter-of-fact dismissal.

"Great feature on Coney Island, Molly," one veteran reporter told her as she walked by his littered desk.

"Couldn't have written it better myself," another called out, throwing her a big smile.

A bald-headed reporter sent her a broad wink. "I didn't think a woman could ever write a story like that, Molly," he kidded her, playfully arching his brows.

She returned his wink with one of her own. "I didn't know bald-headed men could write at all, Willie!" she shot back to the delight of the rest of the reporters, who guffawed loudly.

She walked into her small closet-like office, and sat down at her battered desk, vaguely scanning the *Telegram*'s classified section for agencies that placed domestics. Her concentration now shattered, her mind kept replaying the scene in Lassiter's office.

It wasn't what he'd said, it was what he'd left unsaid that really mattered. By this time, she'd expected him to broach the subject of marriage, but he'd remained strangely silent. Then again, the man was extremely busy, she consoled herself. Why, everyone knew that Burke Lassiter was one of the busiest men in the metropolis.

Give him time, she ordered herself, settling down to

study the classified section in earnest. He'd soon invite her out, and then in that charming, witty, funny way of his, propose marriage, and she'd be the happiest woman in New York City.

Late Friday afternoon Molly strolled into the newsroom, having just interviewed a servant who'd been offered a position in a fine household by a domestic agency on the condition that she give them a bribe. The injustice of it all chaffed Molly's crusader's soul, and she itched to add the startling information to her feature, which was by now three-quarters completed.

She was almost at her office when she heard a voice call out behind her, "Molly, wait. I want to talk to you."

Her heart sank, for she saw Tom Perkins, whom she'd been strictly avoiding since she and Lassiter had made love. Tom had that romantic spark in his eyes, and she wondered how she could explain that she had no intention of ever going out with him again. As she expected, he invited her to dinner, and his face fell when she refused, saying she had to shut herself away and finish her feature.

Just then, a gorgeous blond-haired woman walked into the newsroom, drawing Molly's attention as well as that of the reporters, who looked up from their writing with admiring eyes. The shapely young woman wore the finest clothes money could buy, and ropes of pearls encircled her long neck while jewels sparkled on her long slender fingers. "Who's that pretty woman?" Molly asked Tom, thinking she'd never seen a lovelier example of the female sex.

He gave her a puzzled look. "Why, don't you know? That's Daisy Fellows. She's one of New York's leading debutantes. Her father lives on Fifth Avenue and he's unbelievably rich."

Molly knew she'd seen the woman before, and it gradually dawned on her that this was the female who'd kissed Lassiter the day the *Saxonia* had docked. A surprising connection suddenly clicked in her mind— Daisy Fellows, as socially elite as she was, was Lassiter's beautiful cousin.

The stunning blonde approached Lassiter's secretary, who quickly went into his office. Seconds later, he came out, a startled look on his face as he escorted the gorgeous creature into his private domain.

Molly glanced at Tom. "Well, imagine that. I had no idea Daisy Fellows was Lassiter's cousin."

The accountant put his hand about her arm. "*Cousin?*" he echoed laughingly. "As far as I know she isn't—actually she's his fiancée."

"*His f-fiancée?*" Molly whispered, quick tears stinging her eyes as she remembered Lassiter sitting in her own kitchen and telling her that the beautiful lady was his cousin. For a moment an otherworldly feeling claimed her senses and the newsroom itself seemed far and distant, as if she were seeing it through the eyes of another. She stared at Tom, numb with shock.

"I thought you knew," he said, his expression slightly amused. "They've been engaged for months, and when they marry, it'll be one of the biggest social events of the season. You can bet on that."

Tom's words hit her with the force of a sharp blow, snatching away her breath. Her stomach felt leaden and it seemed her legs might buckle beneath her. *Lassiter had lied to her.* He'd deceived her in the worst way a man could deceive a woman. Her vision blurred her gorge rose. The man who'd so tenderly made love to her only last week was pledged to another.

Scarcely knowing what she was doing, she left Tom and hurried into her dingy little office, holding back her threatening tears until she'd closed the door behind her. She sat down at her desk and shook with sobs. In her mind's eye she saw Lassiter's face as he'd told her all of life was about manipulating others, and the remembered words cut into her heart like sharp thorns.

He'd never had any intention of marrying her. He'd made love to her to manipulate her, to link her more closely to him so she wouldn't take her features to another paper. He hadn't considered their physical union as love—to his way of thinking, he was only getting the best of a business deal.

Molly took a deep breath, feeling totally empty inside, feeling like the biggest fool in New York. Not only had Lassiter taken her virginity, he'd taken her pride, and her plans to be the master of her own destiny. She'd fallen for the charms of a charming scoundrel just like her own mother had done twenty-five years before her. She'd become ensnared in the trap she'd planned to avoid at all costs. She'd tumbled head over heels in love and let that feminine weakness ruin her life. Right then and there, she made a vow to herself that no matter how sorely she was tempted, she'd never let Lassiter make love to her again.

Molly had a long bitter cry, then after wiping her streaming eyes, she gradually felt the steel creep into her soul. She, Molly Kilmartin, was a survivor. She always had been, and always would be. That, she thought with a tight little smile, had been bred into the scrappy Irish soul from thousands of years of grinding adversity.

She blew her nose and slowly stood, feeling her deep hurt and anger coalesce into rock-hard determination. She'd made a great mistake, a terrible mistake, but she couldn't let it ruin her life, for people she loved were depending on her.

Somehow she had to get up from this terrible blow and keep marching straight ahead. As long as there was breath in her body, she'd never stop fighting, never stop struggling. She'd work night and day, until she was the most famous journalist in New York. At that time, she'd have achieved her goal and her success would surely blot out the excruciating emotional pain she now felt.

But, she thought, tightly crossing her arms beneath her heaving bosom, her first order of business would be to confront that black-hearted rascal known as Burke Lassiter.

Chapter Ten

Early the next morning, Molly sailed into Lassiter's office and slammed the door behind her. A look of perturbed surprise on his face, he stood and stared at her. "What in the hell is wrong with you, Irish?"

Molly had only slept in snatches the night before and a headache pounded in both of her temples. So angry she could hardly speak, she walked about the office for a moment, trying to collect herself, then moved squarely before him to meet his questioning gaze. "I know all about Daisy Fellows," she blurted out in a frantic rush. "And I know you're engaged to her."

Lassiter's brow tightened with concern. "Who told you?" he asked, slowly raking a hand through his hair.

"Tom—Tom Perkins told me!"

Lassiter lit up a cigar and threw the match in an ashtray. "That figures."

Molly seethed with anger and humiliation. "What do you mean it figures?" she retorted, disturbed that he was casting aspersions on decent, hardworking Tom Perkins. "Tom told me, but from what I understand it could have been anyone in the newsroom. It seems that everyone in New York knew you were engaged to Daisy Fellows, but me!" She swallowed back her tears. "Tell me it's not true," she finished in a strangled voice.

His eyes roamed over her. "Yes, I'm afraid it's true," he replied with a long sigh. "Technically I'm engaged to her."

Trying to vent her pent-up rage, she started pacing again. "You lied to me about her, lied through your teeth," she went on, trying to steady her broken voice. "And I was trusting enough to believe you."

He gave her a long, measured look. "Listen to me. Listen to what I have to say. I lied to you to protect you—to shield you from a meaningless fact that would hurt you."

Molly stopped to stare at him, her breath quickening. She felt as if she were two people at the same time—one watching the scene with detached interest, while the other trembled with anger. With a fluttering pulse, she suddenly blurted out the question piercing her heart. *"Well, do you love her?"*

Lassiter studied her hot eyes, knowing he could answer that question very easily. "No, I don't," he replied, vocalizing for the first time what he knew in his heart. "Daisy means nothing to me." He felt a tremendous burden lift from his shoulders as soon as he'd spoken the words.

Molly widened her eyes. "Saints above, how could

you be engaged to someone and say you feel nothing for them?"

He studied her milk-white face. "The whole alliance is a sticky matter of expediency. After I met you on the *Saxonia* I started thinking, and I began to realize how foolish I was to become entangled in the relationship." He let his gaze play over her graceful form. "I'll break the engagement before I let her set a date. I'll never marry her."

From Molly's expression, he could tell the words shocked her to the core of her being.

"And I thought you were a decent man," she whispered roughly.

"I like to think that I am."

Lord, how could he make her believe that in fashionable New York society, engagements were often entered upon for reasons other than love, and broken very easily? *Damnation*. In the back of his mind, he realized this very unpleasant scene might arrive sooner or later, but he'd hoped it would be during a better time, at a better place where he could console Molly and make her believe that he'd never loved Daisy Fellows.

He experienced an overwhelming wave of compassion, thinking Molly looked like a stricken child this morning, vulnerable and terribly hurt. Even in her simple blue shirtwaist gown, with her hair loose and disheveled, she was a sight to shake a man's soul.

He drew on his cigar, trying to calm his mind and work out a plan. He wanted to pour out his heart to her, but how could he explain his tangled emotions when he didn't completely understand them himself? And yet there was one thing he knew for a certainty—he didn't want to lose her. Somehow he must soothe her lacerated feelings and keep her in his world.

He snubbed out the cigar and moved closer to her, filled with a powerful need to express his deepest emotions. "Don't you know I care deeply what happens to you? I want you to succeed and will do everything I can to help you."

She glared at him, her chin set in a stubborn line.

He clasped her shoulders, but her body stiffened under his fingers. "You must give me time to work through my problems with Daisy, and here at the *Telegram* too. In the meanwhile, let me provide for you, care for you," he proposed smoothly, studying her large, teary eyes. "I'll see that you want for nothing. I'll find you an apartment—a carriage. You'll live in modest luxury."

Molly felt as if she'd just been hit in the face with a spray of icy water. Totally scandalized, she jerked away from his caressing hands. "If you think I'd become a kept women, that I'd accept an indecent proposal," she spat out with contempt, her eyes flashing dangerously, "you're crazier than I thought!"

He tried to put his arms about her one last time, but she twisted away, her face flushing with anger.

"What I'm suggesting is only temporary," he tried to explain, using a tender voice. "After I've broken off with Daisy—"

"Broken off, my eye!" she interrupted, drawing in a trembling breath. "Do you expect me to believe you'd ever do that? You lied to me once, and I suspect you'd lie to me again."

She swallowed back the sob, not wanting to give him the satisfaction of seeing her cry. Everything had

Thrill to the most sensual, adventure-filled Historical Romances on the market today...

FROM  LEISURE BOOKS

As a home subscriber to the Leisure Historical Romance Book Club, you'll enjoy the best in today's BRAND-NEW Historical Romance fiction. For over twenty-five years, Leisure Books has brought you the award-winning, high-quality authors you know and love to read. Each Leisure Historical Romance will sweep you away to a world of high adventure...and intimate romance. Discover for yourself all the passion and excitement millions of readers thrill to each and every month.

SAVE AT LEAST *$5.00* EACH TIME YOU BUY!

Each month, the Leisure Historical Romance Book Club brings you four brand-new titles from Leisure Books, America's foremost publisher of Historical Romances. EACH PACKAGE WILL SAVE YOU AT LEAST $5.00 FROM THE BOOKSTORE PRICE! And you'll never miss a new title with our convenient home delivery service.

Here's how we do it. Each package will carry a 10-DAY EXAMINATION privilege. At the end of that time, if you decide to keep your books, simply pay the low invoice price of $16.96 ($17.75 US in Canada), no shipping or handling charges added*. HOME DELIVERY IS ALWAYS FREE*. With today's top Historical Romance novels selling for $5.99 and higher, our price SAVES YOU AT LEAST $5.00 with each shipment.

AND YOUR FIRST FOUR-BOOK SHIPMENT IS TOTALLY FREE!

IT'S A BARGAIN YOU CAN'T BEAT! A Super $21.96 Value!

LEISURE BOOKS A Division of Dorchester Publishing Co., Inc.

GET YOUR 4 FREE* BOOKS NOW—
A $21.96 VALUE!

Mail the Free* Book
Certificate
Today!

Get Four Books Totally
F R E E* —
A $21.96 Value!

PLEASE RUSH
MY FOUR FREE*
BOOKS TO ME
RIGHT AWAY!

Leisure Historical Romance Book Club
P.O. Box 6613
Edison, NJ 08818-6613

AFFIX
STAMP
HERE

become very clear to her now, crystal clear, in fact. "I don't think you're capable of loving anything but the *Telegram*. You manipulate people—manipulate them for your own good. Don't tell me you don't because you once said that was what life was all about. Daisy is important to you because her father is rich and can keep the paper stay afloat in bad times. I, on the other hand"—she tapped her bosom—"am less important even though I write features that sell Sunday papers."

"No, that's not it at all," he insisted, a muscle now flicking rhythmically in his jaw. "I truly care about you. I want to take care of you." He came toward her, his face softening with compassion. "You're overwrought now. Don't turn down my offer of help straightaway. Take tomorrow off and sleep late—rest and think about what I've said." He trailed his fingers over her cheek, but she turned her head away. "Just promise you'll consider my offer."

Molly wanted to resign that very second, but she knew her present situation wouldn't permit such a temper tantrum, because she was far from financially secure. Of course she'd never think of becoming Lassiter's mistress, but in her dire financial straights, she had to work out some plan—a plan that would let her keep on working. What she needed was time, just what he was presently offering her, she suddenly decided, staring at his imploring eyes.

"Very well," she coolly replied, already knowing she was going to refuse his insulting proposal. "I'll take tomorrow off, and rest and think." She stood a little taller, anger racing down her spine. "But make no mistake about it, I'll be back the next morning to have it out with you!"

An expectant light shone in his eyes. "Yes, very well," he softly replied, his eyes glistening with compassion. "Just take some time to think things over before you give me an answer."

She moved to the door and put her hand on the knob. Glancing back, she noticed Lassiter's face glowing with hopeful anticipation, and inwardly shuddered, wondering if she had the strength to stick to her principles.

"Ah, Miss Kilmartin," Mr. Babbage said the next morning as he ushered her into his office. "Come in and have a seat," the editor in chief of the *Metropolitan* continued, indicating a big leather chair before his desk. Small and bent, he looked as if he'd never been out in the sun, and his suit hung loosely on his thin frame. He smoothed a hand over his balding head. "To what do I owe the honor of this visit, my dear?"

Molly seated herself, and spreading out her skirt, scanned the bony man whose spectacles now slid down his long nose. It had taken all of her courage to get an interview with the editor, and knowing how valuable his time was, she thought it best to come straight to the point. "I'm seeking employment, sir," she began forthrightly.

Mr. Babbage raised his sketchy brows. "Employment?" he laughed, shaking his head. "Why, that's hard to believe. Everyone knows you're the *Telegram*'s star reporter. Why would Burke Lassiter ever let you go?"

Molly shifted her chair. "Well, it's really the other way around. *I'm* leaving the *Telegram*."

The editor blinked his watery eyes. "Really? Do tell. Surely you and Mr. Lassiter didn't have a disagreement?"

178

Too embarrassed to tell the man about Lassiter's indecent proposal, she calmly replied, "Well actually we did, and I plan on resigning."

The editor studied her with speculative eyes. "I'm afraid we have an investigative reporter already, and if it's a huge salary you're after—"

"*No,* it's not that at all," she quickly interrupted him, suddenly recalling a term she'd heard Lassiter use once. "Mr. Lassiter and I have,"—she swallowed hard at the lie—"we have creative differences."

"Umm, creative differences, is it?"

"Yes, that's it," she affirmed, hoping she sounded believable. Clutching her reticule, she rose and moved to the window. In the street below, a long line of wagons rumbled toward the *Telegram* building, bringing huge rolls of newsprint for its presses. Well, Lassiter will only be needing about half of that, she told herself dryly, sure his circulation would soon be decreasing when she left.

"I thought Lassiter gave all his reporters a free hand," the editor remarked thoughtfully.

She turned to look at him. "That used to be the case, but the man has changed," she stammered, licking her lips. She walked to the editor's desk, and putting her hand on it, leaned toward him. "Look, Mr. Babbage, I need a job, and I need one as soon as possible. Can you give me one?"

The old man got up and walked about, looking so feeble she thought he might topple over at any moment. "Do you have ideas for other features?" he asked, casting her a keen sidelong glance.

"Oh yes," she replied, her voice vibrant with enthusiasm. "I have an idea for a feature concerning the clean-

179

liness of the city's top restaurants, and another about child labor, and one about teamsters' unions, and another one about—"

He raised his thin, veined hand, halting her rambling speech. "Yes, that's all very good."

She neared his side so anxious and driven, she had to refrain from taking him by the lapels. "And then there's my upcoming celebrity interview," she went on, feeling a stab of guilt for stealing the interview Lassiter had labored so hard to arrange.

The old man's eyes sparkled like those of a child in a candy shop. "A celebrity interview? With whom?"

She drew herself up to meet his searching gaze. "John L. Sullivan himself," she answered, consoling her guilt with the idea that after deceiving her, Lassiter was getting no more than he deserved. "I have an exclusive with Mr. Sullivan. He only agreed to the piece on the condition that I do it." She pasted a bright smile on her face. "He said he wanted to be interviewed by someone from the Auld Sod. I'll just explain to him that I'm now working for a different publication."

Mr. Babbage slowly pulled off his spectacles, apparently overcome with the news. "John L. Sullivan, hey? Well, I must say that's impressive indeed."

Molly watched him open his office door and confer softly with his secretary, who immediately rose to see what her employer wanted.

After quietly talking to the woman, he returned to Molly and smiled kindly, putting on his spectacles once more. "I've just asked my secretary to draw up a contract for you, Miss Kilmartin." He patted her hand, and his fingers were so cold, she thought he must have printer's ink running through his veins instead of blood.

"Welcome to the *Metropolitan,* my dear. I want your interview with John L. Sullivan, and after that I'll expect a riveting investigative feature for my Sunday issue each week."

Molly experienced a sharp rush of joy. She was no longer dependent on Lassiter for a salary, and from now on, he'd have to do without her writing talents. Him and his indecent proposal! She'd surely put him in his place, she thought with a warm glow of pride. Without her features, he'd sell fewer Sunday papers and have a much harder time staying in the black.

Yes, she congratulated herself, she'd managed to defeat Lassiter both emotionally and financially, but to her surprised dismay her heart still squeezed with the pain of his betrayal.

Early the next morning, Lassiter and his night editor stood in the huge composing room, talking about a dispute concerning some typesetters' overdue wages. The noisy night crew was just departing, leaving behind dozens of tables littered with type boxes, column forms, and inky aprons.

After everyone was gone, Lassiter turned off the gaslights and prepared to go himself, when, with a bolt of surprise, he spotted Molly entering the now shadowy room. Dressed in her working-girl costume of a plain shirtwaist with a white collar, and wearing a straw hat, she walked toward him, the determination in her eyes matching the spring in her steps.

Since the day before yesterday Lassiter had thought of nothing but Molly. He'd gone over their heated conversation dozens of times, wondering if he could have handled things better. But he presently crossed his arms, deciding he'd let her bridge the distance between them.

She walked directly toward him, her high-buttoned shoes clicking over the planked composing-room floor. What would she say? Would she let him put her up in that little apartment he'd suggested, or would she continue to be the hardheaded little spitfire she'd always been? he wondered, casually leaning against a cluttered table.

Her gaze never wavering, she stopped directly in front of him, her reticule swinging from her slim arm.

"How did you know where to find me?" he drawled, feeling a secret rush of pleasure just looking at her.

"A messenger boy told me where you were."

"It's only six-thirty. What are you doing here so early?"

She arched a delicate brow. "I could ask you the same thing."

"I've been here all night," he answered honestly. "My night editor sent a message about a dispute with the typesetters and I wanted to talk to him before he left."

He walked her to a tall arched window where pale sunbeams slanted into the room, playing over her determined face and making patterns on the worn floor. A poignant air of tension hung between them for a moment; then he began speaking, his heart filled with hope. "Have you had time to think over my offer?" he finally began in a slow, firm voice.

She looked at him boldly. "I suppose you're referring to your indecent proposal."

"Why do you insist on calling it that?"

She narrowed her eyes. "I believe in calling things by their right name, and in truth, that's what it is."

"Now, Molly—"

"Don't 'now, Molly' me," she shot back, standing a little taller. "I refuse to become a kept woman!"

He sighed heavily. "But you wouldn't be. If you'll just give me some time to break off things with Daisy—"

"And how long would that take?" she hotly challenged him. She tightened her mouth. "A month? Six months? A year maybe?" Her eyes deepened until they were the color of jade. "No, Lassiter, you took advantage of my innocence and lied to me, and the truth be told, I believe you're still lying."

He took her shoulders, feeling her stiffen under his hands. "What do I have to do to make you believe me? If you'd just have some faith, if—"

"*No*," she answered, removing his hands from her shoulders. "And under the conditions, I don't believe I can go on working with you."

He couldn't control his burst of laughter. "Now you're really talking crazy."

"Crazy, is it? Well crazy or not, that's what I came to tell you. I'm resigning from the *Telegram*. If you want to go on publishing investigative features, you'll have to find yourself another reporter."

Shock ran through him. "But you need the job. Unless you've just inherited a fortune, I think you're standing on rather shaky financial ground."

An impish grin played over her lips. "That's what you think. I got myself another job yesterday."

"Another job? *Where at?*"

"I had an interview with Mr. Babbage at the *Metropolitan*. He hired me on the spot." Triumph flooded her face. "He's going to publish my interview with John L. Sullivan; then I'm going to start writing Sunday features for him."

"You can't do that," he retorted, his voice raising in outraged surprise. "I'm the one who set up that interview with Sullivan!"

"Oh yes I can. Have you forgotten Sullivan said he wouldn't give the interview to anyone but me?"

The shock of her words hit him like a blow. The thought of Molly writing for his arch competitor, especially stealing the prized interview he'd set up with Sullivan, was too much to bear. "You're going to work for the *Metropolitan*? No," he laughed, "I don't believe you."

She smiled tightly. "That's what I thought you'd say, so I brought this." She pulled her contract with Mr. Babbage from her reticule and waved in under his nose. "Take a look at this. I think you'll find it's perfectly legal."

Lassiter scanned the contract, then shoved it back at her, sick dread swirling in the pit of his stomach. "You can't just up and resign on me, young lady. If you don't recall, I'm the one who taught you to write."

She slipped the contract back into her reticule and laughed merrily. "Oh, I knew how to write long before I set eyes on you, Lassiter."

"But I'm the one who pushed you—the one who made you a star," he insisted, thinking how he'd dubbed her the Angel of Murphy Street.

She shook her finger at him. "You may have edited my work, but *I* wrote it. I'm the one who put the heart and soul into those features." She tapped her bosom. "You said so yourself."

Lassiter wiped his hand over his face, knowing she spoke the truth. He could hire another investigative reporter to write Sunday features, but his readership wanted Molly and Molly alone. Lord, he hadn't expected this, and at the present moment, he had no idea how on God's green earth he could get the little baggage to change her mind. Didn't she feel anything for him? He hadn't completely sorted out his tangled relationship with her, but just looking at her stirred something strong and undeniable within him.

He gently took her in his arms, and before she could protest, gave her a kiss calculated to set her soul aflame. He pressed her closer, his tongue thrusting into her mouth, exploring its moist recesses as his hand caressed her breast. He felt her heart somersaulting against his as he savored the softness of her body, the firmness of her sweet contours.

His lips finally abandoned hers to kiss her eyelids, her cheeks, the curve of her neck. "Tell me you're going to leave me now," he whispered huskily, noticing her body trembling under his touch.

The velvety softness of his voice made Molly's knees weak. Delicious tremors surged through her bloodstream and passion unfurled in her heart and spread through her limbs like hot quicksilver. But summoning all her courage, she took a firm step backward, abruptly pulling away from his encircling arms.

She looked up at his stunned face, relishing his reaction, but at the same time noticing a strange loneliness about her heart. "I won't lie to you," she admitted stiffly. "I feel something all right, but I've decided you never loved me. You only bedded me to bind me more tightly to the *Telegram*."

"That's not true," he whispered, his face a mask of shocked denial.

"Yes, I think it is," she returned, her mind and heart now battling furiously. Heaven knew she secretly yearned to stay with him, to see his handsome face every morning, to hear his mellow voice, to feel his warm hand caressing her arm as they discussed a feature.

But with equal force, her pride insisted this was no longer possible. The man had lied to her, led her on, taken her virginity, then to add insult to injury, made her an indecent proposal. Everything that was strong and moral within her demanded she break off the relationship forever.

Deep concern flickered over Lassiter's proud face. "If it's a matter of money—"

"No, it isn't that, and you know it isn't. You couldn't offer me enough money to write for the *Telegram* a day longer."

An oppressive heaviness settled in his chest. "Surely we can come to some compromise. We *must* come to a compromise."

Molly drew in a long breath. She'd been up half the night herself, pacing her room, trying to plan what she'd say this morning and she had a ready answer on her tongue. "No, I don't think so. Compromises usually don't work out for either side, don't you know."

She walked away, then paused and looked back, realizing she still loved him, but at the same time deciding no love was strong enough to bridge the deep differences between them. "I came to tender my resignation, and that's what I've done. Now I'm going."

He gazed at her, his eyes burning like flames. "Won't you give me a few weeks to find someone to replace you?"

She shook her head. "No, I'm resigning as of today, and I won't let you persuade me otherwise."

Lassiter groaned inwardly. Who would have thought she'd take leave of her senses and resign so suddenly? His heart aching like it had never ached before, he walked to her, amazed at the depth of his feelings for her. "But I've offered you more than most women would ask for."

She stood stock-still and gazed at him with tears welling in her eyes. "Yes, everything but your heart," she whispered roughly. She spoke calmly, but there was no tenderness in her eyes or softness about her lips.

She moved away, then stopped one last time and glanced over her shoulder. "Good-bye, Lassiter. You won't miss me for long. You'll find another writer to replace me, and as far as the rest of it, I never fit into your world, and I never will. I knew that the first night on the ship, but I discarded my common sense because I wanted to believe differently." Her bottom lip trembled. "I've learned a hard lesson, but I've learned it well."

Without another word, she marched toward the half-open metal door, her sharp footsteps echoing through the composing room.

Lassiter watched her leaving and everything in him urged him to take her in his arms again. Lord, how he wanted this woman; wanted to keep her safe and warm and never let anyone or anything hurt her. But he wouldn't run after her like a besotted schoolboy, he thought, his stubborn pride rooting him where he stood.

Sonya Birmingham

How could he go after her when she'd left him high and dry when he needed her the most?

Molly slammed the heavy metal door behind her, and the loud noise it made resounded to the four corners of the empty composing room. Lassiter stood transfixed, staring at the closed door.

The silence was deafening.

Chapter Eleven

Two weeks later Lassiter decided to go riding in Central Park, where he boarded a fine stallion, and to his dismay as he was leading his freshly saddled mount from the stables he met Daisy Fellows, who also kept a horse there. Not being able to dismiss his own fiancée, he was forced to agree to her suggestion that they ride together, but only vaguely listened to her as she harangued him with irritating questions.

"Why are you so cross and ill-tempered today, Burke?" she moaned, edging her blooded mare even with his stallion.

Lassiter fixed his gaze straight ahead, her thoughtless statement vexing him even more. "Things aren't going well at the *Telegram*, if you must know," he finally replied, a knot of annoyance gathering in his chest. "I've lost my star investigative reporter."

"That Kilmartin woman?" Daisy laughed, her voice rising in surprise. "But why has that affected you so drastically? How can one measly writer be so important to any paper?"

He didn't answer, knowing she wouldn't understand. With her limited grasp of finances, she could never comprehend how valuable Molly was to the floundering *Telegram*. Wanting to get away from Daisy's incessant chatter, he clicked to his mount and rode away, enveloped in a swirl of scarlet leaves and the redolent autumn aromas now filling the park.

Molly's career had soared like a shooting star during the last month, he thought as he galloped ahead, his horse's hooves throwing up moist bits of soil. He was certain a front-page notice that she was now writing for the *Metropolitan* and her interview with John L. Sullivan had increased that paper's circulation tremendously. With a hardened jaw, he remembered how the rival publication had boldly displayed a photo of Molly and Sullivan with enormous smiles on their faces when her interview with the fighter was published.

Lassiter kneed his glossy-coated stallion ahead. Damnation, he'd set up the interview in the first place, and by all rights it should have been in the *Telegram*. With an inward sigh, he realized what a downturn his life had taken lately. He'd lost his cash cow, but most important, he'd lost the fun and zest and inspiration Molly had brought into his life. He recalled their fiery argument the last time they'd spoken. No doubt she was so proud she'd never forgive him for making an *indecent proposal* as she called it, he decided sourly.

He heard the jangle of Daisy's bridle and charged down the twisting path, wanting to distance himself from her carping chatter. But pursuing him steadily, she caught up and began whining about their wedding date yet again.

"Burke, you're being so stubborn," she snapped, brushing a gossamer veil from her jaunty hat as they rode side by side. "You put off the wedding all summer, and it's fall already!"

"I've been busy. You know that."

"But you're *always* busy. People are beginning to think about the holidays, and after Christmas they'll be going to their country estates for the winter. We'll never get a big turnout for the ceremony then."

Lassiter really looked at her for the first time that afternoon. He had to admit she was fetching in her smart baby-blue velvet riding ensemble with her polished boots and black kid gloves. It was what came out of her mouth that drove him to distraction. The thought of listening to her whine and complain for a lifetime of *wedded bliss* as she called it made him sick with unspoken dread. He seriously thought of abruptly breaking off the engagement right then and there, but his better judgment told him this wasn't the time or place.

"That's just it," he responded, searching for a way to still her carping tongue. "We need to put off the wedding until the spring when everyone is back in town and you can make a big splash. Besides that, you need to select your gown and trousseau."

She pouted her pink lips. "I've had them selected for two years already. If you hadn't run off to Ireland we'd be married already. Why, I've become a regular laughingstock!"

He reined in his mount to search her angry face. "You, a laughingstock?" he commented satirically, knowing how she valued her father's social position. "Surely you jest. Who'd have the gall to laugh at *you* of all people?"

She simpered prettily. "I suppose you're right there," she demurred, blinking thoughtfully as she basked in his backhanded compliment. "Everyone would be afraid to laugh at Daddy—I mean at me—wouldn't they?"

"Of course they would," he smoothly responded, knowing he'd scored a point by playing on her enormous vanity. He patted her gloved hand. "We don't want to jump into anything. Actually we have all the time in the world. Just be patient."

She gave an exasperated sigh, seemingly realizing he'd won the argument, but not understanding just how. "It's just that I'm so tired of waiting!"

Lassiter wanted to end the conversation while he was ahead and rode on, taking a steep side path. When he looked over his shoulder and noticed Daisy was having trouble with her horse, he picked up his pace, enjoying his temporary freedom.

The cool wind at his face, he thought of the Angel of Murphy Street and wondered what she was doing. Probably thinking up some feature that would put the *Telegram* even further behind in the circulation game, he decided dismally. Either that, or with her crusader's spirit, campaigning for a soup kitchen to feed the masses of poor Irish immigrants who poured into the city daily and struggled to keep body and soul together.

The humorous observation suddenly jogged his brain, and with the sound of sharply creaking saddle leather, he reined in his mount. Wait a minute, he told himself, an interesting idea coalescing in his churning brain. For a moment he totally focused on a plan he thought might be good for the city and also might bring Molly back to the *Telegram*. Slapping his mount's flank with his spread hand, he bolted ahead, really smiling for the first time since the spitfire had slammed the composing room door behind her.

"Gosh, work just hasn't been the same since you left," Tom Perkins told Molly as they walked down Murphy Street one evening later that same week.

She glanced at him and laughed. When he'd knocked on the boardinghouse door after dinner and asked if she'd talk with him, they'd sat on the porch swing for a while, then he'd suggested they take a walk. She was glad she'd agreed, for after being cooped up in the *Metropolitan* building all day, the cool autumn breeze now caressing her face felt wonderfully refreshing. "Oh, I don't think anyone misses me, especially Lassiter," she finally replied, swinging a light knitted shawl about her shoulders.

For a moment there was only the sound of their strolling footsteps against the sidewalk, then Tom slowly ventured, "Well, you may be right there."

Despair tore at Molly's heart, but as they met another couple out for their evening constitutional, she pasted a smile on her face. She told herself it was beneath her dignity to quiz Tom about his employer; still, she'd thought of nothing but Lassiter since they'd parted. "Really?" she commented, trying to make her voice sound casual and disinterested. "What do you mean by that?"

Tom paused, his sparkling eyes revealing he was really delighted to be giving her the information he was about to impart. "Well," he sighed heavily, "I don't think he cares for anyone but himself. He shuts himself in his office, and when he does come out, he's always so ill-tempered and preoccupied that he bites everyone's head off."

Molly guessed that what was keeping Lassiter so preoccupied was his upcoming marriage to Daisy. She closed her eyes, aching despair sweeping through her. The man had been so convincing about breaking off with the socialite, she'd almost believed him. Thank goodness she'd had the wit to listen to her own common sense.

The pair walked past an old house where boarders sat on the front steps talking quietly, and half a block later Molly spotted a bench situated under a street lamp. Suddenly feeling tired and depressed, she sat down and spread out her skirt. A tentative smile on his face, Tom eased down beside her, clasping her arm. "You don't look well. Is there something wrong? Did I upset you?"

"No, there's nothing wrong," she stoutly lied, trying to hide her turbulent feelings. "I'm just a little tired."

"You've been working too hard."

Molly thought of all the hours she'd poured into her present feature on child labor, and had to admit he was right. She'd once loved writing, but it was now becoming a chore, even a drudge. There was no two ways about it—writing for Mr. Babbage just wasn't like writing for Lassiter, who'd encouraged her and was able to give her ideas of his own besides editing her work to perfection.

Tom continued talking about work, but she was so distracted, his voice seemed to come from a long way off, and she scarcely knew what he was saying. Golden light touching his face, he moved closer and gently took her hand in his own. "Lassiter isn't good enough for you. Don't you see that?" he asked in a passionate voice.

A trace of sadness in her voice, Molly laughed softly. "You're imagining things," she rejoined, embarrassed that her emotions had been so transparent. She pulled her hand from his tight grasp. "I have no interest in Lassiter whatsoever."

"Oh, but I think you do," he insisted, his eyes surveying her judiciously. "Your face lights up every time you're around him."

She quickly denied his accusation, but at the same time wondered how many other people at the *Telegram* had made the same observation.

"He's interested in you, Molly, but only in what you can do to increase circulation," Tom continued with a ring of finality.

His words bruising her already tender sensibilities, Molly experienced a sense of nauseating despair. Thinking she couldn't continue talking about the depressing subject a moment longer, she rose and straightened her back. "It's getting chilly," she suddenly announced, pulling her shawl more tightly about her shoulders. "I'm going home."

She stared at Tom's puzzled face for a moment, then turned and, not even bothering to give him a second look, swiftly paced down the block, filled with wretchedness.

A few mornings later Molly swept the main hall of the boardinghouse before she left for work just to help

195

Aunt Agatha, who was busy upstairs changing bed linens. She'd just bent over to position a dustpan when she heard the jingle of a carriage and straightened up.

Shortly afterward, the sound of footsteps resounded on the porch and there were insistent raps on the front door. Thinking the visitor must have come to inquire about lodging, she answered the knock, then gave a soft gasp, for there stood Lassiter with an ingratiating smile on his face. "What do you want?" she shot out, her heart beginning an uneasy thud.

"I thought we might talk. I was sure if I came early enough, I could catch you before you left for work. May I come in?" he ventured, hopeful expectation glistening in his eyes.

Molly stepped onto the porch, still clenching the broom in her hand. "No, you may not. We finished our conversation several weeks ago, and as far as I'm concerned we have nothing more to discuss!"

"But we do," he interposed, lacing his smooth voice with warmth. "I want to tell you about a new project I'm starting."

She tossed back her hair. "In case you've forgotten, I no longer work for the *Telegram*."

"This really isn't about the paper, it's about helping people," he answered in a calm, reasonable tone. "I've given a lot of thought to the idea."

Molly's face went hot with anger. "Don't give me that. I'm sure you're spending most of your time discussing wedding plans with Daisy."

Laugh lines flashed from the corner of Lassiter's eyes. "No, not at all. In fact, that's the last thing I want to do."

She met his amused gaze straight on. "I wasn't

raised on prunes and proverbs, you know. I can put two and two together as well as the next person. I bet you've been seeing her regularly."

Lassiter eyed Molly's stormy face, deciding he'd be forced to continue the rest of his conversation standing on the front porch like some salesman. "And that's where you're wrong, Irish," he replied, his voice shimmering with sincerity. He arched his brows in amusement. "I've only seen her once since we parted, and that encounter was an unfortunate accident."

He gave her another smile. "I've come to realize the *Telegram* should be more active as far as charity works go," he thoughtfully announced, noticing Molly's eyes widen in astonishment. "Many large corporations here in the city try to help out around the holidays with Christmas drives and such, and I want the paper to be a part of that."

He held her skeptical gaze, willing her to really listen to his next words. "I'd like to sponsor a food drive for the homeless. Interested parties could bring canned goods to the advertising office, and I want you to head the team that would be responsible for seeing that charity boxes are distributed. You could write several features about it during the buildup to Christmas." He infused his voice with a warm, conciliatory tone. "With your immense following, I'm sure the project would be very successful."

She stared at him with parted lips for a moment, then her eyes shot green fire. "Soft words will butter no parsnips with me, Lassiter. Shame on you for trying to bribe me into coming back to the *Telegram* by manipulating my emotions!"

He'd thought this was such an appealing offer there

was no way she could turn it down, but damn it all, if she wasn't the same stubborn spitfire she'd always been. He clasped her shoulders, wanting to make her listen to reason. "Don't you see how many people this could help? What a good thing this could be?"

Quick anger blazed in Molly's bosom. "A good thing indeed. A good publicity stunt for *you*," she countered icily. She sent him what she hoped was a scalding glare. "What do I have to do to make you understand there's no way on earth you could tempt me back into your lair?"

"Why are you being so stubborn?" Lassiter inquired, his face tightening with impatience.

"Stubborn, is it?" Near breathless with rage, Molly raised the broom and swatted it against his shoulders. She swung at him repeatedly until he wrenched the broom from her hands, and putting it behind her back, yanked her against his hard chest.

She beat on his shoulders with her balled hands and tried to free herself, but with the broomstick at her back pressing her firmly against him, she was trapped in a vice she couldn't escape. "Let me go!" she demanded, squirming harder than ever.

He jerked his brows together. "*No,* not until you calm down so I can talk some sense into you."

Gasping for air, Molly was forced to stand still for a moment.

Lassiter swung a hot gaze over her, then, his eyes glittering with passion, slowly lowered his mouth to hers. "I've longed to kiss you ever since you left the composing room," he roughly whispered, brushing his lips against hers.

A fiery sexuality simmered between them that shook

her to the roots of her being, and before she could turn her head, he kissed her, still imprisoning her against his chest with the broomstick. Seconds later, she heard the broom clatter to the porch, and he crushed her against him, one hand supporting the back of her head.

She hadn't intended on returning the kiss, but when his warm mouth moved over hers, all her old yearnings for him came rushing back in a powerful tide of desire, and she felt herself torn from her emotional moorings.

Realizing what was happening, she moaned and began struggling again, but he strengthened the embrace and kissed her fervently, plunging his tongue into her mouth. She caught the scent of his bay-rum cologne and felt the stubble on his face pressed against her cheek, and before she knew what she was doing, she lifted her arms and encircled his shoulders.

Her tongue met his in a passionate caress and she felt herself melting as banked fires smouldered and burst into flames somewhere deep within her. At the same time, excitement raced through her, igniting a sweet pulse between her thighs.

Then, just as she was on the verge of breaking the kiss to announce she'd come back to the *Telegram* and head his Christmas drive, she realized what was happening and stiffened her body with outrage. Knowing his offer would be more effective than roses or diamonds, Lassiter had cleverly tried to manipulate her again. *No,* she told herself, already easing from his tight grip—she wouldn't be putty in his hands. She wouldn't let the rascal play on her emotions, and she wouldn't let him win her over with hot kisses and tender caresses either.

She violently wrenched away from him. "I'd be

seven kinds of a fool if I let you break down my resolve now." Anger flaring in her bosom, she slapped him smartly across the face, watching his eyes widen in surprise. "And I'm no fool. Your Christmas drive is nothing but a ruse to tempt me back into your bed and I won't fall for it!"

Lassiter glowered at her. "You're wrong. I need someone to head up the project."

Molly raised her chin. "Let Daisy Fellows head it up then!"

With that, she snapped up her broom, entered the boardinghouse, and slammed the door behind her. Her bosom heaving with emotion, she leaned against the closed door until she heard Lassiter walk from the porch. Then she peeked from the lace-draped hall window to see him drive away in his smart carriage with the yellow-painted wheels.

Aunt Agatha came halfway down the stairs, and stared at her with questioning eyes. "I heard the door slam. Who was that, dear?"

Molly blinked back her tears, hoping her aunt couldn't see them. "Just a salesman," she answered, thankful her voice held steady, "and believe me, you don't want what he's peddling!"

As soon as work was over the next Friday, Molly left the *Metropolitan* building in high spirits, for with her next paycheck, she'd finally have enough money to buy her mother's steamship ticket. On the busy sidewalk, groups of men in vested business suits, most of them wearing bowler hats, stood about talking, waiting for their respective omnibuses.

She'd only taken a few steps when she suddenly

spied Fergus walking toward her, his hands shoved in his pockets and his shoulders hunched forward. She maneuvered through the crowd of businessmen and closed the distance between them, noticing every line of the young man's body foretold bad news. "Fergus— saints above, what are you doing downtown?" she asked, steadfastly holding his worried gaze.

"Trying to c-catch you before you left for h-home, Molly," he replied with a sense of urgency.

"Yes, what's happened?" she breathed, knowing something had gone terribly wrong.

Anguish flickered in his eyes. "It's C-Clara. She was taken to the h-hospital today and sent me to fetch you."

Molly tried to find her tongue. "S-She's in the hospital?" she whispered in a choked voice. "Merciful heavens, what's wrong with her?"

The young man's lips tightened with distress. "S-She's coughing her lungs out. The doctors think it's pneumonia."

"*Pneumonia?* When did all this happen?"

Fergus stared at her, his expression grim. "She started getting sick a few days ago and last night she became seriously ill."

Molly closed her eyes, anxiety washing through her. *Clara sick?* she thought miserably. How could this be? The girl had gained some weight, and since she and Fergus had been seeing each other, she was always in high spirits. Why, the last time Clara had come to the boardinghouse, she'd even looked pink-cheeked.

The clatter of hooves and the *ping-ping* of an approaching omnibus roused Molly from the shock that had temporarily rooted her to the busy sidewalk. "How did you find out about all this?" she asked, hurriedly scanning Fergus's uneasy face.

He eyed the street, then giving her a sidelong glance, took her elbow. "C-Come along with me," he said, escorting her toward the cluster of men now boarding the brightly painted vehicle. "T-This one is going in the direction of the hospital. We can talk on the way."

He climbed onto the noisy omnibus and, putting out his hand, helped Molly up the metal steps. The conveyance was filled to capacity, and she'd just grabbed a swinging hand strap when the driver clicked to his horses and the jolting vehicle rattled away.

As Fergus paid their fares, she stared at his face, thinking it looked like a tightly stretched mask of despair. "Well, go on, then, tell me about Clara. How did you know she was sick in the first place?"

He grabbed a hand strap himself and, swaying a bit, spoke so she could hear him over the noise of the babbling passengers. "I-I went to her apartment to s-see her, but no one opened the door, s-so I t-talked to the landlady. She said Clara was in All Saints." Anxiety flooded his face. "As s-soon as I s-saw her, s-she asked me to fetch you."

Molly stared rigidly ahead, her mind in such turmoil, the other passengers appeared no more than a colorful blur.

"It all started with a chill," Fergus continued, placing his bony hand on her shoulder in an awkward gesture of comfort. "S-She got caught out in the rain and took a cold. The cold w-worsened, and when she began having trouble b-breathing, her b-brother took her to the hospital."

Molly thought of Paddy, who she hadn't seen since the first day she arrived in America, and remembered the words he'd spoken that evening on Castle Island:

"It's obliged I am to you, Molly, for seein' me sister safely through. Don't be worryin' your head about that bond, now. She's a little stick of a thing, but I'll be fattenin' her up soon enough. Just see if I don't."

He'd been true to his vow and had managed to put some weight on Clara, but remembering the bond, sick dread filled Molly's stomach.

With a *ping-ping* of its bell, the omnibus slowed and halted, and she and Fergus stepped to the pavement. Side by side, they began hurriedly walking toward All Saints, a large gray stone building, surrounded with leafless trees, their limbs stark against a dull autumn sky.

Upon entering the hospital, they went up to the women's ward and the sharp scent of a strong antiseptic touched Molly's nostrils, making her slightly queasy. With Fergus leading the way, she hurried down a long corridor filled with bustling doctors and nurses in long starched aprons carrying medical equipment. After more walking, she finally found Clara lying almost lifeless upon a narrow bed, her chest rising and falling rhythmically under a rumpled sheet.

When Molly touched her hand, the girl slowly opened her listless eyes. *"Molly,* I knew you'd come," she murmured, her voice hardly more than a rough whisper.

Filled with compassion, Molly brushed back Clara's limp, tangled hair and kissed her cheek. "Of course I've come," she answered, worrying about her friend's shallow, labored breathing. With a sense of unease, she looked about, and seeing no sign of Paddy, asked where he was.

A frown furrowed Clara's pale brow. "He's out looking for work," she whispered shamefacedly.

"*Looking for work?* But he already has a job."

Clara turned her head away, seemingly embarrassed to meet her friend's gaze. "N-Not anymore, I'm afraid he—he was laid off," she explained in a broken voice.

Molly's heart jolted with the depressing news.

Clara pressed her small, white hands over her face, and her fragile control crumbling, shook with convulsive sobs. She tried to raise herself on one elbow, but Molly gently forced her back upon the rumpled pillow. "No—just rest. Save your strength so you can get well."

"Oh, Molly, you shouldn't have signed that bond," Clara struggled out, tears streaming down her face. "I'm afraid we have nothing saved back. We have no money to pay the hospital bill, and now you'll be responsible for it!"

Molly forced back her despair, then taking out her handkerchief, wiped her friend's tearstained cheeks and held her close.

Fergus swept a questioning gaze over Molly, obviously unaware she'd signed the bond. "I-If it's money that's needed I have a bit that I'll be glad to contribute," he offered, his slightly surprised face slowly hardening with resolve.

Clara coughed and put a thin hand to her cracked lips. "But the doctor says I'll need several weeks to recover," she lamented, looking into his compassionate eyes. She clasped his big hand and held it tightly. "I'm sure it will take far more than you have," she whispered, her eyes bleak with sorrow.

Molly ignored the sick, heavy feeling in her stomach and forced a smile to her lips. "Don't worry your head about money at a time like this. With what I've saved, that will be no problem at all."

Clara burst out in tears again. "I'm so sorry all this has happened," she apologized, pausing to take a handkerchief and blow her nose. "Paddy will find work soon—I know he will."

"I'm sure he will too," Molly returned, bending to gently adjust the girl's pillow. She gave her friend an encouraging smile, her heart tender with feeling. "He can pay me back a bit at a time as he's able. You just concentrate on getting better and don't be giving a thought to that bond, now."

She looked at Fergus, then slowly circled her gaze back to Clara. "I did the right thing, signing that bond, you know," she observed in a light, airy tone. "If I'd let them send you back to Ireland, you'd never have met Fergus, here, would you, now?"

Clara managed a feeble smile. Trying to divert her, Molly prattled on about her job at the *Metropolitan*. But in the depths of her spinning mind, she wildly wondered what she'd do. A suffocating sensation centered in her chest. When she honored the bond, she'd be totally without funds, and in one short month's time, her mother would be evicted.

Chapter Twelve

Molly spent a miserable October worrying about money. As she'd expected, she'd been forced to pay the expensive bond, which had wiped out the money she'd saved for her mother's ticket as well as the rest of her small nest egg. She was totally broke and her only consolation was that Clara was now well and and the girl's brother finally had a new job.

On a fresh, rain-washed Saturday morning, Molly sat on an omnibus headed to the *Telegram* building—a place she thought she'd never visit again. From her reticule, she pulled the letter she'd received from Lassiter only yesterday, and reread it for the tenth time: *Please come to my office on the seventh of November at ten in the morning, as I have a surprise for you. Don't worry, we won't be alone, and my intentions are strictly honorable.*

All the way downtown she told herself she shouldn't obey his summons, but her curiosity had simply gotten the best of her. What kind of surprise did he have in store that made it so important that she see him today? she wondered with a growing sense of interest. She vaguely feared he might have heard of her financial plight and would try to offer her money, but she laughingly told herself that no one she knew would be bold enough to approach the mighty publisher of the *Telegram*, or they'd face her wrath if they did!

As the omnibus rattled its way downtown, she recalled the day after she'd visited Clara in All Saints. During a kitchen conference, Aunt Agatha had offered her a small amount of money, but she knew the old lady was owed back rent and struggled to put groceries on her dinner table. Fergus had gallantly announced he was going to drop out of college and get a full-time job to repay her, but realizing he'd nearly completed his education, she firmly refused his offer, saying he'd only create another problem—one that he'd be years in solving.

When her aunt had suggested she might borrow the money from Lassiter, Molly shot to her feet, crossed her arms, and paced about the kitchen, her temper rising with every step she took. "*Ask Lassiter for a loan?*" she echoed, scarcely believing her ears. "No, never. I'd rather be indebted to Old Scratch himself than Burke Lassiter. I'd die before I asked that rascal for money."

In the end, Molly had been forced to write her mother and suggest she stay with Father Riley until she could send for her. Although he now had a new housekeeper, he would surely take her in. Still, it would be a gesture of charity—charity that Kathleen was loath to accept. How Molly regretted failing her mother; how she grieved for the woman's embarrassment!

The omnibus slowed and stopped near the *Telegram* building and Molly stepped out and walked across the street, steeling her nerves as she went.

Everything inside the building looked and even smelled the same, she thought as she hurried up the sweeping marble steps. Her heart beating a little faster, she entered the smoky newsroom. The reporters sent her a chorus of greetings and welcoming smiles that tugged at her heart and reminded her how much she'd missed all of them.

Some exchanged sly smiles, which made her wonder what they all knew that she didn't. Even Lassiter's secretary gave her a genuine smile, the first ever, and it sent Molly's mind spinning with questions. Saints above, what was going on? she wondered, thinking she'd made a terrible mistake coming here in the first place.

Molly entered Lassiter's office, and when their gazes locked, her heart lurched in her bosom. He rose from behind his desk and slowly walked toward her. His eyes twinkling with delight, he took her hand. She moved back a step, disturbed by a host of pleasurable sensations. Excitement trickled down her spine as he graced her with an admiring glance and kissed the backs of her fingers.

She pulled her hand away, and moved across the room with unhurried purpose. Turning, she straightened her back and met his eyes without flinching. "What are you up to?" she demanded, trying to ignore the spate of tender memories presently tumbling through her mind. "You've got to be up to something.

Everyone in the newsroom was smiling like the cat who'd just lapped up the last of the cream."

"I won't lie to you," he answered, now moving so close she could see the roguish light in his eyes. "I *am* up to something, and it concerns your surprise." He traced the line of her cheek with a long finger, and she braced herself against the warm feelings now racing through her. Damn him, the rascal was at it again. This couldn't continue. She had to show him she was one woman whose will wouldn't crumble beneath his entrancing charm.

With a pounding heart, she removed Lassiter's hand from her face, hating the soft, vulnerable part of her that still ached for his touch. "I'll ask you to keep your hands to yourself," she announced sharply. "Don't think I've forgotten the last time we met on Aunt Agatha's front porch."

His mouth twitched with amusement. "Oh yes, how could I forget? I seem to recall you trying to beat me about the shoulders with a broom."

She tilted her head. "That's right, and you'd better not pull any tricks concerning this so-called surprise of yours."

His eyes dancing, he towered over her, looking very pleased with himself. "Oh, I think you'll be very happy about this surprise." A confident smile hovering on his lips, he opened his office door and asked his secretary to bring in his guest.

Molly's heart nearly burst from her chest as a neat woman with her own sparkling green eyes and auburn hair walked into the office and smiled brightly. Caught off guard, she gasped in utter astonishment and was unable to speak. But when the lady in the plain cotton gown and shopworn little hat decorated with silk roses held out her arms, joy exploded inside of Molly like bursting fireworks. Half blinded by her tears, she ran to her mother and wrapped her arms about her. She sobbed deeply. "Mam, I can't believe my eyes," she whispered between sobs. "I thought you were in Ireland. How did you get here in New York?"

Kathleen laughed and patted her daughter on her back, trying to revive her. "Mr. Lassiter wrote me a nice letter, dear, and the darlin' man included a steamship ticket too. Isn't it wonderful? Father Riley took me in, but oh, we were all so crowded in that little rectory!"

Molly clenched her mother's white-gloved hand, and after leading her toward a leather chair, sat down, thinking her own legs would buckle beneath her. She lowered her head, and touching her fingertips to her temples, took several deep breaths, trying to calm her jangled nerves.

Instead, she burst into tears again and Kathleen knelt beside her, caressing her back and kissing her cheek. "There, there, love. The shock of it all has been too great for you," she crooned in a soft, melodic voice.

Molly pulled in a steadying breath, then clutching her mother's shoulders, moved a bleary gaze over her. How many nights she'd wondered if she'd ever look upon that blessed face again. To see it appear in the *Telegram* building of all places was almost more than she could bear.

Lassiter, his face aglow with pleasure, poured Molly a small brandy and brought it to her. "Here, I think you'd better drink this, Irish."

She accepted the drink with trembling hands and

swallowed it in two gulps. Feeling the liquor burn its way down her throat, she met her mother's gaze that tenderly melted into hers. "I still can't believe it. D-Did you just arrive?"

Kathleen rose and pulled off her crisp white gloves. "No, I arrived yesterday," she answered, tucking them away in her reticule. "Mr. Lassiter was ever so kind. He met the ship, then put me up in a wonderful hotel and bought me a fine meal last night," she answered in a rich Irish lilt. She glanced at her benefactor, a sweet smile spreading over her face. "And the lovely man sent a carriage for me this morning—God bless his soul."

By now some of Molly's shock had worn away and she sat silently, digesting the miracle that had just happened. Conflicting emotions stormed within her. Nothing could have made her more happy than to see her mother, but at the same time, she seethed with growing anger. Lassiter had known how she'd worked and struggled for this moment, and slyly manipulating events, he'd made it happen without even consulting her.

Kathleen slid a bewildered gaze over her. "What's the matter, dear? You're so quiet. I thought you'd be happy."

Molly quickly clasped her hand. "Oh, I am. I'm happier than I've ever been in my life. I-It's just that I'm still so shocked!" She rose and embraced her mother again, gently rocking her back and forth before she traced her hands down her arms and surveyed her face. "Will you wait outside for just a moment?" she asked tenderly, noting the woman's questioning eyes. "I won't be long. Then I'll take you home to Aunt

Agatha." She kissed her mother's forehead and caressed her shoulders. "She'll fair burst with happiness when she sees you!"

Kathleen gave her a radiant smile. "I'll be happy to wait outside. I'm sure you'll be wanting a few words with Mr. Lassiter," she replied, sending an appreciative gaze in the publisher's direction. "We both have so much to thank him for."

"Yes, don't we now?" Molly agreed, putting her arm about her mother's waist and guiding her toward the office door.

As soon as Kathleen was gone and safely out of earshot, Molly turned to Lassiter, struggling with several strong emotions that left her quaking. "How could you?" she demanded, anger and humiliation seething in her bosom as she moved toward him. "How could you do such a thing?" she continued, spitting out the words contemptuously.

He stared at her, his face stamped with utter disbelief. "I thought you'd be overjoyed to see your mother. Isn't this what you've been working for?"

"Yes, of course," she retorted, feeling her temper soaring higher because he obviously didn't understand the situation. She walked around him in a circle. "But I didn't want it to happen this way."

He widened his eyes in astonishment. "What do you mean *happen this way*?"

"I wanted to bring Mam over myself—not be indebted to you for the rest of my natural life!" she flung out, barely keeping her raw emotions in check.

Lassiter poured himself a brandy. "So that's it, is it?" he huffed, quickly downing the amber-colored liquid. "You and your stubborn pride," he retorted, quick annoyance gathering in his eyes. "Well, you needn't feel indebted." Extending his arm, he graced her with an exaggerated bow. "I absolve you from all your indebtedness, young lady," he announced, his tone edged with growing sarcasm. His mouth twisted with exasperation. "I never expect a penny in return for bringing your mother to America."

Her temples pounding, Molly paced about the office, then glanced uneasily over her shoulder, wondering how he'd arranged it all. "How did you find out about this?" she demanded, her husky voice breaking with pent-up tension. "How did you discover that I had to pay Clara's bond?"

He regarded her with hooded eyes. "I believe a young man named Fergus lives in your aunt's boardinghouse."

Molly felt the sting of betrayal. "*Fergus?* He told you?" she blurted out, hiding her trembling hands behind the folds of her skirt. Quick anger erupted within her, then she told herself her friend had only been trying to help. Still, would she give him a talking to he'd never forget this evening!

Lassiter placed his glass aside, his manner now cool and aloof. "Yes, Fergus told me, and thank God he had the wit to come to the *Telegram* and request an interview with me."

Molly turned about, and trying to accept the humiliating fact that both she and her mother were objects of his charity, drew in a deep breath. "And everyone in the newsroom knew this was going to happen, didn't they?" she quizzed in an accusing tone.

"Yes, they did," he tossed at her rigid back. "What's wrong with that? Everyone likes you and they were overjoyed about it."

213

She turned, and mantling herself with her injured pride, swiftly marched toward him. "This is the dirtiest trick you've ever played on me," she snapped, repeatedly jabbing her finger into his chest. "This is worse than trying to bribe me back to the paper with your Christmas drive. You chose the person dearest to my heart, and using her, tried to manipulate me again."

He swept a sharp glance over her. "*No, you're completely wrong,*" he countered, his tone heavy with censure. "I was only trying to help you."

Molly narrowed her eyes. "I don't believe you. You've known all along how badly I wanted to bring my mother to America and you tried to use that knowledge to tip the scales in your favor."

Tight-lipped, she walked to the door with purposeful strides, then turned to scan his glowering countenance. "If I ever harbored even the tiniest desire to come back to the *Telegram,* you've just destroyed it," she exclaimed, her cold voice precise and businesslike.

She swished out of the office and only the sight of her mother's lovely, perplexed face prevented her from slamming the door behind her.

When Molly walked into the boardinghouse kitchen with her mother and announced, "We'll be having one more for dinner tonight," Aunt Agatha not only gasped and widened her eyes, she dropped a bowl of potatoes on the linoleum floor.

"Jesus, Mary, and Joseph," the old lady wailed, tears streaming down her face as she hurried to embrace her sister, "you just took ten years off my life!" Trembling with emotion, she ran her work-worn hands over Kathleen's face and slender arms in a gesture of love.

214

"Saints preserve us all," she went on in a rough whisper, her moist eyes sparkling with surprised delight, "if you aren't just as lovely as you were the last day I saw you."

Molly watched the two sisters and decided this would have been the best day of her life, if she hadn't been so mad at Lassiter. Try as she might, she couldn't forget how he'd tried to manipulate her affections, and when her mother began praising his generosity to Aunt Agatha, it only worsened the situation. Well, if he'd calculated the grand gesture of buying a steamship ticket from Queenstown to New York would make her forgive him, he'd calculated wrong—just as wrong as he could be! she thought resentfully.

For the next fifteen minutes, the kitchen resounded with bright conversation, bursts of laughter, and exclamations of joy. Then Aunt Agatha, still dabbing tears from her eyes, suggested they all go upstairs. Jabbering like magpies, the trio carried Kathleen's luggage to Molly's little dormer room where late-morning light splashed through the windows and made patterns on the threadbare carpet.

After they'd all eaten a bite of lunch, Molly and Kathleen returned to the bedroom and talked for hours as they unpacked gowns and put them away. By three o'clock Aunt Agatha had joined them, to quiz her sister about all the people she used to know in Ireland, valiantly trying to catch up on ten years of gossip before dinner.

Kathleen oohed and aahed at the magnificence of her sister's house, tracing her fingers over the mahogany settees in the parlor and exclaiming at the beautiful tiled fireplaces. Upon seeing the piano, her eyes lit with pleasure. Her face tense with concentration, she sat down on the bench and haltingly began to play. Molly knew she'd played the piano before she married, and emotion now swelled in her throat as her mother's long fingers stretched over the keys, plunking out a sweet melody.

That evening Kathleen was introduced to everyone at dinner, and all the boarders greeted her with embarrassed respect, seemingly recognizing her for the lady she was. As the week rolled on, she asked each man what part of Ireland he came from, and gently drew him out, giving each of the homesick boarders the undivided attention he craved so desperately. And in the evenings there were sing-alongs around the battered parlor piano and laughter-filled card games until bedtime.

Molly soon realized her mother's unexpected arrival had turned out to be a blessing for all concerned. Kind and sweet-spirited, she began to mend the boarders' ragged working clothes, and more important, lend a sympathetic ear to their problems, often offering gentle advice. Molly sighed inwardly, wondering why her father had never realized what a jewel he had in her tender mother, who had such an abundance of love to give to all who asked of her. Still, even as the woman helped her sister and the boarders, the flicker of pain in her eyes plainly told Molly she was still grieving desperately for the son she'd lost.

A week after Kathleen had arrived, she and Molly stepped on the porch one cool morning just as Brian, dressed in ragged clothes and wearing an engaging smile, arrived with a fresh copy of the *Telegram*.

"This is my mam, Kathleen, just over from Ireland,"

Molly told the grinning boy, who gallantly doffed his shabby cap in respect as he handed her the paper.

"Well, ain't she as lovely as the first flowers in May," he piped up, a twinkle in his eyes. "And so young-lookin' she is!" He winked at Molly. "Are you sure she ain't your baby sister instead of your mother?"

Kathleen blushed prettily and began to talk to Brian about her voyage to America. Her face darkened when he told her his mother was gone and he was now living with his stepfather. After he left, a stack of papers thrown over his back, she gazed at Molly, tears brimming in her sea-green eyes. "And doesn't he look like Cossi?" she asked, her voice blurred with emotion.

Molly nodded, swallowing the lump in her throat. "That he does. It's just what I thought the first time I saw him," she replied, giving her mother's shoulders an affectionate squeeze.

After a few more words, Molly hurried off to catch the omnibus that would take her to the *Metropolitan* building. After the front gate had banged behind her legs, she felt an irresistible urge to look back, and she noticed Kathleen still standing on the front porch, clasping a thick, white-painted pillar as she gazed in the direction Brian had gone, a soft nostalgic look on her pale, tear-stained face.

Next Monday, just before his quarterly financial meeting with Tom Perkins, Lassiter sat at his desk reading a scented letter the doorman at the Regency had given him as he left for work this morning. He stared at Daisy Fellows's handwriting, digesting the contents of the letter.

Due to the lack of attention that he'd been giving her,

she'd decided to retreat with her family to their estate in the Hamptons until he came to his senses. There would be no use trying to beg her to stay, for by the time he read this letter she'd be gone. She only hoped when she and her family returned, his attitude would have improved considerably and he'd have already set their wedding date.

He gave a deep sigh. Her snippy ultimatum only increased his desire to break his engagement with her, but that was now temporarily impossible, he thought, rejecting the idea of mailing her an insulting letter as she'd sent him. Even Daisy deserved better than that. But the Lord knew with his paper in such a shaky financial condition, he certainly didn't have time to go chasing after her.

His chest tight with irritation, he tossed the letter aside and thought of Molly, who he considered far more important than the simpering socialite. Would he ever understand women? he wondered dismally. He'd genuinely wanted to help her, but his good deed had backfired in his face like a ton of dynamite. She'd called bringing her mother from Ireland a manipulative scheme. He chuckled bitterly. If it had been a scheme—which it wasn't—it had totally failed, he thought, remembering her flashing eyes.

He rose, and shoving his hands in his pockets, paced about his office. What would he do now? Would he ever be able to get back in Molly's good graces? Was such a thing even possible anymore? he asked himself with a fresh rush of depression.

There was a knock on his door as Tom Perkins quietly entered, a tentative smile on his face. Lassiter noticed a muscle twitch in the young man's jaw, and bracing himself for more bad news, he cocked a brow and quietly asked, "Well, just how bad are things?"

Tom gazed at him with worried eyes. "I'm sorry to report, sir, things aren't going well at all financially." He flipped open a manila folder he held in his hand.

Lassiter studied his harried accountant, wondering how much worse things could get. "All right, show me the numbers," he ordered, unbuttoning his jacket as he walked back to his desk and sat down. After Tom had carefully placed the open folder on a green blotter, Lassiter leaned forward in his desk chair to study the neatly inked entries.

The accountant ran a finger under his stiff collar. "Here is the tally for the reams of paper and hundred weights of ink the *Telegram* has used since I last presented a financial review," he announced, tapping the end of a pencil on the numbers. "I-I'm afraid they're enormous, and the suppliers have been relentless in pursuing payment. S-Several companies have even sent duns."

Lassiter noticed the man actually stuttering, something he'd never heard him do before, and his hands trembled ever so slightly. Obviously he was embarrassed to present this depressing financial report, but his nervousness was totally out of hand.

"Good Lord, why haven't these people been paid?" Lassiter inquired, studying his employee's anxious face.

His gaze vague, Tom peered about the room as if he were searching for the right answer. "W-Well they have been paid, at least partially," he finally answered, transferring his attention to his employer again. "It's just that the creditors expect *full* payment." Moisture sheened his brow. "I send them all something, but it's always late, and I can understand why they're angry."

Lassiter stood and walked around his desk. Already acquainted with the problem, he recalled the recent dispute with his typesetters about their late wages. His hands locked behind his back, he slowly walked across his office, then looked over his shoulder. "Are you telling me I'm broke?"

The accountant gave a dry cough. "Well, just about, sir," he answered, almost wincing as he said the words. "The *Telegram* is definitely running in the red."

Lassiter turned and ran a hand through his hair. "Why didn't you bring this to my attention earlier? How did we get in such a mess?"

Tom tugged his ear. "I did withhold the information a bit longer than I should have, but I kept thinking things would turn around. To answer your second question, sir, there are many variables, but basically we're not selling enough papers to pay the bills. It's as simple as that." He glanced downward, then raised a concerned gaze. "The loss of Miss Kilmartin was a great blow to the *Telegram.*"

"Yes, yes," Lassiter shot back irritably, the thought of his last meeting with Molly still vivid in his mind.

"I-I'm afraid that the paper will fall into bankruptcy, sir," Tom announced ominously, giving a dry cough. "I doubt the creditors will continue to supply us if we cannot make complete payment within a month."

"*A month?*" Lassiter echoed, staring at the man in disbelief. "That soon?"

The accountant's face went white as he picked up the folder and held it tightly in his hands. "Yes, if you could secure a loan, it would put the paper on her feet—give us a little breathing room."

Lassiter had never seen the young man in such a state and wondered what was wrong with him today. "Yes, I understand. You may go now," he said dully, noting the look of profound relief on Tom's face, "but leave the folder on my desk. As soon as I have a chance, I want to study the numbers in detail. Perhaps I can find where we can cut expenses."

The accountant widened his eyes. "You want m-me to leave it here?" he asked, his voice rising in surprise. "You've never asked that before."

Lassiter looked directly at his employee and raised his voice so there would be no chance of misunderstanding. "Well, I'm asking that now. Put the folder on my desk before you go."

"Very well, sir," Tom nervously answered, laying it on the blotter as if he hated to relinquish it. Afterward, he hastily left, his expression announcing he was delighted to be dismissed.

After he was gone, Lassiter went to the window and stared out, so absorbed in his thoughts, he scarcely saw the bustling traffic flowing down Broadway. Lord, did he actually have to go begging for a loan? But who'd give him a loan with the *Telegram*'s dismal financial record? Were all of his hopes and dreams for the paper going to end like this? Was everything, as Tom suggested, really to fall about his ears in one short month? he wondered with a rising sense of alarm.

Kathleen, who sat on Molly's bed knitting, her needles clicking pleasantly, looked at her daughter with a pleading expression. "Why are you going out with this Tom Perkins tonight? Mr. Lassiter seems a perfect gentleman and I'm sure he's interested in you." She gave a little sigh. "I saw it in his eyes the day we were both in his office."

Molly, who'd been arranging her hair, laid the brush on her bureau. How she wanted to tell Kathleen all that had transpired between her and Lassiter, but she pressed her lips together, thinking the blunt facts would shock and dismay her very religious mother. "But I have no interest whatsoever in the man. Haven't I told you that already?"

Kathleen's lips tilted in a sweet smile. "Yes you have, but he's so handsome, and so generous too. Imagine him sending me a ticket to New York because you had to pay that bond."

"If you only knew him," Molly replied, slowly sinking onto the bed beside her mother, "you'd change your mind. If the truth be told, he's very arrogant, and I really don't think he has the ability to love any woman," she explained, a strange emptiness clutching the pit of her stomach as she said the words. "The only thing he loves is his blessed newspaper."

Kathleen laughed softly. "To most men, their work is their life. They're all absorbed in it, but that doesn't mean there isn't a place in their hearts for the woman they love."

Molly took her mother's hand, thinking she would silence her forever on the subject of Lassiter with the revelation on the tip of her tongue. "Mam, listen well," she sighed, squeezing Kathleen's fingers. She widened her eyes to emphasize her point. "He's already engaged to a beautiful socialite named Daisy Fellows. Her father is one of the richest men in New York."

A look of discomfort crossed Kathleen's face, but she gathered her composure. "I'm sure he became engaged before he met you, dear. And engagements have been broken. I've seen it happen many times before," she ploughed on with a determined tone.

"Well, Lassiter won't break his engagement to Daisy. He needs her father's money to keep his paper afloat."

Kathleen studied her silently for a moment, then carefully choosing her words, slowly ventured, "There's something else, isn't there—something you're not telling me?"

Molly rose, thinking her mother deserved to hear the truth. "Yes, if you must know," she suddenly said, deciding a sharp knife hurt the least, "he's too much like Da."

Kathleen batted her eyes. "Too much like your father? What do you mean by that?" she inquired in a soft, interested voice.

Molly sighed, then walked about the bedroom, silently praying she could make her mother understand. "He has Da's charm and gift of gab, and unfortunately his eye for women too." She gazed at the mother's stunned face. "I'd never want to be married to a man like that, for I saw what being married to Da did to you." She slowly approached Kathleen, not wanting to hurt her, but wanting her to accept the truth. "Oh, Mam, the only thing Da brought to your marriage was heartache and grief. I'm sorry to say so, but you know it's true."

223

Her face a welter of emotion, Kathleen put down her knitting, then rose and moved to a battered trunk at the end of the bed. "I have something here I want to show you," she said over her shoulder as she opened the battered luggage and withdrew a packet of letters tied in a blue ribbon. "These are letters that your father wrote while he was courting me," she explained, gracefully rising again. She extended her hand. "I-I want you to read them."

Molly felt herself blush. "No, I couldn't. I'm sure they're too personal."

Kathleen led her to the bed, then asked her to sit beside her. "They are personal, but they hold a lot of truth—truth that I want you to see." She placed a letter in Molly's hand and nodded her head. "Go ahead. It would mean the world to me, if you'd read just one. I'll warrant you, you'll see a side of your father that you never knew."

Just to please her mother, Molly began reading one of the letters, thinking she'd only scan it. Halfway through she became engrossed in the words, and as her mother said, noticed her father possesed a romantic aspect that she wasn't aware of. Could Johnny Kilmartin actually have written such a beautiful letter, a letter so full of love and devotion?

After Molly had read all the letters, which Kathleen had carefully arranged by date, she sat staring at her mother, feeling tears trickling down her cheeks. "I didn't know Da was capable of writing such wonderful things," she murmured in a hushed voice. "All I ever heard come out of his mouth were harsh, careless words."

Kathleen wiped the tears from Molly's face, then bent her head and carefully tied the ribbon about the letters once more. "Yes, I know," she thoughtfully replied, "but the man had a loving side too." She looked up with glistening eyes. "God help me if he didn't."

"But I've heard you cry over him many times."

Kathleen traced her hand over her daughter's back. "It's true life wore him down and sent him looking for pleasure outside the walls of our cottage, but we shared many happy times together, wonderful times that still make my heart sing when I think of them." A wonderfully tender expression claimed her face. "I loved him so much—and I'll love him till the day I die."

Shaken by her mother's openness, Molly felt compelled to ask the question she'd held in her heart for years. "Mam," she whispered, her tone rough with wonder and concern, "how can you say that when Da left you for another woman, then when he was old and sick and broken, came back for you to take care of him until he died?"

Kathleen held her daughter in her arms and looked at her lovingly. "There were bad times and tears aplenty, but for every tear, there was a smile. You must believe that."

Molly clutched her hand. "But I still don't understand," she pressed, not satisfied with the simple answer. "How were you strong enough to ever forgive him?"

Sparkling tears shone in Kathleen's eyes. "My darling Molly," she murmured, her face transformed, "my life has been a long journey, most of it hard, but it's

225

taught me one thing—the power of love. If you love someone enough, you can forgive them anything." A look of dreamy nostalgia gathered in her eyes. "Do you remember when Father Riley used to say love beareth all things and endureth all things?"

Molly nodded, remembering her childhood lessons.

"Well it does, *it really does,*" Kathleen proclaimed, tears now streaming down her own face. When you understand that"—she placed her slender hand over her heart—"really understand it here, it makes you incredibly strong—strong enough to forgive anything."

Molly studied her mother's radiant face, profoundly touched by her words. A quiet peace settled over her, and for the first time, she began thinking about forgiving her father for what he'd done.

Kathleen carefully brushed back her daughter's hair. "Don't let any lingering feelings you have toward your father spoil the happiness you might find with Mr. Lassiter, love. Trust your heart, my darling, for it's always right."

After an attentive waiter had seated Molly and Tom and taken their order, the accountant gazed across the table, his expression marked with gravity. "I gave Lassiter a financial assessment yesterday on the *Telegram,*" he slowly announced, taking Molly's hand in a possessive manner.

She studied his frowning face. "That bad, huh?"

He sighed in agreement. "Yes, I'm afraid the paper is on its last legs. The old man has already made deep inroads into his personal capital and unless he can secure a large business loan, there's nothing ahead but bankruptcy and humiliation. The trouble is," he continued in a dark tone, "with the *Telegram*'s track record, getting a loan is going to be very difficult for him."

Despair spread through Molly, for she guessed what he was going to say next.

He caressed her fingers with his thumb. "The only person who might give him that loan," he added pointedly, "is Daisy Fellows's father."

Molly's throat ached with defeat. "Why are you telling me this?" she challenged, almost angrily pulling her hand from his. "Have you forgotten that I don't work for the *Telegram* anymore?"

A smug look crossed his face. "It seemed someone should warn you what was afoot. I'm sure Lassiter will make a last attempt to lure you back. If he could get you to write features for him again, he might be able to save the paper."

Molly doubted Tom's supposed noble motives in telling her this, but keeping her own council, she bit her tongue. After the waiter brought their dinner, the only sound to be heard for a while was the scrape of expensive silverware, but before the first course was over, the accountant's eyes glistened with intensity. "I've been wanting to talk to you for some time now," he softly ventured, his face full of tenderness. "That's why I brought you here."

Molly's throat went dry with nervousness.

"I've always had great regard for you," Tom continued with great deliberateness, "and to tell the truth, I-I've loved you for a long while."

Molly's heart pitched. "But you hardly know me."

His face glowed with admiration. "I know you better than you think. The old man's right about one thing, you know. You really are an angel, and I'd be the happiest man in the world if you'd do me the honor of becoming my wife." He lifted her hand to his lips. "I know this is sudden, but I just couldn't wait any longer to ask you."

There it was, his proposal of marriage, out in the open at last, Molly thought miserably, already looking for a way to let him down easily. "I'm very fond of you, of course, but—"

"*No,* don't say it," he interrupted, clasping her hand tightly.

She blushed at his eagerness.

"I'm not rich like Lassiter," Tom rushed on, his eyes glistening with entreaty, "but I have enough to care for you—and you wouldn't have to work?"

"Not work?"

"Yes, you could stay at home and take care of our children," he told her, his voice flooded with tenderness.

Molly's head spun as she searched for words to tell him she'd never considered having his children before this moment.

"I'd spend my life trying to make you happy," Tom continued, his countenance imbued with almost pitiable need.

Temporarily speechless, Molly gazed at his pleading eyes. Yes, Tom had many solid, respectable qualities that would ensure a girl a stable marriage. He was presentable, hardworking, and safe, but she wasn't sure if her feelings for him ran deep enough for marriage. "I'm very flattered," she finally began, but I'm really not ready to make a commitment to any man yet."

Tom's face tightened with disappointment; then he patted his chest and pulled a velvet ring box from his embroidered vest. "Just look at this," he said in an excited voice, opening the box to show her a huge diamond engagement ring that glittered like stars in the candlelight. "I wanted to give you this earlier, but you're usually too busy to accept my invitations."

Molly stared at the huge diamond, flabbergasted at what she saw. "That's the largest stone I've ever seen," she whispered, watching the gem blink fiery sparks. "W-Where did you get something like that?

"I bought it at Tiffinay's," he quickly answered, trying to slide the ring on her finger. "It's a beauty, isn't it?"

She pulled back her hand, refusing to let him slip the ring on her finger. "No, I can't wear it, she stated with quiet determination. "You'll have to take it back."

Crestfallen, the accountant put the ring into the box and slipped it inside his vest pocket. "No, I won't take it back," he insisted, his eyes clouded with anguish. "Just remember it belongs to you, anytime you want to wear it." He brushed his lips over her fingers again. "Please tell me that you'll think about my proposal. That's all I ask."

His words made her more uncomfortable than ever.

"I'll take you to Delmonico's in ten days and you can tell me your answer," he smoothly continued, his voice full of hopeful anticipation.

He looked so sad and earnest, Molly had to swallow back her welling emotions. "All right," she conceded, telling herself she owed him the consideration of at least thoughtfully considering his proposal. "I'll tell you in ten days, then."

They continued eating, but Molly's stomach churned with unease. How in the name of heaven could Tom afford that flashy engagement ring he'd bought at the most expensive jewelry store in the city? And most important, why was he pressuring her to marry him so desperately? she wondered with a rising sense of anxiety.

Chapter Thirteen

Thanksgiving Day dawned clear and frosty over the great metropolis. The girl that helped Aunt Agatha had been given the day off to be with her own family, and Molly had been up for hours in the kitchen chopping celery and onion and loaves of day-old bread to be transformed into sage dressing. As the grandfather clock in the hall chimed twelve noon, she lifted a golden-brown turkey from the oven of the wood-burning stove and sat the heavy pan on the table, thinking that with its mingled scents of cinnamon, cloves, and baking rolls, the cluttered kitchen smelled like a little piece of heaven right here on Murphy Street.

Aunt Agatha turned from the counter where she'd just placed several mince and pumpkin pies, and a large bowl of whipped cream, then glanced about the kitchen where every flat surface supported something good to eat. "Do you think we'll have enough, dear?" she inquired in a faintly worried tone.

Molly scanned the counters that not only held dressing and gravy, whipped potatoes, and green beans, but slaw and fresh fruit salad, and jellies and jams her aunt had put up during the past summer. "Yes, of course. They can't possibly eat all of this!"

Aunt Agatha picked up a large decanter of elderberry wine, also made last summer, and hearing the sound of scraping chairs and laughter coming from her dining room, cocked her head. "Well, it's time to go in, I suppose. You carry the turkey and I'll take the wine."

Molly transferred the huge bird to a serving platter, encircled it with garnishes, then added the carving knife and proceeded to the dining room. Once she and her aunt entered the cozy little room, they were met by a sea of merry faces and murmurs of delight.

"Ahh, look at that, will you!" exclaimed Shamus who sat at the head of the beautifully set table that today was decked out with a lace tablecloth and candles. "These Americans invented a fine holiday, did they not?"

Her aunt's boarders, slicked up to perfection with greased-down hair and collars starched so stiff they threatened to behead them, voiced their approval, and following Shamus's lead, tucked their napkins under their chins. Kathleen, her eyes lighting with pleasure, plucked Brian's napkin from the table, snapped it out, and laid it in his lap.

Molly placed the turkey platter on the table, and thought that in truth she did have a lot to be thankful for. First and foremost, her mother sat by Shamus with a smile on her lovely face. Clara held Fergus's hand,

and by the radiant look shining in their eyes, they were more in love than ever. Dressed in a clean white shirt and trousers for a change, Paddy sat beside his sister, looking proud and spirited now that he was working again.

Aunt Agatha put the wine decanter on the table, then catching Shamus's expectant eyes, said, "Go ahead and carve the turkey now, love. It will get you in good practice for after we're married and you're head of the house."

Laughter rippled about the table as the small man rose, and after placing the platter in front of him, rejoined, "I'll be carvin' the turkey, Jelly Bean, but don't take it as a proposal of marriage, now."

The old lady splashed sparkling wine into his glass. "I know," she groaned in a slow, disgusted voice, "you'll marry me when you're financially able."

He placed his gnarled hand over his heart. "I certainly will. I promise on me sainted mother's grave—may she rest in peace."

While the old man carved the bird, Molly and her aunt brought the dressing and the rest of the food from the kitchen, then arranged it all on the table. As Molly set down the last dish she noticed there was an extra plate and an empty chair, but in her haste, decided one of the boarders was absent.

After he'd finished carving, Shamus raised his glass. "I'd like to thank the lovely ladies who cooked this fine feast, and before we begin," he announced dramatically, "I think a toast is in order." Laughter burst out as he sampled the wine and smacked his lips. "The best you ever made, Aggie," he said, throwing her a broad wink.

His eyes gleaming with contentment, he cleared his throat and proclaimed: "Health and long life to you, the wife of your choice to you, land without rent to you, and may you be half an hour in heaven before the devil knows you're dead!"

"Oh, you and your toasts, old man!" Aunt Agatha said. "Everyone knows you only make them to give yourself an excuse to drink."

"And what's wrong with that?" he piped up with a questioning frown. "There's more friendship in a jigger of whiskey than a churn of buttermilk, I always say."

Everyone laughed as he refilled his glass, and Molly noted that although Aunt Agatha pretended to be angry with him, a soft love light shone in her eyes.

Fergus offered grace, and they'd just begun the meal when a knock resounded at the front door. Looking nervous, Kathleen rose. "I'll be getting that," she said, smoothing back her hair with a trembling hand. "I think my company has arrived."

Molly put down her fork. "*Your company?* But everyone you know is already here. Who could it be?"

"Just a friend, love, just a friend," Kathleen said, glancing back for a moment as she left the room.

The apprehension in Molly's bosom turned to shocked surprise when her mother re-entered the room with Lassiter at her side. Dressed in a fine wool suit that emphasized his muscled form to perfection, he sent her a bright smile that made her heart leap wildly. He held a huge bouquet of red roses that he handed to Aunt Agatha, who seemed bowled over by the extravagant compliment.

"This is my friend, Mr. Lassiter," Kathleen announced proudly, a little smile hovering on her lips.

"He's the publisher of the *Telegram*—the man who paid my fare from Ireland. I want you all to meet him."

Everyone gazed at Lassiter with huge wondering eyes as if to ask what someone of his grand social standing was doing at their humble table.

Aunt Agatha sniffed the fragrant roses and momentarily closed her eyes with the luxury of it all. "Thank you so much, you darlin' man," she gushed, blushing like a schoolgirl as she rose to her feet. She pulled out the empty chair by Kathleen. "Mr. Lassiter, won't you be sittin' here?" she inquired, her welcoming voice infused with warmth. Already on the way to the kitchen, she glanced over her shoulder, "If you'll excuse me for a moment, I'll just be puttin' these lovely roses in a vase and addin' a little water."

Lassiter walked about the table and shook hands with all the men, then seated himself by Kathleen, who started offering him turkey and dressing. She kept up a steady stream of conversation, and after her sister returned and put the roses upon the table, she joined in, asking Lassiter simple but thoughtful questions. He answered them all graciously and complimented the old lady on the food, which he ate with relish. Clara and Fergus and even Brian, who seemed agog at meeting the mighty publisher of the *Telegram*, made an attempt to be friendly, but all the working men sat stoically silent, only speaking when they wanted more food.

Lassiter looked about the table, for the first time in his life feeling socially inadequate. Trying to put everyone at ease, he asked some of the boarders questions, which they answered with monosyllables or even grunts and nods. At last he settled his gaze on Molly, who he thought looked particularly delectable today in a simple cotton gown and a frilly white apron. She'd pinned her locks atop her head, but little wisps of hair curled over her brow and rosy cheeks. When he did manage to catch her wandering gaze, her eyes flashed like leaping flames.

Look at her sitting there like a statue, he told himself, noticing she scarcely touched her food. *What am I possibly going to say to her to bring her out of her snit?* he wondered thoughtfully. He held her eyes, silently begging for help, but she scowled, then turned her head to talk to one of the boarders.

Molly watched Lassiter from the corner of her eye, secret sympathy rising in her bosom for the discomfort she knew he must now be experiencing. The conversation went on in starts and fits with Kathleen and Aunt Agatha doing most of the talking, and thinking she could stand no more, Molly finally rose and announced, "Oh my, I've forgotten the cranberry sauce. I'll just be going to fetch it."

She'd just entered the kitchen when she heard footsteps and turned about to find Kathleen approaching her with large eyes. Feeling cross and irritable, Molly faced her squarely. "Why did you invite that man here, today of all days?" she asked in a frankly disapproving tone.

Her mother clasped her shoulders and raised her brows. "Aggie said I could, in appreciation for him bringing me to America."

Molly spread her hands in frustration. "But can't you see how ill at ease he is? If you hadn't asked him, he'd probably be eating dinner with Daisy Fellows and her rich family."

236

"I don't know," Kathleen replied, a thoughtful expression settling on her features. "I've found that the rich are often left out on holidays. The man is probably lonely."

"*Lonely indeed.* Why he could afford the finest dinner in town."

"But he's eating the finest dinner in town right now," Kathleen replied in a quiet, sensible tone. "You know there's no better cook than Aggie."

Molly was stunned into silence by the truth of the statement.

"I'm surprised you're treating him so coldly," Kathleen continued, her usually gentle tone hardening a bit. "It isn't like you at all."

Molly snatched up a bowl of cranberry sauce. "I know you're trying to promote a romance between us, Mam, but I won't cooperate. I've told you I have no romantic interest in him."

"Then just treat him as a welcome guest," her mother pleaded, her voice rising in entreaty. "Talk to him a bit. After all, the man is trying so hard to be sociable."

Molly hung her head, realizing that she had indeed forgotten her manners and her surly attitude was ruining the day for everyone, especially her mother. She looked at Kathleen, and somewhat embarrassed, responded with a smile. "All right," she agreed with a mild sense of regret. "I suppose I am being a little inconsiderate."

"That's my girl," her mother warmly returned, fondly caressing her arm. "Let's go back with the rest."

In the dining room, Lassiter was still struggling, and Molly now helped him out, asking him questions about the *Telegram*. To her great surprise, she noticed he'd gone ahead with his Christmas drive, which the paper was now publicizing, and she quizzed him about this, grudgingly admitting to herself that she'd misjudged him about the project. Fergus, with whom she'd long ago mended her fences, threw out some intelligent questions, and with Brian's bright chatter, the conversation was soon going much better.

After everyone had finished the meal and coffee was served, Lassiter reached into his vest, took out his cigars, and passed them to the other men at the table, who immediately warmed to the gesture, and began smoking and talking, asking him questions about his business.

While the men were enjoying their coffee and cigars, Molly rose to clear the table, and after she'd been in the kitchen a few minutes, she turned with a start to see Lassiter smiling down at her.

He held up a spread hand in a gesture of peace. "I know you're suprised to see me here today, but thanks for saving my life in there."

Molly faced the sink, heaping with dirty dishes. "Don't think I've forgiven you. It's nothing I wouldn't have done for any of my mother's guests."

He turned her about, regarding her gently. "Molly, I need you back at the *Telegram*. I'm not ashamed to say I need you desperately." His mouth tightened in a grim line. "I'm sure you know I'm about to lose the paper. If you'll come back and write for me, I swear on all I hold dear that I'll make sure our association is strictly professional."

She cocked a challenging brow. "Strictly professional? Does that mean you won't try to take me to bed?"

He had the grace to look abashed. "Yes, that's what it means. I won't even touch you." His eyes shone with sincerity. "And I'll pay you double whatever old man Babbage is paying you now."

"You *must* be desperate," she sniffed, irritated with his calm affability. "I'm surprised you can afford it."

He brushed a wispy curl from her cheek. "As I see it, it will be money well spent. Think of all the good you could do with that money—all the people you could help."

Molly had to silently agree with him, for it seemed everyone in the boardinghouse was struggling to keep body and soul together. Then she remembered how Tom had warned her that Lassiter would stop at nothing to get her back. Well, evidently he was right.

She turned to the counter and started scraping plates and throwing flatware in a pan. "How can I trust you?" she asked, eyeing his expectant face over her shoulder. "You once told me you were going to break your engagement with Daisy, and I'll bet you haven't."

He maintained a pleasant attitude, but his tone was now fraught with tension. "No, actually I haven't, but that's simply because she's presently away with her family at their estate in the Hamptons."

Molly poured a pan of soapy water over the flatware. "You could have done it before she left, if you'd wanted, she continued, annoyance spilling over into her voice."

Lassiter moved behind her. "No, not really. At any rate, I've told you before, our engagement is just a technicality. She means nothing to me and I can break off with her anytime."

239

Molly felt his fingers at her waist as he turned her about. His face alive with emotion, he tried to take her in his arms, but she pushed at his chest with her wet hands. "I thought you weren't going to touch me," she exclaimed in a breathless voice as she struggled away.

He stepped back, his eyes full of regret. "I'm sorry. It's just that you look so beautiful with the light catching your hair."

"I suppose you're going to tell me I'm more beautiful standing here in my stained apron than Daisy in all her furs and jewels," she challenged, setting her brows in a straight line.

He smiled tenderly. "Yes, far more beautiful."

Smooth words, thought Molly, smooth words easily said to wear down her already crumbling defenses. He was trying to bend her to his will yet again, and she must guard her heart diligently. How she longed for another taste of honey, but she wouldn't lick it from the briars!

Seized with a fresh rush of anger, she made a sudden heart-pounding decision. "I'm afraid I'll have to decline your offer of employment, Mr. Lassiter, for I already have other plans," she declared, her voice bold with defiance.

Surprise registered in his eyes. "Other plans?"

"Yes," she answered, standing as tall as possible, "I'm going to accept Tom Perkins's proposal of marriage."

Lassiter stared at her, his face stamped with shocked disbelief. He flushed and a small vein bulged at his temple. "Marry Tom Perkins?" he said, his eyes hard with distaste. "But whatever for?"

"I'm going to marry him because he's a good, honest man—not like some I know. He's hardworking, has no bad habits, he keeps his promises, a-and and he's in love with me."

Lassiter met her angry gaze, his sense of loss so acute, he could feel it aching like a pain about his heart. Yes, he wanted her to write features for him again, but more important, he simply wanted her back in his life again. A leaden feeling almost cut off his breath; then he told himself that perhaps he could change her mind before she did something she'd regret all of her life.

He pulled his brows together and clasped her shoulders. "I know how angry you must be, but don't marry Tom because you're mad at me." He inched his gaze over her defiant face. "Don't you see it would be the greatest mistake you could ever make?" Increasing the pressure of his hands, he slid his fingers down her arms, wanting to hold her tight and keep her safe. "The man has been acting strangely lately," he told her, his voice raspy with emotion. "I actually fear for your safety with him."

Wanting to comfort her, he gathered her closer, heartsick at what she'd told him. "Can't you see you're worth a dozen of that dull, stammering bean counter?"

Molly pulled away. "So you say. I hardly think you're an disinterested party in this matter, and I trust my judgment over yours." She squared her shoulders. "You might as well get used to the idea. You may have helped me in times past, but you don't own me, and you can't influence me with your pretty words any longer. I'm going to marry Tom, and that's all there is to it." She tightly crossed her arms under her bosom. "That's my final word on the matter."

Rooted to the spot, Lassiter met her flashing eyes, not knowing what to say. Sometimes, he thought, bitter despair knotting in his heart, there was too much pain between a man and a woman to heal their rift—no matter how deeply they felt about each other.

In front of Delmonico's, the sound of slamming carriage doors filled Molly's ears, and there was the bustle and confusion of men taking off their top hats and the floaty sweep of chiffon as couples brushed past her and Tom, eager to enter the fashionable restaurant.

Dressed in dark evening clothes, the accountant escorted her up a flight of steps, then guided her inside the establishment's great columned vestibule where she mingled with a throng of murmuring aristocrats. In the huge dining room the sounds of muffled chatter and clicking silverware swirled about her, and with an air of excitement, she noticed dazzling chandeliers hanging overhead and heavy wine-colored drapes covering towering arched windows.

They were seated in a palm-sheltered alcove, where a flickering candelabra and fragrant roses decorated a lace-draped table. Moments later the sweet sound of violins wafted toward them from a small orchestra that had just begun to play.

From his slightly slurred speech, Molly noticed that Tom had already been drinking and he immediately ordered the best champagne the restaurant had to offer. Despite his high spirits, he seemed a bit edgy, but she dismissed it as nerves, for before they'd left the boardinghouse, she'd told him she had an answer for his important question concerning their future.

After the waiter had taken their order and left, Tom took the now familiar ring box from his vest and reached for her hand. His face alight with pleasure, he slipped the dazzling piece of jewelry on her finger. "How do you like the ring? Is it all right?"

"I've never seen anything so big and vulgar," she chuckled, twisting it on her finger. "It's gorgeous. But how did you ever afford it?"

"A man owed me a debt and I collected."

"A debt? What kind of debt?"

Tom shifted uncomfortably in his chair. "Actually, it was a gambling debt."

Surprised, Molly nervously adjusted the low-cut neckline of her silk gown. "I didn't know you gambled," she remarked," thinking the indulgence seemed out of character for his clean-cut personality.

"I like to turn a card as well as the next man," he replied defensively. He'd already drank his first glass of champagne, and reaching for the bottle nestled in a silver bucket, he quickly poured himself another.

He slid an eager gaze over Molly. "You're going to tell me yes, aren't you?" Hope suffused his countenance. "Let's get married tomorrow and head for New Orleans."

She blinked several times. "*New Orleans?* You've chosen that city for a honeymoon, then?"

He smiled, trying to cover his apparent annoyance. "No, actually I want to live there."

Molly's pulse beat erratically. Why in God's name did Tom suddenly want to move to New Orleans? Had the man lost all the good common sense she'd always given him credit for? "But you can't just leave the city on the spur of the moment," she laughed, quick apprehension darting through her veins.

243

He shrugged impatiently. "I have nothing holding me here," he casually replied, leaning back in his chair with a long sigh.

"Nothing but your job."

Tom's lips twisted cynically. "That's not much of a loss. Everyone knows the *Telegram* will fold soon anyway." He leaned forward and trailed his fingers over the back of her hand, oddly setting her nerves on edge. "What do you say," he prompted, his face full of hope once more. "I can't wait another minute to hear your answer. Will you marry me?"

Molly's heart thumped with unease. Where was the dependable accountant she thought she knew so well? She frowned as he poured himself another glass of champagne and quickly downed it. She'd never heard him talk so rashly, and deep in her bones, she sensed it had nothing to do with the vast amount of alcohol now flowing through his bloodstream. "I'm not sure yet," she hedged, all her instincts telling her she needed to consider the matter again. "I have obligations here— my job, my mother—"

Sudden contempt flashed in his eyes. "Your mother is a grown woman. You can't be expected to take care of her for the rest of her life, you know."

A chill raced down Molly's arms. With a prick of alarm, she suddenly realized that Tom wasn't the fine, mild-mannered man she'd thought, but a genius at dissembling his feelings and motives. Tonight the liquor had oiled his tongue, and at long last, he'd finally let down the mask he so carefully presented to the world. Gone was the thoughtful, hardworking accountant, and in his place was a selfish, uncaring adventurer bound on having his way, regardless of who he hurt.

Molly slipped off the ring and laid it on the table, thanking God above that she'd seen this side of the man before she told him she'd marry him. She pulled in a calming breath and called on all her courage. "I'm sorry, Tom," she answered in a soft, wavering voice. "I can't marry you. I-I've decided it would be a mistake."

His face went rock-hard as he picked up the ring, put it back in its box, and shoved in into his vest. Every bit of his amiability and good nature had evaporated, and sick with the shock of her unnerving discovery, Molly could tell he was raging mad.

She clutched her reticule and stood, fresh anxiety swirling in the pit of her stomach. "I want to go home now. Please take me back to the boardinghouse."

Tom's eyes dazzled with anger. "I never expected you to act so ungrateful," he stated in a rough, accusing tone that carried to the surrounding tables.

Biting her bottom lip, Molly gazed about with embarrassment, noticing a few of the diners had stopped eating and were now peering through the palms at them with keen interest.

Her heart sank deeply. "Please, Tom," she whispered, sudden tears gathering in her eyes, "I want to go. Take me home—take me home *now.*"

Molly inched back in the carriage seat, watching moonlight gleam over Tom's angry face as he wheeled away from Delmonico's. To her humiliation, she'd been forced to leave the dining room before he finally came stalking after her, and roughly taking her arm, escorted her from the restaurant, drawing shocked stares and murmurs of concern.

Now their carriage blended into the noisy sea of traffic flowing up a main artery lined with ladies' shops and small business with striped awnings. For fifteen minutes, they retraced the route they'd taken to the restaurant, but Molly remained withdrawn and perfectly silent, thinking there was no way she could force herself to make hypocritical small talk after the humiliating scene she'd just endured in Delmonico's.

Suddenly Tom turned onto a shadowy side street. After a short while, the businesses began to peter out and there were rows of large shabby buildings that appeared to be nothing more than old warehouses with boarded windows. "Why have you taken this street?" she asked sharply, becoming more nervous with every passing second.

He stared rigidly ahead, foregoing the courtesy of looking at her. "There's more than one way back to the boardinghouse, you know."

"*No,* go back the way we came," she ordered, her voice rising with urgency.

Ignoring her, he slowed the carriage, then pulled over and stopped in front of a dilapidated warehouse that seemed totally deserted.

Warning bells clanged in Molly's head as she remembered Lassiter's statement that Tom had been acting strange lately. She scanned the deteriorated building, seized with sick alarm. "Why have you stopped here?" she demanded, her breath catching in her throat.

Not answering, Tom regarded her, his hard eyes gleaming in the moonlight. "Now don't start playing the innocent with me. It simply won't work," he answered, his harsh words dripping with ridicule. "I saw you one morning at the *Telegram* before the Coney

Island story came out, and you had a glow on your face like a street lamp. It doesn't take a genius to know what happened. You and Lassiter slept together, didn't you?"

She gave a sharp gasp. "That's none of your—"

"Don't try to explain yourself," he rudely cut her off. "I know you're a plucked rose, and I know who did the plucking," he replied with a depreciating laugh. "You little fool. Did you actually think he'd marry you?"

Molly's heart gave a great lurch. Clutching at her wrap, she tried to get out of the carriage, but Tom forced her back against the seat. He began to stroke her arm, his eyes bright with a lascivious light. With a low chuckle, he caressed her cheek, then let his fingers play over her breast. She cried out and tried to pull away, but he clenched her arm, his fingers biting into it. "What's the matter? Are you afraid? Just relax. I assure you there are a host of women in this city who will attest to my skills as a lover."

A wild pulse pounded at the base of Molly's throat. Tom Perkins was mad, absolutely mad, she thought, shocked tears gathering in her eyes.

"You should be honored," he hissed, fondling her breast. She tried to push his hand away, but he grabbed her wrist. "I courted you, bought you a ring, and even offered you marriage." His face twisted with contempt. "Well, your attitude this evening made me decide that marriage isn't necessary. I'll simply take what I want and be on my way to New Orleans."

She raised her hand to slap him, but he forced it to her side. With his other hand he continued to paw at her breast. Summoning a strength she didn't know she possessed, she tried to rise and leap from the carriage, but Tom caught her and slammed her against the seat.

"You led me on, so you deserve everything you're going to get" he snarled, before brutally slanting his mouth over hers. He kissed her forcefully, bruising her lips. Trembling with revulsion, she beat her balled fists against his shoulders and tried to kick at his legs. As she struggled against him, she felt something hard under his vest and with a fresh burst of alarm, guessed it was a gun. Her heart pounded with wild fear.

In the back of her mind, she heard the rattle of a carriage, then from the corner of her eye, noticed it had rolled to a stop behind them. There were running footsteps, and before she knew what was happening, a large man had pulled Tom from the carriage and thrown him on the pavement. Scooting to the edge of the seat, she quickly scanned the figure, finally able to make out his face in the shadows. "*Lassiter*," she sobbed, with a rush of relief that left her weak.

Tom tried to get up, but Lassiter struck his jaw and the man crumbled in a twisted heap by the carriage wheel, blood trickling from the corner of his mouth.

Strong hands pulled Molly from the seat, and in a matter of seconds, Lassiter had lifted her in his arms and carried her to safety.

He widened his eyes, which dazzled with alarm. "Are you all right?" he asked, quickly settling her in his own carriage.

Trembling, she leaned back against the seat. "Yes, I'm all right now that you're here," she told him in a tear-smothered voice. She let her gaze play over him, wondering how he could have suddenly appeared out of the darkness. "B-But I don't understand," she stammered, still tightly clutching his shoulders. "Where did you come from? Why were you following us?"

He wiped a tear from her cheek. "I came to the boardinghouse so we could talk, and found Perkins had taken you to Delmonico's. I arrived there just as you two were leaving."

Hearing a groan, she swung her gaze back to Tom, and to her horror, saw he was grasping a carriage wheel, pulling himself to his feet. "H-He's getting up," she cried, noticing one of his hands fumbling under his dinner jacket.

Lassiter had just started for Perkins when the man produced a pistol. Tousled hair hung over Tom's panicked eyes as he leveled the weapon at Lassiter's heart. "Take another step toward me, and I'll kill you—so help me I will!" he growled, his breathless words slurred with desperation.

Faced with the pistol, Lassiter paused for a moment, and taking advantage of the situation, Perkins scrambled into his carriage. Slapping the reins against his horse's rump, he started down the street, then careened away into the darkness.

Lassiter hurried back to his carriage, and climbing aboard, took Molly in his arms where she sobbed against his chest. "There now, just calm down," he murmured in a reassuring voice, gently caressing her shoulders and running his hands over her trembling arms. He clutched her against him, whispering words of comfort as if he were speaking to a frightened child. "Hush, everything will be all right now," he promised in a tender, consoling tone.

She lifted her head, meeting his concerned gaze. "Where do you think he's gone?" she choked out, trying to pull her scattered thoughts together.

Lassiter frowned, his eyes stony under drawn brows.

"Only the Lord knows," he answered, holding her a little tighter. "After what happened, he surely won't return to his apartment. He was probably carrying a great deal of money and will hide out for a few days before he tries to leave the city."

Molly snuggled against him, shuddering inwardly at the memory of the incident she'd just endured. "Please, take me home," she whispered, swallowing back the last of her tears.

He held her slight frame against him and let her take her comfort until she issued a long, quivering sigh; then he eased her away and ran a finger over her cheek, wiping away a tear. "Yes, of course, my darling. But first we must alert the police."

Pulling in a steadying breath, she nodded and he nestled her against him and kissed her forehead, comforting her until she'd stopped shaking.

Chapter Fourteen

The moon had risen high in the sky by the time Lassiter and Molly left the police station and drove toward the boardinghouse, the chilly autumn air touching their faces. Exhausted and still reeling from her unbelievable experience with Tom Perkins, Molly mulled over all that had happened during the last hour.

A walrus-mustached detective had informed her that the railroad stations as well as Perkin's apartment would be watched, and with a bit of luck, he'd be apprehended before he left the city. She'd blushed as she described the details of the attack, but seemingly reading her mind, the detective had told her, "Have no fear, Miss Kilmartin. We'll keep your name out of this, but as soon as we nab Perkins, he'll be jailed for assaulting you."

Now as Lassiter turned a corner, only a mile or so from their destination, all was quiet except for the sounds of the clopping horse and the whir of the spinning carriage wheels. Trying to sort out everything in her mind, Molly slowly stole a glance at his shadowed face. "I can't believe tonight even happened," she remarked in a rough, shaking voice. "It all seems like a bad dream. Who would have thought solid, predictable Tom Perkins was a gambler. Did you have any idea what was going on?"

Lassiter let his gaze wash over her, thinking every line of her lovely body bespoke utter weariness. "No, I didn't," he replied with a decisive shake of his head, "but I agree with the detective. He's probably been pilfering money from the *Telegram* for some time now. I'd just started going over his account books," he added, remembering how shocked Perkins had been when he was forced to relinquish the records, "and found some puzzling entries."

Anger surged through him as he recalled the sight of the man assaulting Molly and he had a great desire to strangle him with his bare hands. "I think he sensed everything was coming unraveled and decided to collect you before he left the city," he explained as he clasped her cold hand in a gesture of comfort.

She ran an incredulous gaze over him. "I still can't believe it. He had me totally fooled. How clever he was."

Lassiter let the reins slip through his hands. "Most scoundrels are," he answered, thinking he'd take the *Telegram*'s account books to the police station the first thing in the morning.

Molly sat back and gave a thoughtful sigh. "Do you think they'll catch him?"

Lassiter considered her question, feeling deeply betrayed because he'd trusted the accountant so implicitly. "Yes, I do," he finally answered, wishing he'd become suspicious of Perkins much sooner, "and when they do, I hope they throw the book at him."

Faced with the horrible truth about Tom, Molly realized he'd tried to poison her mind against Lassiter, and with a twinge of guilt, decided Lassiter's motives for bringing her mother from Ireland might have been more noble than she'd first thought.

She gazed at his shadowy features. "Thank you," she whispered, gently touching his arm. "Thank you for tonight and thank you for bringing Mam from Ireland."

He regarded her with a smile, his face soft with appreciation.

They turned a corner and the carriage slowly rocked to a halt before the boardinghouse, where a welcoming light glowed from the parlor window. To Molly the flickering light suggested a protecting sanctuary, and she told herself the old house had never looked more appealing.

Lassiter wrapped his reins about the brake lever, and regarding her with an expression of deep relief, expelled a long breath. "Thank God you're safe," he murmured with a quiet smile.

He held her captive with his sapphire-blue eyes that glowed with desire, and a rush of sweet tingles tumbled down her spine. When he tenderly brushed back a lock of her tangled hair, the look in his eyes told her he was going to kiss her. She told herself that was the last thing she wanted, but in the privacy of her heart, she wondered how she could resist.

A look passed between them that shook her deeply. Then he slid his arm around her waist and drew her to him, his touch persistent yet incredibly tender, and with a thudding heart, she felt herself surrendering.

He skimmed his lips over her cheeks and feathered them over each eyelid before his raven head tilted forward and he pressed her against his hard, muscled form. She silently cursed the power he seemed to have over her and suddenly blurted out, "Lassiter, please don't, I—"

His lips firmly covered hers, silencing her attempted protest, and his probing tongue darted into her mouth, exploring its moist recesses. Sweet, sweeping feelings tangled up inside of her, leaving her limp in his embrace. His body was warm and strong and the rhythm of his heart did impossible things to her self-control. His touch set off a fiery chain reaction within her, and ever so slowly, her arms crept about his broad shoulders.

Moving his lips from hers, he pressed hot kisses over her cheeks, her closed lids, and the throbbing pulse at the base of her throat. "I've missed you so much," he whispered against her neck as he swept his hand down her back. Excitement sang through her, and with a shiver of delight, she felt her nipples harden and swell against her bodice. "My little love," he whispered in a caressing drawl as he pulled her closer. He kissed her again, stifling a warning voice that told her she should slip from his arms. Clutching his shoulders, she quivered at the power and tenderness of the kiss as his lips ignited banked fires buried deep in her heart.

His warm breath was upon her cheek and she could feel his pounding heart. Raising his head, he swept back her hair and gazed tenderly at her. His eyes were shining with passion and there was a constriction in her throat that forestalled another protest from her lips. He kissed her deeply and at that moment, Molly's whole body took on a warm, sensual glow that left her weak and trembling.

How she wanted him to keep holding her in his arms. How she wanted to completely forgive him. Still, a nagging question burned in her heart—one that her pride forced her to ask. Grasping his biceps, she pushed herself away and looked into his questioning eyes. "There's something I must ask you," she murmured, her voice soft and shaky.

He traced his finger over the curve of her cheek. "Yes, go ahead. What is it?"

Her throat went dry, then in a tremulous breath she said, "Have you been able to get your loan—your loan to save the *Telegram*?"

He widened his eyes. "Who told you about that—Perkins?"

"It doesn't matter," she whispered, mentally bracing herself for his response. "Just answer my question."

She could see him struggling for words. "I can't lie to you," he finally replied, his face lined with deep despair. "No—I haven't."

The spark of hope Molly had so carefully kindled flickered out, leaving her desolate. Sadness sweeping over her, she told herself his paper meant more to him than anything or anyone, and he was on the verge of losing it. Yes, he might have deep feelings for her, feelings that went beyond simple physical attraction, but in the end, she knew he'd marry Daisy so he could save his beloved *Telegram*. It was as simple as that.

"I have to go now," she said, trying to untangle herself from his arms."

"But why?"

A flash of overwhelming pain stabbed at her heart. "You heard the detective," she replied bitterly. "You'll never get that money back that Tom gambled away. It's time to cash in your insurance policy. It's time for you to marry Daisy."

He held her tighter. "No, you don't understand."

Before he could say another word, she tore herself from his arms, and twisting about, scrambled from the carriage, her silken gown flashing in the shadows. She lifted her skirt and ran toward the boardinghouse, hot tears streaming from her eyes.

Two weeks later, December's first snow fluttered down from the leaden sky, covering the great city with silvery patches of white. Molly buried herself in her work, trying to numb the pain that tore at her heart every time she thought of Lassiter marrying Daisy, which she was sure would happen very soon now.

A few days after Tom Perkins had assaulted her, a police officer came to the boardinghouse, took her onto the front porch, and told her the accountant had been apprehended. The police had been watching the railroad station, and on a hunch a man had been posted at Tiffany's. It was there he'd been nabbed, trying to return the costly engagement ring.

The officer had revealed that Tom had a surprisingly checkered career, and at long last Molly finally understood why he'd been so close-mouthed about his past. True to his word, the detective who'd originally interviewed her hadn't released the details of the assault to the press and she'd been spared an experience she feared might prove embarrassing to her employer as well as her family.

A few mornings after the officer had visited the boardinghouse, Tom's photo in the *Metropolitan* caught her eye. Above it blazed the headline, ACCOUNTANT CHARGED IN EMBEZZLEMENT CASE. Her eyes glued to the page, she devoured the story and learned Tom was accused of embezzling more than twenty thousand dollars from the *Telegram* over a period of a year and a half. Lassiter would be called as a witness when the trial, scheduled for late spring, took place.

This sickening news Molly couldn't keep from her mother or Aunt Agatha, and she heaved a sigh of relief that she hadn't hinted to either of them that she'd ever considered marrying the accountant. She knew they'd discuss the newspaper article for days and be in a state of deep distress that the "nice Mr. Perkins" they knew was really a sly, hard-hearted criminal. Molly once again experienced a nauseating sense of regret at the thought of how he'd so cleverly deceived everyone, including her. Truly, it was almost too much to believe.

As the days slipped past, the shock about Tom began to fade a bit, and everyone in the boardinghouse began looking forward to Christmas. Kathleen sat up late at night to knit a scarf and pair of mittens for Brian, who she became more attached to with each passing day. Determined that their first Christmas in New York would be memorable, Molly bought a small tree and placed it before the parlor window where she decorated it with red bows and small white candles.

One bitterly cold night just as she and Kathleen had started to drape the tree with popcorn chains, a knock resounded from the foyer. Molly opened the front door, then drew in her breath at the sight of Brian standing there bundled in damp rags and shaking with cold. "Brian, merciful heavens, come in. You look half frozen."

His eyes lowered, the boy stamped his boots, then awkwardly entered the boardinghouse, his whole manner apologetic. Snow clung to his matted hair, and swiftly scanning him, Molly noticed his lips trembled and his hands were chapped and red with cold.

Kathleen walked into the foyer, her mouth forming a horrified *O* at the sight before her. "What in God's name are you doing out on a desperate night like this?" she murmured, running her eyes over the child in alarm.

The silence lengthened between them as the boy shifted his gaze to the side, then slowly back at her, and in a small, frighted voice answered, "I-I didn't have anyplace else to go." He swallowed hard. "I came home and my stepfather was—was gone."

Kathleen put a hand to her throat. "Jesus, Mary, and Joseph," she whispered in a stricken tone.

Molly, realizing what the admission had cost the boy, awkwardly cleared her throat, then put her arm about his shoulders and drew him close. "Come into the parlor where it's warmer," she suggested, escorting him across the room to the blazing fire. Filled with disturbing thoughts, she brushed clotted snow from his wet hair, then smoothed it back, studying his lackluster eyes. "Why, you're near frozen," she exclaimed, rubbing his hands between hers and manipulating his stiff fingers. "You need to thaw out."

Catching up with them, Kathleen snatched a knitted throw from the sofa and draped it about the boy's thin shoulders. Her eyes dark with distress, she cupped his face in her hands. "Go on, dear, and tell us what happened when you got home today," she urged, her worried gaze tenderly playing over his face.

Brian regarded her with anguished eyes. "When I got home, the apartment was locked tight," he confessed, his face clouded with uneasiness. "I talked to the landlord and he said my stepdad had"—he paused, gathering strength to force out his next words— "had left for good."

"Saints above," Molly exclaimed, sinking to the floor and wrapping her arm about his waist. "Didn't he leave you a word about where he was going?" she asked, studying his pale, drawn face.

The boy coughed, and with quaking hands, pulled the throw tighter about him. "No, I reckon he didn't want me to know." He gazed at the carpet with embarrassment. "I-I don't think he'll ever come back—me bein' a burden to him and all."

Kathleen put a hand on his shoulder. "Do you have a place to stay?" she asked, blotting moisture from his face with the end of the throw.

Brian's lips trembled. "No. I walked around, tryin' to figure out what to do, and couldn't think of anythin' but comin' here," he said, managing a feeble answer. His voice drifted to an agonized whisper. "Y-You see, the landlord's rented the room to someone else. Guess he knew that I couldn't pay for it." He went into a coughing fit, gasping for breath.

Molly heard his labored breathing and traced her fingers over his clammy brow, deciding he was burning with fever. The boy started to speak, but with a look of defeat, closed his flickering eyelids and grasped a chair arm.

Seeing his legs buckle, she put her arms about him to break his fall. "He's going to faint," she said as she positioned him in her arms. "I'll bet he hasn't eaten in days." Sick with worry, she rose, lifting his thin, light body with her. "I'm taking him upstairs," she told her mother, who stared at her with a stricken, wide-eyed expression. "Quick, fetch Aunt Agatha."

Molly carried Brian upstairs, and maneuvering him through her half-open door, gently laid him on the bed she shared with her mother. Light from a softly glowing lamp spilled over his pale face and his chest heaved as he fell into another coughing fit.

There were hurried footsteps on the creaking stairs, and seconds later, Kathleen and Aunt Agatha entered the little dormer room, their large, concerned eyes immediately focusing on the bed.

Seemingly in a state of shock, Aunt Agatha stood there still puffing from her swift climb to the third floor.

"The boy is burning up with fever," Molly explained in an urgent tone. "He's very sick and needs a place to stay."

Kathleen looked at her sister with pleading eyes. "He has no other place to go, Aggie," she said, her voice charged with emotion. "He can sleep on a cot in the hall and I'll look after him."

Molly studied her aunt's troubled face, knowing she already shouldered more burdens than any one woman should have to bear. "His stepfather left the city without a word," she quietly informed her, anger knotting inside of her at the very thought of it. "He's on his own now. *We're all he has.*"

Kathleen clutched her sister's fleshy arm. "Oh, let him stay, Aggie," she begged, kneeling by the bed. She glanced up, her eyes full of entreaty. "We can't put him out in freezing weather like this. See how thin he is?" she said, running her hand over his slim, stick-like arm. "If we put him out, he'll take pneumonia and die."

"But the expense of a doctor—" her sister began in a sorrowful voice.

Kathleen traced her fingers over the boy's gaunt face. "There'll be no need for a doctor. He just needs love and care and some of your good cooking, and he'll be well in no time." She regarded her sister, her eyes blazing. "Please, Aggie, we have to take him in!"

Aunt Agatha looked on the verge of making a decision, and Molly, who stood on the other side of the bed, managed to catch her eyes and nod, silently suggesting she agree to the proposal. "Yes, let him stay. I'll pay for his board somehow. I promise I will." She realized Brian would now be a permanent member of the household, for in her mother's mind, he'd replaced Cossi, and she would never let him go. At the same time, she held her tongue, knowing this was the worst possible time to reveal the news.

Aunt Agatha's face became a welter of conflicting emotions. But at last the old woman sighed and wagged her head. "Guess I know when I'm outnumbered," she announced, her once stern face softening in the glow of the lamp. "I reckon the little beggar can stay—at least till he gets well," she conceded in a gruff voice, trying to hide her own tender emotions.

Three days later, on a cold December morning, Molly sat at the kitchen table lingering over her last cup of tea as she searched the paper for Lassiter's wedding announcement. Strange, she couldn't find it, she thought, knowing Daisy Fellows would certainly have insisted on a large article and several photos on the society pages.

All the other boarders, except her mother, who was with Brian, had left the dwelling and the kitchen table was piled with clean-smelling clothes, now being folded by Aunt Agatha, who smiled pleasantly as she worked.

"You're in high spirits today," Molly commented, wondering why she was so gloriously happy on such a raw winter day.

The old lady balled a pair of Shamus's socks together and gaily tossed them into a basket of garments she was going to take upstairs. "Yes, I am," she replied with an air of bright cheerfulness. "Don't know when I've ever been so happy."

Molly decided her aunt had been acting strangely since she'd first seen her this morning, in turns preoccupied, then laughing outrageously, as lighthearted as if she might be tipsy on her own elderberry wine. What was making her act like a girl of sixteen; what was wrong with her? Molly wondered, watching her lovingly smooth out Shamus's striped nightshirt before she carefully laid it atop the heaping basket of clothes.

Her face aglow, Aunt Agatha picked up the basket and balanced it on her broad hip. "I'll just be goin' up and takin' these clothes to Shamus's room, now," she announced, leaving the kitchen with a sprightly step.

Molly put down her cup, thinking she'd best leave for work, when she spied a pair of socks that had tumbled from the table. Knowing her aunt had missed them, she snatched up the socks and hurried up the stairs to Shamus's room, where the door was half open. Aunt Agatha stood in front of an open bureau drawer, and hearing her niece, whirled about, an embarrassed expression on her face.

"And what might you be doing?" Molly asked in a light tone, noticing she was trying to hide something she held in her hand. "You look like the cat who just ate the canary."

The old lady's hand flew to her heaving bosom. "W-Well, I just thought—I-It's just that—" she stuttered, a panicked light in her widened eyes.

"*Yes?*" Molly prompted, thinking she'd soon be finding out why her aunt was so happy this morning.

Aunt Agatha heaved a guilty sigh. "Well I might as well tell you," she answered, opening her clenched hand to reveal two lottery tickets. "The news is just too good to keep." She studied her niece with keen speculation. "I *can* trust you to keep a secret, can't I?"

More curious than ever, Molly walked to her side, "Yes, of course," she laughed, clasping her aunt's soft shoulder.

Sonya Birmingham

Aunt Agatha's face lit with delight. "Well, I checked the newspaper this mornin', a-and I won the lottery—a thousand dollars no less!"

"*You didn't!*"

The old lady's eyes glinted with mirth. "Yes, can you imagine, after buyin' tickets all these years, I finally won!" A satisfied smile graced her lips. "Did you notice Shamus didn't have time to check his lottery number in the paper this mornin'?"

"So that's why you rushed him away so quickly," Molly replied, becoming infected with her aunt's joyous enthusiasm.

"Yes, that's right," the old lady answered, actually trembling with excitement. "Now I'm goin' to exchange my ticket for his."

"*Oh, I see.* You clever puss. But do you think the trick will work?"

A light shone in Aunt Agatha's eyes. "Yes, I'm sure it will." She held up both of the tickets for her niece to inspect. "See, both of the numbers begin with nine. He'll be rememberin' his ticket started with nine, but I'll wager you, he'll never be able to remember the rest of the numbers."

Molly caressed her aunt's plump arm, impressed with her daring plan, but at the same time a little startled with her boldness. "Don't you have any qualms about doing this?" she laughed, amazed at what she was witnessing. "It'll change his life forever."

The old lady arched her brows. "And mine, too, if I'm lucky," she chuckled mischievously. Joy danced in her eyes. "The switch may not be honest, but it's just. The man has been enjoyin' my pamperin' for years now, and the old fool needs someone to take care of him anyway. Without me he'd be lost."

Molly had to agree. It was apparent to anyone with eyes that Shamus did indeed love his Aggie, he just needed a gentle shove over the dreaded threshold of matrimony. For years he'd promised marriage, but never thought he'd have to make good on his vow. Now judgment day had come in the form of a winning lottery ticket, and Aunt Agatha's long-awaited ship had finally docked.

The old woman gazed at her with pleading eyes. "You won't tell, will you, darlin'?"

Molly hugged her tightly, then clasping her aunt's hands, pushed her to arm's length. Mimicking Shamus's thick brogue, she looked her full in the face and answered, "Of course I won't tell. I promise on me sainted mother's grave—may she rest in peace!"

That evening everyone had left the dinner table but Shamus, who lingered to smoke his pipe, and Fergus and Clara, who sat holding hands and looking into each other's eyes, scarcely cognizant of what was going on about them. Flushed with excitement, Aunt Agatha cleared dishes from one side of the table, while Molly, a tray in her hand, removed things from the other.

She walked behind Shamus, and after she'd placed his dishes on the tray, casually inquired, "Have you checked your lottery ticket today?"

He looked up and grinned, reminding her of a good-natured gnome wearing a smoke halo. "Blessed if I haven't. Aggie rushed me away so fast this mornin' I haven't had a chance."

She handed him a copy of the *Telegram,* and he quickly scanned the first page where the winning numbers appeared each morning. His bushy eyebrows shot up in surprise. "Jesus, Mary, and Joseph, it begins with a nine," he whispered in an incredulous tone. He stood and headed toward the dining-room door, the fluttering paper in his hand. "I'll just be goin' upstairs for a bit."

As soon as he'd left, Aunt Agatha sent Molly a sly glance and Molly had to bite her lip to keep from laughing.

Moments later thundering footsteps resounded from the stairs and Shamus half slid into the room, his face stamped with an expression of shocked joy and disbelief. He held up a lottery ticket with a trembling hand and swallowed hard, his Adam's apple bobbing in his scrawny neck. "I've won," he croaked, half dancing across the room. He yelped with excitement and threw his stubby arms into the air. "Glory be to God. I've won the lottery. I finally won!"

Fergus, shaken from his romantic trance, stood, his eyes shining with disbelief. "You've won? *How much?*" he inquired, hurrying to Shamus's side to inspect the ticket.

The little man tilted his head backward and closed his eyes, his face bathed in ecstasy. "A thousand dollars," he answered, kissing the ticket, then pressing it to his heart. "I've never had that much money at one time in all me life."

Clara rose, and her face pale with shock, hugged him in congratulation. "Oh, that's wonderful. I've never known anyone who's actually won!"

Aunt Agatha laughed and Molly joined in, only to see Kathleen and Brian, who'd apparently heard the merriment, come into the room with wondering eyes. One by one, all the boarders drifted in, questioning smiles on their faces.

Pandemonium ensued as the men laughed and shook Shamus's hand while he strutted about like a proud bandy-legged rooster, jabbing his finger at the winning lottery number and taking little jig steps across the dining-room floor.

Dressed in an oversized nightshirt and robe, Brian caught Shamus's gnarled hand and smiled up at him. "This calls for a toast for sure, don't it? Ain't you gonna give us one?" he chimed in, his eyes glistening mischievously.

"Right you are, lad!" Shamus replied, turning to the sideboard to fill a glass with wine. Looking dazed, he held the glass in front of him, then ruffled Brian's curly hair. "But God help me, I'm too stunned now to remember one!"

"Then just make up one," Brian laughed, playfully arching his brows.

"All right, lad, you asked for it." Shamus smoothed down his mustache and blinked rapidly as if he were trying to put some words together. "Very well, here we go, then: May those that love us, love us; and those that don't love us, may God turn their hearts,"—he paused, scratching his head—"and if he can't turn their hearts," he went on, a relieved expression claiming his face, "may he turn their ankles so we'll know them by their limpin'!"

Everyone burst out laughing again, and pushing up his sliding spectacles, Fergus slapped Shamus on the back. "Saints preserve us, how are you going to spend a thousand dollars, old man?"

Shamus rolled his eyes heavenward. "A new suit, a pair of shoes, and a box of cigars," he answered, circling his gaze back to the young man, "and I might even look at a carriage!"

When the laughter had died down, Aggie cleared her throat and crossed her arms. "Don't you think you should be consultin' your future wife about such extravagance?"

Every head in the room swiveled toward Shamus, who looked as if he'd just been poleaxed.

The old lady tapped her foot. "You wouldn't be tryin' to weasel out of your vow, would you now, darlin'?" she asked with a suspicious frown.

Shamus, who'd gone milk-white, put out his trembling hand. "N-No, no, Jelly Bean," he croaked, scarcely able to speak. "I promised on me sainted mother's grave, didn't I?"

Aunt Agatha stared into the distance, a soft smile on her face. "I think a spring weddin' would be nice. We'll be married at Saint Anne's when the first lilacs bloom." She glanced at her sister and smiled. "Kathleen can be my maid of honor."

Fergus stood and took Clara's slender hand. "This may not be the time, b-but I graduate this spring, and you know how I feel about you. Would you care to make it a double wedding?" He scanned the gathered boarders, then circled his gaze back to her face, which was now bathed in glowing delight. "You wouldn't turn me down in front of all my friends, would you now?"

Clara threw her arms about him, shiny tears glistening in her eyes. "No, of course not. I thought you'd never ask. A spring wedding would be lovely!" She skimmed a questioning gaze over Shamus. "Don't you think so, Shamus?"

The little man flopped into his chair and sat there like a statue, too stunned to answer.

Aunt Agatha poured him another glass of wine and placed it in front of him. "You look terrible. Drink this, old man."

Shamus downed the wine in two gulps, then studied her with teasing eyes and kissed her plump, work-worn hand. "Saints preserve me, woman. There you go—already tryin' to boss me about!"

Molly, standing at the door, watched her aunt kiss his cheek, provoking raucous laughter among the boarders. She was blissfully happy for the pair as well as for Fergus and Clara, who stood gazing at each other with adoring eyes.

Then without warning, a sudden feeling of sadness and loss settled over her, chilling her spirit like the coldest winter's day. Would she and Lassiter ever be blessed with the same happiness? she wondered, blinking back quick tears. She prayed it might be so with all her heart, but as things now stood, she had to admit their future looked like a dark horizon, covered with angry storm clouds.

Chapter Fifteen

The next morning Molly softy closed Mr. Babbage's office door behind her, wondering why he'd sent for her.

"Oh, Molly, there you are," he said, his voice warm with welcome as he gazed at her from behind his cluttered desk. "Come right in."

Experiencing a flicker of apprehension, she walked across the room, and claiming a comfortable leather chair, sat down to face him. "Your secretary said you wanted to speak to me," she began tentatively. "I was wondering—"

"Yes, yes," he interrupted her, leaning forward to take off his wire-rimmed spectacles and put them aside. A flash of excitement crossed his face. "I want to talk to you about making a trip to San Francisco," he announced with a little laugh.

"Y-You want to do what?" she stammered in a bewildered voice, thinking she hadn't heard him correctly.

Mr. Babbage stood, his eyes glistening with a steely sense of purpose. "I want you to take a series of express trains to San Francisco," he explained with a benevolent smile, "then return to New York, giving me your impressions of the various states and cities along the way. I'm sure your features will enthrall your readers and we'll undoubtedly sell thousands of papers."

Jolted with the news, Molly rose and put out her spread hand. "I'm not sure I understand," she breathed, becoming increasingly uneasy at the prospect. "You have other feature writers. Why are you offering me this assignment?"

Holding her gaze like glue, Mr. Babbage rounded his desk and cleared his throat importantly. "Because everyone in New York loves your writing, that's why," he answered with a soft chuckle. His eyes sparkled. "You already have a large following that will be eager to read about your new adventure," he added, walking to a huge globe of the world and tapping his finger on the western coast of the United States.

He looked at her over his shoulder. "The *Metropolitan* will pay all of your expenses, of course, and I've made arrangements for you to travel in special Pullman Palace cars, usually rented by the richest men in America."

Stunned, she sat down again, and held his gaze. "Pullman Palace cars?" she echoed, the words stirring her interest.

"Yes, the owner of the Union Pacific was quite agreeable, for he knows your trip will focus everyone's attention on his line. Other people will be traveling on the trains of course, but private cars and personal stewards will afford you the comfort and privacy you'll need to write your features."

He moved to her chair and looked down at her. "The express trains will have commissary cars, and to expedite your trip, other slower trains will be shuttled aside." He picked up his spectacles, and hooked them about his ears, studying her intently. "You'll change trains in Chicago and Omaha, Cheyenne and Virginia City, and no doubt there will be cheering crowds in all the terminals."

Molly nervously licked her lips. "I never heard of such a thing." She let her gaze inch over him. "Where did you come up with such a wild idea?" she murmured, thinking she hadn't given him enough credit in the imagination department.

He shot her a satisfied grin. "I'm friends with the publisher of the *San Francisco Chronicle*. He's read some of your features and knows how popular you are here in New York. He thought the story would increase circulation for both of our papers, and so it shall," he explained in a buoyant mood.

Dozens of questions assailed her floundering brain. "But how would I get my articles back to you?" she asked, his idea unfolding a little too fast for her.

His passionate expression made it clear he'd thoroughly thought out the plan. "All the large train stations have telegraph offices," he answered in a reasonable tone. "When you change trains, you can send reports about your journey to me and the *Chronicle,* and we'll publish them, no doubt on the first page." He fondly patted her shoulder. "Your name will go down in the history books, my dear."

"But from what you've told me, I wouldn't have time to catch my breath. Would there be no layovers at all?"

He sat down at his desk again, favoring her with an indulgent smile. "You'll spend one night in San Francisco so the *Chronicle* can hold a reception at the Palace Hotel where you'll be staying. No doubt you'll meet some city dignitaries and the newspaper there will do a special interview to maximize the publicity of the event. After a good night's sleep you'll be leaving bright and early the next morning for the east."

He beamed, seemingly proud of his intricately engineered scheme. "When your trip is over, you'll be met by a representative of Union Pacific on the City Hall steps here in New York for a welcoming ceremony." He chuckled with relish. "It should be quite a spectacle."

Molly, bubbling over with a mixture of fear and excitement, stood, mulling over the idea. Remembering that most of the nation was now covered with a blanket of white, she guessed the weather might pose a problem. Still, when all was said and done, she was being presented with an idea that, if the editor was right, would change her life.

Mr. Babbage rose and took her shoulders. "Don't you see this could be the journalistic event of the year? No doubt other papers will pick up the story and your name will be on the lips of every reader in America."

He walked about the office rubbing his hands together. "We'll publish the idea in the Christmas Eve issue, and you can begin the journey on Christmas Day." He gave her a quick smile. "Quite a good idea, don't you think? I'm sure your feminist backing would be behind you all the way, as well as this city's large Irish population." He chuckled with satisfaction. "You're not the Angel of Murphy Street for nothing, you know."

Molly moved to the huge globe and traced her finger between New York and San Francisco, wondering what lay between the two great cities. Since arriving from Ireland, she'd never been out of the city, and this would be a fine chance to see the heartland of America, she thought. She'd pass through several large American cities, but what really stirred her interest was the chance to see the great prairies with their antelope and buffalo herds, and the sweeping forests and towering mountains of the far west. Yesterday she'd have scoffed at the idea that she might be involved in such a fantastic trip, but now it not only seemed possible but plausible.

She walked to the window, weighing and assessing everything in her mind, and as she looked across Broadway, there, dominating her view, was the great *Telegram* building, steam rising from a row of smokestacks jutting from its roof. What memories the sight of that building stirred within her! She closed her eyes, trying to get Lassiter out of her mind. Then with a rush of happiness, she realized the trip across America would be a way to do that very thing. It would be a way to start living again.

She heard Mr. Babbage cross the office and she knew he was now standing behind her. "Well, what do you say, my dear? Are you ready to become the toast of the nation? Will you accept the assignment?" he challenged, his voice vibrant with glowing hope.

Still amazed she'd been presented with such a glittering opportunity out of the blue, Molly turned and met his pleading eyes. "Yes," she finally answered, feeling a great mantle of responsibility settling on her shoulders, "I'll accept the assignment and I'll try my hardest to make the features my best writing ever."

Christmas morning arrived and the air was cold and crisp, a light snow having fallen the night before. Outside of Grand Central Terminal, located on lonely Forty-second Street, far from downtown, most of the snow had melted away, clinging only to the north side of the buildings that surrounded the imposing domed edifice.

As Molly and her entourage, which included Mr. Babbage, Kathleen, and Aunt Agatha, swept into the noisy terminal at six-thirty, a porter followed at her heels, pushing a handcart stacked with two suitcases filled with lovely new clothes, compliments of her employer, who'd insisted she needed them for the trip.

Dressed in a perky hat and the red velvet gown and fur muff she'd always dreamed about in Ireland, she marched ahead, swinging a tote bag full of writing supplies on one arm while two corded hatboxes dangled from the other. She clutched her mother's arm, suprised to see such a large crowd gathered inside the terminal so early in the morning. Some of the people carried signs and placards, and not only were there working men and women, but also many of the city's elite, excited to see her off.

A band had turned out, and pale wintery light filtered into the glassed building and softly glinted from the musicians' brass instruments as they played a gay march that further enlivened the already eventful morning. Caught up in the spirit of the moment, Molly stopped to acknowledge the happy crowd that cheered loudly with every wave of her gloved hand.

"I didn't think there would be so many people," she told Mr. Babbage as she scanned the excited crowd.

The editor patted her hand. "You underestimate yourself, my dear. I told you the whole city loves you, and I was right," he chuckled appreciatively.

Kathleen clutched her daughter's shoulder, her radiant face wreathed in smiles. "I knew you'd be famous someday, love," she gushed, the feathers on her little hat trembling as her bosom heaved with emotion.

Molly squeezed her hand. "It's a wonderful country, is it not?" she laughed, relishing the glow on her mother's face.

Kathleen's eyes twinkled. "The most wonderful in the world!"

Aunt Agatha, who was bundled up in a long coat, presented Molly with a small box tied with a string. "I fixed you a bit of food," the old lady stated matter of factly. She sniffed knowingly. "You never know what you might get while travelin', and you need to keep up your strength, you know."

Molly kissed her, thinking it was just like the old lady, who'd go straight back to the boardinghouse to finish Christmas dinner for all her hungry boarders.

Mr. Babbage took Molly's elbow. "We must to go to the train now, my dear," he softly urged, looking in the direction of the puffing locomotives, located just outside the terminal building near a maze of platforms and tracks.

Molly, along with her mother and aunt, accompanied him out of the building, attracting the attention of the cheering crowd, which streamed behind, brandishing their placards and signs. The long, hissing Union Pacific locomotive waited just ahead on platform seven. The scent of oil and soot and sulphurous smoke touched Molly's nostrils and the sound of shrieking whistles rang in her ears as the editor guided her toward an imposing Palace Pullman car.

She paused at the metal steps leading to the entrance of the car and gazed at her mother's tender face, knowing she must say good-bye. From her bag, Kathleen withdrew a fine knitted scarf of the softest lilac wool and draped it about her daughter's neck. "Merry Christmas, love. "I'm so proud of you. We'll be reading your features every day. You will take care of yourself, won't you?"

Molly swallowed back a rush of emotion. "Of course I will. And you take care of Brian," she ordered, giving her mother a tight hug.

"I'll take care of him like my own son," Kathleen murmured against her daughter's shoulder.

The words made tears gather in Molly's eyes, and she kissed both her mother and Aunt Agatha. Then, led by Mr. Babbage, and followed by the porter, she walked up the metal steps and entered the waiting train.

The editor proudly showed her the parlor car, and after putting down her things, she traced her fingers over the smooth green-striped chairs and like-colored curtains that were decorated with an abundance of gold fringe. There was a little table before one of the seats, where Molly could write and eat, and she was so impressed with the comfortable car outfitted with glowing lamps with green shades that she let out a sigh of appreciation. "I never expected anything so grand," she exclaimed, studying her employer's pleased countenance.

"Yes, it's the finest the Union Pacific could give us," he returned. Knowing who you are, they were only too happy to cooperate. It seems nothing is too good for the Angel of Murphy Street."

He went on to show her the adjoining sleeping car, decorated with the same luxury and containing a washstand with a china bowl and pitcher, dozens of soft linen towels, and a round gilt-framed mirror. Then, still talking, he took her back to the parlor car.

His expression growing serious, he gave her last-minute instructions, admonishing her to send him a telegraphed report as soon as she arrived in Chicago, where she'd board another express for Omaha.

The train let out a piercing whistle and Mr. Babbage graced her with a fatherly peck on the cheek. "I must be on my way now," he announced in a businesslike tone. "We can't delay your schedule, you know." A look of gravity slowly moved over his face. "Remember, through your eyes, all of America will be seeing this great country, Molly. You can't let them down."

"Yes, I'll do my best," she smiled up at him. She watched him leave the car, then waved at him as he stood on the platform looking as if he might burst with pride beside her teary-eyed mother and Aunt Agatha.

After sitting down, she pulled a tablet from her tote bag, already getting an idea how she would begin her first feature. At exactly seven o'clock, she felt the vibration of the train wheels beneath her feet and the locomotive began to inch slowly away from the station. Through the window she heard the roar of the throng, which had spilled from the terminal and now lined the platform, and she rose to wave at everyone.

Anticipation gathered in her bosom, for she was beginning the most exciting journey of her life, and as Mr. Babbage had said, she'd be taking thousands of readers with her. The whistling train slowly picked up speed and she waved a last good-bye at the cheering crowd, which went wild with excitement.

As she scanned the crowd, her pulse suddenly fluttered. There, standing on a raised part of a platform two rows over, she caught a fleeting glimpse of a tall man dressed in a top hat, long dark overcoat, and a muffler that snapped in the breeze. A piece of luggage rested by his feet, and there was something strikingly familiar about his masculine stance and the cigar that jutted from his lips. *Lassiter*, she thought, her heart pounding out of control.

A gust of steam billowed up from the side of the train and she pressed her hands against the window trying to get a better view, but the billowing mist was too thick. The train gained momentum, and to her dismay, the mysterious male figure as well as the cheering crowd became only a blurred mass obscured by gray smoke.

She slowly sank to her seat.

Had Lassiter made the trip to the station with the rest of the excited crowd to see her off? Had he come to bid her good-bye and wish her luck? No, it was impossible, she decided, taking a deep breath to calm her overwrought nerves. What would he be doing at Grand Central Terminal?

Surely Daisy had returned from the Hamptons, and

on today of all days, he'd be with her and her family in their Fifth Avenue mansion eating Christmas dinner and talking about marriage plans. The tall man had to be just another traveler. How foolish of her to even imagine anything else.

Shaking off her depression, she flipped open a tablet, then began writing what she hoped would be the best feature of her life.

Lassiter shoved his hands in his overcoat pockets and watched Molly's train as it disappeared into the billowing smoke. Even with the caboose out of sight, the crowd still cheered, seemingly not wanting to relinquish this magical moment they'd shared with the Angel of Murphy Street. No doubt the excited people knew this day would go down in the history books, and they wanted to tell their grandchildren they'd seen Molly Kilmartin leave New York City on her journey to San Francisco on Christmas Day of 1883.

What a grand moment it was, he thought, pride gathering in his chest as he picked up his bag and walked to his waiting train. He fondly remembered the first time he'd seen the feisty Irish heller aboard the *Saxonia*. Even then he knew she'd make something of herself, and that she had, becoming the toast of the city.

When he'd read about her trip yesterday morning in the *Metropolitan*, it had set his imagination aflame, for he knew it was a fantastic idea—one he could capitalize on. The paper had published her itinerary, and after looking at some maps and rail schedules, he knew that with only a little luck, he could probably beat her time, a feat that would sell thousands of papers.

Lassiter now handed his bag to a porter to be carried aboard his train, and sweeping off his top hat, entered a special parlor car belonging to Henry Vanderbilt, son of the late Cornelius Vanderbilt, and owner of the New York Central line. His eyes widened as he entered the long car paneled with richly carved oiled walnut. The car was appointed with plush cushioned seats and boasted marble washstands, damask curtains, and massive mirrors with gilded frames.

There was a round mahogany table with a decanter of brandy and a humidor of premium cigars, and under a large window stood a French desk glittering with brass ornamentation. Overhead, a brass chandelier with green shades hung from a ceiling depicting Greek goddesses and bordered with rococo plaster ornamentation picked out in gold. Lassiter let out a low whistle, marveling at the luxury in which the rail king usually traveled.

He inspected the adjoining sleeping car decorated in the same ostentatious fashion, lit with magnificent flaming brass sconces and outfitted with a bed covered with a red silk coverlet fringed with heavy gold tassels.

He strolled back to the parlor car, sat down, and helped himself to a cigar. Smiling to himself, he lit the expensive brandy-scented cheroot and settled back to recall the scene yesterday when he'd visited Vanderbilt in his office and approached him with the idea of turning Molly's trip across America into a race.

When he'd pointed out how much publicity the event would bring the rail line, the tycoon had immediately warmed to his idea. After they'd both inspected rail schedules, Vanderbilt agreed with Lassiter that to expedite the trip to California, he should switch to the

Kansas Pacific line at Omaha, then farther west to the Atchison, Topeka, and Santa Fe line for the rest of the journey.

With a little effort, Lassiter had even persuaded Vanderbilt and the owners of the other lines to pay his expenses and put up a tremendous sum of fifty thousand dollars to be given to the winner on the steps of New York City Hall. For the first time since learning of Tom Perkins's treachery, he now felt a sense of relief, knowing the huge purse could save the *Telegram,* which was only weeks from bankruptcy now.

Lassiter propped up his feet on the table before him, thinking how stunned the whole metropolis would be when the *Telegram* published his plans in a late edition of today's paper and everyone found out the trip was now a race, not only between rail lines, but between a man and a woman. With the feminist cause on everyone's lips, the event would surely capture the imagination of the whole country, and set everyone's tongues wagging. It was the Union Pacific against the New York Central; Kansas Pacific; and Atchison, Topeka, and Santa Fe—a colorful train race that would rivet America's attention like nothing before it.

The locomotive hooted its whistle and the train slowly moved out, then picked up steam and swiftly rumbled down the tracks. The powerful express was quickly out of New York and Lassiter sank back into the plush seat and felt the mighty rails sing under his feet.

He chuckled to himself, then blew smoke rings into the air, anticipating what he expected to be an extremely enjoyable adventure. It was fabulous—the journalistic stunt of a lifetime. And how surprised

Molly would be when he met her in Chicago and discovered she now had to race him across the whole continent and back again.

After her train was out of New York, Molly made some notes about her send-off, then started composing the ideas into paragraphs. She glanced up occasionally, but lost in her work and the clickety-clack of the train wheels, was surprised when she reached the outskirts of a New Jersey town, which was announced with a long blast from the locomotive's wailing whistle. Outside the window, fluffy snowflakes floated down, sticking to the sides of the grimy factories and warehouses that lined both sides of the tracks.

She noticed a pair of ragged urchins chucking pieces of coal at the train. The children had the same hard, pinched faces she'd seen on many of the ragamuffins in New York. With a burst of compassion, she thought of all the struggling immigrants who'd come not only from Ireland, but all over the world to make a fresh start in a new country, and she wondered how many would get their share of the American dream.

As the train bisected the northern part of New Jersey, it cut through land forested with fine hardwood trees powdered with white, and passed neat farms tucked in the hilly dairy land. Molly scribbled hard and fast, and before she knew it, she'd crossed the swirling Delaware River and was in Pennsylvania.

She moved closer to the window, and pushing back the gold fringed drapes, peered out, her eyes devouring everything she saw. Overhanging clouds obscured the light for a moment, then winter sun broke through one spot and cast a soft glow on the rolling land. She saw tidy farms and cattle grazing over white-powdered stubble, and when the locomotive rumbled over a switch crossing, she noticed a crossroads and rutted tracks glistening with snow.

As the train roared though a small town, she spied children rolling hoops and wondered if they'd just received them that morning as Christmas gifts. The thought made her remember her loved ones in the boardinghouse, and she fought back a wave of homesickness.

Later a steward knocked and brought Christmas dinner. As they talked and laughed together, she felt her spirits rising, and after he'd left, she removed the domed silver cover from her plate to reveal a fine meal of turkey and dressing and all the trimmings.

She ate leisurely, watching the rolling hills forested in birch, maple, and oak slide past outside her window. She thought of last Christmas in Ireland when she and her mother had shared a meager meal of porridge and bacon, and could scarcely believe all that had happened to her since she'd left the port of Queensland. When she'd finished the meal, she opened Aunt Agatha's little parcel and helped herself to a wonderful apple tart oozing juice.

The steward came back to take her tray and serve coffee, and she sipped the steaming brew, relaxing against the soft seat and looking at the beautiful Pennsylvania farmland covered in a mantle of white. She spotted farmhouses with smoke drifting from their chimneys and barns with hex signs, and neat little black buggies traversing the undulating roads. Gripped by the hand of winter, the silvery land projected an ethereal look, and reminded her of the expensive Christmas cards she'd seen in New York's exclusive stationery shops.

The train rushed through small whistle-stops and she spotted farmers and their wives patiently waiting upon platform benches for other trains. She was struck with the vastness of the land that spread out like a huge series of patchwork quilts before her, thinking all of Ireland would fit into this one state of Pennsylvania. She unfolded a map and looked at all the land she still had to cross. What a huge country America was and what a vast assortment of people it contained!

Sighing, she began writing again and was so absorbed in her work, she didn't stop until a glance at her dangling bodice watch told her it was five o'clock. Surprised it was twilight already, she wrapped a throw about her legs to protect herself against the chill seeping in around the window, then feeling a wave of creativity, began working again, filling one page, then the next, with bold handwriting.

At seven the steward served another meal, and after he'd taken the mostly untouched food away, she added a few more lines to her feature, thinking she had twelve long hours to go before she reached Chicago. She reread her work, made a few changes, and satisfied with her first effort, pushed the tablet aside and gazed from the window, rather tired from the day's excitement.

She retired early that evening, and comparing the fancy sleeping car to her little dormer bedroom, felt somewhat out of place surrounded by such luxury. After reading awhile, she extinguished the lights and lay in the dark listening to the clickety-clack of the train wheels.

The thought suddenly surfaced in her mind that when she returned she'd be more famous than ever and could no doubt get a job as a feature writer at the revered *New York Times*—but the realization strangely failed to satisfy her. So this is fame, she decided in a deep, pensive mood.

When she was starving in Ireland, fame and fortune was what she'd craved. Well, she thought dryly, it wasn't all that she'd supposed. She now understood that fame could clothe a person in fine raiment and fill their stomach—but it couldn't mend a broken heart.

Wiping a tear from her cheek, she sighed and surrendered to comforting sleep while the rail joints clicked off the hastening miles.

Awakened at six the next morning by a wailing whistle as the express passed through a small hamlet, Molly sat up in bed, then bubbling with anticipation, pulled an ornate bell cord, signaling for her steward. After washing and dressing and hastily arranging her hair, she walked into the parlor car, just as the smiling steward knocked and entered with breakfast and pungent coffee, all served on a silver tray.

Too excited to eat, she carried a cup of the dark brew to the window and pushed back the silken drapes, getting her first glimpse of the great state of Illinois.

Beams of crisp morning light slanted down on the suburbs of Chicago. She noticed the houses were coming closer together now, and seeing strings of buggies and business vans along the roads that paralleled the tracks, she knew she'd soon be in the city proper. She began gathering her writing supplies and smoothed back her pinned-up hair, wondering what kind of reception she'd have at her first stop.

Fifteen minutes later the train slackened its speed as it passed a series of row houses, factories, and tall brick buildings. At last the locomotive decreased its pace even more, and shrieking its whistle again, glided into a huge domed station. From the terminal came the muffled sounds of jolting cars and the chugging hiss of departing locomotives.

Molly sat forward, interested in all she saw. Elegantly dressed ladies and gentlemen walked along the wide platforms toward their waiting trains as white-jacketed porters followed behind with pushcarts full of baggage. There were station restaurants, ticket offices, and newsstands, all busy with returning passengers on this day after Christmas.

Bundled-up children, some carrying toy wagons and dolls, held their mothers' hands as they hurried along trying to keep up. On the brick walls, large signs marked the way to the platforms and Molly caught a glimpse of the telegraph office, her intended destination as soon as she left the train.

The locomotive came to a slow, grating halt, and as conductors slammed portable steps beneath the train's compartment doors, her fellow passengers exited their respective cars and streamed onto the platform. With a burst of excitement, she saw her welcoming committee, a large crowd of people, some with signs saying, WELCOME TO CHICAGO, MOLLY. Everyone was smiling and cheering and waving newspapers with her photo on the front page.

She gathered her things and rose, and seconds later a porter entered and picked up her bags and hatboxes.

"This way, Miss Kilmartin," he said, ushering her to the end of the parlor car where she'd disembark.

Molly emerged from the train, completely unprepared for the cheer that reverberated from the high station dome the moment she stepped onto the platform. *"Molly, Molly,"* the people chanted, some reaching across the ropes that held them back in an attempt to touch her. Lost in the excitement of the moment, she spoke with a local reporter, then shook hands with some of her fans, showering her well-wishers with smiles.

Afterward, she briskly walked along the busy platform, feeling strong and rested after a good night's sleep. The porter at her heels, she headed in the direction of the telegraph office, eager to transmit her feature to Mr. Babbage and the editor in San Francisco.

She'd just rounded a corner when her heart leaped wildly. "Jesus, Mary, and Joseph," she gasped, trembling with disbelief. She swallowed back her shock, for there, lounging against the telegraph office, stood Lassiter, looking as if he had all the time in the world as he leisurely smoked a fine cigar.

Chapter Sixteen

Molly stared at Lassiter through a thick mist of emotion. She was only vaguely aware of the milling passengers moving past her as she stood in a state of shock, her reeling mind trying to comprehend what her eyes were now seeing. For a moment the platform, the train station, and even Chicago itself seemed distant and far away as if they didn't exist at all.

Saints above, what was Lassiter doing here when he belonged in New York? she wondered, temporarily rooted to the spot. Could he be in this city on business or visiting friends? He had no ties with Chicago that she knew of.

Slowly, as if in a dream, she walked toward him, never taking her eyes from his amused face. When she got near enough, he grinned, and after tipping the porter, took her bags and hatboxes and placed them on the platform. "Well, hello, Irish," he greeted her, scanning her ensemble with appreciative eyes. "I see you finally got that red velvet gown and fur muff you talked about back on the *Saxonia*." He put his hand on her shoulder. "Lord, am I glad to see you. Seems like I've been waiting for hours. I thought you'd never get here."

She tried to speak, but when she opened her mouth the words stuck in her throat. "W-What are you doing here?" she finally squeaked out, thinking the question might strangle her.

He gave her a bright smile. "I'm on my way to San Francisco, just like you."

"*San Francisco,*" she whispered, feeling herself go cold about the heart. "Why on God's green earth are you going to San Francisco?"

His eyes twinkled mischievously. "Trying to race you there and back to New York."

Molly's anger quickly escalated to white-hot fury. "Trying to race me back to New York?" she cried, trembling with emotion. "What do you mean by that?"

He lifted a cocky brow. "Just what I said. I'm making your trip across America into a contest between us."

She pulled in a sharp breath. "No one gave you permission to do that—least of all me!"

He chomped his cigar. "Permission? Who needs permission? This is a free country where a person can do anything he's big enough to do. You can't prevent an American citizen from traveling to San Francisco and back, you know. And if he happens to do it faster than you can, well, I say good for him."

She jerked her brows together. "You must be out of your mind," she ranted as she surveyed his pleased face. "I don't want to race you across the country and back again. I *can't* participate in a race, anyway." She tapped her bosom. "Once I arrive in San Francisco, I have to attend a reception and spend a night there for publicity purposes."

"Oh, I know that," he replied with a casual shrug. "It was all in your itinerary in the *Metropolitan*." He pursed his lips thoughtfully. "I wouldn't want to take advantage of your fixed schedule. So just to be fair, I'll lay over one night in San Francisco myself." He gave her a lighthearted expression. "It won't make any difference. We both know the trip west will just be a publicity stunt. It's the trip back to the east coast that really counts." He rubbed his chin. "Of course, it would be a great psychological victory to arrive in San Francisco first."

She narrowed her eyes at him. "You started this race because you're still mad about me taking that Sullivan interview to the *Metropolitan*, right?

"*No*," he chortled, I got over that a long time ago." His eyes lit up as if he'd just remembered something important. "Oh, you'll be glad to hear this. I talked the owners of the New York Central; Nebraska Pacific; and Atchison, Topeka, and Santa Fe into putting up a cash prize for the winner of the race."

"A cash prize?" she echoed, her voice ringing with surprise. "How much?"

He shot her a lopsided grin. "Fifty thousand dollars."

Her mouth flew open. "*Fifty thousand dollars?* she said in a barely audible whisper. "Why, you must be crazy to think I'd believe that."

His eyes snapped. "I am crazy—crazy like a fox to engineer that deal."

"No one has that kind of money to give away," she

exclaimed, angry that he was now teasing her with such an outlandish tale.

He gave her a friendly wink. "Yes they do. You just haven't met them. In fact, officials from the various lines will be at New York City Hall to present the prize money. Whether you know it or not, Irish," he continued in a confident tone, "you're now in a race, and the contestant who reaches the top of those City Hall steps first is the winner."

With this statement, reality hit Molly square in the face and she finally realized that he was serious about every blessed thing he'd told her, as outrageous as it all sounded. She stood glowering at him with parted lips, for the thought of racing him across the country, no matter what the prize, filled her with an outrage she could scarcely contain. She swallowed hard, searching for words strong enough to express her boiling emotions. "But this is completely unfair. No doubt Mr. Babbage knows nothing of this!"

"He does now," Lassiter replied with a laugh. "The whole east coast knows about it, and probably the west coast too. I gave my staff orders to print a front-page story about the race in yesterday's late edition. Old man Babbage is probably pulling out what hair he has left, but there's not a damn thing he can do to stop it. It's a fact you'll both have to deal with."

Molly felt weak and dizzy.

"You don't look well," he said in a consoling voice, taking her elbow and ushering her toward a bench. "I think you should sit down for a while."

"*No,* I need to get to the telegraph office," she cried, pulling against him arm.

"Oh, there's no rush about that," Lassiter retorted, a

proud grin touching his lips. "I've already telegraphed my story back to New York. There's no way your story will beat mine."

"*Your story?* Now you're after telling me *you're* writing features about the trip too?"

"Sure. I'm having them telegraphed back to the city just like you."

Molly sank onto the bench, not believing what he'd just told her. "B-But you couldn't have got here before me," she finally stammered, rubbing her throbbing temples as she tried to sort things out. "It was impossible," she said, throwing him a sharp glance. "I saw you standing on the platform when I pulled out, so you had to leave New York after me."

He laughed deeply. "That I did, but I arrived here a good twenty minutes before your train crawled in, and I've already sent my story."

She blinked rapidly, more confused that ever. "I still don't understand," she moaned, trying to digest the exasperating experience that had left her staggering with disbelief. "H-How could you possibly do it?"

Lassiter puffed on his cigar. "It was easy," he explained, looking at her through the smoke. "I left ten minutes after you, but I used a slightly shorter route and a more powerful locomotive. When it comes to speed, eighty-six-inch driving wheels do make a difference, you know."

She stared at him, thinking she was trapped in a nightmare.

He chuckled happily. "Old man Babbage contracted with the wrong railroad line. When I studied the New York Central timetable, I knew I could beat you to Chicago."

Molly's whirling mind grappled with all the agonizing facts he'd just presented. How dare the rascal copy Mr. Babbage's idea and ruin his scheme. How dare he brazenly upstage her!

Lassiter gently cupped her chin. "You look pale. Shall I buy you some breakfast?"

She pushed his hand away. *"No,"* she snapped, quickly rising to her feet. "I have to get into the telegraph office."

"Here, let me carry your bags, then," he offered good-naturedly as he hoisted them from the platform. "My luggage has already been transferred to my new train."

She looped the hatbox cords on one arm and wrestled her bags away from him, determined she'd carry them herself. She took a few steps, and practically bursting with rage, turned to look back at his satisfied face. "I see what you're about—manipulating people again. You think you'll win that fifty thousand dollars and save your newspaper, don't you? Well, I'm not going to let you get away with it!"

The dangling hatboxes bumping against her legs, Molly lugged her heavy bags into the telegraph office and gave her feature to the operator, who immediately started sending it. On an impulse, she also sent Mr. Babbage a message about what Lassiter had done and asked him to reply as soon as possible.

As the operator transmitted her article and personal message, she nervously paced about the windowed office, often stopping to peer through the glass and watch Lassiter casually smoke his cigar as he studied train schedules, a smug smile enlivening his countenance.

Thirty minutes later, she finally received a surprising reply from Mr. Babbage saying that although he was angry, there was nothing they could do about the race, and actually as far as publicity went, it might work to their advantage. As soon as she'd read the message, a sense of steely determination seized her soul. *All right, Mr. High and Mighty Burke Lassiter,* she thought, *if it's a race you want, I'll give you the race of your life!*

As soon as the telegraph operator was finished, she picked up her bags and boxes, and wobbling back and forth, left the office, barely able to carry everything. Knowing she must walk past Lassiter to get to her new train, she raised her chin to a proud angle, promising herself she'd ignore anything he might say, and above all, not let him get under her skin. Her heart pounded faster as she hobbled past him, then leaped in her bosom as he caught up with her and started walking by her side.

"I have to go this way too," he announced amicably. "You don't mind if I walk along, do you?" He took one of her bags. "Here, let me help you."

"*No.* Give that back to me," she cried, stubbornly wrenching the piece of luggage from his hands.

It seemed nothing could sour his good mood, for he continued to smile brightly. "Well, I'll walk along and keep you company then."

"Suit yourself," she replied in an icy tone. "As you said only a short while ago—this is a free country."

About this time, one of her hatboxes got tilted to the side and came open, spilling a lovely green feathered chapeau to the platform. Lassiter picked it up, and lightly dusting it off, thoughtfully admired it. "Why this is gorgeous. It should really set off your eyes."

Blushing hotly, Molly snatched it from his hands. "Here, let me have that," she retorted, putting it back into the box and closing the lid with a slap of her hand.

Lassiter continued smiling at her, offering to help her with her luggage as she stubbornly struggled ahead. "I'm going to Davenport, Iowa," he remarked leisurely, then across to Des Moines, then on into Omaha, Nebraska, where I'll change to the Kansas Pacific. I'm taking the southern route to the west coast. It's less treacherous than crossing those snow-packed mountains the Union Pacific winds through, and the flat land and straight tracks should save me time too."

"You think you're so smart," she burst out, forgetting she wasn't going to lose her composure. "I hope your train blows up in the middle of Iowa and you're savaged by a herd of rabid swine!" she flung at him as she hobbled on with her bags, finally setting them down to rest a minute.

Laughter burst from his lips. "Do I detect a little sharpness in your voice, Irish?" He arched a questioning brow. "I don't see why you're so upset. The race and the purse will only make the event more enjoyable. You'll still get a lot of notoriety out of this, you know. Of course, you won't win the race, but coming in second in such an event has its own rewards."

"I'm sorry," she returned, giving him what she hoped was a blistering glare, "you'll have to marry Daisy to get the money to save your precious paper. You may have beat me to Chicago, but you won't beat me to San Francisco, that I promise."

Seeing her new express was only a few yards away, Molly picked up her luggage and marched ahead, the bag handles cutting into her palms. "*You* may have made this trip into a race," she called over her shoulder, wishing she could wipe the self-satisfied smile from his face, "but *I'm* going to win it and that's all there is to it!"

By noon Lassiter's train had passed over the Mississippi River and through the rich farming country around Davenport, Iowa. Excitement building in his chest, he pulled out his maps and rail schedules and began studying them again. He smiled to himself, thinking of the *Telegram*'s printing presses running off extra papers that would undoubtedly sell out. Lord, how did old man Babbage ever come up with such a good idea anyway?

After mulling over the material to his satisfaction, he moved to the window and looked out, peering at the outskirts of Davenport, now visible on the horizon. With only the sound of the train's clicking wheels to keep him company, he thought of the dramatic scene that had played itself out the day before he'd left New York.

Daisy had returned from the Hamptons for the Christmas season, and he remembered the shock and outrage on her face when he'd told her he was breaking their engagement. He'd felt little remorse, for she'd skillfully maneuvered him into the situation, and when all was said and done, he simply couldn't marry her— even to keep the *Telegram* afloat.

No doubt she'd throw fits for weeks and claim he'd betrayed her to everyone who'd listen, but he also knew that she'd never really loved him, only his position and the excitement she felt he'd bring into her shallow life. Next year at this time she'd be chasing some other eligible bachelor whose head had been turned by her doll-like appearance and her father's millions.

Excitement seized his soul as he thought how tempted he'd been in Chicago to tell Molly he was now a free man. But what fun would that be? For the time being, her flashing eyes and saucy tongue provided such wonderful sport, he thought with a chuckle. And after all, he had the rest of the trip to break the news. He'd just choose the right time—a time when she'd calmed down enough to be in an amicable mood.

In a deep thoughtful moment, he sat down and ran a hand through his hair, trying to predict the future. In truth he felt as if he were walking a tightrope over some yawning chasm. If he won the race, which, barring some unforeseen event, seemed a good probability, would Molly ever forgive him?

From the fiery look in her eyes in Chicago, it didn't seem likely. Was it possible to beat her to those New York City Hall steps and still manage to get back in her good graces? he asked himself, for the first time wondering if he'd done the right thing in starting the race.

That afternoon crowds hailed Molly at every whistle-stop on the way to Omaha. She could see the excitement on the people's faces and hear it in their cheering voices as her express steamed past them, belching gray smoke and fiery sparks.

It was a sight to behold. Some folks whipped American flags above their heads while others waved newspapers with banner headlines. Farmers tossed hats into the air, their red-cheeked wives fluttered white handkerchiefs, and children jumped up and down in a frenzy of joy.

With a feeling of glowing pride, she realized she was involved in the adventure of a lifetime. She knew that with Lassiter's entry into the trip, this event had not only become a race between railroad lines, but it had transformed itself into a heated battle of the sexes, man against woman, and all of America was enthralled.

Then with a renewed sense of outrage, she wondered if he was receiving the same glorious reception she'd experienced this afternoon. A dull feeling settling about her heart, she remembered this morning as her train had pulled away from the Chicago station. People had stood beside the tracks cheering and waving, but in her anger, she'd scarcely seen them. How dare Lassiter horn in on Mr. Babbage's idea, and most of all, how dare he find a quicker route to San Francisco!

With a blush, she remembered her disturbed sleep the night before. In her dream, she and Lassiter were in his suite as they had been that rainy night months ago. His eyes glistening with desire, he kissed her, sending a rapturous river of pleasure rushing through her bloodstream.

As their passion had flared, he settled her upon his bed and caressed her body with his warm hands, using them expertly. She was nude, and unashamed, and gloriously happy as he unleashed wondrous sensations within her that left her throbbing with pleasure. After a session of long, rapturous lovemaking, they'd climaxed together as one. Even today as she relaxed against the seat, her body pulsed with the exquisite memory of the dream.

The train rumbled over a switch crossing, bringing her back to reality. She couldn't help what she'd dreamed, but she'd be damned if she'd let herself revel in the memory, no matter how sweet it might be. She bit her bottom lip, deciding she must divert her thoughts somehow. Disciplining her mind, she pictured her loved ones back in the boardinghouse and wondered what they might be doing.

Then unbidden, the image of Daisy's face filled her mind's eye. She thought of the blonde ensconced in her father's Fifth Avenue mansion, no doubt eagerly keeping up with the race and planning her trousseau at the same time. Well good riddance to her and Lassiter, too, for *she'd* win the race and set them both on their ear.

She pulled out a Union Pacific schedule, and taking out a pencil, studied it with growing interest. She noticed she'd be crossing not only the Continental Divide, but also the Sierra Nevada range—in the dead of winter no less. Anxiety nibbled at the back of her mind. Would the mountains really present as much of a problem as Lassiter had suggested? She pulled in a long worried breath, noting how imposing the black-colored mountain range looked on the map. Did Lassiter and the owners of the rail lines who were sponsoring him know something she didn't? Would his southern route actually be faster this time of year as he'd suggested?

She sat back and threw down her pencil. No, the rascal was just taunting her, playing a wicked battle of minds with her, trying to shake her confidence.

Still, as she carefully folded up the map and put it away, she pictured the foreboding mountains that lay ahead of her and felt a chill race down her spine.

That evening about six-thirty Lassiter was reading when a steward softly knocked on his door, then entered. "Mr. Lassiter," the man announced, lifting his bushy brows, "we'll be pullin' into Omaha in about an hour and a half. Just thought you'd want to know." He put his hand on the door lever. "I'll be servin' dinner soon."

Lassiter glanced up from his book. "Yes, all right."

After the steward had left, Lassiter moved across the parlor car, lit with softly glowing lamps, and raised the fringed shade covering the window. The night was dark and windy with hundreds of glittering stars overhead. He surveyed rows and rows of dry, cut-back cornstalks powdered with snow and barely visible in the darkness. He thought of the people who'd settled the land, hearty, broad-shouldered immigrants with German, Dutch, and Czechoslovakian names who'd poured their sweat, toil, and hopes into the black land and planted it with corn and wheat.

Lassiter reseated himself and relived his long day. Taking thirteen hours, the train had cut across the width of Iowa, passing over the Des Moines river and the Nishnabotna, chugging through miles and miles of rich, fertile farmland until it was now making a beeline for Omaha.

Minutes later, the steward returned to present him with a dinner of roast chicken, savory vegetables, and flaky hot rolls, all served on the finest china as if he were in a first-class hotel somewhere on the east coast. After he'd eaten and his dishes had been removed, he settled back with a last cup of coffee, studying the swiftly moving landscape outside the window. In the distance he could see the lights of Omaha, and after he'd finished his coffee, he began gathering his things, putting his latest feature into a folder.

The silhouette of Omaha's buildings now loomed closer on the flat night-blue horizon as the train steamed to its destination. Judging from the scattered outskirts of the town, it looked much like the other plains villages he'd passed through, only bigger and laid out in neat blocks lined with white frame houses that glittered with ice and snow in the light of glowing street lamps.

Here in this provincial mid-western town there was no sprawling domed terminal, only a wooden depot with offices and benches, and a large train yard filled with crisscrossing tracks. All about the depot he noticed clusters of surreys and heavily bundled farmers sitting on wagons, their plain, bonneted wives hunkered in the cold beside them.

When the hissing train slowed down in order to stop, he spied an excited crowd filling the platform. Obviously impressed with the importance of his mission, the engineer tooted his whistle and the clamoring people gave forth with ringing cheers. Lassiter picked out signs bearing his name, and with a flash of pride, realized not everyone was rooting for Molly to win. Could he be here first as he'd predicted? he wondered as the train finally came to a slow, gliding halt.

A smiling porter came for his bag and ushered him toward the vestibule where he'd exit the luxurious sitting car. A frosty evening breeze hit his face as he walked down the train's metal steps, and carrying the folder that contained his feature under his arm, he tugged down his top hat with a gloved hand. On the busy platform, the assembled crowd greeted him with wild cheers, their voices clear and bright on the icy winter air.

A young man dressed in a white starched shirt and a neat suit rushed to Lassiter and scanned him with excited eyes as he fumbled to open a tablet and take out a pencil. "Mr. Lassiter, I'm from the *Omaha Standard,*" he announced importantly, his muffler fluttering in the icy breeze. "May I ask you a few questions?"

Lassiter, turning up his overcoat collar, nodded and waited for the reporter's first question.

"As you must know, you've arrived here in Omaha before Molly Kilmartin. How do you feel?"

Lassiter chuckled at the question. "I feel damn good," he answered in a booming voice, speaking loud enough that those standing behind the reporter could hear his remark.

The laughing crowd burst into applause.

When the ruckus had settled down, the reporter said, "Everyone in Omaha is waiting for a few words from you, sir. What are your impressions about your trip so far?"

Lassiter held back his response to build up the drama of the moment. "My most immediate impressions," he finally answered, "are that it's a hell of a long way across this country of ours and Omaha is colder than Siberia."

The crowd laughed appreciatively.

"Do you have anything else to say?" the young reporter asked, writing furiously as he spoke.

"Yes," Lassiter announced in a more serious tone. "This journey has made it only more evident to me that

America is the greatest country in the world, and I'm glad I had a chance to visit Omaha, the breadbasket of our nation."

The patriotic statement drew another round of applause.

"How are you going to spend the prize money?" the young man asked, his hair ruffling up in the wind.

Lassiter began walking away, knowing he needed to get to the telegraph office. "I haven't won yet," he called over his shoulder to the eager reporter, who hastily scribbled down his words.

The telegraph operator had just finished sending Lassiter's feature when Molly's train pulled in, billowing rolling steam. Smiling to himself, Lassiter walked to the office window and rubbed a circle on the clouded pane to watch her exit her special car, today dressed in a green velvet outfit with gold fringe and the hat he'd retrieved from the platform on their last stop.

Her gaze ran over the modest crowd of women who was there to greet her. The assembly of severely dressed ladies looked like bluestockings and reminded him of the group who'd once gathered under his office window to rally for the vote. He knew he wasn't wrong when mixed with the signs wishing Molly good luck, he noted a placard reading, WOMEN DESERVE THE RIGHT TO VOTE.

While Molly paused to speak to the women, he took the opportunity to leave the telegraph office and walk in her direction. From her fiery expression, he decided she'd already spotted him and realized she'd be boiling mad. After shaking hands with some of the women, she left the crowd and swiftly walked toward him, a trailing porter pushing her luggage on a handcart.

"Well, hello, Irish," he tossed out, watching feathers flutter atop her charming chapeau. He gently touched her face. "What took you so long? I've been here the better part of an hour and already transmitted my story." He glanced at his pocket watch. "In fact, my train leaves in fifteen minutes," he added, snapping the timepiece shut and putting it away.

Molly knocked his hand from her face. "So does mine, so get out of my way."

"Now what's all this?" he asked good-naturedly, thoroughly enjoying their banter. "I thought travel was supposed to soothe the soul. Why are you so fretted up?"

She glared at him as if she wanted to cut his throat. "Why am I so fretted up, the man asks. Now I wonder why that should be. First you butt in on my trip, then you have the gall to taunt me about it at every possible chance."

"Taunt you? Why I've just come to greet you, make you feel at home, if you will. Seems like that's my duty—me being here first and all."

Her eyes blazed green fire. "Enjoy yourself while you can, because it's I who'll be greeting you in San Francisco."

He met her smouldering gaze with an unblinking stare. "I don't know about that. I'm headed for Kansas where there's lots of flatland, but the mountains are going to be mighty tricky this time of year." He tugged on his gloves. "If you think it's cold here, just wait until you get out west.

She flung him a hot glower, then lifted her head proudly. Her back ramrod straight, she strode toward the telegraph office, her bustle swaying behind her.

He quickly passed the porter and caught up with her.

"You'll never have time to send your story and catch your train, too, you know," he challenged with a satisfied chuckle.

Molly whirled about, and the look she gave him would have burned a normal man to a crisp. "I don't have to stand over the man while he sends the feature, you know. I'll just leave it with him."

He smiled and manacled her elbow as she breezed past him, turning her about in her tracks. "Good thinking."

She tried to wrench away, but he held her tight. "Oh, I almost forgot. I want to issue an invitation. Since we have that layover in San Francisco, I want to invite you to dinner at the Palace Hotel. I've decided to stay there too."

She stared at him, her mouth agape with shock. "I wouldn't want to trouble you!" she finally answered, her words blistering the icy air.

"Oh, I wouldn't be any trouble." He rubbed his hand over his chin. "I beat you to Chicago, I beat you to Omaha, and no doubt I'll beat you to San Francisco. I'll be there early and make reservations for us." Such a expression of rage flooded her face, he thought she might explode right there before his eyes. "Oh, you don't have to decide now. You can tell me in San Francisco," he added with a gracious smile.

Molly gritted her teeth. "I don't have to think about it. I'd rather eat supper with the devil himself." Quick tears clung to her thick lashes. "I hope those plains Indians derail your train, then scalp you and feed your fingers to the grizzly bears!"

She pulled away and marched off in a huff to the

telegraph office, looking as if she would knock aside anyone who got in her way.

Lassiter pelted her with laughter, then called out, "See you in San Francisco, Molly. Don't forget, dinner's at eight!"

Chapter Seventeen

Molly left Omaha at nine that night, but try as she might, she couldn't get her mind off Lassiter's smiling face as he'd invited her to dinner at the Palace Hotel in San Francisco. How dare he ask her to dinner! Well, she'd show him, she thought with a feeling of growing satisfaction. She'd get to the west coast first and be standing on the platform waiting for him, ready to deliver a salvo of stinging barbs, like those he'd so recently thrown at her in Omaha.

Frustrated beyond measure, she read for a while, then finally went to bed and rode all night, the sound of the train's clicking wheels lulling her to sleep.

When she woke the next morning, she was still in Nebraska with miles and miles of unbroken plains stretching before her. Looking out, she occasionally noticed a sod house, and sometimes in the distance, herds of roaming buffalo moving like a huge dark sea over the treeless land.

She wrote for a while, putting down her impressions of the flat, barren state, and at about ten a steward told her they'd just crossed into Wyoming Territory. Scanning the horizon, she saw her first mountains, looming blue and hazy in the distance, and she experienced a mixture of dread and tingling anticipation.

At noon she arrived in Cheyenne, hardly more than a rough railroad outpost, and found a modest cluster of people waiting to greet her. After she'd sent her feature, she glanced about the icy little depot with its potbellied stove and few other amenities, and realized she'd left civilization in Omaha and was finally in the real west.

Ensconced in another opulent private car, she began her journey across the southern half of Wyoming, taking a winding route past rustic Fort Laramie, through the rocky Black Hills, then out into the Platte River Valley. Vast panoramas of majestic country peppered with deer and antelope delighted her eyes at every turn, and always in the distance there were the mountains, tall and imposing, stretching to the sky.

Her imagination stirred by the awesome scenery, she wrote late into the night, wanting to impart to her readers the sense of grandeur that was so apparent in this fabled land that Easterners only read about in dime novels written by people who'd never been out of New York City.

The next morning, she noticed the train was going up a grade, winding itself into some foothills, and she experienced a pang of anxiety. When the steward brought her meal, he told her they would soon be going through South Pass, a great natural gateway in the Continental Divide.

She rode quietly for a while, looking at the snowy pines and every now and then catching a glimpse of a nimble deer bounding through the silvery forests. Although she knew the locomotive was laboring, it slowly managed to negotiate its way through the mountains, passing through many tunnels as it crept to the summit of the pass.

Once the train traversed South Pass, it veered into the northeastern corner of Utah Territory with its thick forests, and chugged westward for Ogden, now crawling through the Uinta and Wasatch mountains. The locomotive was forced to proceed at an agonizingly slow speed, and worried about Lassiter steaming westward on the flat, southern route, she constantly checked the dangling watch pinned to her bodice.

Trying to calm her rising anxiety, Molly looked at the breathtaking scenery and considered the seemingly endless tracks spanning the country and the men who'd laid them. She thought of the anvil chorus that had played across the nation in triple time: three strokes to a spike, ten spikes to a rail, four hundred rails to a mile. How great this country was, how immense.

She'd seen so much: the neat Pennsylvania farms; the lush Ohio farming country sleeping under a blanket of white; flat, lonely Nebraska with its prairie-dog towns; the vast grandeur of Wyoming. She said a silent prayer of thanks that so far there had been no trouble on the tracks. But what, she wondered with a growing feeling of unease, would she find on the dangerous last leg of her journey across the treacherous Sierras?

* * *

Molly's train steamed past Promontory Point where the golden spike had been driven, joining tracks from the east and west and forming the first transcontinental railroad. Then it cut through the Utah desert and crossed into the state of Nevada. Puffing straight ahead, it sliced through the great basin that lay between the Rockies and the Sierra Nevada Range and passed through Elko and Winnemucca, finally reaching Virginia City, sprawled over treeless hills that had been stripped of lumber to build mining shafts.

After visiting the telegraph office, Molly walked about the small platform, gazing at the rough mining town with its backdrop of foothills, and beyond them the great Sierras, rising majestically to the west in the noonday sun. She stared at the daunting snow-capped mountains, thinking she'd never seen anything so grand and imposing. So this was the last, perilous barrier Lassiter had been talking about, she thought, realizing the train would have to creep for hundreds of miles to negotiate its way through the mighty range that separated Nevada and California.

Taking a deep breath, she told herself the only way to San Francisco was straight over those mountains, no matter how high they were, so squaring her shoulders, she boarded a new Union Pacific parlor car for the last leg of her journey. Its bell clanging loudly, the express chugged from the Virginia City depot and steamed toward the edge of town. As it negotiated a curve, Molly noticed another brightly painted locomotive had been added to provide extra power for the upcoming mountains.

Gradually the train gathered speed and stormed into

the foothills. For two hours Molly looked from her parlor car window, watching snow fall fast and furious over the steadily rising foothills, where scarlet-leafed manzanitas made a striking contrast against the puffy snowbanks.

She wrote for a while, and by the time she closed her tablet, the terrain had become increasingly steep. To make matters worse, a wind had risen and swirled flakes down in huge gusts that blew over the tracks. The train slowed as it ascended into the mountains and crept along a dizzying shelf, two thousand feet above the thread of the American River.

She was writing when a light rap sounded at her door, and a tall, rawboned steward entered carrying a tray with a lovely silver service.

"Just thought I'd bring you some coffee, miss," the rough-hewn man said in a western-flavored voice. "Thought it might warm you up."

Molly thanked him as he placed the service on the table before her and poured coffee. Hungry for a little conversation, she chafed her chilly arms and smiled up at him. "*Brrr,* it's getting colder, isn't it?" she asked with a little shiver.

The steward threw her a nervous smile. "And it will be gettin' colder still, I'm afraid."

She peered out as the train negotiated a treacherous curve and saw a wooden structure that reminded her of a covered bridge over the tracks. "What in the world is that?" she remarked, transferring her attention back to the man's amused face.

The steward chuckled. "Why, that's a snowshed, miss. Altogether there's forty miles of them here in the Sierras. We get drifts through these mountains up to

312

thirty feet, and need somethin' to protect the tracks, you know. The snow is bad, but what makes it worse is the wind."

Molly nervously fingered the rim of her coffee cup. "Do you think there'll be trouble?"

A thoughtful look crossed the man's face. "Could be, there's some bad weather comin' in." He leaned over and pointed at a snow cornice down the tracks. The windswept arch, looking like a gigantic frozen wave, hung precariously over the rails. "With the wind blowin' like this, you never know when one of them cornices is goin' to crash onto the tracks."

The steward turned up the parlor car lamps, then slid his gaze back to Molly. "Well, I'd better be gettin' on now," he commented, touching his hat respectfully. He paused at the door and threw her a smile. "Just ring if you need anythin' else, miss."

Molly drank her coffee, then nestled down under a satin throw and put a tasseled pillow behind her head. Left alone with the sound of the singing rails, she closed her eyes and was soon fast asleep.

Weary from her long trip, she slept deeply, then as the train began to slow, she gradually awoke and noticed the parlor car was much darker than when she'd dozed off. Straightening up, she checked her bodice watch, and with a flicker of surprise, realized she'd been asleep for more than an hour.

Outside the train, she heard the whining wind, and she wiped off a space on the clouded windowpane, seeing that the heavy snowfall had turned into an outright blizzard. Twilight had settled upon the mountains, and paths of fuzzy light glowed from the front of the locomotive, diffusing in the swirling snow. From the way the train was laboring, she told herself it must be approaching a summit.

The Union Pacific slowed even more, and suddenly she heard the sound of screaming brakes and saw bright sparks flying from the rails. Seconds later, the train jerked to a stop that almost threw her from her seat. Clutching a dangling hand strap by the window, she righted herself and peered out, wondering what had happened.

The locomotive was stalled on a curve, and with a sense of horror, she saw a huge snow cornice had broken away from its base and crashed in front of the first engine. With its impact, a small avalanche had been set off on the steep incline behind the cornice and snow now tumbled down the mountainside, thundering rocks and debris over the rails.

She placed a hand over her heaving bosom, wondering why this tragedy had to happen now of all times. The train still chugged rhythmically, as if impatient to be moving again. Work crews from both locomotives spilled to the ground, shovels in hand, and attacked the mound of snow and rocks, their figures silhouetted against the headlights' orange glow.

Molly's heart ached for the bundled-up laborers whose actions were impeded by the numbing blizzard. Wind whipped at their jackets and mufflers, and cloudy vapor floated from their open mouths. The men scooped snow aside, where it was scattered like blowing foam by the high wind. Some of the workers slid and fell, only to be quickly pulled up by another man.

Stunned, Molly sat for a good ten minutes, watching the men work frantically. Despite their efforts, it seemed they'd hardly made a dent in the mound of snow and debris. At last she laid her head against the back of her seat and closed her eyes, knowing Lassiter had been right about the risk of crossing the mountains in the winter. Heartsick, she calculated it would be hours before the tracks were cleared and the train could continue.

The small avalanche would cost her dearly, she decided, fighting back a powerful feeling of depression. But when all was said and done, she thought, her spirits lifting a bit, being first to San Francisco really didn't matter a whit. She pressed her lips together in determination, then slowly straightened up and pulled in a long, calming breath. It was being first back to New York that really counted, she sternly advised herself. She had as good a chance as Lassiter to win this race—and win it she would.

Seated in his comfortable parlor car, Lassiter scanned the vast panorama before him: the deeply incised canyons, natural bridges and arches, towers and turrets, all lightly powdered with snow. So this was the great west he'd heard so much about, America's manifest destiny, the land first mapped by fur traders and Indian scouts, he thought as he took out a tablet and pencil and began writing another feature.

After seeing this country firsthand instead of merely reading about it, he now had an idea of the immensity of the nation, of its boundless plains, its awesome wild mountains, its thick, sweeping forests, and he struggled to put his thoughts and impressions into words, thinking the journey had been an experience he would remember the rest of his life.

He felt extremely removed from the great city where he lived, even more so than when he'd been in Ireland, for that green land was sprinkled with villages, while here in the wide open west, where a person could travel for days without seeing another soul, one had a sense of being completely isolated from civilization, of being alone, not only with his most private thoughts, but with his maker.

There had been a few tank towns, mere whistle-stops, he thought as he described them on paper. He'd seen saloons with swinging doors, and there were men in buckboards with grime-stained Stetsons, and laughing women dressed in garish gowns. All in all, the west appeared to be a hard, unforgiving land, where men lived desperate, blood-splattered lives, their daily existence so different from that of the average inhabitant of New York, they might as well be on another planet.

New York, he thought, with a warm sense of nostalgia. He laid aside his pencil and lit a cigar, trying to imagine what was going on there. No doubt the police were still digging into Tom Perkins's shadowy past and piling up evidence they'd present next spring in a court case that was sure to draw a large, interested crowd. And surely everyone in the metropolis was keeping up with the race now, buying not only the *Telegram,* but every paper they could get their hands on. Of course with the great New Year's balls imminent, the city would also be stirring with a flurry of social activity.

He thought of Daisy searching for just the right gown to wear to the Gould's soiree—that is if she'd been able to find someone from the crowd that hung out at Delmonico's to take her there. He smiled to himself,

316

deciding that if she didn't have an escort, she'd be forced to feign illness and stay home—a social tragedy that would hardly go down well with the proud, head-strong Daisy.

And what of Molly? What was she doing now and where was she? he wondered, leaning back and crossing his legs before him. Had she made it over the Sierras or had she run into trouble as he'd expected? He considered Omaha, knowing he'd missed another opportunity to tell her he'd broken off with Daisy, but after all, the moment just didn't seem right when she was telling him she hoped the Indians fed his fingers to the grizzly bears.

A soft knock interrupted his thoughts and a white-jacketed steward quietly entered his parlor car. "Mr. Lassiter," the man announced in a respectful tone, "I thought you'd be interested to know that we just entered California."

Lassiter stood and nodded at him. "Good, very good indeed."

He watched the man leave, then moved to a window and eased the gold fringed shade a little higher, seeing his first eucalyptus grove. He chuckled to himself, thinking he'd been right. By taking the southern route through the northwest corner of Kansas, then swinging through the Colorado plateau and the flat, arid west, the train had been able to proceed at full chisel, and he'd made excellent time. This last leg of his journey should go by in a breeze, he decided, knowing the powerful locomotive was gradually turning north to storm up California's San Joaquin Valley on tracks that were straight as an arrow.

He took a draw from his cigar and blew out a smoke ring. In a matter of hours he'd be in San Francisco.

Lassiter's train made its way north, chugging past San Jose. The express veered west and the gulls wheeling in the sky above the rice fields told him he had to be near the coast. From there on, the land was gently rolling and dotted with orchards and vineyards, all brown and dormant until spring.

He read for a while, then looked up and spied the smudgy outline of San Francisco. Closer in, he was struck with the sight of forested hills and rocky cliffs tracing the coastline, and a melange of businesses and fine Victorian homes built of redwood and decorated with spindles, arches, and bay windows, their leaded panes glittering in the afternoon light.

The train entered the city proper and Lassiter noticed carriages and freight vans packed the steep, twisting streets, and well-dressed pedestrians walked up the terraced sidewalks to lovely hotels boasting ornate balconies. To him, it was apparent that the city some called the Paris of the West was bursting with prosperity, energy, and a taste for luxury.

The railroad station itself was a massive, domed building, typical of many he'd seen in large eastern cities. Here, as in New York, a brass band played and people lined the platform, jostling signs in their excitement. As the express slowed and finally came to a hissing stop, he spotted a group of Molly's fans, who all looked tired and dejected as if they'd been waiting for hours. Instantly, he took out a Union Pacific timetable and saw that her train was hours late.

Farther up the platform, there was a crowd yelling his name and holding a huge banner reading, SAN FRANCISCO WELCOMES BURKE LASSITER. Once he'd exited the train, he was besieged by a battalion of eager reporters and photographers, who immediately went to work setting up their standing cameras.

After Lassiter had been interviewed and photographed, the crowd still cheered, trying to reach over the ropes to touch him. He spoke to several of the people, then carrying his own bag, made his way through the busy station. With a little looking, he found the station agent's office and discovered the Union Pacific had telegraphed that the train had been delayed in the Sierras by a small avalanche and would be arriving three hours behind schedule.

With the knowledge that Molly was safe, Lassiter smiled to himself, imagining how angry she must be as the express tried to make up for lost time. Picturing the welter of emotion that must be stamped on her face this very minute, he sent his feature, then walked through the packed depot, which was filled with a babble of voices and the noise of throaty train whistles.

At last he emerged into the bright light, and the tang of the bay hit him in the face. On the busy street he hailed an open-sided victoria, and the driver deposited the luggage in the boot, then raised his cap, regarding his passenger with curious eyes. "Where to, sir?"

"The Palace Hotel," Lassiter announced, settling back against the soft leather seat.

The driver took his box, and within seconds they were off, wheels rattling against the brick-paved street. In the harbor, white-sailed ships bobbed and creaked, and on the busy docks there was the screeching of winches and the whining of tackle, but Lassiter's mind dwelt upon Molly alone. Lord, how he longed to see her, but when she did arrive, tired, dispirited, and disgusted, would her pride be so wounded she couldn't face him? Then recalling her fierce pride, he smiled to himself, thinking of a way he might persuade her to have dinner with him.

After her express had come to a complete stop at the San Francisco depot, Molly rose and checked her reflection in the mirror, preparing to leave the train. A small but ardent band of people met her as she stepped off the express just as twilight was falling over the city by the bay. Her fans cheered politely and one of them cried, "Good luck, Molly. We're still betting on you!" Some waved signs, but from the mood of the crowd, she knew that just as she'd expected, Lassiter had arrived before her. Depression almost overwhelmed her for a moment, but mindful of her duties to the *Metropolitan,* she raised her chin and smiled, acknowledging the crowd's attention.

An elderly, silver-haired gentleman wearing a fine suit came forward and introduced himself as the owner of the *San Francisco Chronicle.* Knowing the man had given Mr. Babbage the idea for the trip in the first place, she greeted him warmly and posed for several pictures with him.

When the crowd had thinned out a bit, the publisher handed her an envelope with her name on it. "Since you were running several hours behind schedule, I took the liberty of picking this up for you at the telegraph office," he announced with a gracious smile.

Molly found the message was from Mr. Babbage and she devoured it with hungry eyes.

> *My dear,*
>   *I have been informed there was some trouble on the tracks in the Sierras, and only hope you have arrived in San Francisco safely by now. The delay was unfortunate, but please don't lose heart. Your features about crossing America have been wonderful. You've sold thousands of papers and business has never been better. Keep your pretty chin up, my dear. Lassiter may have beat you to San Francisco, but it's the trip back to the east coast that really matters. You still have a good chance to win.*

After she'd read the message, the publisher called an assistant forward. "The mayor and several other dignitaries are waiting at the Palace Hotel for your long-postponed reception, so I suggest you let my assistant send your feature. As soon as the piece has been keyed in, he can whisk it to the Chronicle to be set into type."

Knowing she couldn't keep the mayor waiting any longer, Molly agreed; then the publisher called a porter, escorted her from the station, and guided her to his waiting victoria.

She sat back in the open carriage, watching San Francisco pass before her in the rosy dusk as the kindly publisher pointed out various sights. How hilly the city was! Some of the steep streets seemed to go up to the pink-tinged sky while others dropped sharply to the sea where square-rigged ships floated in the harbor.

They passed through the edge of China Town where shrill music drifted over grilled balconies, and the scent of sandalwood mingled with that of dried fish and gingerroot. Vendors wearing broad hats of woven bamboo carried flexible poles over their shoulders, and slung on either end of them, huge baskets of vegetables bobbed rhythmically with the men's swinging gait.

The sun was just sliding into the bay, and its last rays glinted from the windows of the fine mansions atop Nob Hill. Even in winter there was a profusion of fruit stands lining the main arteries, and in the residential districts, lights began to glow in the fine Victorian homes that loomed over the twisting streets.

The carriage slowed as it turned onto Market Street, and there in the distance, Molly saw the magnificent Palace Hotel, rising seven stories and silhouetted against the sunset. Soft lamplight shimmered through hundreds of windows and American and California flags snapped from the huge entry arch.

She blinked in surprise when the carriage passed under the high arch and into a huge atrium covered with an amber dome. Glossy-leafed plants, gurgling fountains, and flickering lanterns filled the beautiful enclosed garden. After the publisher drew the victoria to a halt, he helped her from the carriage and summoned a porter to carry her luggage into the hotel.

Escorted by the newspaper owner, Molly entered the Palace's grand columned lobby, amazed at its elegance. Her heels clicked over gigantic squares of black-and-white marble, and on every gleaming console there were massive flower arrangements flanked by golden candelabras. With chandeliers sparkling from the high frescoed ceiling, the effect was spectacular.

A large group of reporters and photographers stood back respectfully as a portly man approached her, an elegant entourage at his heels. A fine dark suit with an embroidered vest clad the official's thick body and a gold watch chain swung diagonally across his round stomach.

The publisher introduced the gentleman as the mayor of San Francisco and the dignitary immediately broke into a litany of congratulations. "I want to welcome you to this great city," he proclaimed, his fleshy face glowing with goodwill. "Like the rest of the nation, everyone in San Francisco has been keeping up with your journey across America"—he gushed with a wide smile—"and we believe your efforts should be rewarded."

The official asked one of his assistants for a long jewelry box, then handed it to Molly, who discovered a large gold key resting upon red velvet. "I want to offer you the key to the city. This key is made from California gold, all taken from the Golden State," the mayor announced proudly.

Knowing what was expected of her, Molly smiled brightly. "Thank you," she said graciously, "I'll always treasure it."

Photographers now disappeared under velvet covers to take pictures of her receiving the memento and shaking hands with the dignitary. Flash pans flared, leaving white spots dancing before her eyes, but when they cleared, her heart leaped for she suddenly spied Lassiter walking down a sweeping staircase behind the press, a cheerful smile on his face.

As he moved to the edge of the crowd of journalists, a lock of jet-black hair fell over his forehead, giving him a careless, devil-may-care look. Saints above, if the man didn't have the gall of ten men, she thought, her heart thumping against her ribcage. She knew he'd be ensconced in the hotel, no doubt in a fine suite, smoking an expensive cigar, but she had no idea he'd appear at her reception!

Feeling the heat of Lassiter's gaze upon her, she met representatives from the Chamber of Commerce and other dignitaries, then the eager reporters rushed forward with tablets in hand to besiege her with questions. All the time the men quizzed her, asking her about the avalanche and her impression of the trip, she shot slanted glances at the back of the crowd, noticing Lassiter was still watching her with amused interest.

At last the reporters wound up their questions and milled away to write their stories. After a little more conversation with the newspaper maven, she refused his invitation for dinner, wanting to go straight to her room for a relaxing private meal.

"Very well," he graciously replied, affectionately patting her hand. "I'll see you bright and early tomorrow at the terminal with more photographers who'll be wanting to take pictures of your departure."

When he'd left, she raised her chin several notches higher, and aimed herself in the direction of the reception desk, trying to sweep past Lassiter as if he didn't exist.

"Irish!" he greeted her, clasping her shoulders and running his fingers down her arms to her wrists. "I think you handled that reception just fine." He shook his head, feigning disbelief. "Imagine getting the key to the city."

Molly tried to pull away from him. "Get out of my way," she sniffed, twisting her head so she wouldn't have to look at him. "I want to go to my room."

"Wait a minute," he laughed, turning her face toward him, "I understand you had a bit of trouble in the Sierras. Want to tell me about it?"

She met his curious eyes, her heart beginning an uneasy thud. " 'A bit of trouble,' the man says," she chanted, cocking her head to the side. "Yes, there was a small matter of an avalanche over the tracks. It took hours for the work crew to dig us out."

Lassiter clucked his tongue sympathetically. "Now that's a damn shame. I didn't have any trouble at all."

"Ah yes, the devil is always good to his own, is he not?"

Lassiter raised the back of her hand to his lips. "Still the same old Molly, I see. Oh, don't take it so hard," he advised, a teasing light in his eyes. "You may still beat me back to New York. Of course it's highly unlikely, but it's technically possible."

Her sensibilities pricked, Molly found the strength to break away from him. "It's more than technically possible—it's what's going to happen!" she said, spitting out the words contemptuously.

He laughed richly. "Very well, then. Will you have dinner with me to celebrate your victory in advance? I've already made reservations for us."

She stared at his smiling face, thinking he'd lost his mind. "Of course not. I told you that the last time I saw you." She started walking away. "Now leave me alone."

He caught up with her and grabbed her arm. "Well, I should have known it," he commented, affecting an air of deep disappointment, "but I thought you had more courage than that."

"What do you mean—more courage than that?" she came back, stiffening her body at the insult.

He grazed a knuckle under her chin. "I just thought you'd have the courage to eat dinner with me tonight. I've been looking forward to it since Omaha, you know."

She tossed her head in disgust. "Courage has nothing to do with it," she hooted, her voice heavy with derision.

"Oh, yes it does," he insisted, his eyes glistening with challenge. He traced his finger over her cheek. "You're afraid to eat dinner with me, aren't you? Why don't you just admit it?"

She put her hands on her hips. "Afraid?" she echoed in a loud, incredulous tone. "I'm not afraid of anything or anyone—especially you."

He smiled showing strong white teeth. "Well, eat dinner with me then and prove it. I dare you."

Too angry to speak, Molly took a deep breath to gather her wits.

Lassiter sighed and assessed her judiciously. "Yes, I was right. You are afraid, I can see it in your eyes."

"I am not," she whispered, tightly crossing her arms under her bosom. She let her scathing gaze crawl over him, and provoked beyond her endurance, narrowed her eyes. "All right, then, I accept your dare." She arched her brows and jabbed her finger at his chest. "But if you think you're going to get anything but the pleasure of my company this evening, you're sadly mistaken!"

Chapter Eighteen

Fresh from a relaxing bath and dressed in black silk stockings, bloomers, and a corset, Molly went to a carved armoire, opened its heavy doors, and eyed the ensembles she'd brought from New York. She selected a peacock-green dinner gown with dainty puffed sleeves and a fashionably large bustle that Mr. Babbage said would be appropriate for dinner in San Francisco and held it before her.

She stood in front of a gold-framed cheval glass studying her reflection. With a prickle of excitement, she knew the off-the-shoulder creation would make her skin even whiter and the single satin rose pinned at the center of the daringly low-cut neckline would accentuate her cleavage to such an extent that Mam would blush even just to know she was wearing it. But feeling somewhat rebellious and angry at herself for accepting

Lassiter's dare, she put it on anyway, then stepped into a pair of like-colored satin slippers.

At the vanity dresser, she sat down to brush her hair until it glowed with red highlights, pinned it back with some decorative combs so it would cascade over her shoulders in loose waves, and finally teased little curls out about her hairline. After applying a tinge of powder, rouge, and lip gloss, she moved to the cheval glass again to get the full effect of her labors.

Her eyes widened at the image the glass flashed back. The gown's color made her hair dazzle with coppery fire, and with the sleek bodice and large bustle, her waist had never seemed so small nor her bosom so voluptuous. Her heart raced when she thought of Lassiter, who by now had to be waiting for her in the first-floor dining room. Surely even *he* would be affected.

After dabbing perfume on her wrists and cleavage, she pulled on a pair of long white kidskin gloves and picked up her reticule. Her petticoat rustling pleasantly, she left the gorgeous room in cloud of musky, tantalizing scent and a sweep of silk.

On the first floor, she peeked into the hotel's magnificent dining room with a tingly sense of dread. All about the grand chamber, hung in rose-colored silk and illuminated with glittering chandeliers, were classic statuary and bowers of greenery and exquisitely scented blossoms.

A tall maître d', holding several of the largest, most ornate menus Molly had ever seen, approached and bowed his sleek head. "Ah, Miss Kilmartin, there you are. Mr. Lassiter said you'd be joining him. If you'll just follow me, please."

The man walked away with stiff dignity, and taking a

deep breath, Molly trailed him into the elegant room, feeling dozens of inquisitive eyes trained upon her. Seated about scores of round tables with snowy tablecloths and bouquets of flowers was the cream of San Francisco society, dressed in the height of fashion. The women wore elaborate dinner gowns and sported plumes in their hair and jewels at their throats, while the distinguished-looking men were decked out in dark dinner jackets and white ties.

The couples smiled up at her as she passed, apparently having seen her photo in the *Chronicle* during the last few days. One of the gentlemen stood and raised his wineglass, saying, "Congratulations, Miss Kilmartin," and a bit flustered with all the attention she was getting, she simply smiled back her acknowledgment.

Lassiter sat at a lovely table illuminated with flickering candles, his strong hand resting on the white cloth. He was dressed in a superbly tailored dinner jacket, and the white tie about his neck accentuated his bronzed features to perfection. She'd never seen him looking better or more confident. When their eyes met, his face brightened, and as the maître d' respectfully stood aside, he rose, a smile flashing on his pleased face. He extended his hand to guide her gently to her chair. "My, don't you look ravishing tonight? I'm so glad you decided to accept my invitation. I hate to eat alone. Don't you?"

Lassiter let his gaze play over Molly, his eyes devouring her. Lord, how beautiful she was. There was a bloom on her cheeks and that familiar fire in her eyes that always made his blood race a little faster. And what that gown did for her figure, gently kissing each tempting curve, he told himself, his eyes irresistibly drawn to her creamy bosom, which was displayed so delectably.

After he'd seated her, he ordered the best champagne in the house, then focused his attention on her exquisite face. They engaged in a little small talk about their respective rooms, then he gently clasped her slender wrist. "I must admit," he commented with quiet emphasis, "I was a somewhat concerned when I heard about that avalanche you had in the Sierras." He held her gloved hand, tracing his thumb over it. "Thank God you arrived safely."

She splashed a hot gaze over him. "Yes, if it hadn't been for that three tons of snow and rocks, I would have beat you here," she quickly returned, stripping off her long gloves and laying them aside. "You can mark my words about that."

He tilted back his head and laughed, thinking her spunk was what he liked best about her. Few women could have made her journey without emotionally collapsing, and there she sat, still full of sass and fight. "Your honesty is one of the things that endear you to me," he confessed, leaning forward to playfully trace a finger down her pert nose. "With you, it's impossible to be bored. You *do* keep life exciting."

Molly regarded him with a look of cool disdain. "I wish I could return the compliment by saying you have noble motives or something like that, but we both know it wouldn't be true, don't we?"

He chuckled softly, enjoying their verbal sparring. "Oh, never trust anyone who operates from noble motives," he warned, a trace of mirth in his tone. "In the end, you're sure to be disappointed."

She cocked a knowing brow. "Well, I'll never have to worry about that with you, will I now? From what I've seen, you're as ambitious as they come."

He settled back, permitting his gaze to wander over her challenging countenance. "Right on both counts. Why be poor when it's so easy to be rich?"

She gave him a weary frown. "For *some* of us, it's easy to be rich. But most of us weren't born with a silver spoon in our mouths like you, don't you know."

"Now, don't pout," he warned, wondering how he could broach the subject of their future together when she was in such a murderous mood. "Remember we're here to enjoy ourselves."

The maître d' served their champagne and as Lassiter raised his glass, Molly looked into his provocative eyes, bracing herself for the rush of tender feelings now pouring through her. Even now in the back of her mind she thought of the race, and was forced to secretly admit that in one respect it might be to her advantage if Lassiter won, for with the prize money he wouldn't have to marry Daisy—then in her deepest heart of hearts, she told herself he'd marry her anyway.

It seemed there was just no way she could come out of this situation with a winning hand. Trying to salvage her pride and soothe the intense longing for him, which secretly burned in her heart, she tasted the wine, masking her face with what she hoped was an expression of icy disinterest.

After they'd sipped some champagne, a waiter approached, and Lassiter opened his tall menu, pondering it carefully. "Now what will you have? The sky's the limit."

Molly cast a glance at the menu, which featured

everything from caviar and turtle soup to grizzly-bear steaks, glad to be eating a meal that wasn't moving for a change. After a moment of perusal, she casually announced, "There's no need for anything fancy. I think I'll just have a salad and a Kansas City steak." She closed the menu and laid it beside her folded gloves.

"Good choice," he concurred, tossing her an approving grin. "You can't go wrong there." He glanced up at the waiter. "I'll have the same," he said, turning to refill Molly's wineglass.

The meal was served, and more hungry than she thought, Molly ate her salad and steak with relish, noticing that Lassiter kept splashing champagne into her glass with every sip she took. "Now, don't be trying to get me drunk," she ordered, already feeling delightfully tipsy. "I want to have a clear head in the morning."

He glanced at the near empty bottle and pulled a face. "Get drunk on this stuff? Why, it's hardly more than springwater."

Before she could open her mouth to protest, he signaled the maître d' and ordered another bottle. A warm, fuzzy feeling crept over Molly as the meal progressed, and when Lassiter said something funny about his trip, she found herself laughing like a schoolgirl. He offered her more champagne, but she waved away the bottle. "I've had too much to drink already."

Ignoring her, he filled her glass to the brim, saying, "No, not quite enough. Just relax and enjoy yourself, Irish. You deserve it, you know."

He went out of his way to amuse her, mimicking some of the pompous officials he'd encountered on the trip, and to her chagrin, she was besieged with a fit of giggles that she couldn't quell. She hiccuped, and feeling herself blush, covered her mouth with her napkin.

"Don't worry. What's one little hiccup?" he advised, refilling his own glass. "Just let your hair down and relax tonight. You're with a friend, you know."

"*Friend?*" she echoed, tossing her napkin back onto her lap. "For an editor, I'd say you're being sinfully loose with words, Mr. Lassiter!"

They had cherries jubilee for dessert and when the waiter set the concoction aflame, it struck Molly as being so hilarious, she had to cover her mouth with her hand to stifle her giggles.

Lassiter chuckled, happy to see her enjoying herself. How beautiful she was with a glow on her lovely face and those delectable little curls fanning about her hairline. He hadn't meant to make her tipsy, but he definitely wanted to get her in a good mood and he congratulated himself on his success.

He poured her yet another glass of champagne, smiling at her relaxed exuberance. Lord, he'd longed to hold the feisty bundle of mischief in his arms since the first of their string of transcontinental skirmishes in Chicago. Would he be able to charm his way into her room tonight? he wondered, a sense of sharp desire welling up within him as he surveyed her lush bosom swelling so temptingly over the top of her silken gown. Only the Lord knew, and the Lord wasn't talking tonight, at least not to rascals like himself, it seemed.

Molly scanned Lassiter's smiling face. She knew she was tipsy, but for one glorious moment she didn't care and all her troubles seemed far away. How wonderful it felt to be relaxed, just enjoying herself, not worrying about writing another feature or catching another train.

Yes, it was so grand to simply let go and enjoy life, she decided, letting her usually high defenses slip precariously low.

When they'd finished dessert, Lassiter leisurely caressed her bare arm, running his finger under the edge of her puffed sleeve and sending a potent burst of desire exploding through her veins. "This has been a wonderful evening—the best I can remember," he allowed in a deep, vibrant voice alive with feeling. A slow smile touched his lips. "Let me escort you back to your room," he suggested, his passionate eyes roaming over her.

Something intense flared up inside of Molly. "No, I—"

"But you're quite a celebrity now and need protection," he interrupted, a touch of amusement clinging to his face.

"Protection from *you* most of all, I'll wager," Molly quipped, a sense of shocked delight darting through her even as she said the words. The erotic glitter in Lassiter's eyes told her she should immediately refuse his offer, but her racing heart quickly silenced the warning.

Perhaps he *would* kiss her at the door to her room, but what was one kiss when she'd longed for the feel of his lips on hers for weeks now? Surely she had the wit to dismiss him and simply close the door behind her after that, she decided, telling herself she was clever enough to handle the situation.

"I'm waiting for an answer," Lassiter prompted as he inched an appreciative gaze over her face, which was by now quite warm.

Molly smiled at the look of hopeful expectation glazing his handsome features. "I can hear your mind clicking all the way over here. It's quite noisy, you know."

He arched his brows. "Oh, really," he laughed. "Well what am I thinking, then?"

"Will she or won't she let me into her room."

He leaned back in his chair. "My, how you run on," he scoffed, his eyes soft and compelling. "Well, how about it, now," he continued, sitting forward and tenderly caressing her arm once more. "May I escort you back to your room?"

Molly picked up her gloves, and telling herself she was totally capable of withstanding his charming ways, met his searching gaze and answered, "Very well, if you insist, but expect the door to be slammed in your face as soon as I say good night."

As Lassiter and Molly strolled down the hall to her room, he continued telling her humorous stories about his trip, giving her another fit of the giggles. At the door to her room, she fished the key from her reticule, but he quickly took it from her hand. "Here, let me open that door, young lady. You're much too busy giggling."

After turning the lock, he dropped the key back into her reticule, and in the space of a heartbeat, slipped his arms about her waist. Before she had time to protest, he placed a gentle kiss on her forehead and both of her cheeks, then looked into her eyes, sending a shudder of excitement spiraling through her. "Thank you for a wonderful evening, Molly," he said in a tone that shimmered with underlying sensuality.

The caressing warmth of his voice quickened her blood. "No, thank *you*," she whispered, trying to ignore the pleasant tingling in the pit of her stomach. For a moment, his eyes sparkled with questions she was afraid to answer, then he slowly lowered his head and she felt his warm breath upon her cheek. Before she had time to protest, his arms tightened about her, and she was overcome with sweet, tender feelings, making her knees go weak beneath her.

His sensuous lips whispered over hers in the lightest caress; then he kissed her more deeply, and little sparks of fire started speeding through her bloodstream. He plunged his tongue into her mouth and traced it about her teeth, and blushing hotly, she felt her nipples harden and swell against her gown. As the fiery kiss continued, her heart set up an uneasy thud, and knowing there would soon be no denying him, she twisted in his arms and pushed against his chest with her spread hands.

Ignoring the futile attack, he smothered her lips with his, at the same time opening the door behind her. Then lifting her into his arms, he carried her into the softly lit room, where a pleasant fire crackled in the marble-faced fireplace.

Hearing the door close, she knew he'd pushed it shut with his heel and squirmed in his arms, finally forcing him to place her feet on the floor. "Don't try that trick with me," she warned, putting out an arm to balance herself as she backed up a few steps. She smoothed her rumpled skirt and adjusted her bodice, then flung him a pointed glare. "You weren't coming in, remember?"

Trembling with emotion, she drew back her hand to slap him, but he caught her wrist and gently but firmly placed it by her side. With a little chuckle, he raised a dark brow. "Not again, you little spitfire," he said, his eyes gleaming with amusement.

Molly gave an audible gasp. "Spitfire, is it? How dare you call me names when you've just forced your way into my room?" she challenged, widening her eyes in outrage.

He shrugged dismissively. "Forced my way into your room?" he remarked in a light, offhanded manner. "Why, there was no forcing about it. I simply opened the door and carried you in. And if you remember, *you* were the one who said I wasn't coming in, not me."

Enraged by his clever answer, she hurled her reticule at him, but he ducked, and the purse landed with a soft thunk behind him.

"Now Molly, dear," he said with a pleasant smile, glancing at the reticule, then back at her, "you shouldn't be so inhospitable to a sightseer from the east."

"Sightseer from the east?" she hooted, tossing back her disheveled hair. "I'd hardly call you that."

"Oh, but I am." He steered his gaze toward a huge window that faced the city and was gorgeously draped in gold-fringed crimson silk. "When I checked in to the Palace today they told me the view of Nob Hill from this floor was quite spectacular." He strolled to the window, then brushed back the silken drapes and peered out at the city, nodding his head appreciatively. "Yes, they were certainly right. This is quite a romantic sight." He glanced over his shoulder, flashing a beguiling smile. "You should come over here and take a look for yourself. You might want to add your impression of the city lights to your next feature."

Molly rolled her eyes. "Do you really think I'm going to fall for that old trick?"

He widened his eyes. "It's no trick. It's gorgeous out there. Come and take a look, then you can call a porter to throw me out if you want to. Believe me, you don't want to miss this."

Lassiter caught Molly's interested gaze, and smiled to himself. She was crumbling, and he knew she only needed a few more sentences of encouragement to come to the window. He continued to rhapsodize about the beauty of the view, and one step at a time, she slowly began to cross the room. He experienced a twinge of guilt, for he knew the champagne had lowered her inhibitions a bit, but at the same time he realized that he needed all the help he could get.

When she was by his side, he held back the drapes, urging her to look at he breathtaking view of the lights of San Francisco, highlighted by the blazing spectacle of Nob Hill, which all lay before them like a sack of spilled diamonds on black velvet.

"San Francisco is fantastic," he commented with a true burst of enthusiasm, remembering the sights he'd seen on the way from the railroad station. "I wrote a fine feature on this place after I checked in today." He thoughtfully rubbed his chin, noting her skeptical expression. "I can hardly wait to see it in print."

Her face softened and she suddenly burst out laughing. "Saints above, I've never seen anyone so in love with writing as you."

He cupped her chin, watching her soft eyes dance with emerald fire. "I do love it." He slowly traced his finger over her cheek and her soft lips, aching to take her in his arms. "It gets in your blood, you know"—he lowered his voice to emphasize his next words—"the same way some people do."

A rush of pink stained her cheeks, and with smooth assurance, he slipped his arm about her slender waist.

Ever so gently, he turned to lightly hold her in his arms while he looked into her luminous eyes. "Did anyone ever tell you how perfect your features are—what wonderful skin you have?" he asked, letting his gaze caress her face, her graceful neck, the milky expanse of her luscious bosom.

Molly slid him a sly glance from beneath her smoky lashes. "No, they haven't. Did anyone ever tell you what a silver-tongued rascal you are?"

Lassiter laughed deeply and caressed her shoulders, working his hands down her slim arms.

She laughed a little herself, then a serious expression gradually stole over her face. "What are we going to do about each other, you and me?" Her face sobered even more. "I—I think we need to talk."

Tenderly, Lassiter brushed back the hair from her pale forehead and placed a kiss there, one on her temple, and one on her cheek. He knew that with a few more moments of conversation, she might be hurling something else at him, so he lowered his head, and pulling her against him, whispered, "No, I think we need to do this."

He took her mouth in a long, ravishing kiss. At first she struggled against him, but as he deepened the kiss, forcing his tongue deep into her mouth, she surrendered and melted in his arms, slowly placing her arms about his neck.

Lord, how he'd missed her! he thought, the softness of her body spurring his ever-growing passion. During that exquisite moment, desire ran through him in a great torrent, urging him to make love to her, and he pulled her more tightly against him, thinking the best place to tell her that he'd broken off with Daisy would be after they'd made love and were wrapped in passion's tender afterglow.

Molly's pulse raced out of control. For the dozenth time that evening, a warning voice sounded in the back of her head, but carelessly surrendering to the moment, she chose to ignore it. Feeling strong muscles ripple across his back, she twined her fingers in his glossy black hair. His mouth slanted across hers in another blazing kiss and she moaned softly, relishing the feel of his thudding heart against her chest.

She noticed the heat of his hand on her breast and she relaxed against him, swept away by overpowering desire. He slowly moved his lips from hers and fluttered moist little kisses over her face and quivering eyelids. "You're a dream come true," he whispered huskily, trailing his warm fingertips over her throat. "I love touching your soft skin. It's like the finest silk." He slipped his fingertips under the top of her bodice and brushed them over her nipple, making it harden with aching pleasure. "And your breasts are perfect."

A warm, languorous glow crept through Molly's body, destroying the last of her crumbling will, and when he ravished her lips again, she moaned with the rapturous pleasure of it all. Gently, he picked her up and moved toward the bed, and a rational part of her brain advised her she should tell him to put her down. Seemingly reading her mind, he deepened the kiss, forestalling her intended cry of protest. Seconds later she felt herself sinking onto the soft mattress, and Lassiter lying down beside her.

"I love holding you in my arms," he murmured, fluttering kisses over her face. "Lord, I want you so badly."

"No, we shouldn't. I—"

"Hush, everything will be all right," he said in a soft, consoling voice that helped to assuage the last of her lingering doubts. "After all, no one will know but us. Let me make love to you again, my darling."

By now helpless with desire, she completely forgot the vow she'd made to herself when she found out he'd lied about Daisy being his cousin, and simply moaned her acceptance of his passionate proposal.

His hands swept over her body as he kissed her ears, her cheeks, and the throbbing pulse at the base of her throat, and she trembled with pent-up excitement. He took her mouth and her tongue battled with his in a firestorm of desire that left her weak. With practiced hands, he undid the back of her dress, then slid it from her shoulders and over her waist and hips. Within moments the peacock-green gown lay on the Aubusson carpet beside the bed in a silken tangle.

With tender hands, he unlaced her corset, and feeling his warm fingers upon her flesh, she shivered with tingling anticipation. Soon the corset was on the floor beside her gown and he firmly drew on her nipples with his lips, teasing and pulling them until they became pebbly hard.

He kissed her savagely, then removed her shoes, and pushed down her bloomers and threw them aside. He gently rolled down her garters, then lovingly ran his hands over her legs, making her shudder at his delicate touch. Her silk stockings made a pleasant swishing sound as he stripped them from her legs and let them fall to the floor.

Lost in a haze of misty passion, she relaxed into the soft mattress and watched him stand and undress. Once out of his shoes, he stripped off his dinner jacket and white tie and shirt, then slipped out of his trousers and undergarments. Her heart jolting, she noticed his long, aroused manhood nodding ever so slightly as it jutted provocatively from his shadowed groin.

He lay down beside her and ran his hands over her curves, and she sighed with pleasure, his tantalizing touch doing incredible things to her sanity. His eyes deep and languorous, he fluttered kisses over her breasts, leaving a trail of fire wherever they touched. She groaned and skimmed her hands over his hard muscled back, a shiver of wanting racing through her that left her shaken to the depths of her soul.

"You're exquisite. I love your breasts, your legs, every part of you," he murmured throatily, moving his lips to hers as he left her half mad with unfulfilled desire. The heart-melting tenderness of his gaze was irresistible, and he kissed her wildly, sending a delicate fire flickering through her body.

Now he drew on her nipples and she felt a lurch of excitement that left her weak and trembling. He nibbled and suckled her breasts until she moaned with a frenzy of sexual excitement. At the same time, he trailed his fingers over the triangle between her legs, parting the silky nest covering her womanhood. Gently he inserted a finger and explored the very essence of her femininity, teasing it until she closed her fluttering eyelids in swooning pleasure.

Tantalizingly, he flicked over her swollen bud of desire with his finger, and when she gasped in a spasm of delight, his lips met hers in a kiss that sent her blood rushing through her veins like hot quicksilver. He

343

relentlessly carried her to the very brink of erotic pleasure, and nearly breathless, she clutched at his broad
shoulders, pressing her fingertips into them.

All her senses aglow, she felt his hard maleness
brush against her, heard his ragged breathing, and was
keenly aware of his warm, musky scent. When he broke
the kiss, she opened her eyes and stared up at him. His
eyes shone like jewels, and weak with love, she trailed
her fingers over his rugged face. "If you're trying to
seduce me, you're doing a good job of it," she whispered huskily, her pulse beating at a crazy gallop.

Lassiter scanned Molly's lovely face, her half-closed
eyes, which now glittered with desire. "Me seduce
you? What conceit, you little baggage." She started to
say something, but he placed his finger over her soft
lips and raised his brows. "Let's not talk anymore, darling," he suggested, gently pushing back a silky tress
from her cheek, "for I'm going to pleasure you as
you've never been pleasured before."

Molly's hair was spread out like a fiery halo on the
silken pillow and her eyes held the expression of a
naughty angel. "Oh, Lassiter," she replied with a little
smile, trailing a finger over his lips, "didn't your
mother tell you that no one likes a show-off?"

"I'm not bragging, Irish, merely reporting the facts
like any good reporter should." He chuckled, reaching
down again to leisurely work his fingers over her moist
womanhood. Playfully, he kissed her ears, her smooth
eyelids, her glorious hair that slid through his hand like
silk. Lord how he wanted to make love to her, to feel
her velvety softness tightly clenched about him, throbbing in blissful spasms as she totally yielded herself to

him. Determinedly putting everything out of his mind but Molly, he studied her finely molded face, and an incredibly tender feeling akin to awe wrapped itself about his thudding heart.

The erotic gaze in Lassiter's smoky eyes filled her word with bliss, and as he lowered his mouth to her breasts again, she completely surrendered her heart to him. How she wanted the rogue, wanted him as she'd never wanted him before. He kissed her throat, her ribcage, her stomach, then with a jolt of surprise, she realized his mouth was working its way lower, searing her skin with fire and eliciting wanton sensations deep within her soul.

She moaned as he gently moved her legs apart and began nuzzling the inside of her parted thighs, stirring up wild, unnamed feelings within her. He swept his hands up to her breasts and his fingers teased her swollen nipples, while his wet tongue inched closer to the throbbing seat of her desire. He bathed her femininity with his warm, moist breath, and crazed with passion, she clutched at his strong arms, every muscle in her body tingling with bursting excitement. Blood heated her cheeks and a sense of confused modesty momentarily overcame her. "*Lassiter,*" she whispered, her voice a ragged cry of protest.

He momentarily continued his gentle ministrations, then raised his head a bit. "Just relax and enjoy it, darling," he murmured in a thick voice disturbed with passion. "Take it as your due."

He found her pulsing womanhood once more and firmly flicked his tongue over it, producing hot, sweet sensations that made her breath come in ragged gasps.

She threaded her fingers through his thick hair, moaning his name, thinking she would swoon with ecstasy. Still he continued, and his swirling tongue worshiped her with soft, nuzzling kisses until she shuddered with a convulsive passion that made her think her very soul would dissolve with pleasure. She cried out his name again, and as exquisite sensations rippled through her, twisted her head back and forth on the pillow in an abandoned gesture of ecstasy.

Just when she thought she might faint with the pleasure of it all, he positioned himself over her, resting his weight on his arms. She felt the tip of his hardened manhood probing, pressing against her femininity, teasing but not yet penetrating her. A deep hunger for his loving had brought her to a white-hot pitch of excitement, and feeling the accelerated beat of her heart, she softly groaned, "Please, make love to me now."

He lowered himself closer, but to her dismay, she felt his manhood entering only the first fold of her welcoming flesh, teasing her with the pleasure to come. Thinking she could stand it no longer, she instinctively arched upward and wrapped her legs about his hips as he slid into her in one masterful stroke. Digging her fingertips into his muscled back, she began moving against him as each of his rhythmic strokes filled her with pulsing rapture.

An aching need unfurled within her, growing and stoking a passion that threatened to blaze out of control. There was no time to think, only time to respond, to ease this deep craving that had blossomed from somewhere deep in her soul. Now her hips twisted beneath him as she struggled to meet his faster pace, and hot pleasure rushed through her, leaving her with the sensation that she might burst with exaltation at any moment.

Lassiter thrust forward as if to reach the very core of her being. She could feel his body warmth, hear his raspy breathing, and a wild, primitive feeling surfaced in her pounding heart, frightening and delighting her at the same time. Masterfully controlling his strokes, he increased the cadence of their lovemaking, until helpless with desire, she unconsciously pulled him closer.

When the first wave of ecstasy crested over her, her breath caught in her throat. Even now at the zenith of her excitement, she yearned for more than a physical coupling, and wanting to be one with him in every respect of the word, struggled to meet his faster pace. Whimpering for surcease, she tightened her softness about him, but he kept steely control and pounded into her again and again until she was almost breathless. At last consumed by a passionate fire she couldn't deny, she felt herself losing control and surrendered to each exquisite sensation claiming her throbbing womanhood.

Lassiter now jetted into her with one mighty thrust and groaned his satisfaction in a long, shuddering sigh. Pulsing with womanly fulfillment, she clutched his shoulders, luscious aftershocks rippling through her. Kissing her hair, he cradled her in his arms, murmuring endearments, and she clung to his warm body until her racing heart slowed.

Love's glorious afterglow stole through her as he eased to his side and held her against him, kissing her face and tenderly caressing her back. "You're the most exciting woman in the world, you fiery little minx," he whispered against her ear, his voice still rough with passion.

Molly raised a finger and lovingly traced it over his firm lips. True to his word, he'd taken her to the very heights of passion, and her body still glowed and tingled from his skillful touch. "Thanks—you're not so bad yourself," she murmured dreamily, feeling his protective arm draped over her waist.

Tenderly, he fluttered kisses over her throat and teasingly rolled one of her sensitive nipples between his fingertips, still delighting her with his touch. Floating on a warm sea of love, she noticed a deep sense of security claiming both her body and spirit. She heaved a huge sigh of contentment as she leisurely savored the exquisite sensations thrumming through her satiated body.

On the cusp of light sleep, she thought of how tender Lassiter had been tonight, how he'd patiently fanned the embers of their passion until they'd burst into glorious flames. He'd been strong, but also gentle, she decided, locking away the memory of their lovemaking deep in her heart. No, he'd never told her he loved her, but he *must* love her, she reasoned, her worries and doubts about Daisy somewhat dimmed now. Undoubtedly he'd soon confess his love for her. Despite the train race, despite his engagement, everything would work out, she consoled herself, at last sinking into a deep, peaceful sleep.

Lassiter gazed down at Molly, noticing her bosom rise and fall rhythmically, and to his surprise, realized she was already asleep. He thought about kissing her awake, so he could tell her the good news about his engagement, but she looked so relaxed and satisfied he decided the news could wait until first thing in the morning.

Tender memories flooded his mind as he envisioned her as he'd first seen her on the *Saxonia,* all fire and sass and flashing green eyes. He remembered her in her ragged gown when he'd first appeared at her aunt's boardinghouse, and when she'd defiantly walked away from him in the composing room, leaving him feeling as if his heart had been torn from his chest.

He caressed her face and arms, considering their lovemaking with a sense of awe. Never had a woman touched his mind and spirit as Molly had done this evening, and never had he wanted to please a woman as he had her. Then with a sudden burst of acuity, he realized that he was not only infatuated with her, or mesmerized with her. God help him, he thought with a soft chuckle, he was actually in love with her—deeply, completely, insanely in love with her.

The insight touched him profoundly, and he let out his breath in a long sigh, considering its ramifications. The realization not only pointed out his future actions, it explained a lot of things that had happened since he'd first met her. Now he understood why his heart leaped with joy every time he saw her sparkling eyes, and more important, he now completely understood why he'd broken his engagement with Daisy. He had to free himself to be with Molly forever, for she'd become as essential to him as the very air he breathed.

Suddenly beset with a great, unfulfilled urge to tell her he loved her, he kissed her slim hand, then placed it over her waist, thinking he'd pour out his heart to her as soon as she woke. He let a silky lock of her hair slip

Sonya Birmingham

through his fingertips, wondering what her reaction would be. Could she find it in her heart to forgive his "indecent proposal" as she called it and accept his new proposal of marriage and a life spent together living as one in every sense of the word?

What would he see in those lovely eyes tomorrow morning—love and longing or sorrow and regret?

Chapter Nineteen

Molly slept deeply for hours, then groggily opened her eyes and saw the hotel bedroom bathed in soft light pooling from several china lamps. The fire had burned low and a chill hung over the large chamber, making her snuggle down and pull the silken counterpane over her bare shoulders. Although she wasn't sure what time it was, she realized it was before sunup, for there wasn't a speck of daylight glowing through the silken draperies.

With a prickle of excitement, she instantly remembered that she and Lassiter had made love again, then fallen asleep in each other's arms without extinguishing the lamps. She turned her head on the pillow and saw him sleeping deeply, one bronzed arm thrown over his head. Dark hair caressed his forehead, his chest rose and fell rhythmically, and his face was relaxed in sleep, making him almost irresistible. He'd never looked more appealing and her heart lurched at the very sight of him. Then, as her mind gradually cleared from sleep, she suddenly remembered the train race back to New York.

Now fully awake, she propped herself up on one elbow and considered her actions of only a few hours before with a sense of growing disbelief. She'd made a vow never to let Lassiter touch her again, but he'd charmed his way into her room and had his way with her yet again, making her carelessly cast that vow aside. She flushed with distress and humiliation. How could she have succumbed so easily, even *asking* him to make love to her? she wondered with a fresh wave of mortification. Had she taken leave of all her common sense and better judgment? Distress and embarrassment brought a flush to her face. Saints above, she wondered, smoothing back her tousled hair, how could she have behaved in such a rash, utterly foolish manner?

Then the faint ache in her head reminded her of all the champagne she'd consumed at dinner. A sense of outrage gradually rose in her bosom as she carefully reviewed the past evening, which had once seemed so glorious. No doubt the rogue had made plans well ahead of time to ply her with champagne to lower her resistance to his persistent advances.

Still, that was no excuse for her deplorable actions, she thought, now seeing the lovemaking session in a completely different light. She'd let Mr. Babbage down, let the Union Pacific down, but most important, let herself down by surrendering to Lassiter's allure. Beset with regret, she swallowed back her tears. *Why did I behave so wantonly?* she wondered, thinking it

almost impossible that she'd permitted Lassiter to take
her to bed.

Full of deep contrition, she quietly slipped from the
bed. Her bare feet padding over the soft carpet, she
went to the dresser, and finding her dainty bodice
watch, discovered it was five-thirty in the morning. She
picked up her discarded undergarments and quickly put
them on, a hot blush claiming her cheeks as she
remembered how Lassiter had so deftly removed them.

Her mind now clear and composed, she analyzed all
that had happened. Although he'd heaped on the compliments last night, he hadn't told her if he was still
engaged to Daisy. No doubt he was, for his kind didn't
change, she decided, the realization making her heart
squeeze with pain.

Lassiter sighed deeply, then rolled over and continued sleeping. Remembering what they'd shared, her
heart swelled with love for him, but she warned herself
that she'd made that mistake before and must ignore
her womanly feelings. She had to be strong and listen
to her head, for giving her heart to a man like Lassiter
would only cause more trouble and heartache. She tried
to console herself with the fact that she'd been
exhausted last night and had experienced a weak
moment, and he'd callously taken advantage of her.
Still, she'd made a great mistake—a tragic mistake.

It was time for her to do some deep thinking, to
make some decisions, she reasoned, once again considering the race back to New York. She'd acted like a
moonstruck schoolgirl last night, and due to her own
foolishness, lost a great deal of her precious pride—but
that didn't mean she had to lose the race. This wasn't
the time for regrets—it was the time for action, and

clever planning, she decided, her mind spinning with possibilities.

An idea suddenly blossomed in her brain that flooded her heart with excitement. If she was quiet enough, she might be able to slip from the room without waking Lassiter, for he'd also consumed a great amount of champagne. In fact, if her luck held, he might keep sleeping and miss his train, giving her a tremendous jump on the race.

After Molly was dressed in her traveling clothes, she ran a brush through her hair, letting her locks hang loosely down her back. Silently, she packed her bags, carelessly dropping in her garments and personal items in a rush to leave the room.

After she was finished, she softly snapped the bag closed and stole a glance at Lassiter, who was still sleeping soundly. She experienced a little rush of guilty pleasure. Yes, he might miss his train, but as she saw it, she was under no obligation to wake him.

Then on the spur of the moment, she decided to write him a note, telling him just what she thought of him. Gliding open the dresser drawer, she found some hotel stationery and a pencil and scratched out her message, underlining words and using the exclamation marks he hated so much at the end of almost every sentence. She placed the note on the dresser where he was sure to find it, then looped the cords of her hatboxes over her arm, and one by one, quietly dragged her bags from the room.

Once in the hall, she managed to lift the bags from the floor and struggled toward the staircase leading to the lobby. Feeling better by the minute, she breathed a sigh of relief and thanked God she'd awakened when she did. How suprised Lassiter would be when he finally stirred from his slumber and found she wasn't even there.

With a little luck, she decided as she made her way down the carpeted stairs, her bags bumping against each step, she might win this race after all.

Lassiter awakened slowly, taking time to stretch. He experienced a few moments of grogginess, then immediately thought of Molly stretched beside him. After more lovemaking, he'd tell her he loved her and propose, then they'd enjoy a leisurely breakfast and share a carriage to the railroad station, making plans for their future. His eyes still closed, he thought of the warmth of her body and the matchless passion they'd shared the night before. Wanting to take her in his arms that very moment, he slowly rolled over and reached out for her.

When his searching hand touched thin air, he slowly opened his eyes. He blinked not once, but twice, for she'd vanished. Where she'd been sleeping, there was only a tangle of crisp white sheets. He immediately sat up and scanned the room but she was nowhere in sight. Somewhat alarmed, he swung his gaze about the chamber and saw that her discarded clothes had been picked up. Getting out of bed, he decided she'd simply awakened first and was taking a bath. With a smile, he imagined her in the huge marble tub soaking in water and surrounded in bubbles up to her chin.

He chuckled softly. He'd surprise her and join her in the tub, he thought, imagining what fun they'd have sharing the warm, soapy bath, which if he was lucky might lead to another round of lovemaking. He knocked on the bathroom door and when there was no answer, he softly pushed the panel open. Once in the room, his heart sank to his stomach, for she was nowhere in sight. Quickly, he left the bathroom, and went back into the bedchamber, becoming more anxious by the minute.

His mind spinning faster, he inspected the big armoire and found her clothes gone, then noticed her bags and hatboxes, which had been stored at the bottom, were also gone. He slammed the armoire door, deciding she must have dressed, taken her luggage, and gone downstairs for an early breakfast. She'd be at a table drinking coffee when he came down, and probably shoot him a cocky smile and ask him why he was so late joining her.

He had his undergarments and shirt on when a piece of sharply folded paper on the dresser caught his eye. A fresh rush of anxiety built in his chest as he crossed the room and picked up the note, swiftly reading it:

Lassiter,

I hope you've enjoyed your sleep, because you're going to need it. I'm appalled that I fell into your carefully laid scheme last night, you scoundrel! How dare you ply me with champagne to get me into bed with you! You're no gentleman, but I already knew that! You took advantage of me being tired and my discipline being at a low ebb. Only a cad would have behaved in such a despicable fashion, but after all is said and done, that is what you are!

I hope that it's nine o'clock when you read this note, and you've already missed your train. Good luck in beating me back to New York because I

*now have the jump on you, you black-hearted ras-
cal! I'll win the prize, but I suppose that doesn't
matter for you'll still have Daisy's millions to fall
back on. But from now on, remember the early
bird gets the worm—you contemptible worm!*

Lassiter crumpled up the note and threw it on the floor,
cursing his luck. He raked back his tousled hair and
tried to gather his wits. Damnation, why hadn't he followed his impulse to rouse Molly last night? Why in
God's name had he let her go to sleep without telling
her he couldn't live without her?

He swiftly found his pocket watch and with a spurt
of alarm saw it was already seven-thirty. Lord, he'd
botched everything royally last night, he thought with a
deep, gut-wrenching feeling of regret. But he couldn't
be thinking of that now.

Moving faster than he'd ever moved before, he
scooped up his trousers and started hastily pulling them
on. He had to get back to his room and pack, then rush
to the station and tell Molly he loved her before her
express pulled out for New York and she refused ever to
speak with him again.

Molly had arrived at the San Francisco station in plenty
of time to sit calmly on a bench and write her impressions
of the city, which she sent back to Mr. Babbage along
with her assurance that she'd win the race. But worrying
that Lassiter might arrive at any moment, she checked her
bags and hatboxes with a porter so he could put them
on her train, then nervously paced about the station,
fretfully looking for the publisher of the *Chronicle*.

To her dismay, her mind kept dwelling on Lassiter

and her cheeks heated at the way her body had betrayed her. Mortified, she couldn't believe she'd succumbed to his charms, not once but *twice* now. Then she told herself it wasn't her fault. Like a spider spinning a sticky web, the rogue had set out to ensnare her with champagne and silken words, and to her deep chagrin he'd succeeded.

Yes, Lassiter had used her sorely, but how surprised he'd be when he finally awakened to find her gone. How panicked he must be about now. She pictured him tangled in the sheets as he scrambled out of bed and into his clothes, and smiled at the cleverness of the trick she'd played on him.

Simmering with nervousness, she searched the crowd for the publisher of the *Chronicle*, wondering why he wasn't there yet. Then her heart lurched as she saw Lassiter walking down the platform, carrying his bag. He paused, and with a deep frown ploughing his brow, searched with keen eyes the crowd that was already gathered there.

Gasping, she scurried away, but her heart sank when she noticed that he'd spotted her and was headed in her direction. Straightening her shoulders, she marched away with swift strides, having no desire to talk to him. As she glanced over her shoulder, seeing he was gaining on her, her heart beat faster.

"Wait a minute, Irish, I want to talk to you," he yelled, maneuvering his way through the milling people.

She hurried ahead, hoping she could lose herself in the noisy crowd before he caught up with her. Her breath coming faster, she ducked behind a huge pillar, and holding herself against it, remained perfectly still.

After five minutes, she slowly crept from behind the concealing column, and giving a sigh of relief, began to edge away.

Just as she thought she'd lost him, their eyes met, and she scrambled away again, seeking another place to hide. When she noticed he was gaining on her, she began to run, but he was soon at her side and had firmly grabbed her elbow.

He spun her about and smiled down at her. "I got your note," he said, dropping his bag on the platform.

Molly narrowed her eyes at him. "Good," she spat out, anger knotting in her bosom like a tangled ball of twine. "I meant every word I wrote and a lot more that I didn't have time to write."

She started to move away, but he pulled her back. "That wasn't very nice, sneaking away like you did."

"I can't help it that you overslept!"

He pulled his dark brows together. "Waking me up would have been the decent thing to do, you know."

She let out an outraged sigh. "Well, well, look who's talking about being decent," she huffed, so angry she could hardly speak. "If I'm not mistaken, *you* were the one who tried to get me drunk last night."

He rolled his eyes heavenward. "I wasn't trying to get you tipsy," he groaned, "I was trying to show you a good time."

"Show me a good time? I'll never believe that. You were trying to have a good time yourself, you cad!"

Lassiter looked down into her frowning face, his mind churning with frustration. Lord, how he wanted to tell her he loved her, but how could he when she was mad enough to strangle him with her bare hands?

He firmly clasped her shoulders. "No—you don't understand."

She tore away from his fingers. "I understand perfectly. Now leave me alone before I call a policeman!"

Lassiter held her firmly, trying to calm her down enough so he could reason with her. "I have something important to tell you. I'd hoped you'd listen."

"I don't want to hear it!"

Sudden anger flooded his chest. "I'd hoped I could make you understand how I feel." He tried to caress her shoulders, to communicate his love for her with some action, but as he feared, she was as surly and hard-headed as a Kansas mule this morning.

Molly stared at his serious face, her temper refueled with memories of the previous night. "I don't want to understand how you feel. The only time I ever think of you," she lied through her teeth, holding back the fact that she thought of him almost every waking moment, "is when I picture how wonderful it will feel to beat you to the top of those City Hall steps!"

Lassiter grabbed her arm, his fingers like a band of steel. "If you'll just calm down and listen a minute—"

"Let me go, you big bully," she hotly interrupted, struggling against him. "It's a long way across the plains and I wish you nothing but bad luck. I hope your train runs off the tracks on a thousand-foot bridge," she cried, kicking at his legs. "Better yet, I hope it gets caught in the biggest snowstorm in the history of the United States. Then I hope you wander for days in the wilderness without a bite of food and take a bad case of pneumonia. When you're coughing your lungs out," she cried, aiming her foot at his shin, "I hope the Sioux capture you and slowly torture you to death with red-hot mesquite thorns. Then when you're dead, I hope the squaws pulverize your bones to powder with their corn grinders and throw the powder to the four winds!"

He tried to take her in his arms, but she hit his shoulders with her balled fists. When he was on the verge of subduing her, she had a brainstorm, and stamped her high-heeled shoe on the arch of his foot as hard as she could.

He dropped his arms and winced in pain. Seeing her chance, she scurried away, but not before pausing to look back over her shoulder to see him hopping about on one foot, his face twisted in pain.

"I'm losing patience with you, you hellcat!" he yelled after her.

"*Wonderful,*" she cried, turning about to shoot him a nasty glare.

An expression dark as a thundercloud settled over his face. "I ought to paddle your behind, you little brat."

She gave a crack of laughter. "You and who else?"

He scowled darkly. "All right, Irish, if you want war, war it shall be!" He tapped his chin. "Take a look at this face, because it'll be looking at you from the top of those City Hall steps when you roll up in your carriage—far too late to win the race."

She hooted with laughter. "Don't make me laugh, you conniving scoundrel. I'll be waiting for you in New York—that is if the Sioux don't get you first!"

Her heart lifting, she spied the publisher of the *Chronicle* walking toward her with a concerned frown on his face. A squad of photographers trailed behind him, carrying their large cameras, and she hurried toward the group, knowing that she'd be safe from Lassiter once she was in their protecting fold.

When the Union Pacific passed Sacramento and started winding into the foothills again, Molly finally began to relax. With a long sigh, she laid down her writing and looked from her window, seeing a steep ravine peppered with piñon pines and red-leafed manzanitas powdered with white. The train was negotiating a curve, and ahead of her, she spied the high Sierras, their rugged peaks gleaming with snow.

Once in the mountains, the train encountered heavy snow and slowed to the agonizing crawl Molly remembered so well. Constantly checking her watch, she started worrying about Lassiter beating her time, and as the Union Pacific locomotive inched along, eating up precious time, she pictured his express streaming full chisel over flat tracks.

The train passed through the familiar snowsheds, and on many of the twisting curves proceeded so slowly she was afraid it might come to a complete stop. Hour after long tedious hour, the train slowly puffed through the treacherous mountains, trying Molly's patience to the very limit.

For a while, she thought she'd never get out of the mountains, but at last, the train pulled into Virginia City, leaving her almost limp with relief. Her spirits sinking, she realized the eastbound trip across the Sierras had taken almost as long as the westbound, but helpless to change things, all she could do was board another express and silently pray it would make better time across Nevada.

After dinner the next day, she wrote another feature, then emotionally exhausted, went to her sleeping car, wanting to get a good night's rest. She dreamed of Lassiter that long night, dreamed of his glittering eyes and warm fingers, and the way her body tingled under his practiced touch, then she woke at dawn, angry at herself because she couldn't control her dreams.

She spent another tedious day as her train slowly chugged its way through the Wasach mountains and South Pass, devouring yet more precious time. Trying to calm her rising anxiety, she looked at the mountain scenery and thought of New York, wishing she were already there. Her mind drifting, she considered Tom Perkins, still scarcely believing he'd been able to deceive her so completely. Trying to push the unpleasant memory from her mind, she smiled and thought of how much happier Brian had been since he'd come to live at the boardinghouse.

Then lost in a private world of introspection, she recalled her mother's lovely face the afternoon she'd told Molly she should try to forgive her father. Scanning the rugged slopes, Molly sighed, and in this quiet place, examined her heart, gradually realizing that without consciously making the decision, she'd somehow been able to do that very thing. Amazed with the secret workings of her own heart, which had wrought the life-altering decision, she felt a great burden lifted from her shoulders.

Filled with a sense of spiritual renewal, she traveled through the magnificent Platte Valley and arrived at the Cheyenne rail station about dusk. Snow was peppering down steadily as she exited the train and paused to talk with some of the people who'd come out to bid her good luck. As she passed a rough counter stacked with a few newspapers, she eyed the publications that were all from the west, and yearned for the moment she was far enough east that she could buy an armload of the thick New York papers and see what they were reporting about her.

Despite Molly's best efforts, she kept thinking of Lassiter, and facing up to her emotions, wondered if she'd see him in Omaha. Hearing a long, wailing whistle, she walked toward her express, a porter pushing a creaking luggage cart at her heels. She had to admit that in one sense she yearned to see Lassiter again, on the other hand, she hoped she'd never have to face him until she could look him in straight in the eye, knowing she'd beaten him.

Squaring her shoulders, she forced him out of her mind and boarded the puffing express. Fueled with steely determination, she sat down in another magnificent parlor car and concentrated on the race, for to her, it had now become her total reason for living.

At that very moment, Lassiter's train steamed through the plains, and he laid back his head thinking Molly had probably already arrived at Cheyenne and was streaking toward Omaha.

Retrieving a cigar from his vest, he lit it, visualizing the Irish hoyden who'd turned his life upside down. He recalled the way her hair dazzled like burnished copper in the sunlight, and the way her laughter stirred his deepest feelings. He remembered the first time he'd made love to her and how it had lifted his spirits to the stars and touched his soul like nothing before it. Then with a stab of regret, he also remembered how he'd come close to telling her he loved her several times, but hadn't been completely sure until that night in San Francisco.

How she'd changed him since he'd first met her. She was so special—so completely unique and filled with exuberant life. He took a long draw from his cigar, deciding that with her special brand of faith and hope, she'd taught him what it was to really dream again, and make that dream into a reality. She taught him to live again—live with hope and purpose and excitement. Most of all, she'd taught him that real love existed and was within his reach, if he was only willing to latch on to it.

He closed his eyes and sighed. What a mess he'd made of their whole tangled relationship. But how could he tell her that he adored her more than life itself when she was flailing at his shoulders and kicking at his legs?

After riding awhile longer, he straightened himself up on the seat and looked at the scrubby land that now passed by in a blur of browns and grays. Could he ever convince Molly that he loved her? Could he ever persuade her to accept his proposal of marriage? Somehow, someway, he thought, grinding out his cigar in frustration, he had to make her talk to him.

Full of despair, he listened to the sound of the clicking train wheels, then with a glow of hope, realized the challenge was simple. All he had to do was get to Omaha before her. That was it. He'd be waiting for her in the station as he'd been on the way west, and forcefully sit her on a bench until he had poured out his heart, holding her there by brute force if necessary.

With a little luck, maybe he'd get another chance to talk some sense into the wildcat.

Lassiter gazed from his window as the Kansas Pacific wound its way across the endless prairie, dotted with herds of graceful antelope as well as shaggy buffalo. He watched the animals with some interest for a while, then for the dozenth time went over in his mind what he wanted to say to Molly in Omaha.

He knew there wasn't any hope of being romantic or subtle, for she'd amply demonstrated she was mad enough at him to shoot him on the spot. He'd just take her in his arms, and warding off her blows to his chest, blurt out that he loved her. No doubt she wouldn't believe him, but he'd tell her again, then kiss her until she lost her breath—kiss her until she was silent enough and compliant enough to listen to his confession of love.

Lost in hopeful anticipation, he rode for another thirty minutes, too distracted to write, then he noticed that the train had begun to slow. Getting up, he left his luxurious parlor car, went through a vestibule, and walked into a regular passenger car, attracting the attention of several interested travelers, who turned their heads to stare at him. At last finding a steward, he clasped the man's arm and inquired, "Is there some problem? Why has the train slowed down to a crawl?"

The man shook his head, then pointed out the window at the gently curving tracks ahead of them. "Buffalo, that's the problem, sir," he answered as the train now came to almost a complete stop.

Lassiter peered from the window to see a gigantic herd of buffalo slowly crossing the flat, scrubby landscape ahead of them as they leisurely nibbled on winter-burned grass poking through the thin coating of snow glazing the earth.

He blinked at the lumbering sea of reddish-brown buffalo passing over the tracks, their shaggy manes shaking in rhythm to their rolling gait. There were big cows, and bulls with cracked, craggy horns, standing six to seven feet at the shoulder hump, as well as an assortment of calves whose thick hair was a soft yellowish color. Lord, there were hundreds of the animals, thousands of them in fact, and they were taking all the time in the world as they aimlessly wandered over the tracks in their progress to God knew where.

Some of the other passengers were at the windows, pressing their hands against the panes, oohing and ahhing as they enjoyed the strange spectacle gradually unfolding before them. Children laughed and talked, and several little boys extended their arms and pointed their fingers at the buffalo, pretending to shoot them. Even their parents seemed mesmerized, and not at all worried that the locomotive had now come to a complete stop as the engineer waited for the animals to pass so the train could be underway again.

A man stood to open his window, and the sound of the snorting bulls, who occasionally pawed at the earth and bellowed deep in their throats, could be plainly heard. A woman two rows back shot up, marched to the window and slammed the pane shut before huffing back to her seat. The beady-eyed buffalo lowered their heads, horns thrust forward, and continued their agonizingly slow progress, blissfully unaware that they'd temporarily halted civilization's march of progress.

Lassiter noticed a sick feeling in the pit of his stomach. "Do you have any idea when the train will be moving again?" he asked the steward, hoping against hope the man would give him some encouraging news.

The man let out his breath in a rush. "Nope, I haven't any idea at all, sir."

"Has this ever happened before?" Lassiter asked, irritated that nothing was being done to clear the tracks.

The man laughed. "It sure has," he answered, tugging down his billed hat. "Why, just last year we had to stop for five hours one time before the blasted animals crossed the tracks."

"*Five hours?*" Lassiter repeated, watching several of the buffalo pause to stare directly at the train, foam streaming from their open mouths. Devastated, he looked back at the steward. "Can't *anything* be done?"

The man shrugged. "No, not a damn thing. You can't hurry the animals, and if you try to spook them, it just makes it worse. Some of them bulls weigh better than two thousand pounds and none of the crew is fool enough to get out among them. All we can do is just sit here until they're all over the tracks."

For thirty minutes, Lassiter watched a wide stream of buffalo amble over the tracks, then continue into the arid prairie that was riddled with bushes, rocks, and shallow washes. Finally tiring of the sight, he went back to his parlor car, and after pacing about for a while, flopped down and checked his watch, noting the train had already been halted for an hour.

He bit the end off a cigar, then lit it up, thinking of all the calamities Molly had wished upon him, including being tortured to death by Sioux squaws. No doubt, she'd have included an endless herd of buffalo in her litany of curses, if she'd only thought of it. But even with her vivid imagination, she hadn't imagined such a calamity as this.

He propped his elbow on the armrest and supported his head, deciding Molly would beat him into Omaha for sure now. Had a man ever been so sorely tried as he? he wondered, silently cursing his astonishing bad luck.

At dusk, Molly's train slowly puffed into the Omaha train station. She looked from the window and saw the usual crowd, all waving signs and shouting her name. Her spirits lifted by their gay mood, she fluttered her handkerchief at them and gathered up her things, getting ready to depart the parlor car.

She marched along the platform, a porter following her swinging bustle, acknowledging the cries of her fans with thank-yous and waves of her gloved hand. From the corner of her eye, she spotted Lassiter's welcoming committee, and laughing to herself, walked right past them.

She sent her feature, and as she exited the telegraph office, heard a loud whistle and saw a Kansas Pacific locomotive pulling into the depot. She paused, and her pulse fluttered wildly as she waited to see if Lassiter would exit the train. Several agonizing minutes dragged by, then a stream of passengers emerged, but he wasn't with them, and to her surprise, instead of being elated, she experienced a strange rush of depression.

Wondering what could have happened to him, she boarded her new express, which steamed across the middle of the Iowa farmland, quickly eating up the miles. Trying to ignore the uneasy feeling she had about Lassiter, she wrote and ate and slept, and after many weary hours, at last reached Chicago. Anticipation simmering within her, she gathered up her writing, shoved it into her tote bag, and walked to the end of the car, eager to stretch her legs.

Several dignitaries met her on the platform, and after talking with them, she made her way to the telegraph office. Her mind still filled with Lassiter, she thought of the argument she'd had with him in the San Francisco depot. He'd seemed so intent on talking to her, but she'd cut him off at every turn.

The sound of the clicking telegraph key ringing in her ears, she began to wonder if she'd been too hard on him. Her womanly instincts told her yes, but her hardheaded practical side told her no. The man had wantonly manipulated her once again, and her pride had demanded that she rebuff him. He'd gotten everything that was coming to him and deserved even more.

She left the office, realizing she was beginning the last and most important leg of her journey. For the first time since Lassiter had made her trip into a race, she was glad for what had happened. She would have never agreed to the event in a million years, but as things had turned out, she stood to profit from his underhanded scheme tremendously, and with a little glow of triumph, she decided that also served him right.

On the way back to her new express, she noticed a newsstand, and with a rush of excitement, saw the first New York papers since leaving that city. She bought an armful, then boarded the train, planning to read them all the way back to the Forty-second Street depot.

After the Union Pacific had pulled out of the Chicago station, she settled down and started devouring the papers, scanning the *Metropolitan* first. She quickly found the feature she'd written on San Francisco, and with a feeling of pride, noticed that Mr. Babbage had printed it just as she'd written it. She studied a photo of herself and one of Lassiter printed beside it, grudgingly admitting to herself that the scoundrel looked as good in newsprint as he did in person.

She flipped through the paper, reading some of the columns, then on a whim, turned to the society pages. Like a slap in the face, a photo of Daisy Fellows in a fantastic lace-edged wedding gown leaped out at her, taking her breath away. At first fearing Lassiter might have married her before he began the race, she tore through the story, but to her utter astonishment, discovered Daisy was now Mrs. Edwin G. Longstreet of the Long Island Longstreets.

Dumbfounded, she read the story three times to make sure she'd understood everything correctly. The pair had been married in Saint Patrick's Cathedral only a few days ago, then enjoyed a lavish reception at Delmonico's before leaving on a steamer for an extended honeymoon in Paris.

Molly drew in a long, steadying breath. Daisy was a married woman and no longer engaged to Lassiter. Her mind spun with disbelief, for she knew the socialite would never give him up of her own accord. *He* must have broken his engagement with *her,* and she'd quickly married on the rebound. But why would he break off with her when he needed cash so badly to keep his paper afloat? Joy began to seep through her. Could he have possibly broken the engagement because he loved her? Was this what he'd been trying to tell her when they'd had their terrible argument in San Francisco?

Her throat tightening with emotion, she tried to piece everything together. If that were the case, why hadn't he given her that important information when they'd made love in San Francisco? The possibility that Lassiter might actually love her filled her with such emotion that tears now streamed down her face. Saints above, why hadn't the great fool told her about all of this earlier?

Molly read the other New York papers and as she perused all the articles about Daisy and her new husband, her spirits rose with every word. Then she thought of how Lassiter always tried to manipulate people, and doubt and suspicion stole into her soul like a slow poison. There must be some other reason why he'd broken his engagement with Daisy. Perhaps he and her father had argued about a loan, and seeing he would get no help from the millionaire, he'd broken the engagement so he could marry another rich socialite.

She blinked back fresh tears, for she simply couldn't believe that it was possible for Lassiter to love her more than his precious *Telegram*. Still the thought that he was now a free man, unencumbered with a previous romantic commitment, made her heart leap with hope and excitement. What would happen when she saw him in New York? Was there a slim chance that he might tell her he loved her? she wondered, folding up the newspapers with trembling hands.

Chapter Twenty

Molly's heart beat a little faster as she caught her first glimpse of the buildings of New York. She'd stayed the course, and if luck was with her, had won the race, but she'd only know that when she arrived and heard the reaction of the crowd.

The buildings were coming faster and thicker now, and when the express began to slacken its pace as it approached the great glassed train terminal, she sat back and tried to calm her nerves. She breathed a sigh of relief that she'd soon be seeing her family and getting back to her normal life. With a sense of bubbling anticipation, she thought of her mother and Aunt Agatha and the others from the boardinghouse and wondered if they'd be in the station to greet her.

She noticed a maze of tracks beside her own and

heard a long wailing whistle as the engineer announced the arrival of the Union Pacific. Her train glided past others that had just pulled in and were still belching steam, then slowed even more. When the locomotive finally came to a quivering stop, Molly smoothed down her skirt and settled her hat upon her head, preparing to leave the train.

New York, she thought, her pulse fluttering with excitement. *Home at last.* She peered from the window, seeing throngs of people waving signs emblazoned with her name. Some of the placards read, WELCOME HOME, MOLLY, and when she spied one reading, YOU'VE WON! she experienced a sweet rush of joy. Could it really be true? she wondered, barely able to control her burgeoning excitement.

Her heart singing with pleasure, she stood and exited the express, then walked down the car's metal steps, an obliging porter carrying her luggage. She was immediately immersed in the scents of oil and soot and the sounds of hissing trains, slamming compartment doors, and screeching whistles.

The instant her feet hit the platform, thunderous cheers filled her ears, and for a moment she had a flashback of the rolling prairies, high mountains, and the steep streets of San Francisco. What a journey she'd made; what an experience she'd had—the experience of a lifetime.

Behind a long series of restraining cords interspersed with metal posts, a brass band lustily played "When Irish Eyes Are Smiling," and there were people everywhere—women with children, and shouting men, some dressed in working clothes, others garbed in fine attire and sporting fur-trimmed overcoats and brass-handled walking canes.

An eager host of reporters dipped under the cords and made their way toward her. Momentarily overwhelmed, she wondered how she should handle them, what she should say. Then with a sense of relief, she spied Mr. Babbage striding down the platform, his face wreathed in a welcoming smile. As soon as their gazes met, she told the porter to put her luggage on a handcart and follow her, then hurried toward her employer.

With a joyous expression, the editor of the *Metropolitan* closed the distance between them and pressed her against his slight frame. His face was radiant and there was a sheen of tears in his watery eyes. "Welcome home, my dear," he finally managed, patting her back, then easing her away to sweep an appreciative gaze over her.

She burst out with laughter. "Is it true? Have I really won?"

"Almost," the little man chuckled, taking the handcart from the porter and tipping the man, "but I checked on the progress of the New York Central and Burke Lassiter's train is only half an hour behind yours. We have to get to City Hall as soon as possible."

Mr. Babbage waved off the pack of clamoring reporters and photographers who were trailing Molly and began shoving the squeaking handcart toward the terminal building. An excited crowd followed the pair as Mr. Babbage pushed the luggage down the platform with Molly by his side, leaning close as she answered his questions about the trip.

"I've hired an open carriage to take you downtown, my dear," Mr. Babbage advised her as they left the platform and walked through the teminal itself still accompanied by a band of Molly's admirers. "It's a long way to City Hall, so we have no time to spare," he added, walking a little faster.

"But what about Mam and Aunt Agatha? When will I get to see them?"

"Don't worry," he replied, speaking louder so she could hear him over the cries of the fans, "they'll be waiting for you at City Hall."

As they left the terminal with her luggage and walked toward a line of victorias, she noticed a stream of people following them out of the building. Once the driver put her bags and hatboxes in the back of the carriage, she and Mr. Babbage claimed a place on the leather seat, but the crowd was so thick about them the victoria couldn't proceed. Molly experienced a moment of panic. What would happen now? she wondered as her euphoric fans stretched out their hands and frantically tried to grab her legs.

Her anxiety steadily built as they sat stalled. Then a mounted policeman clattered into view, and by waving his gloved hand and blowing a whistle, managed to push back the crowd. Calling to the frightened horse, the driver was finally able to control him, and with the policeman now leading the way, the carriage started to roll slowly from the railroad station and bound away for downtown.

As they made a turn off Forty-second Street, Mr. Babbage put his mouth close to Molly's ear and said, "Don't be frightened, my dear. The *Metropolitan* published your route to City Hall yesterday, and I'm sure we'll encounter crowds all along the way, but the police should be able to clear our path."

It was a perfect winter's day with a light breeze and only a few clouds, and as Molly scanned the noisy crowds lining the street, she could scarcely believe her eyes. People jostled one another to get a better view, and looking up, she spotted welcoming banners stretched across tall buildings. One especially colorful banner, printed in orange and gold, read, CONGRATULATIONS TO THE ANGEL OF MURPHY STREET FROM THE ANCIENT SOCIETY OF HIBERNIANS.

On the sidewalks pandemonium reigned, and overhead excited people leaned from open windows, waving American and Irish flags. At the same time, children raced behind the carriage, raking sticks over its wheel spokes. Gentlemen on fine steeds galloped past, smiling and tilting their top hats in respect, and one gallant even tossed a bouquet into the rolling carriage. Pride glowed within Molly's bosom for it seemed this day belonged to her alone.

Then sudden tears stung her eyes as she recalled another day—the day she'd arrived in America only six months ago. At that time she'd been unceremoniously loaded onto a barge and taken to Castle Island to be questioned and prodded, and treated more like an animal than a human being. Now all of New York was shouting her name. She smiled to herself, knowing Father Riley would never believe what had happened to the girl who'd once cleaned his parsonage and washed his dinner dishes.

Molly's carriage slowed to negotiate a corner and the

shouting throngs surged forward, completely surrounding their mounted police escort and once again stalling the victoria's progress.

A sea of people stared up at Molly with longing expressions, calling her name and trying to touch her. Mr. Babbage put his arm about her to comfort her. As the people became more insistent, some of the men swinging their arms in an attempt to grab the horse's bridle, he rose, and scanning the crowd with an anguished face cried, "Please! Step back and let us pass!"

Ignoring his pleas, the people pressed closer, raising adoring hands toward Molly. The frightened horse shied and reared and the driver stood, trying to unsuccessfully rein him in. People screamed and clutched the carriage wheels in an attempt to get to Molly, and as the vehicle began to rock back and forth, she held to the seat, terrified they would be overturned.

Her mind whirled frantically as she imagined Lassiter only miles from the train station now. Would he win the race that had now come down to a matter of crossing the city, simply because she couldn't make her way through the frenzied mob?

Lassiter gathered his things as the New York Central slowly steamed into the Forty-second Street terminal. Peering from the window he saw milling crowds, some with signs to welcome him, but his heart dipped when he noticed placards bearing Molly's name scattered on the platform. He had the distinct impression that he'd arrived at a gigantic party, but too late to be a part of it. Newspapers and other litter were strewn on the platform as if a massive crowd had waited hours for the guest of honor, then left in a hurry to follow their idol.

Scores of people still filtered from the platform in the direction of the terminal, undoubtedly trying to make their way downtown to see the Angel of Murphy Street claim her prize. What had the little baggage thought about her grand reception? What had she felt? he wondered, truly happy for her fame.

Lassiter gathered his belongings and left the hissing train to meet a modest crowd who congratulated him on his trip. He shook hands with representatives from the New York Central; Kansas Pacific; and Atchison, Topeka, and Santa Fe, and after briefly speaking with the men, discovered Molly had indeed arrived to a tumultuous welcome usually reserved for war heroes.

Mixed emotions clashed within him as he left the officials and hurried down the platform, carrying his bag. In one respect, he experienced a feeling of defeat, but then he quickly decided that simply speaking to Molly was more important to him than winning any race, no matter what the prize. Once she'd left City Hall and was in the arms of her family, she might refuse to see him again, so he had to get downtown with all speed.

Swiftly pacing from the terminal, he selected a waiting hack and ordered the driver to take him downtown, using back streets he was sure would be less crowded than the route Babbage had probably chosen for publicity reasons. After tossing his luggage into the boot, he got into the hack and it bolted away.

Lassiter leaned against the seat, harboring a burning desire to take Molly in his arms and talk some sense into her. It was all a matter of time now. Could he make it to City Hall before she marched up those steps and out of his life forever?

With the assistance of an additional squad of New York's Finest, the crowds were finally dispersed and Molly's carriage started rolling toward its destination once again. She sighed with relief, but at the same time could not forget that if the New York Central was on schedule, Lassiter was now in the metropolis and had probably started toward City Hall himself.

Molly and Mr. Babbage rolled across the heart of the city for twenty minutes, acknowledging cheering crowds lining both sides of the wide boulevard. They passed through the financial district filled with newsstands, and when Molly finally caught her first sight of City Hall Park, her heart pounded deeply. The park was so filled with people all trying to catch a glimpse of her that she couldn't see the ground upon which they stood.

The carriage slowed, and she noticed the huge marble-faced City Hall building was surrounded by an even greater throng than she'd found at the train station. There were photographers and another brass band playing, and the excited people all screamed her name, making such a noise she had to stifle an urge to cover her ears.

Once the carriage came to a complete stop, Mr. Babbage got out and helped her to the pavement. "This way, my dear," he urged, taking her elbow once again as the photographers' flash pans flared. "Hurry, for we don't have a moment to waste."

Scanning the sea of faces, she spotted her mother and almost everyone else from the boardinghouse standing behind a roped-off enclosure at the base of the great marble steps. Her heart went out to them, for she knew that to get such a privileged position they must have been waiting since dawn. Impulsively she broke away from Mr. Babbage's grip and ran toward them. She reached her mother first, hugging her tightly, then noticed Brian at her side and quickly kissed his cheek.

"Oh, Molly," her mother gushed, thank God you're home safely. We've been keeping up with your adventures in the paper every day. Are you all right?"

For a moment Molly was so overcome she couldn't speak. "Yes, I'm fine!" she finally managed.

Slipping away from Kathleen, she hugged Aunt Agatha, who was wearing her treasured hat, its black feathers swaying gently.

"Molly, you've won the race, my girl," she exclaimed, clutching her so tightly she thought her ribs would crack.

Brian gazed up at Molly and tugged at her arm, his face glowing with pride. "That's right, now you're as famous as ole John L. hisself!" he cried, speaking the man's name as if he were a saint.

Shamus, Fergus and Clara stood behind the the trio, their expressions bubbling over with joy. Molly quickly grabbed their outstretched hands and squeezed them, and laughing through her tears of excitement, cried a special greeting to each of the others from the boardinghouse over the roar of the crowd.

Kathleen held Molly's arm, her expression bright with anticipation. "What about Mr. Lassiter? Did you talk to him? Where is the darling man?"

"I don't know where he is," Molly said more sharply

than she'd intended. "I don't want to talk about the wretched man. *I hate him.*"

Kathleen caressed her face. "*No,* I think you really love him."

Out of respect for her mother, Molly bit off another tart reply. If the woman only knew how he'd behaved in San Francisco. If she only knew what a rascal he really was. "Oh, Mam," she groaned, caressing her mother's back. "If you only understood!"

Kathleen drew her delicate brows together. "Darling, more than anything, a mother wants her child to be happy." She smoothed her hands down her daughter's arms. "Too much pride is a dangerous thing," she continued in an earnest voice. "You're young. You have your whole life in front of you. Don't be thinking of your father. You'll never understand all that happened between us, so let it go. Don't be afraid to love." Tears glimmered in her eyes. "Do that, for it would be the finest gift you could give me."

Molly swallowed back a rush of tears.

Kathleen clutched her arms a little tighter. "Have you found it in your heart to forgive your father?" she suddenly asked, her eyes deep and imploring.

Too emotional to speak, Molly could only nod.

"Well then," her mother said with an encouraging smile, "you can also forgive Mr. Lassiter. Just look into your heart and you'll find all the forgiveness you need. All you have to do is take it."

Molly had no time to consider the suggestion for Mr. Babbage was at her side frantically tugging at her arm. "My dear, please hurry. I beg of you!" He glanced at the top of the steps where a group of railroad officials dressed in dark suits and top hats waited impatiently, pacing about and nervously glancing at their pocket watches. "Walk up those steps and claim your prize!"

Molly looked up the steps and felt a glow of resolve. Her mother just didn't understand. Lassiter didn't love her or he'd have told her about his broken engagement in San Francisco. Obviously his plans for the future didn't include marrying her. It was time to put him from her mind forever. Her heart pounding as if it would burst from her bosom, she raised the hem of her skirt and moved away from Mr. Babbage.

Seeing her actions, the crowd roared its approval.

She was only on the second step when she heard another great roar from the crowd, and wondering what had happened, turned about with a start. A carriage had just stopped beside hers and as a man exited the hack and raised himself to his full height, her heart jumped to her throat.

There as big as the devil himself stood Lassiter, a flashing smile on his handsome face.

Lassiter scanned Molly, and as their gazes locked, he knew she only had to continue up the steps to win the prize. His breath came a little faster. Lord, what a moment this was. For an instant the great noise about him dimmed and it seemed that time itself had stopped. The whole race had come down to something as simple as walking up a flight of stairs.

He slowly neared the gleaming steps, knowing he could easily bound up them ahead of Molly, but she'd won the race, and if the truth be known, he was proud of her. He held her fiery gaze. What was wrong with her? Why was she standing there still as a statue, seemingly trying to make some type of important decision?

The little hellion should be scrambling toward the officials this very instant, he thought, stifling an urge to shout at her to move ahead.

Molly continued staring at him, an expression of intense concentration lighting her countenance. What was she thinking? What was she trying to decide? Most important, what would she do now? he wondered, watching her face for a sign of what might be going on in her pretty head.

She suddenly shot him a look of challenge, and turning, straightened her back and continued up the steps. *Good girl.* She was going to accept what was rightfully hers, but had he expected any less of the feisty Molly Kilmartin? The prize was hers, and of course she would claim it.

He watched her quickly pace up the steps, a picture of feminine grace and dignity. The crowd's noise was deafening, and halfway up, Molly turned to acknowledge the people's acclaim with a wave of her hand—then a horrified expression flew over her face as she stumbled and fell on the hard marble. Lassiter's heart lurched, for she doubled over and clutched one of her ankles, and her agonized expression told him she was in terrible pain. The crowd groaned, their voices one great cry of distress, and Mr. Babbage's face went chalky white.

Lassiter's heart squeezed with alarm. Without thinking, he raced up the steps and knelt to gather her soft body in his arms. From his side vision, he caught a glimpse of the editor of the *Metropolitan* clamoring up the steps, his eyes filled with shocked disbelief behind his sliding spectacles. The crowd's once exuberant roar had diminished to a murmuring buzz of alarm, and their stunned expressions were stamped with curiosity and disappointment.

Lassiter put his arms about Molly and pulled her close. "Good Lord, Irish, what have you done?" he demanded, hastily cupping her face and searching her pain-filled eyes. "Are you all right?

Molly bit her bottom lip. "I've twisted my ankle," she wailed, sucking in her breath. "Ohh, it hurts so much." She winced and pulled her brows together. "Who would have thought *this* would happen? I don't think I can stand, and I know I can't walk."

"Let me see how bad it is." Lassiter ran his hand over her ankle and she gave a long moan.

"No, don't touch it!" Her eyes glittered with sparkling tears. "Go on—*you win*. Get up there and take the prize," she hurled at him, her voice rough with the agony of her injury.

Lassiter stared at her speechlessly, not believing what he was hearing. "I think you must have cracked your head instead of twisting your ankle," he exclaimed, now really beginning to worry about her. "Do you know what you're saying?"

She scowled up at him. "Don't you remember the rules? The first contestant to the top of the steps is the winner."

"Of course I remember the rules," he shot back, starting to lose patience with her in earnest. "I helped write them."

She winced again. "Then quit babbling and go get the prize."

"*No*. It belongs to you." He let his gaze play over the impatient crowd, then looked back at her. "These people are here to see you win. You're not going to disappoint them, are you?"

By now Mr. Babbage was at Molly's side. Huffing and puffing, he knelt on one knee and gazed down at her, his eyes wide with alarm. "My dear, what in heaven's name is wrong with you? You only have a few more steps to climb. Surely you can make it!"

She gave him a wan smile. "No—I can't. I can't put any weight on this foot at all. Surely you wouldn't have me crawl up the steps."

Shock drained the blood from his face. "No, it's just that I didn't think—I mean—I—" he stammered, his anguished voice finally wobbling to a halt.

Lassiter put Molly's arms about his neck. "Damn it to hell, you'll go to the top of those steps if I have to carry you." He scooped his arms under her, then rose and started up the steps.

She slipped one arm free, and balling her fist, hit at his shoulders. "No, put me down!"

He quickly strode up the steps toward the wide-eyed official with the envelope whose mouth was agape in shock. "I'm trying to save your bacon."

"I'll save my own bacon!"

"Shut up, you hardheaded little mick. You're going to take that blasted envelope if I have to put it in your hands and close your fingers around it myself."

The crowd went wild with excitement and roared its approval while Mr. Babbage slowly plodded after them, dabbing at his forehead with a folded handkerchief.

Molly squirmed in Lassiter's arms, but holding her a little tighter, he managed to carry her to the official with the envelope, who drew in a sharp breath of astonishment. "Now stand up and take the prize before I throttle you" Lassiter ordered, forcefully subduing her flailing arm.

"I can't stand up."

"Yes, you can. Put your weight on your good foot and lean on me."

Apparently knowing she was beaten, Molly grudgingly obeyed, clutching tightly to his shoulders as the other officials hurried toward them, shocked expressions racing over their faces. "I-I don't understand," one of the men blurted out, sweeping his confused gaze over both of them. "Which one of you is here to accept the prize?"

"*He* is!" Molly cried, cutting a hard gaze at Lassiter.

He scowled and jabbed his finger at her. "No, *she* is. She was in the city first."

Mr. Babbage finally made it to the top of the steps himself. "He's right," he affirmed, a thread of hysteria in his voice. "She was in the city a good thirty minutes before the New York Central arrived."

Their voices rising in debate, the railroad officials conferred with one another at length; then the gentleman with the envelope studied Lassiter, his countenance still worried and perplexed. "This is most irregular," he murmured, his tone irritated that he was being subjected to such a spectacle. "Do you concede the race, sir? I must hear it from your own lips before I'll believe it."

"Yes, I concede the race," Lassiter answered with staunch determination, becoming digusted with how hard it was to give away fifty thousand dollars. "Now give the prize to Miss Kilmartin."

"Very well, if you insist," the official whispered in a baffled tone, "Molly Kilmartin wins the race across

America and the prize that goes with it." Struggling to maintain a dignity appropriate to the occasion, he pulled himself up to his full height and placed the envelope in Molly's hand. She tried to shove it at Lassiter, but he laid it in her palm and tightly closed her fingers over it.

When the official placed his hand above her head to indicate to the crowd that she'd won, they burst out with thunderous cheers that washed up the steps in reverberating waves.

After the railroad mavens questioned Molly and Lassiter awhile longer, they began to drift away, still hotly conferring with one another and shrugging their shoulders. His spectacles now resting on the tip of his nose, Mr. Babbage trailed after them, and in an insistent voice continued to assure them that they'd made the right decision.

When Molly and Lassiter were finally alone, she looked up at him with a faintly puzzled expression. "With all those flat tracks, I was sure you'd beat me back. What in the world kept you?"

"Buffalo," he groaned, widening his eyes at the memory of the experience. "A herd big as the state of Texas blocked the tracks for four hours, if you must know."

She giggled merrily. "Now why didn't I think of that? It's almost as good as the Sioux squaws torturing you to death and pulverizing your bones."

Her laughter finally drifted away, and as he tightened his arm about her, her expression gradually stilled. Her eyes now glittered with the familiar fiery light he knew so well. "On the way back to New York, I read that Daisy had married someone else," she said, a suspicious expression settling over her face. "Why in heaven's name didn't you tell me that night in San Francisco you'd broken your engagement!"

Lassiter ran his finger down her nose and sighed. "I kept intending to," he smiled, "but it was rather difficult while you were raining curses on my head and kicking at my legs, you know." He laughed and steadied her arm as she swayed in his grip. "I should have shaken you into submission. Can you forgive me?"

Her face softened. "Oh, I'll think about it," she replied with a teasing grin.

The band struck up a sentimental rendition of "Danny Boy," and Lassiter picked up Molly and started carrying her toward his waiting hack to the roared approval of the crowd. Among the photographers' glaring flash pans, he noticed Kathleen looking up at them with a pleased smile, and gave thanks that there was one sensible woman in the Kilmartin clan. "Your family may be waiting," he sternly told Molly, "but we have a lot to talk about and you're going home with me, you redheaded hoyden."

When they were at the base of the steps, the crowd cheered as never before, and Brian suddenly ducked under the ropes, and whooping for joy, hurled his shabby cap skyward. Cupping his hands to his mouth, he leaned forward and shouted, "Well, why are you just standin' there, Mr. Lassiter? Ain't you gonna kiss her?"

Lassiter placed Molly on her good foot, and holding her tightly so she wouldn't fall, lowered his lips to hers. "Sounds like a good idea to me," he chuckled, "but I swear I'll throttle you if you try to slap me again."

Molly gave him a crooked grin. "Don't worry, sir, this hellcat has had her claws clipped." Showing no

389

resistance, she let him slant his mouth across hers. He kissed her deeply, feeling her melt in his embrace. Lord, he was really in love for the first time in his life and it was fantastic. He'd found the fulfillment he couldn't put a name to—the companionship and warmth of a woman he cared about with all his heart and every fiber of his being.

He knew she'd remain the same colorful Irish hellion the rest of her life, but as his heart brimmed with love, he decided that's just the way he liked her. Yes, he thought with a reassuring sense of contentment, he may have lost the race across America, but he'd won the most important contest in his life—the contest for Molly's heart.

A delicate fire ran through Molly's flesh and a glorious sense of excitement rolled over her as she accepted the forgiveness she readily found for him in her pounding heart. Light-headed with pleasure, she finally admitted to herself that she loved him with a love beyond her control—a love that would last into eternity.

When Lassiter finally broke the kiss and eased her away a bit, she clutched his shoulders and looked up at his amused face. "How do you like being famous?" he asked sweeping his hands over her back and pulling her closer.

She wrinkled her nose. "It's not bad," she said, laughing softly, "but it's really noisy. I've decided I'd rather be happy than famous any day."

His eyes grew incredibly tender. "I love you, Molly Kilmartin. I love all of you—your mind, your spirit, your heart, your gorgeous hair and eyes, and even your fiery temper." He clutched her shoulders, his eyes sparkling with excited anticipation. "Will you marry me, Irish?"

She gasped at his confession of love. "Yes, God help me," she answered with all her heart, weak with joy that he'd finally uttered the words, "I'll marry you any day of the week. You'll never get rid of me now!"

"Wonderful," he laughed, crushing her to him and fluttering kisses over her forehead and both of her cheeks.

After he'd ravaged her lips again, she struggled away and searched his smiling face. "I'll marry you on *one* condition."

He raised his brows. "Yes, anything, my darling Molly."

"I'll marry you if you'll use the prize money to keep the *Telegram* afloat."

His face softened, and she sensed he wanted to respond, but for the first time since she'd met him, she saw threatening tears brimming in his eyes.

"And one more thing," she continued, giving a little hop on her good foot to balance herself.

Lassiter cocked a dark brow. "Uh-oh, I think I should have read the fine print on this contract," he groaned, a surprised expression slowly stealing over his face.

"Yes, you should have, but it's too late for you to back out of this deal now, so you're stuck with it. I want to write a matching editorial for each one of yours— and my byline must be two points larger than yours."

Lassiter burst out laughing. "Still the same spitfire I met on the *Saxonia,* I see." His eyes warm and dreamy, he lowered his lips once more to sear her mouth with a kiss full of wild desire.

Sonya Birmingham

Blood roared in Molly's ears, drowning out the cheering crowd. A tremulous urgency ran through her, and sighing, she leaned close against him, noticing the thud of his pounding heart. Filled with a glowing warmth, she felt as if she'd scooped the winter's sun from the sky and it was now shining in her heart. Smiling inwardly, she realized that Lassiter now thought he knew everything about her—but how little he really knew.

During this glorious moment she decided she'd go to her grave keeping her secret: She'd purposely stumbled on the City Hall steps and her ankle wasn't twisted at all. Well, saints above, she thought with a satisfied chuckle, the darling man didn't need to know everything, did he now?

SCARLET LEAVES — Sonya Birmingham

Bestselling Author of *Frost Flower*

From the moment silky Shanahan spots the buck-naked stranger in old man Johnson's pond, she is smitten. Yet despite her yearning, the fiery rebel suspects the handsome devil is a Yankee who needs capturing. Since every able-bodied man in the Smoky Mountains is off fighting the glorious War for Southern Independence, the buckskin-clad beauty will have to take the good-looking rascal prisoner herself, and she'll be a ring-tailed polecat if she'll let him escape. But even with her trusty rifle aimed at the enemy soldier, Silky fears she is in danger of betraying her country—and losing her heart to the one man she should never love.

_4081-6 $5.50 US/$6.50 CAN

Dorchester Publishing Co., Inc.
P.O. Box 6640
Wayne, PA 19087-8640

Please add $1.75 for shipping and handling for the first book and $.50 for each book thereafter. NY, NYC, and PA residents, please add appropriate sales tax. No cash, stamps, or C.O.D.s. All orders shipped within 6 weeks via postal service book rate. Canadian orders require $2.00 extra postage and must be paid in U.S. dollars through a U.S. banking facility.

Name_____
Address_____
City_____ State_____ Zip_____
I have enclosed $_____ in payment for the checked book(s).
Payment <u>must</u> accompany all orders. ❑ Please send a free catalog.

LEIGH GREENWOOD'S
SEVEN BRIDES
Laurel

Although Hen Randolph is the perfect choice for a sheriff in the Arizona Territory, he is no one's idea of a model husband. After the trail-weary cowboy breaks free from his six rough-and-ready brothers, he isn't about to start a family of his own. Then a beauty with a tarnished reputation catches his eye and the thought of taking a wife arouses him as never before.

But Laurel Blackthorne has been hurt too often to trust any man—least of all one she considers a ruthless, coldhearted gunslinger. Not until Hen proves that drawing quickly and shooting true aren't his only assets will she give him her heart and take her place as the newest bride to tame a Randolph's heart.

_3744-0   **$5.99 US/$6.99 CAN**

Sylvie Sommerfield

FOREVER

After serving two years at Yuma Prison for a crime he didn't commit, Steven McKean is released on a mission in Montana Territory. Experience has taught him women can never be trusted—and he is not about to let another close to his heart. Rachel knows Steve is trouble by the way his steely gaze catches and holds her like a panther stalking its prey. Against her better judgment, she finds herself hiring him to work on her father's ranch. But as dangerous as he seems, as much as his kisses make her forget all reason, she knows there is more to this man than meets the eye. And she senses that she has found a love to last forever.

___4491-9 $5.99 US/$6.99 CAN

THE LADY'S HAND
BOBBI SMITH
Author of *Lady Deception*

Cool-headed and ravishingly beautiful, Brandy O'Neal knows how to hold her own with the riverboat gamblers on *The Pride of New Orleans*. But she meets her match in Rafe Morgan when she bets everything she has on three queens and discovers that the wealthy plantation owner has a far from gentlemanly notion of how she shall make good on her wager.

Disillusioned with romance, Rafe wants a child of his own to care for, without the complications of a woman to break his heart. Now a full house has given him just the opportunity he is looking for—he will force the lovely cardsharp to marry him and give him a child before he sets her free. But a firecracker-hot wedding night and a glimpse into Brandy's tender heart soon make Rafe realize he's luckier than he ever imagined when he wins the lady's hand.

_4116-2 $5.99 US/$6.99 CAN

Dorchester Publishing Co., Inc.
P.O. Box 6640
Wayne, PA 19087-8640

Please add $1.75 for shipping and handling for the first book and $.50 for each book thereafter. NY, NYC, and PA residents, please add appropriate sales tax. No cash, stamps, or C.O.D.s. All orders shipped within 6 weeks via postal service book rate. Canadian orders require $2.00 extra postage and must be paid in U.S. dollars through a U.S. banking facility.

Name_____
Address_____
City_____ State_____ Zip_____
I have enclosed $_____ in payment for the checked book(s).
Payment <u>must</u> accompany all orders. ☐ Please send a free catalog.

WILD LAND, WILD LOVE

CONNIE MASON

Australia in 1812 is a virgin land waiting to be explored, a wild frontier peopled by even wilder men, a place where a defenseless woman risks both her virtue and her life. But hot-tempered, high-spirited Kate McKenzie is sure she can survive in Australia on her own ... until she meets her match in Robin Fletcher. In the brawny arms of the former convict she discovers that a defenseless woman can have the time of her life losing her virtue to the right man.

___52278-0 $5.50 US/$6.50 CAN

Dorchester Publishing Co., Inc.
P.O. Box 6640
Wayne, PA 19087-8640

Please add $1.75 for shipping and handling for the first book and $.50 for each book thereafter. NY, NYC, and PA residents, please add appropriate sales tax. No cash, stamps, or C.O.D.s. All orders shipped within 6 weeks via postal service book rate. Canadian orders require $2.00 extra postage and must be paid in U.S. dollars through a U.S. banking facility.

Name_____
Address_____
City_____ State_____ Zip_____
I have enclosed $_____ in payment for the checked book(s).
Payment <u>must</u> accompany all orders. ☐ Please send a free catalog.
    CHECK OUT OUR WEBSITE! www.dorchesterpub.com

SONYA BIRMINGHAM

Song of the Lark

When the beautiful wisp of a mountain girl walks through his front door, Stephen Wentworth knows there is some kind of mistake. The flame-haired beauty in trousers is not the nanny he envisions for his mute son Tad. But one glance from Jubilee Jones's emerald eyes, and the widower's icy heart melts and his blood warms. Can her mountain magic soften Stephen's hardened heart, or will their love be lost in the breeze, like the song of the lark?

___4393-9 $5.50 US/$6.50 CAN

Dorchester Publishing Co., Inc.
P.O. Box 6640
Wayne, PA 19087-8640

Please add $1.75 for shipping and handling for the first book and $.50 for each book thereafter. NY, NYC, and PA residents, please add appropriate sales tax. No cash, stamps, or C.O.D.s. All orders shipped within 6 weeks via postal service book rate. Canadian orders require $2.00 extra postage and must be paid in U.S. dollars through a U.S. banking facility.

Name_____
Address_____
City_____ State_____ Zip_____
I have enclosed $_____ in payment for the checked book(s).
Payment <u>must</u> accompany all orders. ☐ Please send a free catalog.
    CHECK OUT OUR WEBSITE! www.dorchesterpub.com